DATE ME

date me

THE KEATYN CHRONICLES: BOOK 3

JILLIAN DODD

This book is a work of fiction. Any references to historical events, real people, or real locales are used fictitiously. Other names, characters, places, and incidents are the product of the author's imagination, and any resemblance to actual events or locales or persons, living or dead, is entirely coincidental.

Jillian Dodd Inc.
N. Redington Beach, FL

3rd Edition
ISBN: 978-1-940652-19-1

This book is for

The KC Addicts.

I heart you all.

Books by Jillian Dodd

The Keatyn Chronicles®

Stalk Me

Kiss Me

Date Me

Love Me

Adore Me

Hate Me

Get Me

Hollywood Love Series

Fame

Power

Money

Sex

Love

That Boy Series

That Boy

That Wedding

That Baby

The Love Series

Vegas Love

Broken Love

Spy Girl Series

The Prince

The Eagle

The Society

Monday, September 26th

YOU HAVE A WILD SIDE.

FRENCH

I FLOAT MY way to French class on cloud nine.

When I take my seat, Aiden says flatly, "Well, that was something."

I turn around. I'm beaming. I think my smile will be on perma-blast all day long. "Wasn't it outrageous? The way he asked. I loved it!"

"You like stuff like that? Being the center of attention." He rolls his eyes toward the ceiling and laughs in a deep, sexy way. "Never mind. Don't answer that. Of course, you do. You seemed to be enjoying yourself. So, how come you never danced like that when we danced? It was pretty sexy."

"Oh gosh, did I look stupid?"

"No, everyone loved how you played along. You looked shocked. Were you?"

"I had no clue. I thought I was in trouble. Even when the dean started dancing, I thought it was some new girl hazing or something."

"You have a wild side."

"Everyone does. Do you?"

"You have a boyfriend now. You probably won't be finding out."

"If I was wild, that wouldn't stop me," I fire back.

He gazes at me for a beat. "No, I guess it wouldn't," he finally mutters.

"You're right though," I say. I'm practically bouncing in my seat. "I would never cheat, but he only asked me to Homecoming. Not to be his girlfriend."

Annie sits down and grabs my arm. "That was so adorable! I can't believe you danced with Jake like that! Whitney was seething! It was awesome!"

"Just before it all started, Whitney was telling me that Dawson was going to ask her to Homecoming. Telling me how they bonded in the limo. How they will be king and queen."

Annie sighs. "Don't do anything to make her mad at you, Keatyn. She's not a nice person."

I nod. Because I think I know that.

What did I say about Vanessa? *Been there. Seen it. Burned the T-shirt.*

I turn back around to face Aiden. "You know, it's because of you that Dawson and I are still together. I haven't thanked you properly, but what you did—how you told Riley. Seriously, thank you."

The look that crosses his face is indecipherable. He nods his head, agreeing with me and giving me a little smile, but he's grinding his pencil into his notebook. Like it's a horcrux and he's trying to kill it with a basilisk fang. He leans closer to me and says quietly, "I told you in the chapel that I'm done pretend punching your head."

I smile. "I'm glad, Aiden. I don't like when we fight."

He gives me the sweetest smile, but then says flatly, "I'm done fighting."

I turn around and try to focus on class.

But I can't.

He's completely given up on us. Hasn't he?

That's why he told Riley about what Whitney did.

After my breakdown in the chapel, he knew it for sure.

No way a lunatic like me could be his true love.

LIFE TWISTS AND TURNS.
2:45PM

AFTER SOCCER PRACTICE, I run up to Aiden, who is practicing kicking a football through the goal.

"Hey, would it be okay if we did tutoring in your room tonight? Everyone is talking about lunch, about how Dawson asked me to Homecoming, and I know if we go to the library we won't get anything done because people will come up to gush about it."

"Uh," he says, hesitating, "I'm sure the library will be fine."

I look at him funny. He's acting quite strange today. Maybe I should let him go to the library to get his aura recharged or something. But I don't want to. He's easier to deal with when his powers are weak.

"Please," I say with a pout.

He sighs. "Oh, fine."

AFTER DANCE, I knock on his door.

He doesn't answer.

I check my phone to see if he's running late.

There's nothing from him.

I knock again, wondering if maybe I caught him in the bathroom or something. He still doesn't answer, so I slide down the hallway wall and sit on the floor. Sitting here reminds me of one of my first nights here. I close my eyes and remember the party. The night Dawson gave me the worst kiss ever and how I ran out to this very spot and slid down the wall. I remember Aiden sliding down next to me. Me fighting back tears and telling him how Dawson ruined my lips. How Aiden kissed them and made them better.

How perfect it felt.

It's funny to me now. Life twists and turns in ways you never expect it to. I could practically see my future with Aiden. I thought he spoke to my soul, for god's sake!

I'm suddenly aware of a body sliding down the wall next to me. I open my eyes and see him. He looks out of breath. Like he ran all the way here.

I fight the urge to reach out and put my hand on his chest. To feel his heartbeat.

"Sorry, I'm late."

I nod. "It's okay. I haven't been waiting that long."

He takes a deep breath and gives me one of those smiles that almost blinds me. The kind of smile that makes me want to drag him to a little chapel in the woods, say *I do*, and make him the last boy I ever kiss.

"This is familiar."

"What is?" I say, pretending not to know exactly what he's talking about.

"Don't you remember the party? When I kissed you right here?" He reaches up and gently touches my lips with his finger. "Fixed your lips."

"Yeah, I remember, Aiden," I say. What I don't say is, *And it makes me sad. Sad to know that you knew so quickly that I wasn't the one.*

I start to get up.

He grabs my arm. "Why don't we just sit out here and study? Um, my room's a mess."

"You're such a liar. Your room is always perfect." I almost say, I love that about you, but I don't.

He rolls his eyes at me again, then says firmly, "I think out here would be better."

"Aiden, what is in your room?"

"I just . . . there's something I don't want you to see, okay?"

I grin, wondering what he's hiding from me and now totally curious.

I get up and open his door. Look around. "It looks normal."

He looks around his room, like whatever used to be there is gone, maybe?

"Okay, well, let's get to it." He sets his backpack on the ground and pulls his French workbook out.

I grab mine too and set it on his desk. "It's been an exhausting, crazy day," I say, and then flop down on his bed.

He gets all nervous-looking again.

He's acting very strange. I'm half expecting a naked girl, or a blow-up doll, or something embarrassing to appear. I look around his room again. All is completely in order, so I close my eyes. "Okay, so I worked on the first page of our homework during drama today. Do you want to copy it and just go over it? It's mostly review."

"Uh, sure," he says. "Give me a minute."

I hear him turning pages and then writing.

I open my eyes and look up at his ceiling.

"You don't have the twinkle lights on," I say. "It looks weird."

He looks up from his workbook and makes a sort of coughing sound. I glance at him, but he appears to be fine. My eyes go back up to the twinkle lights. Then I notice there's something new on his ceiling. Stars.

"Aiden! Oh my gosh! You put up stars. Are they the glow-in-the-dark kind? I love those! My little sisters had them all over the ceilings of their bedrooms." I study them more and realize they aren't just randomly scattered. They are in some kind of pattern. It's hard to tell since they are sort of blending into the ceiling right now.

"Yeah, they're in a pattern." He taps his pencil on his workbook and says in an irritated tone, "You were the one who wanted to come here so we wouldn't get distracted. Let's focus on French. We have a lot to do."

"No. I want to see them lit up first. I'm gonna turn your lights off for a minute." I start to hop up but, in a flash, Aiden is sitting on the edge of the bed, blocking me.

His eyes bore into mine. The gold surrounding them seems to be brightening, speaking to me. His eyes are trying to tell me something.

Something I can't translate.

Finally, I say, "What?"

"I didn't want you to see this, but I know you won't stop bugging me."

I smirk at him. I love getting my way. "That is true. Can I turn off the lights now?"

"No. We're gonna do this my way. Scoot over to the edge of the bed and then close your eyes."

I don't really like to be told what to do, but fine. I do it.

"You promise to keep them closed until I tell you to open them?"

"Sure."

"Okay," he says. He gets off the bed, walks over to his door, and then flips off the light. Then he walks back toward me and pulls down his window blind.

Obviously getting it dark enough for the stars to glow.

He lies back down next to me.

I swallow, suddenly realizing I am lying on a bed next to the God of all Hotties. His shoulder and arm touch mine, causing my whole body to feel like it just got plugged into an outlet and its current is running through me. I wonder if this is how my cell phone feels when I recharge it? Like it's alive.

His pinkie reaches out and grabs ahold of mine, like we're pinkie swearing.

He whispers, "Open your eyes now."

I look up at his ceiling and see that the glowing stars are definitely in a pattern. They spell out *Homecoming?*

My first reaction is, *That's so adorably romantic.*

But then, I feel a little sick.

Like I could throw up.

That's why he didn't want me to come here.

He didn't want me to see this.

He didn't want me to know he's going to lie next to some other girl. That he's going to touch her pinkie. That she's going to say yes and kiss him.

I launch myself off his bed, grab my workbook and backpack, and bound toward his door.

In my haste, my foot catches under his desk chair.

The chair and I do a sort of slow-motion dance before it darts out from underneath me and sends me crashing to the ground.

I pick myself and my bag up quickly. "I'm fine," I say to Aiden. He's getting off the bed to come help me. "I'm not feeling well all of a sudden. I'm sorry. I, uh, I have to go. Call Annie if you need help."

I rush out of his door and shut it quickly behind me.

I run down the hall to the stairs. When I get there, I realize I'm not lying. I don't feel very good. I look down at my knee. It's gushing blood and turning my white knee-high sock all red.

I limp down the staircase then collapse three steps from the bottom to inspect the damage.

I hurt.

I hurt a lot.

And at this point, I can't determine which hurts more. My knee or the pain in my heart when I think of Aiden with another girl.

I know it's not a rational thought, but it's there.

I start to get hot and feel like I'm going to pass out.

I examine my knee closer.

Just below my kneecap is a large gaping cut that is bleeding heavily.

Something tells me I should probably try to stop the bleeding. I pull my other shoe and sock off, thinking I'll wrap my sock around the wound.

A shadow passes over me, causing me to look up.

Jake bends down in front of me and looks at my knee. "Damn, that's really bleeding. Like. A lot."

"You gonna pass out at the sight of blood?"

"Nope, but you need to see the nurse. What'd you do?"

"I tried dancing with a chair. It wasn't a very good partner," I sort of chuckle.

"Nice," he says, as he wraps his arm around me, picks me up, carries me to his room, and sets me on his bed.

"I was going to wrap my other sock around it," I say, holding up my sock.

"Don't do that, Monroe. Your sock is furry and the fibers will get in the cut. Which will then have to be cleaned out before you get stitches." He walks over to his perfectly organized closet and grabs a washcloth.

"You're so neat," I say, taking in his room.

"I'm not sure how I managed to room with Dawson all these years. He never makes his bed." He cuts into their shared bath, bangs a couple of cabinet doors, runs the water, and then walks out and sits next to me. He has a bottle of vodka in one hand and a damp washcloth in the other.

He takes a drink of the vodka and hands me the bottle. "Take a big drink. This is gonna hurt."

I take a little drink. "How much worse can it get? It's already throbbing like crazy."

He takes off my sock and shoe then puts the wet washcloth across my knee.

"Jake!" I yell and take a big swig of the vodka. "That hurts!"

We hear Dawson's door open and shut.

"Hey, Dawes!" Jake yells. "C'mere."

I take another swig of vodka, bracing myself for how my heart will feel when it sees Dawson. I'm afraid that, after what just happened, I won't be happy to see him.

But I am.

So happy.

When Dawson sees me sitting on Jake's bed, vodka bottle in hand, he gets a big grin on his face. "You two better not be partying without me."

Jake holds up my bloody white sock, which looks a bit like an oversized used tampon.

"Oh my god. Gross. *What* is that?" Dawson asks.

Jake points down and takes the white—well, now pinkish red—washcloth off my knee.

"Keatie!" Dawson rushes over to the bed and gently sits down next to me, quickly wrapping an arm around me. "What'd you do?"

I lean into his chest and feel safe. Safe and happy. Happy he wants me and no one else. "I fell."

He grabs the vodka bottle out of my hand, takes a swig, and then kisses me. "You need stitches."

"Why do you two keep saying that? I don't need stitches. I just need a couple of those butterfly bandages. Run down to the field house and get some. I'm sure they'll work fine."

He hands me back the bottle and looks at me seriously. "You need stitches. Nothing else will hold on your knee. Drink."

I take another drink. "Why the vodka?"

"Because it's gonna hurt," Jake says. Like, *duh*.

"Really? I've never had stitches before. Isn't the cut, like now, the worst part? It hurts. A lot." I start to get tears in my eyes.

Tears about everything that feels hurt.

Jake pulls back his hair, showing me a hairline scar. "Six stitches." He holds out his wrist. "Four stitches." He points to his own knee. At a thin white line across the top. "Eight stitches."

Dawson points to a scar above his right eyebrow. "Four stitches. Camden threw a golf club at me." He shows me his elbow. "Five stitches. Sliding into home plate."

I touch Dawson's cute little eyebrow scar. "That doesn't look bad."

He leans in and gives me a sweet kiss.

I don't care that Jake is watching. I give him a deep kiss back. I want him to know that I appreciate him. Appreciate the way he asked me to Homecoming. Appreciate how sweet and perfect he's been to me. Appreciate that he's not a hottie god.

Jake grabs another clean washcloth, puts it across my knee, and wraps bright yellow athletic wrap around it to hold it in place.

Dawson kisses me while he does it. He's trying to distract me, but I still cringe and make a pitiful *ouch* sound into his mouth.

"I'd say another," Jake says to Dawson.

Dawson hands me the bottle. "Big drink this time."

I actually take a bigger drink this time. I want the pain to go away.

Dawson stands up. "It's time to get you to the nurse." He picks me up and carries me to the student center, and into the nurse's office.

Jake says to the nurse, "We need some stitches."

"Well, let's get her in here and take a look," the nurse says. I remember meeting her briefly during my orientation tour. She looks like a sweet grandmother who would never hurt a fly.

She undoes the wrapping and removes the washcloth. "Oh, my, sweetie, that *is* a nasty cut." She smiles at Jake, almost flirtatiously. "You were right. She needs stitches."

She cleans the cut, which hurts like a bitch. I squeeze Dawson's hand tightly, tears streaming down my face.

Then I watch as she goes over and prepares a shot.

"What's the shot for?" I say, in a panic, to Jake and Dawson. "My tetanus shot is up to date. I don't think the chair was rusty."

When she walks out of the room for supplies, Dawson explains, "She has to numb your knee to do the stitches."

Jake agrees. "That's why I gave you the vodka. So it won't hurt as bad."

HE LIED.

Even with the vodka, it hurts a lot.

She sticks my kneecap about a thousand times, each time sending burning medicine into my already hurting knee.

Then I watch in horror as she shoves a needle threaded with blue thread into my skin.

I bury my head in Dawson's shoulder. I have one of his hands in a death grip and Jake is squeezing my other hand every time she pushes the needle in again.

Eventually, the nurse says, "That should do it. Five stitches." She covers it with a big gauzy bandage and rattles off a bunch of instructions I don't quite catch.

I think the vodka is finally starting to kick in.

Dawson carries me back to his dorm and lays me on his bed.

Jake pats me on the arm. "You were a trooper, Monroe. And she gave you pain pills. Score."

"Thanks for taking care of me," I tell him as he walks through the bathroom door to his room.

"Five stitches," Dawson says. "That is pretty impressive."

He kisses around my knee, up my thigh, and to my waiting mouth. He gives me a yummy kiss, then says, "You were brave."

I roll my eyes at him.

He laughs. "I should have asked for a shot to numb my hand. You were squeezing so hard I think you killed it." He holds his hand up, making it look limp and dead.

"That's cuz Jake was squeezing my other hand every time she did a stitch."

"He was trying to distract you."

He leans up on one arm and grins at me. "So, everyone seemed to like the way I asked you to Homecoming."

"It was amazing, hilarious. Awesome. I loved it. I'm so excited to go with you. I really didn't think you were going to ask me. I was so surprised."

He scrunches up his nose. "You think I'd let anyone else take you wearing that dress? No fucking way."

"You like my dress?"

"I love your dress. Love your loft. Loved the whole weekend." He touches my face gently and his brown eyes look at me with such sweetness. These eyes look so different from the ones I saw that night at the Cave. There's no more hurt in them.

I push my lips hard against his.

And kiss him.

"Dawson, remember the night at the Cave? How you told me your goal was to take Whitney to Homecoming."

"A lot's changed since then."

"I know, but we had a great weekend, and you helped me pick out my dress, but you never said anything about us going together."

"That's because on the long drive back to get you, we decided I should ask you in a big public way. We had it all planned out. I wanted you to be surprised."

"When I was sitting there waiting for you, Whitney told me that you bonded in the limo. How you had gone to the last three Homecomings together, how you wouldn't want pictures with me, and how you'll be king and queen. That's part of why I wouldn't take the key. I didn't believe you yet."

He smiles. "Does that mean you believe me now?"

"I'm starting to."

Tuesday, September 27th

HE CAN'T BE A GOD.

7AM

I DIDN'T TAKE a pain pill last night before I went to bed because I had that vodka, so I woke up at three this morning with a throbbing knee. I tried for a couple hours to go back to sleep and finally gave up.

I hobbled into the bathroom, got some water, and took a pill around five. I got ready, thinking it would help me forget that it hurts. It didn't really work then. But now, as I walk into the Social Committee meeting, I'm feeling completely relaxed and pain-free.

I sit down, pull my over-the-knee sock down, and inspect the gauze, making sure it's still in place.

Aiden sits down next to me. "Five stitches, huh?"

"Yeah," I slur a little.

"Why did you run out of my room and pretend you weren't hurt, when you obviously were?"

"I felt sick. I didn't really know about the cut until I saw it was bleeding."

Peyton and Brad start the meeting, so Aiden stops talking.

I listen to Peyton go through all the details for the Homecoming after party. It's interesting and I can't wait, but I'm really struggling to keep my heavy eyelids open.

Maybe I can close them for just a second.

I'm lying in Aiden's bed looking up at his ceiling. He touches my pinkie and tells me about the sexual dream he promised to tell me. I'm turned on by his dream and he knows it, so he rolls over, pulls me hard up against his chest, and says, "Since it's a dream, we can act it out and, technically, it's not cheating."

Then he kisses me. A mouth open, full-on tongue, hot, hard kiss. The kind of kiss I didn't know he was capable of. I feel like fire and energy are rolling through my body. When he bites my bottom lip and tugs on it gently, that fire pulses directly between my legs. He rolls on top of me, but is holding himself above me. Like he's doing a push up. I run my hand across his arm, across the muscles that are all pumped from holding up his weight.

He slowly lowers his lips to my neck without letting any part of his upper body touch mine. I feel the fire on my neck, but all I can think about is what is touching. His hips have mine pinned to the bed. His legs are between mine.

He runs his tongue slowly from my neck, down my chest, and straight down to . . .

"Boots," he whispers with grin. "I think you dozed off."

"Oh, I'm sorry," I say breathlessly, as I try to push the feel of Aiden's tongue and hips out of my mind.

I listen as Brad goes over more details.

Aiden leans toward me. "Will you save me a dance at the after party?"

"I don't know," I tease. "Can you dance?"

He puts his head down. Like he can't.

And I feel bad. Embarrassed for him. "Oh my gosh. Is that why you only wanted to dance to slow songs? Is that all you know how to do?"

He can't be a god. I'm certain of it now.

Happy Homecoming to him and whoever he asked to go with him.

Although, I'm a bit surprised I haven't heard about it. Or seen the stars glowing from the ceiling on someone's Facebook page.

"I'll get my French homework done before tutoring. You can teach me to dance instead."

"I don't really feel like dancing, Aiden. The knee and all."

"I've gone above and beyond the call of duty in Social Committee. It's not something I really had the time to do, but I did it for you. So you owe me."

I STOP FOR a latte on the way to history and as I'm walking up the stairs, I decide that I'm very concerned that my subconscious believes that acting out a dream in real life is not cheating.

But then I think about it. If you *were* pretending to be dreaming or *were* possibly in a heightened state of consciousness, *would* it be cheating? Like, technically?

That sounds like a question for Brooklyn. If I were ever to speak to him again.

Surely, if this were the case, someone would have figured out that loophole before me. So, probably not.

Then I have an odd sense of déjà vu. I think I said those exact words to Aiden in the dream, and he said, No, you think outside the box. You color outside the lines. For you, it's not cheating.

I wonder if Aphrodite was good in bed.

I mean, we know she was clearly capable of seduction but, technically, once they were seduced, was she?

I have the sudden need to find out.

PASSION, NAKEDNESS, AND SEX.
HISTORY

RILEY AND I are working on another stupid history project.

Our project is: *How did transportation affect the Industrial Revolution?*

Uh, hello. Who thinks up this stuff?

The answer is pretty simple: *The use of widespread transportation allowed the Industrial Revolution.*

Project done.

But, no.

We have to waste our time cutting out little pictures of trains, highways, cars, and boats to glue on a poster. I'm supposed to be looking on my phone for some statistics.

But instead, I just googled: *Was Aphrodite a good lover?*

Just as I hit the enter key, Riley grabs my phone looking for statistics. He sees my search and says, "What the hell?"

I bury my face in my palm. "Shut up."

"Didn't you just have an amazing weekend with my brother?"

"Yeah, so?"

"You're still obsessing over the god."

"No, I'm not. I've just developed a scholarly interest in Greek mythology."

"Bullshit."

I roll my eyes and pretend to put my phone away but, later, when he goes to refill his water bottle, I peek at it.

Aphrodite represents the power of love. The kind of love from which you cannot escape.

No wonder she had so many guys captivated.

She rules all aspects of love, desire, beauty, and sex.

And, oh my.

She is considered the mistress of pleasure. She symbolizes passion, nakedness, and sex.

Oh, wait. There's more.

Once Aphrodite enters into a relationship, her powers go beyond love and sex to include deep friendship and the connection of souls.

Oh. My. Gosh! *That's* why I thought he spoke to my soul. It *is* just a stupid godly love trick. He can do it to anyone he smiles at!

And now, thanks to my research, I know.

I'm not crazy.

Riley says, "I think I know how I want to ask Ariela to Homecoming."

I light up. I'm so excited for him. "How?!"

"Well, I want to do something at the football game Friday night. While I'm in my uniform and she's in her cute little cheerleading skirt. What should I do?"

"I thought you said you knew?"

"I know *where*. I just need to figure out *how*. Something all her friends will see. And I was thinking it'd be cool if whatever I do had, like, something she could keep. A memento."

"So cupcakes and balloons are out."

"Yeah."

"You could write it on her megaphone."

"Would she see it?"

"Probably not. Plus, she'd probably get in trouble. Um, what else is out there?" I think for another minute. "Oh, I know! You could change the sign the guys run through. I could even help with that."

He shakes his head. "She'd keep ripped paper?"

"This is hard."

"I know. I want it to make her melt. For her to think it's super sweet."

I raise my eyebrows at him in surprise. "Who the hell are you and what have you done with my friend?"

"Shut up and think. What else is on the field?"

"The scoreboard?"

"Only has numbers."

I get an idea. "A football! You could write it on the football and while you're warming up, call her name and toss it to her. And you could both sign it and date it afterwards. That'd be really cute. It'd be cool to have a keepsake. Speaking of that, I'd like a keepsake to remember how Dawson asked me. Can you stand in my room with your shirt off and an M painted on your chest?"

He flicks my nose. "Hey, that was for you. I was embarrassed to be seen shirtless."

I laugh out loud. "Now that is bullshit. You'd walk around shirtless all day if they'd let you."

He smirks at me. "I'd be better off if they'd let me walk around with no pants. Now that *is* impressive.

HOLLYWOOD ROYALTY TO TRASH.

MATH

WHILE WE'RE SUPPOSED to be doing some math problems towards the end of class, I poke Logan, who sits in front of me.

"Hey, I heard you're trying out for the play. What part do you want?"

"I'm trying out for the Bad Prince. You know, the guy that screws everything up for the trashy girl you want to play?" He looks down his nose at me, like I'm actual trash, then turns his back on me.

I purse my lips and scratch my temple.

I have to admit, this kind of response from a guy is sort of new to me. At my old school, well, anywhere really, boys who I didn't know seemed thrilled, almost honored when I talked to them.

What happened to me?

Why isn't he flirting with me? Is he like Whitney? Does he think I'm trash too?

I look down and scrutinize myself. Run my hand down a chunk of my hair. It's still blonde and shiny. My clothes are still cute. I check my reflection in my phone. My teeth are still white. My legs still long and tan.

How did coming to a new school cause me to go from Hollywood royalty to trash?

CLASSY IS OVERRATED.

CERAMICS

JAKE FOLDS HIS arms across his chest and sits on the stool next to me. "So now I have to figure out a way to ask Whitney to Homecoming that is classy but compares to what Dawson did for you. You're stealing her spotlight, Monroe. She doesn't like it."

"You must be high if you think I'd help plan anything for her."

He shakes an adorable freckled finger at me. "See, that's where you're wrong. I am asking you to help *me*. Because I gave you vodka for your knee. Because I came back with Dawson and because I helped him ask you. That's what friends do. They help each other."

I sigh. He's right. I need to be a friend back.

"I doubt I'll be much help. No one did this kind of stuff at my old school. My last boyfriend didn't even ask me to the dance. He just told me to tell him what color my dress was so we could match."

"Come on. You have good ideas. Brainstorm with me. Think romantic."

"You could spell out Homecoming in rose petals on her bed. She could take a picture of it. She'd like that, wouldn't she? It'd be private. Classy."

"I think she's thinking classy is overrated."

"She wants you to top the dean's sizzling ass and a bunch of naked chests?"

"I think so."

"Hmm. You could jump out of a plane with a heart-shaped parachute. You could streak across campus in nothing but a raincoat. You could . . . You know, it's really hard because she isn't really in anything. Like, guys have put stuff in the girl's dance locker. Or one guy asked on stage during drama. It was so cute. So that leaves you with lunch or maybe at a football game."

"Keep going," he says. "You're thinking big now. And it's good you haven't been here to see all the ways people have asked. That means you should be able to come up with something new and creative."

I shake my head. Trying to come up with something.

"Paint it on the football field?"

"I can't do that."

"Do it with rose petals then."

"They'd blow away."

"Balloons?"

"Not original."

I throw my hands up in the air in frustration. "Then why don't you just hire a freaking airplane and fly a banner over the field?"

He gets a big smile on his face and fist bumps my ceramic deer. "I knew you'd come up with something."

EMBARRASSMENT PROTECTION PROGRAM.
4:40PM

AIDEN IS STANDING in front of me, expecting me to teach him how to dance. Why did I ever agree to this?

"This is silly," I say. "I can't teach you how to dance. Plus, I'm injured."

"I saw you jogging at soccer practice, even though I doubt you were supposed to."

I laugh. "I took another pain pill. Felt healed."

He stands there and stares at me. Knows he wins whatever game he's trying to play. If I could jog, then I should be fine to dance. I sigh and figure I'll just get it over with. I turn on my favorite dance playlist, grab his hips, and move them to the beat. Move them with mine.

He moves awkwardly. Strangely. With no rhythm whatsoever.

Um, okay.

This is not working.

I turn around, stand in front of him, push my back into his chest, and pull his arm around to my stomach, where it presses against my bare skin.

Leaving a scar, I'm sure.

I shake my ass into him, and he finally seems to be getting it. He's moving with a little more rhythm.

What can I say? I'm a good teacher.

I put my hands on top of his and move them around on my body in the name of dancing.

This would be even funner if we were naked.

Shit.

Hello? You can't think that.

This is you helping a dance-disabled friend.

It's practically philanthropic. I bet I could get community service hours for this.

AFTER ABOUT SIX songs, Aiden spins me out of his arms and breaks out boy band dance moves.

"What the hell?" I say, shocked. "Do you used to be in a boy band? Are you here in some embarrassment protection program?"

He gives me a radiant smile.

I shake my head at him. "Don't tell me you can sing too."

He walks close to me. "We'll have to save that for another day, Boots. I don't want to overwhelm you with all my talents at once."

"Everyone says you have great hands," I blurt out.

"These?" he asks, holding them in front of my face.

I look at his hands.

Really look at them.

They're beautiful.

Seriously, is there any part of him that's not complete perfection? I run my hand across them, searching for something. Then I find a scar that runs across his pinkie and middle finger. "What happened here?"

He laughs. "Knife attack. In the war."

"Very funny."

"Fine. Cleat attack."

"Now I know why you're such a good goalie," I say, further examining his hands.

"Because I'm fast." He quickly slaps the top of my hands. Like the game Damian and I could play for hours when we were kids.

I slap his hands back quickly before he can pull them away. "Not fast enough," I say with a smirk. I grab his hands again and hold them up, scrutinizing them. "They're too big for your body."

"What do you mean?"

"Proportionately. They're off. They're too big." I tilt my head and look at him. Size up his six-foot-two-inch frame. "That, or you're not done growing yet."

"I'm probably not done growing yet," he shrugs, then starts doing the robot to the music.

It makes me laugh. "You *so* know how to dance."

"Naw, you're just a really good teacher. I couldn't do this until today."

"You're such a liar. How do you know how to dance like this? You dance alone in your room to music videos or something?"

"No. I have a bossy older sister."

"So?"

"So, instead of wanting to play school or Barbies, she wanted to play dance instructor. If I played nice, she snuck me cookies."

"So everyone at school knows you can dance like this but me, right? Very funny. Ha. Ha. You tricked me."

He takes a step closer to me, wraps his arm around my waist, and pulls me in. His leg moves between mine. Our lower halves have never been entwined like this except for in my daydream. His leg feels even warmer than it did in the dream. Like it's radiating energy into my thighs.

"You're the only one at school who knows I can dance like this. Well, besides my sister."

"Why?"

"Because it's embarrassing. You asked me if I was in a boy band witness protection program or something."

"Ohmigawd, did your mom video tape it? I'm so asking your sister."

He tries not to laugh. "You are not. Or you'll be in trouble."

"Oh, really?" I sass, putting my face right in front of his. "What kind of trouble?"

He grabs my butt cheeks firmly in each hand, squeezes them, and raises an eyebrow at me in challenge.

Oh, two can play this game.

I grab the back of his jeans.

Jeans I hardly ever see him wear. Jeans that sit low on his hips. The Cougars soccer T-shirt that he's wearing just barely meets the thick band of his underwear.

I pull his shirt up over his head and toss it on the floor.

As he slides his hands down my sides, I take a moment to touch those hips. Touch the edge of the deep-V that is now visible.

I try not to think about what isn't visible.

"You gonna do that at the dance?"

"Maybe." I place my palms firmly on his pecs. Close my eyes and dance with him.

I run my hands over his chest, grind on his leg, move to the beat.

We dance well together.

I seem to know what he's going to do before he does it.

ANOTHER ONE OF my favorite songs comes on, so I push off his chest, jump up and down, then turn around and give him a booty shake. He spins me around and puts his knee back between my legs.

Which means he likes it there.

I grab his shoulders and run my hands across the muscles I have only admired.

He starts a very fast, exaggerated version of a waltz. He pulls me toward him. Spins me out, then spins me so that my back is now pulled tightly against his chest, our arms intertwining.

His hand glides across my bare stomach. I'm still in my dance clothes, and this bra top doesn't seem as solid a wardrobe choice as it did earlier.

I need more insulation from his electric touch.

I reach up and wrap my arm around his neck. He drops his head, placing his cheek next to mine. Even though the music is still fast, our bodies have slowed way down. His hands move slowly across my body, leaving little shocks of pleasure in their wake.

The music stops.

My ten-song playlist is over.

I turn around and face him.

Our faces are so close.

Our lips torturously closer.

His hand tangles in my hair, and he looks at me. His eyes are kissing my soul. Caressing me like a lover. They sparkle and shine with both fire and tenderness.

I realize I've been holding my breath.

I suck in a big breath of air and back away from him.

I need to get out of here.

Like, now.

"I think you're ready for the dance," I say, as I grab my jacket off his chair.

He steals it from me and plops down on his futon.

"Dance for me," he commands.

"Dance for you?"

"Yeah."

"You wanna see my Kiki stripper moves?" I laugh. "Cuz I really don't have any."

"No. I want to see you move. Show me your new routine. My sister's been telling me about it."

"I can't show you. It's totally top secret."

"It's either that or I pull you on this futon and make a cheater out of you."

At first, I think he's kidding. But the way he's leaning on the futon. The shadows playing across his face. His hooded eyes. That freaking mouth.

It stops me dead in my tracks.

I would be both pissed and hurt if Dawson danced with someone the way I just danced with Aiden.

I used to be the kind of girl that flirted with everyone and anyone. The old me would flirt with Aiden and lead him on. Vanessa would say it's smart. Smart to have a few guys in reserve that want you. That it keeps the guy you're with on his toes. And if he turns out to be a jerk, you just tee up the next guy.

That might be the kind of girl I was, but it's not the kind of girl I want to be.

And why is he dancing with me like this when he's asking someone else to Homecoming? It's not fair to her either.

I should do the right thing.

"Look, Aiden. It's nice that we're getting along better. But I like Dawson and I shouldn't have danced with you like that. I don't want to give you the wrong idea. So if I'm going to keep tutoring you, it'll have to be in the library. No more dances. No more almost kisses. No more talking on my neck."

"But you and Dawson aren't exclusive. You still aren't wearing the key. So go on a date with me. Date us both."

I look at him. Stare into those eyes.

But, I can't.

I don't want this.

"I'm sorry, Aiden, but I can't date a guy like you. A guy that can't decide if he loves me or hates me." He's getting ready to counter my argument, but I don't give him the chance. "And I know we had some crazy love at first sight thing, but we obviously would be a disaster together."

He grins at me.

Just keeps grinning.

Then he taps his foot like he knows a secret and can hardly keep it inside him. His whole body is practically humming.

And his stupid grin keeps growing.

Damn that smile. I wish he would just put that thing away.

"Why are you grinning?"

"Love at first sight, huh?"

"No. It's just an expression. That stuff doesn't happen in real life," I say, even though I know sometimes it does.

He stands up close to me. His broad naked chest is so close to mine I can feel when he breathes. I hold my breath and move slightly backward, trying to increase the space between us.

But when I take a step back, he takes another step forward.

I take another step and back into his wall. There's nowhere else for me to go.

He puts his palms against the wall on each side of my head. I've never seen this look in his eyes before. It's hunger. And it looks so fucking sexy on him.

I let out a little breath. Almost a sigh. And close my eyes.

I can't let him look at me like that. I won't.

His cheek grazes mine as he whispers in my ear. "I think being just your friend will be fun."

I don't open my eyes. I just pant out, "How so?"

Where are those damn magic Spanx when you need them?

He places his open mouth on my cheek, slowly closing it into a pucker. He gently pulls his top lip off my cheek first, the bottom lip staying in place and then—bit by agonizing bit—receding.

It's then that I open my eyes.

And need to move.

"I have to go."

"See ya, friend," he says playfully.

But he doesn't move. He just raises one hand off the wall, giving me a small pathway to squeeze through.

He's such a jerk, I think, as I squeeze past him.

I get my stuff together and then take one last look at his room. The twinkle lights. The smell. The memories of our dances and his kisses.

Then I glance up at the stars that are still in place. Waiting to ask a girl to the dance.

When I close the door, I know I'm closing the door on us and not coming back.

I'm not coming back here.

Ever. Again.

And I feel surprisingly good.

Like a weight has lifted off me.

Like I just battled an addiction and won.

No, it's better than that.

I just kicked fate's ass. And won.

It's freeing.

And it's official.

My silly schoolgirl crush on the god is over.

I STOP AND sit on the stairs, feeling proud of myself and happy with my decision. I really like Dawson and I think it's time I let him know it.

I don't text him. I call.

"Where are you?" he asks.

"In your dorm. Where are you?"

"Hang on." I hear a bunch of noise. A chair sliding across the floor, rustling. "I'm in my bed. Almost naked."

Just thinking about him almost naked makes me feel warm. "Should I start stripping my clothes off as I walk down the hall?"

"Damn, that sounds hot. Can I watch?"

"No one is in your hall right now," I say as I round the corner. "Maybe you can."

I wait by the stairs at the end of the hall for him to open his door.

When he does peek out, I see he's shirtless, wearing a pair of athletic shorts, and probably nothing else.

I'm shaking. Half excited and half scared of what I think I'm about to do.

He winks at me, which sets me in motion. I take a step forward, pull my top off, and toss it down the hall at him. He grabs it and throws it into his room.

I say a quick prayer I don't get caught.

I walk by another door, pull my shorts off, and throw them at him.

Now I'm in nothing but a bra and a thong.

I take another step. I'm two doors away and breathing heavily.

What on earth possessed me to do this?

But the fire in Dawson's eyes, and the fact that his shorts are now saluting me, keep me going.

When I'm one door away, I stop and undo my bra.

He grabs me and pulls me into his bedroom.

He doesn't close the door, so I kick it shut behind us. When he hears it shut, he slams me back into it.

"Fuck, Keatie. I can't believe you just did that!"

I don't get to reply. His mouth is on mine. His hands are in my hair, then down my back, then cupping my ass and pulling me up toward him. He leans me back against the wall and pushes his shorts down. I wrap my legs around him and kiss his neck. Hard. When he thrusts into me, I gasp and kiss him again. He's as out of control as I feel.

I'm trying to be quiet. But I'm having a hard time. I don't want anyone walking in the hall to hear us. Dawson stops suddenly and says into my hair, "Not yet."

Then he locks the door and carries me to his bed. We're still attached in every way when we fall onto the bed.

"Ohhh, god," I say.

Apparently that was all he was waiting for. He's out of control again.

Finally, he says, "Holy shit." And collapses on top of me.

He kisses my cheekbone, down by my ear, and then rolls off me. He lies spread out on the bed like he just finished a marathon.

"That was so fucking hot," he says, kissing my fingers. Then he sits up and shakes his head. "No, that was hotter than hot."

"It was molten lava hot," I say, thinking about how he always makes me feel.

"You're gonna kill me. Two and a half hours of football and then this."

I smile at him and snuggle into his shoulder. I know I need to get dressed quickly. You never know when someone is going to knock on the door.

But instead, I lean across his chest and kiss the key necklace. "Do you still want me to have this?"

"You can have each and *every* part of me."

I know what part he is specifically referring to and it's safe to say that it's *not* his heart.

I ROLL OFF the bed, grab my shorts, and pull them on. He's watching me, so I throw him his shorts before he can get any ideas.

He slides on his shorts, sits on his desk chair, and pulls me onto his lap before I have a chance to find my bra.

"Does that mean you're ready for my heart? Are you in love with me?"

I run my hands through his gorgeous dark hair and sigh. "I'm not sure about the whole love thing yet, but I like you a lot, Dawson, and I don't want anyone else kissing you or doing anything else with you."

"Keatie, are you asking me out?" he asks playfully, as he tickles my sides.

I giggle and squirm. "No!" I scream a little too loudly, which causes Jake to burst through the bathroom door.

"What's wrong now?" He has a freaked out look on his face. "God, I thought Dawson died or something."

I push my still naked chest into Dawson's, trying to cover myself up.

Jake says, "She said no, bro. No means no."

They both laugh hysterically.

"What's so funny?"

"Inside joke," Dawson says.

Jake agrees. "Yeah, old joke from freshman year. Back when we were both virgins."

I laugh. I love their friendship.

Jake pulls a red bra off his bathroom counter and swings it by the strap. No wonder I couldn't find it.

"This belong to you, Monroe?" he asks with a smirk.

Dawson laughs heartily and buries his head in my shoulder.

I want to say no, but it's a new bra and I want it back. I sheepishly nod.

"And what exactly was it doing in the hall?"

"I'll let you two discuss that after I leave. I'm gonna go back to my dorm and change for dinner."

I cover my boobs with one arm and grab the bra out of Jake's hand with the other. Then I grab one of Dawson's sweatshirts off the pile at the end of his bed and pull it over my head.

Dawson motions for Jake to leave and pulls me into a hug. He gently touches my cheek with the back of his hand and looks sweetly into my eyes. "I love you, Keatie." He adds quickly, "Don't say it back. I'm glad you're ready for the key. And I do want you to go out with me, but I want to ask properly."

"Properly? Does that mean I get more naked chests?"

He kisses me. "Only my naked chest. *Whenever* you want." He pulls me in tighter for a steamier kiss. "God, you're hot. I don't know how I got so fucking lucky. So, tomorrow, we'll go out for dinner. Just the two of us."

"That sounds nice," I say.

He smacks my butt in response. "Hurry and go change. I'm starving."

PROMISE NOT TO FREAK.
10PM

AFTER THE GAME, the girls are hanging out in my room. Annie is practically bouncing off the walls.

"Can you believe Ace asked me?" She holds her phone to her chest and dances with it. "Can you believe he was sitting right next to me at the game and asked me on Facebook? It was so cool. I about died when I read the notification!"

"You also screamed out loud!" Maggie laughs.

"I know. I'm sure people just thought I was cheering about the game. But, whatever, I have a bigger concern now."

"What's that?" I ask.

"I need a great dress. I don't really like the dress I picked out with my mom. It's black and conservative. All of a sudden, I want to be one of those girls."

Maggie stops texting whoever she is texting. "One of what girls?"

"You know, the kind of girl that gets a pink sparkly dress. The kind of girl that feels like a princess when she goes to the dance. Not the kind of girl to wear the black shapeless dress her mother bought. The kind of girl that's going to make out on the dance floor and not care about getting in trouble."

"Damn," I say. "Ace has got you all messed up."

She spins around again. "I know. Isn't love amazing?"

"Love?" Maggie, Katie, and I all say at the same time.

NOW I'M LYING in bed thinking about love. About how to know when you're in love. None of the girls have much experience with love, so I can't really ask them for advice.

I grab my phone, go into the stairwell, and call Mom.

"Hey, sweetie," she answers. "How's my girl?"

"I'm good, but I have a question. How do you know when it's the right time to tell someone that you love them?"

"I suppose you would want to tell them when you feel it."

"Yeah, but feelings are tricky."

"You like this Dawson a lot, huh? Are you thinking about telling him? Has he said it?"

"He has. And I feel really bad for not saying it back."

"Well, why didn't you say it back?"

"Because I'm not sure what love is."

"Then you probably aren't ready to say it."

"But I feel like I love him. It's just hard to admit. It opens you up to more hurt. And Brooklyn said it to me all the time and he—look Mom, I need to tell you the truth about something. I hate lying to you."

"What are you lying about?" she says in a tone that makes me know she's panicking.

"Promise me you won't freak."

She makes a little sniffle noise. I can tell she's doing that thing where she takes a deep breath in through her nose when she's trying to stay calm. "I promise I won't freak. No, that's a lie. I'm already freaking because you just made me promise not to freak. Which means you think I will freak. So, now I am."

"Over Labor Day weekend, Brooklyn had a tournament in New York. I went to see him."

"Keatyn! All we've done to try and keep you safe and you went to a scheduled event? What if Vincent had been there?"

"He was there, Mom."

"What?! Why don't I know about this? What happened?"

"I saw him. He didn't see me. I'm fine. I got out of there. But I need to tell you about B. What he did."

Mom takes a deep breath. "Tell me that you won't try to see him again."

"I won't. You don't have to worry. I just never thought Vincent would go that far to try and find me. It's still hard to believe."

"I know, sweetheart," she says gently. "This is all pretty unbelievable. But please, don't make any mistakes. I love you. That's the only reason I even agreed to this plan. I wanted you to be able to have a somewhat normal life."

"I want a normal life too. Do you think sometime I could come there? Like spur of the moment, no one knows kind of thing. Like even you would be surprised?"

"If no one knows you're coming, there is no way Vincent could know. But if he found out you were here, I'd be worried about getting you back safely."

"Yeah, that's true," I say defeatedly.

"So, back to love," Mom says. I can tell by the way her voice shakes that she's getting choked up.

"So when B asked me to come see him, he told me that he still loved me. He talked about us, you know, doing things sexually that weekend. How me missed me. All that."

"And so you went . . ."

"And while I was there, he snuck into a cabana and had a quickie with a groupie."

"Really? That just doesn't sound like something Brook would do."

"Well, he did. He told me he had to take care of something but looked all sneaky about it. I followed him. Watched him meet the girl. Watched her drag him into the cabana. Stood there for about five minutes and watched them both come out still sort of getting dressed."

"Oh, baby, I'm so sorry. I know that you loved him."

"You know, Mom. You taught me all about protection and how not to get pregnant, but never once did you teach me how to protect my heart."

"That's because you can't protect your heart. Your heart feels what it feels.

Your brain helps you decide if that person is worthy of your love."

"So you can love someone who's wrong for you?"

"Of course. Your heart is capable of loving lots of different people in lots of different ways. The way you will love your children is different from how you love your pets. The way you love the man you marry is going to be different than the love you felt for an old boyfriend."

"So you loved and married my dad, but now you love Tommy. How is the love you felt for my dad different from what you feel for Tommy?"

"That's a hard question. Um, your dad was my best friend. He was gorgeous and he made me feel beautiful and he could always make me laugh. When I walked into a room with him, I knew every woman there was jealous that I was with him. He was caring and sweet."

"And Tommy?"

"I don't want to diminish what I had with your father, so don't take it that way. When I married him, there was no one I wanted or loved more. But Tommy felt different. He felt like my destiny. I don't know if it's because I needed to experience life before I was ready for Tommy or what, but he came into my life at just the right time. You liked him right away too. I never would've been with someone you didn't love. You were always my first priority."

"I don't know if Dawson is my destiny. But I love being with him. He's sweet and sexy. He makes me feel happy and, I don't know, I have been through a lot lately. When we first started hanging out, he told me that he felt like he was healing every time we were together. He had a really rough breakup that he was trying to get over. And I feel that way about him."

"Keatyn, you're seventeen. You don't know what your future holds. If you feel like you love him and you want him to know it, you should tell him."

"Thanks, Mom. I think I just wanted someone to tell me it was okay. I don't really trust my feelings. I never would've thought B would do something like that. I thought I loved Cush because of a pair of boots. And I thought Vincent was my friend. I must be a really bad judge of character."

"Part of life is making mistakes and learning from them. I've made plenty of them."

"You have? You're, like, perfect."

Mom laughs. "I am far from perfect and I make mistakes like everyone does. So are you going to tell him?"

"Yeah, I think so. Night, Mom. I love you. Give the girls a kiss for me."

"Love you too, sweetie."

Wednesday, September 28th

GETTING TANGLED UP.

LUNCH

"SO, MONROE," JAKE says, setting his tray between Whitney's and mine. "I hear you're trying out for the play."

"Yeah, I'm planning on it."

Whitney starts talking loudly to the table just as Peyton sets her tray down. "Okay, people. Voting for Homecoming Court is this afternoon and every vote counts. You know that Jake and I will be the perfect King and Queen." She leans over and kisses him on the cheek. "Won't we, baby?"

"I don't really care about that," Jake says, shrugging his shoulders. "But I do want to play the Good Prince in the drama production." He turns to her. "Remember, I told you tryouts are tomorrow?"

She waves her hand, dismissing him. "Jake, who cares? This is Homecoming Court I'm talking about. It's important."

He gives her a defiant look and turns to me. "So, anyway, Monroe. You know, if you get the part of the Cheerleader Bachelorette, we're going to have to kiss a lot." He stops, licks his lips, and gives Dawson a smirk.

Whitney's face goes blank and she shuts her eyes tight, just for a second.

She rubs her hand up Jake's arm. "If it's the lead, then I'm sure you will get it. You're talented at everything you do. You didn't mention though that the role calls for kissing."

I smile and happily inform her, "Oh, it's not *just* the Cheerleader Bachelorette he has to kiss. He will be kissing—what was it, Jake, four or five bachelorettes?" I turn and say to Whitney, "But, you know, it's just acting."

I notice Peyton isn't wearing her normal boring pumps. Today she has on an adorable pair of kitten heels. "Peyton! I love your shoes. They're so cute."

"Yeah," Whitney says. "If you want to look like a tramp."

"Better than looking like a grandma," Peyton fires back. "And personally, I think Dawson is going to win Homecoming King this year." She gushes to me. "Wait until you see it, Keatyn. Eastbrooke does Homecoming up big. You and Dawson will dance together in front of everyone. It's a big honor. And you two are just so darn cute together."

Jake says, "As long as Dawson understands I may be borrowing her. We're going to have to do a lot of practicing."

Whitney shoves her tray away. "If you're trying to piss me off today, Jake, it's working. Excuse me."

She gets up and leaves her tray on the table. Rachel and the minions immediately look concerned and follow her, all leaving their lunches on the table for someone else to pick up.

Peyton snickers and flirts with Jake. "It's kinda fun to piss her off, isn't it?"

Jake rolls his eyes, shoves the rest of his pizza in his mouth, and says, "I better go talk to her."

AS DAWSON WALKS me to French he says, "Keatie, do you really have to try out for the play? Jake had a part last year and they have a ton of practices. You won't have any time for me."

"We'll find time, Dawson. Even if I have to sneak to your room in the middle of the night."

He grabs me and pushes me up against the wall in front of French class. "We should skip class, sneak into my room, and spend the afternoon getting tangled up."

Miss Praline walks by and says, "Mr. Johnson, I think you better get yourself to class."

STOP GRINNING.

FRENCH

I'M THINKING ABOUT the play. About how if I do get the part of the Cheerleader Bachelorette that I'm going to have to kiss both princes. Jake thinks he will get the part of the Good Prince and says that Logan will get the part of the Bad Prince. Kissing Jake will be no big deal. We're friends, but Logan will barely speak to me.

I spin around in my desk and say to Aiden, "Isn't Logan one of your best friends?"

"Yeah. Why?"

"I heard he's trying out for the part of the Bad Prince."

Aiden nods and makes a little frown.

Even though I wish I could control the wattage of his smile and its effect on me, I really don't like to see Aiden frown. It just doesn't look right on his face.

"Is he nice?"

"Logan?"

"Yeah. He's in my math class. Sits right in front of me. He has a nice looking back but that's all I know about him. I tried to talk to him yesterday about the play. I don't think he likes me." I sigh. "And I'm not sure why."

"Uh, that's probably my fault."

"Your fault?"

Aiden moves his pencil around in a tight circular motion before raising his head. "I may have told him about some of my past frustrations with you."

"So he hates me," I say flatly, putting my head down and turning back around.

I'm completely, one hundred percent over the hottie god but, for some reason, knowing that his best friend hates me because of things Aiden has said about me makes really sad. That and his stupid stars.

Annie looks at me. "What's wrong? You look like you're going to cry."

I wipe a stray tear from the corner of my eye. "I think I have something in my eye."

Aiden leans up and whispers in my ear. "He doesn't hate you."

I turn back around because now I'm kinda pissed. Pissed that this idiot who I've been wasting my time tutoring for almost a month is saying bad things about me.

"You must have had wonderful things to say about me to make him hate me when he doesn't even know me."

"He thinks you kind of played me."

"Played you? Are you kidding me? You're the one that got all pissed off and didn't call."

"He's also sort of down on love."

"That must be why he wants to play the Bad Prince. He'll get to be the cynic."

Aiden nods. "He is kind of cynical about love."

I do not want to talk about love of any kind with Aiden, so I change the subject to something more pleasant. "I think it's funny that Jake is trying out for the part of the Good Prince. He's so not good."

"He's a Prefect," Aiden counters.

I remember Jake's first words to me. "Yeah, but he's naughty. I love that about him."

"You said that so easily."

"Said what?"

"That you love him."

"Well, not in love. That's different."

"Have you told Dawson you love him yet?"

I fidget and rub my feet together nervously. "I told him that I'm ready for the key."

"That's not what I asked."

"Well, that's all I'm answering because it's none of your business what I say to him."

Aiden smiles. The four-ton radioactive smile.

"Stop grinning," I say and swivel back around in my seat. "It's annoying."

I'M LASHING OUT.

DANCE

"OKAY, LADIES," PEYTON says. "That's enough for today. Have a seat. We need to go over what's expected of you for Homecoming week. For those of you who are new this year, Homecoming at Eastbrooke is a time-honored tradition. Alumni will be on campus all week and you are expected to be on your best behavior. We'll be working on our parade float with the alumni dancers this Sunday afternoon. After that, we'll be teaming up with the cheerleaders and spirit club to make all the signs and banners that will decorate the halls this week. These are required activities."

She looks down at her notebook and continues. "You're expected to go all out on dress-up days. Monday is Groovy 70's. Peace. Love. Cougars. Think tie-dye and bell-bottoms. Tuesday is Pajama Day. A lot of girls will wear those zip-up onesies. They make your ass look horrible. Like you're wearing a diaper with a load in it. I don't want to see *any* dancers in one of those ugly things. Wednesday is Western Day. Think cowboy boots, bandanas, and hats. Thursday is Sports Day. You'll need to borrow a Varsity player's football jersey for that day and pair it with your red sequined skirt. We'll perform at the pep rally, bonfire, and for the JV game. Friday is School Spirit Day. Normally, that's the day we would wear the football jerseys but I'd like to do something different this year. Shake some things up. Anyone have any ideas?"

Katie whispers to me, "How cute would it be to dress as little cougar kitties? Like all in leopard or something?"

I whisper back, "Tell her. That's an awesome idea! Although I've never understood why they have leopard print mixed with their school colors when a cougar is different than a leopard."

"Probably because leopard print is easier to find?"

"Oh, yeah, that's true. So tell her."

"No, it's a stupid."

I raise my hand.

"Yeah, Keatyn?" Peyton says.

"Katie and I think it would be cute if instead of wearing school colors, we dress as cougar kitties."

Peyton's eyes light up. "That would be cute. We could wear leopard ears and tails. Those would be easy to buy. What about the outfit?"

"We have those black tanks and flutter skirts that are required for our dance competition. We could wear those."

"That's perfect. Good job, girls. On Saturday, we'll all be attending the Ladies' Luncheon. Please dress appropriately. Nothing low cut or too short." She glances down again. "All right. I think that covers it all. I'm looking forward to a fun week."

AFTER PRACTICE, PEYTON pulls me aside. "Jake really pissed Whitney off at lunch today. It was awesome."

"What's gotten into you lately? Are you mad at her?"

She shrugs. "I hate how she just assumes that she'll win Homecoming Queen. Like I don't even have a chance. It pisses me off. I guess I'm lashing out."

"I thought you were best friends."

Peyton rolls her eyes. "We have a weird friendship, I guess. Maybe I'm just getting sick of feeling like I'm always supposed to come in second. I'm probably too competitive." She turns to Katie. "Great idea on the little cougars. We're going to look hot."

MY SUPPOSED REBOUND.
7PM

DAWSON TAKES ME to the cute little Italian restaurant he brought me to on the day we bought my car. I know he's going to ask me out tonight, so I wanted to look extra cute. I straightened my hair but then teased it to look a little messy and sexy. The dress I'm wearing is a multicolored, crocheted Free People dress with a fringy hem. I couldn't decide if I wanted to wear the tall teal suede boots I got to go with it or the strappy purple suede heels. I went with the heels.

We have a nice dinner, chat pleasantly about Homecoming, about his family coming, but not once about our relationship.

I hope I didn't waste this adorable outfit on nothing.

After dinner, he parks his car down by the field house and leads me out onto the big green commons ground, where we played football and he kissed me in the grass.

My heels are sinking into the damp grass and I'm worrying about ruining the suede when he says, "This is where I first laid eyes on you."

"No, it's not. We met at dinner, when you said Riley was a cheap imitation of the real thing."

He scrunches up his nose. Kisses me. "You tease me about the worse kiss ever, but you're lucky I even talked to you. You were so mean."

I laugh. "You were a jerk, and, besides, I apologized."

"Still, this is where I first saw you. When you stole the soccer ball from me."

I remember that day so vividly. Like it was a scene out of a movie. I felt free and fearless. I could never have done something like that at my old school.

I glance over at the goal. The spot where I first saw Aiden.

I can still feel that instant connection.

But I've learned that instant connections aren't enough. Sparks aren't enough.

My mom always says that life is about the choices you make. And I know that I've made the right choice. The smart decision.

Because I'm here with Dawson.

"You didn't have a shirt on that day. I thought you were gorgeous."

"I thought you were crazy." He laughs and grabs a piece of my hair, twirling it lightly on his finger. "Crazy, but hot. So, Keatie, will you be my girlfriend?" His big brown eyes glitter in the moonlight.

Our relationship has been all backwards. Bad first impressions. Bad manners. Bad kisses. Sex way too soon. My supposed rebound could have gone horribly wrong in so many ways.

But it hasn't. It's been better than I could have scripted.

"I'd love to be your girlfriend, Dawson."

He undoes the necklace. I turn around and lift my hair up, while he clasps the key to his heart around my neck.

Of course, once he has it clasped he attacks my neck with his mouth.

COOL YOUR ORANGE PANTIES.
11PM

I'M LYING IN bed lazily sliding the key back and forth on the chain and thinking about tonight. How Dawson attacked my neck. How he stopped hugging me and started rubbing his hands up and down my sides. How he slid his hand up under my dress and inside my panties. How I stood there in the dark thinking, *What if someone can tell what he's doing to me*, but not caring enough to stop him. How by the time he was done all I could think about was having him come to my house for a wild playdate. The kind of playdate where the parents aren't home so the kids eat sugar, jump on the beds, and color all over the walls. How I dragged him to the lacrosse field. How the bleachers felt cold on my naked ass and how it contrasted so perfectly with the hotness of him on top of me.

He texts me at the same time a Facebook notification pops up.

Dawson Johnson and Kiki Kiki are in a relationship.

It shows a photo timeline of us together. Kissing on the bench. At the Hamptons partying. Holding my hand at lunch. Kissing after he asked me to Homecoming. I accept our relationship and change my profile picture to the one of us kissing. You can't really see my face, just how I leapt up into his arms and gave him a kiss worthy of the sexy way he asked me.

KATIE POPS UP out of her bed. "Keatyn! Dawson asked you out? Why didn't you tell me?"

"Everyone already thinks we're going out. We just made it official tonight."

"How did he ask? Was is dreamy?"

"I'm not sure about dreamy. He was just sweet. We went to dinner, and then he took me down on the soccer field where he first saw me. Asked me there."

"Then what?"

"Then he was being naughty, so I dragged him to the lacrosse field."

"I want to go to the lacrosse field. I've heard it's a nice, private place."

"I little cold but, yeah, it was."

"So are you finally going to admit that you and Dawson are having sex?"

I laugh. "Probably not."

"But you are, right?"

I nod my head and laugh. "Probably."

She leaps across the room and onto my bed. "Tell me about it, please. Let me live vicariously through you. I don't even have a date for Homecoming and it's only a week away!"

"I have an idea of someone you could go with. I know you've been hanging out with Jordan, but I heard him say that he didn't want a date."

She slumps her shoulders, picks up one of my pillows, and hugs it. "I was hoping Tyrese would ask me, but he's been seeing that Macy chick."

"Yeah, he hasn't hung out or partied with us in a while. Dawson says he does that. He gets all into a girl and forgets about his friends."

"So you have an idea of someone I could go with?"

"What about Dallas?"

"He is so cute. Do you think he would want to go with me?"

"I know he thinks you're cute."

Her face brightens. "Ohmigosh, really? He's adorable. Can you talk to him?"

"Should I call him now?"

"Oh, I don't know." She smooths her hair down with her hand. "I look like a mess."

"He's not going to see you through the phone, silly. I'll text him."

Me: *You gonna ask anyone to Homecoming?*

Dallas: *Probably go stag.*

Me: *What if you had a real date? Like with someone that has been crushing on you since school started.*

Dallas: *Katie???!!*

Me: *Yes, Katie. She was hanging with Jordan, but he says he doesn't want a date.*

Dallas: *Must be gay. Call me. Then make her talk to me.*

Me: *Uh, okay. What are you gonna say?*

Dallas: *First, I'm gonna ask if she wants to hang out tomorrow night. Then if she puts out, I'll ask her to HC.*

Me: *DALLAS!!!!*

Dallas: *Cool your orange panties and call me. I won't try anything but if she attacks me I will NOT resist.*

I dial Dallas' number and hold the phone out to Katie. Her eyes get big then she sits up straighter and brushes her fingers through her hair. She nods at me and takes the phone.

She goes, "Uh, huh." Laughs. "Oh!" Giggles. "Well, I'm not wearing any right now." Major blushing and more giggling. "No, you don't have to. Yes, I'd love to."

She hands me back my phone and screams, "AHHHHH!!!!! I have a date for Homecoming!" Then she stands up and jumps up and down on my bed singing, "I have a date. I have a date!"

I think about how Gracie used to jump on my bed. It's weird how someone doing the simplest thing can bring tears to my eyes. How it can remind me of home.

She does one more bounce then lands with a thud.

"Did you tell him he didn't have to ask you in a cute way?"

"Yeah, I don't care about that. I just want a date. Plus, he kinda caught me off guard when he asked about my panties. He's really sexy. Like, he has a sexy voice. Had any other guy asked me that, I probably would've hung up on him. But he's just so damn cute. I gotta call Annie and Maggie and tell them!"

She bounds back over to her bed and calls Maggie.

Me: *She's screaming in joy.*

Dallas: *I'll have her screaming in ecstasy ;)*

Me: *You are SO bad!*

I read Dawson's text.

Dawson: *I think we need to celebrate. Let's get some people together tonight and party.*

Me: *I thought our celebration was pretty damn good already but, you know me, I'm always up for a party.*

Dawson: *Bryce and Jake are up for it too. Meet me at 1, my sexy, hot, amazing girlfriend.*

Me: *Your girlfriend. I like that. <3*

HEARTING ME.

1:30AM

I'M SITTING IN Aiden's room.

Yes.

The place I said I was never going back to.

Lucky thing number one: Aiden is not here.

I'm happily sitting on Dawson's lap, drinking a Corona, and gabbing with Peyton.

Lucky thing number two: Whitney's not here.

I think tonight might just be my lucky night.

I've gotten lucky twice.

Well, three times if you count the lacrosse bleachers with Dawson.

And you most definitely should.

Jake walks in, grabs a beer, and tries to sit on my lap.

"My knee?" I half yell at him. I don't need him popping open my stitches. Although, I'm ready to. The things itch like crazy.

He hops up, picks Peyton's skinny ass up, sits in her chair, and sets her on his knee. "So I asked her," he announces.

"Asked who what?" Peyton asks.

"Whitney to Homecoming," Jake says matter-of-factly.

"But I thought you were doing my airplane idea?"

"Yeah, great idea. Big expense. Not doing it. So, I got creative. I wrapped a note around a certain body part. Told her she might want to find it."

"Ohmigawd, Jake! That's a horrible way to ask!" Peyton says as she hits him on the shoulder.

But I'm thinking just the opposite. A little treasure hunt around the body of a hot guy sounds like fun to me.

"I'd like a treasure hunt across your body," I whisper into Dawson's ear.

He squeezes me tight. "That sounds like fun."

Jake responds to Peyton by tickling her sides. "Wow. You think so highly of me. I wrapped it around my ankle." He grins. "Fortunately, for me, her mind is in the gutter like yours. She didn't look there first."

"I was gonna guess your bicep," I tell him.

He gives me a high five. "*That's* what I like about you, Monroe. You're sweet, even though you're a bad liar. I swear, you can't lie about anything. When you try to fib, it's written all over your face."

I think about the lies I've told them. How I'm a better liar than anyone knows.

But I smile and shake my head like I'm a ditz and he has me all figured out.

"Did she apologize to you yet?" he asks me.

"No," I scoff.

"She's not going to," Peyton says.

"I know. And I was thinking . . ."

"Uh oh," Jake says. He must have been drinking earlier because he seems kinda tipsy. He puts his fingers into Peyton's sides again, which causes her to squirm around on his lap.

The look on Jake's face and his own squirming tells me he's enjoying it.

They seem oddly comfortable touching each other, and I can't help but wonder if they have some kind of history.

"What I was going to say is that Katie, Maggie, Annie, and me are going to start an underground *Vote for Peyton* campaign. I found out that 90% of the freshman class voted for me for student council. I want to make sure they all vote for you."

"Better not let Whitney hear about that," Jake says, as he bounces Peyton on his knee and leers at her. "But I agree. Peyton would look gorgeous in a crown. And don't drink too much tonight, Monroe. We have some kissing to do on stage tomorrow." He giggles, sticks out his tongue at Dawson, and then licks up the side of Peyton's face.

She lets out a little screech, but Dawson frowns.

"Stop saying that! I will not be kissing anyone during tryouts. It's not part of the audition."

Luckily, Bryce walks in and hands Jake and Dawson a shot of something dark.

"Where are our shots?" Peyton asks, now totally flirting with Bryce. He rolls his eyes at her, so she says to me, "Keatyn, be a pal. Go across the hall and find us something yummy."

"Uh, okay," I say.

I walk across the hall. Bryce's door is slightly ajar and there is a little light glowing. I open the door slowly, hoping not to walk in on someone hooking up.

As my eyes adjust, I see Aiden's long body sprawled across Bryce's bed. His head is propped up on his arm and there are books spread out in front of him, but his eyes are closed and he appears to be asleep. I walk over, close his French textbook, and move it to the desk. As I do, a sheet of paper floats to the ground. I pick it up and hold it under the light. Random French words and scribbles are written across it like always. It seems to be how he studies. There's a list of words he can't remember. Some doodles. But just as I set the paper down, a phrase written in English catches my eye.

Why should I bother?

Underneath that, written in French is:

Elle ressentait la même chose.

Which translated means: *She felt the same way.*

Wow. Looks like his godly tricks have already worked on some other poor unsuspecting girl. The girl probably thinks they have an amazing connection and was thrilled when he asked her to Homecoming. At least I'm assuming he asked. I noticed the little stars aren't on his ceiling anymore.

I bet this is an old note. He was probably trying to decide if she was worth the hassle of hanging all those stupid little stars. Because what a pain in the ass that must have been.

I shove the note under his textbook with a little too much force, which causes a container full of pencils to crash onto its side.

Shit.

I glance at Aiden, praying I didn't wake him. Thankfully, I didn't, but he moved a little and now he's snuggling an extra pillow.

He looks adorably sweet.

Not so much god-like and much more boy-like.

I glide the back of my hand across his cheek, pull the blanket up over his shoulders, grab the bottle of cake vodka I know he started buying just for me, and then turn off the light.

"What took you so long?" Dawson says upon my return, pulling me back on his knee and kissing my neck.

"I couldn't find the cake vodka and Aiden was asleep, so I couldn't turn on the light." I hold up the bottle. "But the good news is that I found it."

Peyton grabs the bottle out of my hand, takes a big slug, and hands it back to me.

I do a quick shot before Dawson grabs it and chugs at least two shots worth.

We sit around for a while. Talking. Drinking. Laughing.

Finally, Bryce says he's tired and going to sleep.

"I'm tired too," I tell Dawson and pull him out the door.

As I turn around to say goodbye to Peyton, I see her and Jake start to drunkenly make out.

I quickly shut the door behind me.

WHEN I GET back to my room, I text Dawson.

> **Me:** *Tonight was really fun. I heart you.*

He calls me right away. "Is hearting me close to loving me?"

"Maybe. You swear you're over Whitney?"

"I swear."

"Then I think I need another goodnight kiss."

"I'm on my way."

I crack the window, letting in the chilly night air, then run into my closet, using my phone as a flashlight and jumping over the pile of textbooks that are scattered across my floor.

I throw on a soft knit nightie as I hear my window open and shut. I grab a cashmere blanket off my chair, wrap it around my shoulders, and walk toward my bed where Dawson is diving under the covers.

"It's cold out," he whispers.

I slide under the covers, wrapping him up in the blanket with me.

He's a little tipsy and looks really tired. "Are you tired?"

"Very, are you?"

"Yeah."

"So you just wanted a goodnight kiss, huh, Keatie?"

"That and . . ." I run my hands through his hair, stalling. Then I decide to be fearless and go for it. "I wanted to tell you something."

"And what's that?"

"I wanted you to know that I more than heart you, Dawson."

I can feel him smiling as he kisses me. "Hearting me is good enough."

"No, it's not, and it's not how I feel." I kiss the side of his neck, just below his ear, and finally say it, "I love you, Dawson."

Thursday, September 29th

DO I LOOK GUILTY?

LUNCH

WHEN MY ALARM went off at 6:30, Dawson was gone. But when I got in the shower and shut the shower curtain, I noticed something on the top of my hand.

In black permanent marker, he drew a heart.

And I've been smiling at it all day long.

I've been smiling at my shoes too. I'd been saving these Prada two-tone black and red Mary Jane platform pumps for a worthy occasion. And a new relationship with sexy Dawson is just such occasion. I paired them with a black Burberry stretch silk cinched-waist blouse, my red cardigan, plaid skort, black over the knee socks with ribbon ties, and an adorable Longchamp furry red clutch.

I'm getting ready to walk into the cafe, when Peyton grabs my arm and says, "Oh my god. Why did you let me drink so much?"

"Why did you let yourself drink so much?"

She pulls me into the girls' bathroom, looks under all the stalls, and then leans against the counter with a thud.

"Jake and I hooked up."

"Hooked up, hooked up? Or, like, made out hooked up?"

"We hooked up." She throws her arms in the air. "In my brother's bed!"

"Eww. What if he had walked in?"

She grabs my shoulders and gets in my face. "What. If. Whitney. Finds. Out?"

"How would she? Jake's not going to tell her. I'm certainly not gonna tell her. Dawson didn't see you kissing. What's up with you and Jake anyway? You seemed very familiar even before you got drunk."

"We used to go out. It was a long time ago."

"You're cute together," I say with a grin.

She buries her head in her hands and cries, "You don't even understand. She knows things."

"Oh, I understand perfectly. But don't worry, I won't say anything. You have my word."

"I just pray she doesn't find out."

"Don't act guilty then."

She looks at herself in the mirror. "Do I look guilty?"

"Mostly, you look hung over but, yes, right now, you do. But that's probably because you're kind of freaking out."

She runs her hand through her perfect long blonde waves and says, "Shit. I cannot let her find out but, at the same time, I would kind of like her to know. It just really pisses me off how she's prancing around with Jake and acting like them being Homecoming King and Queen is a given. Which is funny since this was always supposed to be her and Dawson's big year." She rolls her eyes. "The culmination of all her work."

"Her work?"

Peyton purses her lips. "I shouldn't have said that but, in a way, sleeping with Jake feels sort of freeing." She stops and laughs. "Plus, he is really fun. Maybe I should just tell her." She nervously bites on the edge of a manicured nail. "You know, she did that to me. Found out that my college boyfriend was cheating on me. Embarrassed me in class by passing around a photo of him kissing another girl."

I think about how I could help. What could she do that wouldn't be a direct challenge, but would still piss Whitney off?

I smile. "Maybe you should find a Homecoming date who is hotter than Jake."

Peyton narrows her eyes. "Who here is hotter than Jake?"

"I don't know," I say. "Come on. Let's get out of here."

WE STAND IN line, grab a couple salads, and then sit at the table. Dawson and Riley walk over and set their trays down next to me.

Peyton's face lights up, and I half expect her to say Dawson is hotter and she'll take him.

She stands up quickly and throws her arms around my shoulders in a hug. "You're brilliant."

"Why are you brilliant?" Dawson asks, just as Whitney sits down and scoffs,

"Yes, why *are* you brilliant?"

"Because I helped a friend with a problem, I think."

Whitney sneers. "So brilliant that you don't even know. Classic." She turns her back on us and starts chatting animatedly to Rachel about Jake's Homecoming proposal.

I face Dawson. "I think maybe Peyton wants to be your date."

He runs his hand up my thigh. "Peyton is hot, but she's been with my brother. I could never be with someone who's been with one of my brothers. Speaking of brothers. Cam wants me to hang out with him this weekend."

"That sounds fun."

"You won't be mad if I go?"

"Should I be mad at you for wanting to see your brother?"

He wraps his arm around my neck and kisses my forehead. "You're the coolest girlfriend ever."

I'm about to ask him what he's going to do there that I would need to be cool about, but the dean stands up at the podium. "Before I announce this year's Homecoming Court, I'd like to remind you all to be on your best behavior while the alumni are our guests. I expect no shenanigans." He stops and stares directly at Riley. "The alumni are to be treated with the upmost respect. Now it's my honor to announce this year's Court."

He starts reading freshman and sophomore names off a list. "Riley, why did he stop and look at you?"

Riley whispers, "Remember I told you I got kicked out Freshman year?"

"Uh, huh."

"It may have been due to an incident during Homecoming."

" . . . Junior boys: Aiden Arrington, Logan Pedersen, and Nick Cosse. Junior Girls: Maggie Morgan, Keatyn Monroe, Ariela Ross. And lastly, our Senior Court: Jake Worth, Dawson Johnson, and Brad Stewart. And our lovely Queen candidates: Whitney Clarke, Peyton Arrington, and Mariah Sauer. Remember, if you are a football player, you will wear your uniform on the field during half time. And, as per tradition, all girls will wear a formal gown. All members will be accompanied on the field by their parents. Congratulations to this year's Homecoming court, and Go Cougars!"

I watch Whitney ball her hand into a fist and shake it when they call her name. She must really want this. She never shows such excitement over anything.

Dawson hugs me. "Congrats, Keatie! I can't believe you made it. You've only been here a month!"

Whitney says, "Why you think she's dating you, Dawson? She wants to be popular."

I want to leap over the table, grab Whitney by the shirt, and wipe the smug look off her face.

But, I don't.

"I'm not dating Dawson to be popular, Whitney." I say. "I'm dating him for hot sex."

Dawson drops his head onto my shoulder to hide his snickers.

"Classy."

"Hot sex isn't supposed to be classy, Whitney. But speaking of classy, I heard how Jake asked you to Homecoming last night. How he tied a note to a *certain* body part."

Rachel and the other minions look at Whitney in surprise. I have a feeling she didn't tell them the complete truth.

Whitney recovers quickly. "He wrapped it around his ankle."

I laugh. "So I heard. I also heard that wasn't the *first* place you looked." I turn to Dawson. "Come on, my future Homecoming King. Walk me to class."

"My pleasure," he says, getting up and escorting me out of the cafe.

AS I'M SITTING in French class, waiting for the bell to ring, I'm thinking about texting Kym and asking her to find me a gown. But I decide that it might be fun to go shopping in New York this weekend instead. Dawson will be out of town, so I'll ask the girls if they want to make a weekend out of it. I'm also wondering who in the world I'm going to get to escort me on the field.

Me: *I need your help.*

My phone rings.

"What's wrong?" Garrett asks me.

"Um, nothing. I made Homecoming Court. My parents are supposed to escort me. It's a big deal here, so I just thought maybe . . ."

Aiden and Annie sit in their desks next to me. ". . .Um, maybe, my *uncle* could come."

"I'm sorry. Your mom is planning a trip, so I have a lot on my mind."

"Is something going wrong with the trip?"

"It's my job to make sure nothing goes wrong."

"Oh, okay. So it's next Friday night. Will that work?"

His voice softens. "I'll make it work, Keatyn."

I smile. "Thank you."

Annie screams, "Congrats on Court! Oh my gosh, Keatyn, I'm so excited for you. And a little jealous, too. I wish I could get a gorgeous long gown."

SCRIPTED OUT HER PERFECT LIFE.

SOCCER

WE'RE FINISHING UP soccer practice when Peyton smiles and whispers to me, "Done."

"What's done?"

"I have a date who is hotter than Jake and, no offense, hotter than Dawson."

"Who?"

"Dawson's older brother, Camden. But don't tell anyone. I want it to be a surprise. I've been telling Whitney that I don't have a date. That I'm probably going stag. She's been pitying me."

"Why don't you want her to know?"

"Because that's who Whitney really wanted." She leans in close and speaks quietly. "Dawson doesn't even know this. He thought she was a virgin when they did it, but her first time was really with Cam."

As we jog into the locker room, I think about Dawson. How hurt and disgusted he would be if he ever found out the truth.

While I'm changing out of my soccer clothes, Peyton is still spilling. "He totally used her then ditched her. So she settled for Dawson. Told me that she knew he'd grow up to be almost as hot and planned their perfect senior year in detail."

"She scripted out her perfect life?" Wow. Whitney and I aren't really that different.

I mean, except for the whole bitch part.

Peyton nods, "Exactly."

"So you're taking Cam to rub her face in it?"

"Yep," she says proudly, tightening her ponytail. "I'm tired of her crap. Tired of her telling me who I should date. What I should do. How I should dress. I'm going on record right now." She stands in the center of the locker room and yells out, "I hate square-heeled grandma shoes!" Then she takes a pair of sensible navy pumps out of her locker and whips them into the trash.

I can't help but flash back to Cush taking off the boots that were trying to kill me and how freeing it felt. How it was about more than just a pair of shoes that didn't fit. I was trying to free myself of Vanessa.

She goes on. "I'm popular. I'm in every freaking activity there is. I should just make my own group. Tell her to fuck off."

I scrunch up my nose. "Um, yeah, that might not be the best idea."

She wraps her arm around my shoulder. "And you are just the girl to be my new best friend."

"Um . . ."

She holds up her hand, shushing me. "No. Please. Don't say anything. Let me revel in the freedom."

"Uh, okay," I say, but I'm thinking, *Shit. What did I just get myself into?*

BE A ROCK STAR.

4:45PM

I STOP TO get hot chocolates for the girls after dance practice and when I get to our room, Katie, Maggie, and Annie are surrounding Katie's desk.

Katie turns to me. "Keatyn, come here! You have to listen to our new favorite song. And you should see the video. Hang on, I'm going to pull it up. The lead singer. Holy shit. He is so freaking hot. But, like, dreamy. And, I swear, it feels like he's singing to you. Like you're the only girl in the world."

As she pulls up the video, I see the name *Twisted Dreams* dance across the screen.

I slowly drop down onto her bed.

"It's not a real video," she continues. "Apparently, they played this song for the first time at a concert in Stockholm and the crowd went crazy. So the next concert—well, watch. You'll see."

The big stage is completely dark except for a spotlight shining down on Damian, who is sitting on a stool holding a microphone. His guitar strap is across the front of his chest; his guitar pushed around to his back. His head is down and his dark bangs are shagging over his closed eyes. The song starts out slow with only his soulful voice.

She's the kind of girl
Everybody wants be.
But no one sees what's inside,
Or that she cries herself to sleep.

But I see, baby, yeah, I see.

She's Miss Popular,
Floating with the crowd.
But it all feels so empty
That she wants to scream out loud.

But I see, baby, yeah, I see.

Suddenly, the stage lights up. The band starts rocking as Damian stands up, kicks the stool away, and sings loudly.

So forget about them,
Come surf the crowd with me.
It ain't the water,
But, baby, it's plain to see.

You gotta do your own thing.
Forge your own path.
Climb up to the top.
Any way you can.

You gotta do your own thing.
Do it up big.
Launch us to the moon.
Now, everybody sing.

The band joins him singing the chorus and so do Katie and the crowd. My eyes fill with tears. I know this is the song he talked about writing when we were in France this summer. About doing what makes you happy. About not following the crowd.

Be yourself.
Do what you love.
And soon we can all
Be a rock star.
Be a rock star.

You gotta do your own thing
Who cares what they think.
Rocket to the moon.
Come on, everybody sing.

Be yourself.
Do what you love.
And soon we can all
Be a rock star.
Be a rock star.

All three of them are still singing, *Be a rock star, be a rock star,* even after the video is over. Katie swivels on her chair. "Aren't they awesome? I heard they're going to tour Japan next and then, finally, they will be touring here. We have to go see them. Promise me."

I swallow the big lump in my throat and nod at her. "Yeah. We will definitely go."

Katie's phone beeps. She reads it and pops out of her chair excitedly. "That's Dallas. I'm meeting him for dinner, then we're skipping the JV game to study in the library." She laughs. "Actually, I'm hoping *not* to study. If he doesn't kiss me tonight, I don't know what I'm going to do. I want to kiss him so badly. Will you be in the library tutoring Aiden tonight? Or did you already?"

I laugh. "Let's see. I think you should get him to kiss you. Stare at his lips. He'll get the hint. And I am not tutoring Aiden tonight. I think he's going to study with Annie."

"Aiden said he has something else to do tonight," Annie says. "I'm meeting Ace at the game. Are you and Dawson coming?"

"I have those play tryouts."

"Oh, I suck as a friend." Annie says, "I completely forgot. Good lu—"

"Don't say it," I interrupt her quickly. "You say, *Break a leg.*"

Katie goes, "But you already hurt your knee. Why would we want you to break your leg? A cast would suck. You couldn't dance. It'd be tough to, you know, have fun with Dawson, and you could only wear one shoe."

"Katie."

"Oh, sorry. I'm rambling." She gives me a hug. "Why don't you wish me luck on the kissing, instead?"

"Good luck," I say.

Maggie says, "She is totally right about the shoes, because you'd probably have to wear flats with a cast. And that would suck."

"Hey, speaking of shoes. Should we all go shopping this weekend? I guess I need to find a gown and stuff for dress up days. Annie, you said you wanted a new dress."

Annie starts bouncing up and down. I think she and Katie have been hanging out too much. "That would be so great!"

Maggie screeches, "Yes! I'd much rather have you guys help me pick out a gown than my mother!"

"Where should we go?" Katie asks.

"New York. Dawson will be at Columbia, so I thought we could have a girls' weekend. Shop all day. Stay at my loft. Party all night."

"That sounds perfect!" Maggie exclaims.

"Hey, Ariela made Court too. Would you mind if I invited her?"

Katie says, "But she's a cheerleader? Isn't she supposed to be our mortal enemy during Homecoming?"

"Technically, yes, but she's really nice," Maggie says wistfully. "We were best friends until I accidentally slept with her ex-boyfriend."

"*Accidentally* slept with him?"

Maggie laughs. "I was drunk."

"Do you hate each other?"

"No, she forgave me, but we really haven't been close since."

"Do you have her number?"

"Yeah, here. I just texted it to you."

I open the text, add her to my contacts, and text her.

Me: *Hey! It's Keatyn. Congrats on Court! Me, Annie, Maggie, and Katie are going to NY on Saturday morning to go shopping. Maggie and I need dresses and we all want to find stuff to wear for spirit week. We're staying at my loft. Wanna join us?*

Ariela: *Is Maggie okay with that?*

Me: *Completely. She says she misses you.*

Ariela: *Awww. Tell her I miss her too. I hoped to make Court again this year, but I was afraid to buy a dress early and jinx getting nominated. So I need to shop too. I'd love to go!*

Me: *We plan to shop all day and drink all night. A happy, boy-free night.*

Ariela: *I could use a boy-free night. Riley pisses me off sometimes.*

Me: *Why?*

Ariela: *He hasn't asked me to Homecoming yet!! It's only a week away! Is he going stag?*

***Me:** I'm not sure. I'll ask him.*

Yes, I lie to her. But after tomorrow night, she won't be mad anymore.

***Ariela:** Thanks :) I can't wait!*

"She's on board, and, Maggie, she says she misses you."

"Oh, that's so sweet. This is such a good idea. All right, I have to get going too. I'm working on a date of my own," she says as they breeze out the door.

AS SOON AS they leave, I send an email to the concierge service for my loft with a long list of food and drinks I want delivered. Then I look at the clock.

Let's see. It's six here, so it should be well after midnight, depending on where he is in Europe.

I push Damian's number and, as usual, he answers right away.

"Keats, what's up?"

"A friend just showed me your video. The new song. It's really great. Catchy. She already has it memorized." I sing, "Be a rock star. Be a rock star."

"I've been wanting to call you. I'm sorry I haven't. You should've been the first one to hear it, since you inspired it with all your drama this summer."

"It's good to know my screwed up life is so inspirational," I say sarcastically.

"Hey, you're the one who told me people could probably relate. And you were right. We performed it one night just to gauge the crowd's reaction. It was nuts. They were singing it with us before it was over. And the label's not stupid. They knew we had a hit on our hands, got us some studio time, and we recorded it quickly. We released it a week ago and it's already hit number two in Japan."

"And there are over a million views on the concert video. Damian, I'm so proud of you. Where are you anyway?"

"Helsinki. We have a show here tomorrow night. That will round out the European tour. We'll be doing some promotional stuff, maybe get some studio time, then back at it in Japan. How's it going there?"

"I'm doing good. I'm dating a guy. He's really sweet . . ."

"Not to interrupt but I think I'm going to be in Miami soon. Special gig. I'll let you know. It'd be great to see you. I miss my Keats."

"I was your Keats before I was anyone else's."

He clears his voice. "You talk to him much?"

"I did something stupid, Damian. Vincent almost found me."

"What did you do?"

I tell him about the surf tournament.

"THAT'S IT. I'M kicking his ass."

"All that I just told you about Vincent and that's what you got out of the story? That you need to kick B's ass?"

"Yes. I'm definitely kicking his ass. And if I do Miami, it will be a very last minute surprise-the-audience thing. Not planned like Brook's tour. I really want to see you. What are you doing for the holidays?"

"I don't know. I haven't really thought about it yet."

"I think you should go to The Crab." *The Crab* is our nickname for their house in St. Croix.

"Could I? Will your dad be there?"

"No. Marisa is pregnant again."

"Awww!"

"Yeah. It's a boy this time. She wants to name him Rain."

"Well, his sister is named Stormy. I guess that would fit."

"He'll get his ass kicked on the playground with a name like that. Why can't they name him Lightning or Thunderbolt or something tough?"

"Speaking of names. My sisters got a dog like Buoy. They named her Kiki."

He laughs out loud.

I miss making him laugh. I miss him.

"My dad told me about that. All I have to say is Kiki must be one patient dog. I heard the girls painted her with pink and purple paint, then poured glitter all over her. When Tommy got pissed, Ivery took him aside and told him that Kiki was sad because she didn't have pretty tutus or glitter shoes and they wanted to her feel pretty. They're so funny. Everyone says they are going to have to call you Buoy when you come home." He stops laughing and is quiet for a minute. "I miss you, Keats. Everyone misses you."

"I miss everyone too. Garrett doesn't think I'll ever be able to go home. But I'm doing okay, Damian. I'm starting over."

"That's bullshit. If this goes on much longer, screw Garrett, you and me will figure out something together."

"Like old times, huh? You helping me write the scripts of my life?"

"Exactly. So, hey, we have a morning radio interview in a few hours and I haven't even been to bed yet."

I hear a girl's voice in the background say, *Baby, hurry up.*

"Who's that? Damian! Do you have a girlfriend?"

He laughs loudly and then whispers to me. "More like groupies. Touring is *awesome.*"

"Then I better let you get back to that."

"Actually, I was just getting ready to leave. I really do need to get a few hours of sleep. Are you sure you're doing okay, like, really?"

"I think so."

"Any guys giving you shit?"

"I love you."

"You're avoiding that topic. Does that mean one already is?"

"No. It's more like the opposite."

"A guy is treating you too well?"

"Yeah, maybe."

"Maybe you should marry him," he laughs. "No, wait, you can't. We're already married."

"It will be easy to annul. We married under false pretenses. You told me you were a prince."

"Only because you wrote the script and made me wear that girly crown."

"True, but I also cast you as a frog because hopping around like a maniac and singing songs was something you were actually good at."

"Are you saying I wasn't a believable Prince? You've just dashed my dreams of winning an Oscar."

"I'm saying you played a much better frog." I hear the girl whine again in the background. "Case in point," I say and hang up.

YOUR ARM CANDY.

6:45PM

AFTER DINNER, JAKE walks by us, puckers his lips at me, and makes a loud kissing noise. "Come on, sweets, let's go."

Dawson flips him off, wraps his arms around me, and kisses my neck. "How 'bout you skip tryouts and come to my room? I guarantee it will be more fun."

"Why don't you come watch me?"

"I really don't want to watch you kiss a bunch of guys on stage."

"You know Jake is exaggerating that part just to piss you off. I kiss Jake three times in the play. And they have to be perfect fairytale kisses. They aren't hot kisses."

"Like this?" He lays his lips gently on mine in a chaste fairytale-style kiss, but then grabs the back of my hair and shoves his tongue in my mouth.

"Are you sure you don't want to try out? Those are the kind of kisses I would like to practice over and over again."

"So Jake's not going to kiss you like this?"

"Um, not even close."

"But if you do the play, we won't have much time for our kind of practicing," he pouts as he slides his hands down my back and squeezes my ass.

"We'll have plenty of time for that. I promise," I tell him as we head out of the cafe.

What I don't tell him is that this is something I really want to do. And that for the first time in my life, I can try out for a role and not worry about being an embarrassment to my mom.

I can just be me.

I PRACTICALLY SKIP to the auditorium. I'm so excited.

I see Jake and Peyton ahead of me. They appear to be having a heated discussion. He walks through the auditorium doors and leaves Peyton outside.

She looks upset. "Are you okay?"

She takes a deep breath. "Yeah. Jake isn't going to say anything, but I'm pretty sure he already told Bryce. Whitney cannot find out."

"Congrats on Court. I meant to tell you earlier, but you were reveling in the freedom of throwing away your shoes."

She brightens. "That felt really good. And you too. I'm so happy for you."

"What's the deal with wearing a formal dress on a football field? That's the weirdest thing I've ever heard."

"Really? It seems normal to me. So I saw Maggie and Katie earlier. They said you all are going to New York to shop this weekend. Do you think I could come with you? Is that bad? My totally inviting myself."

"We'd love it! I would've asked you. I just figured you already had a dress."

"Whitney has had her dress for months. She's been planning for the perfect dress since she started dating Dawson."

"Do you have one?"

"I do, but she helped me pick it out." She scowls. "I don't love it."

I give her a grin. "You're going to win, so you need to be in a dress that you love."

She bounces a little. "Wouldn't that be amazing?"

I glance at my watch. "Hey, I gotta get in there."

"Break a leg." She looks at me sincerely and says, "Thanks for letting me come with you."

"You're welcome. Um, do you want to invite Whitney? I felt bad when she left me out, I don't want to make her feel that way."

"Hell, no," she says and marches off.

"KEATYN MONROE," THE drama coach says, calling my name off a list in his hand.

It's time! I was a little nervous while I was standing here waiting for my turn, but as I walk across the stage, it's gone.

I'm ready.

I have my lines memorized.

The accent down.

I know how I want to portray the character physically.

I've even dressed the part in a sweet but flirty skirt and cowboy boots.

I recite my lines and forget about everything else.

AFTER MY TRYOUT, I step slowly off the stage. I know I have to let the next person audition, but I'm not ready to leave. I could stay up here all night.

Dance. Talk. Pretend to be someone else.

I don't want to leave.

I send Dawson a quick text, telling him I'll meet him later, and work my way through the seats to the darkened back of the auditorium.

I'm surprised to find Aiden sitting right where I was headed. "Are you trying out?" I whisper as I take a seat next to him.

"No, I watched Logan and Nick try out earlier. They had to get to the JV game. I decided to stay and watch for a while."

"Shouldn't you be there too?"

"Cole was the starting receiver and he got hurt, so I'm filling in for him and will only be playing Varsity for a while."

"That's exciting. Congrats."

He cocks his head at me. "So just *who* was that up there?"

"What do you mean?" My heart sinks. "Oh my gosh, did I suck?"

He smiles gently and shakes his head. "No, you didn't suck. It was like watching a different person. The accent. The way you flipped your hair."

He knows how I flip my hair?

He continues. "And you put your hand on your hip when she was being sassy. You only do that in real life when you're mad. You even held your jaw differently. Like, not as tight as usual and your face looked softer. Sweeter, maybe."

I break out in a grin. "That's because she's not a bitch like I am."

"You're not a bitch."

"No? But I can play one." I straighten my back. Tilt my chin and look down on him. Roll my shoulders slightly forward in a model pose. Get a defiant look in my eye.

"Damn, you haven't even said anything yet, and I'm already scared," he says with an adorable laugh. He studies my face for a minute. "You know, you have a very expressive face."

My mind flashes to Vincent saying those same words. I remember thinking it was sweet that he noticed. Of course, that was before he tried to kidnap me.

"Thank you," I say to Aiden.

"You belong up there. On stage. You made it look completely effortless, like you're a natural."

My heart aches to tell him that I should be a natural at it, having an actress for a mom and a model for a dad. I think about my dad. How he always used to tell me to think of something happy and then would snap a photo. How we would pose for silly pictures. How he could think about something sad and look like a different person.

I nod my head and whisper the words I've been afraid to admit to anyone. "I think it's what I want to do. Like, for a living. Like, if I'm good enough."

"If I didn't need you here to tutor me, I'd suggest you quit school, go to Hollywood, and start auditioning. I'm serious, Keatyn."

My heart skips a beat. He just called me Keatyn.

God, my name sounds beautiful on his tongue.

I get all flush and flustered. Why do I still get that way around him? I kicked the Aiden addiction.

"Um, uh, thanks," I stammer. "But I think I need some practice first. Some classes, maybe."

"Well, I know you'll get the part."

"You can't know that. I was the first one to audition for it."

"Why did you pick that role and not the lead?"

"I like how she affects the story, I guess. I like how she has to follow her heart and how she finds true love. How even though the Bad Prince tries to keep her and the Good Prince apart, their love prevails."

Aiden lets out a deep, sexy growl. The kind of growl that makes a girl want to rip off her panties.

Not me, of course. I'm just saying most girls. Well, some girls would, maybe.

I think.

"I always knew you were a romantic at heart," he says.

For the first time tonight, I start to sweat. I move my arms out wide on the armrests to give my pits some air to breathe.

No. I will not do it.

I will not talk to the hottie god about true love or romance.

I will change the subject.

"I've heard it's hard to be an actress. Dealing with the paparazzi. The filming locations. Kissing your cast mates. I can see why Dawson is having a hard time with it."

Aiden leans closer to me and puts his big hand on top of my knee.

It's a casual gesture, leaning in toward me, his hand on my knee for balance. "Dawson should be here supporting you. And if he had come, he'd know. It's not you up there."

Electrical shivers shoot up my leg.

And my knee is *such* a slut!

She likes it! She's that friend you have. The one who you tell you're on a diet and the next day she shows up with cupcakes and says, *Aww, just one won't hurt.*

But when I look down at my knee, I realize that she's not only a slut, she's an enabler. She's all, *Look at your knee. How small it looks under his big hand. How safe it feels.*

God, I hate my knee.

And Aiden is talking to me. Something about a premiere and a red carpet. But I don't really catch all he's saying.

Because. His. Hand. Is. On. My. Knee.

"You'll walk the red carpet with me?" I ask unbelievably. Is that what he said?

It's dark back here, but I instantly see a flash of brilliant white teeth.

"I said I'd *watch* you walk it, but if you're offering . . ."

"Oh. I, um, just, you know, a hot guy in a black suit is, um, well, it's like the ultimate accessory."

I get another radiant smile. "It's agreed then. I'll be your arm candy."

I have the sudden urge to lick him. To see if he tastes as good as he looks.

He leans back to watch the next audition, taking his big hand with him.

I close my eyes and shake my head.

How the hell does he do that?

Damn him!

He's like a goddamned walking love potion.

I quickly grab the key necklace, hoping it's like an antidote, and slide it back and forth across my chin while we watch the rest of the auditions in silence.

AN OBSESSION WITH BRAS.
9:30PM

AFTER AUDITIONS, I have a little time before curfew, so Dawson leaves the JV game and meets me in his room.

"I think my tryout went pretty well."

"Speaking of pretty . . ." He kisses my neck hard, unbuttons my blouse, and grins. "This is the bra from the day at the library."

"You have an obsession with bras. What are you, like thirteen?" I laugh, but I love that he likes them.

He throws me on the bed and shakes his head. "I know a lot more now than when I was thirteen."

My phone buzzes with a text and I peek at it over his shoulder.

"Dawson! Ohmigawd! Yay! I got a callback!"

"A what?"

"A callback. From the director! I mean, the drama coach!"

"What does that mean?"

"It means he liked my tryout enough to want me to read another scene tonight, probably with one of the princes to see if we have chemistry on stage."

"Chemistry? Like the kissing parts?"

"It's not just the kissing. It's are we believable to the audience? Am I a good enough actress to pretend like I have feelings for him? Haven't you ever seen a movie where two people are supposed to fall in love but you just can't picture them together? I mean, take *Twilight* for example. I think when most people read the book they loved Edward. But when the first movie came out a lot of people started switching to Team Jacob because it felt like they had good chemistry." I laugh. "And, well, his abs didn't hurt either."

"But aren't the people who played Edward and Bella a couple in real life?"

"I'm not sure, but I think they were a couple during some of the filming."

"So, some people do fall in love with their co-stars." He hangs his head a little.

I wrap my arms around his neck. "Dawson, I love you. Please don't be jealous."

He pushes me back a little to read my face.

"Is Jake just giving me shit?"

"Yes."

"It's just he has Whitney, and I was a little nervous he'd get you too."

"You're jealous Jake has Whitney?"

He runs his hand through his hair and sighs. "No, it's just he was telling Bryce and Tyrese about other night. About how she was drunk. How hot the sex was. I guess she's different with him."

"Our sex is different than it was with you and her, it would stand to reason that theirs would be different too," I say, even though I know that Jake was talking about sex with Peyton, not Whitney.

"Yeah, I guess. Maybe she just wasn't that attracted to me."

Knowing what I know about her wanting his brother instead, I'd say he's probably right. "Not to bring up my past, but I'm not the same with you as I have been before. You make me feel a whole lot sexier."

He tries to pull my bra off. "You are sexier."

"And I have to go. I'll call you when I get back to my dorm."

Friday, September 30th

STRANDED ON SECOND BASE.

BREAKFAST

I'M SITTING AT breakfast with Riley and Dallas.

"So, I'm giving up on boobs," Dallas says.

Riley is like, "You going gay, dude?"

"Ah, no. But apparently some girl complained to a teacher about it, like I was sexually harassing her or some shit."

"That's kinda lame," I say.

"It's not like you were touching them or anything. Were you?" Riley asks.

"Naw, I mean, not unless she wanted me to later." Dallas grins. "But I decided that basically the psychic panty network and the boob guessing were really just pickup lines. Ways to talk to a girl, get her attention."

I nod my head. "I could see that."

"So, I have a new approach."

"Oh, boy, what's that?"

"I'm going to try a different pickup line every few days."

"Interesting idea."

"Maybe we could go off campus and try out a few," Riley suggests.

"Riley, are you trying to meet new girls? I thought you were crazy about Ariela?"

"I am, but, shit. I told you. I'm stranded on second base. I haven't been stranded on second base since seventh grade!"

"Which means you like her."

"Yeah, maybe. We'll see."

I turn to Dallas. "So does it start today? What's your line? Try it out on me."

"I can't just say it. I need to work it into the conversation."

The bells rings, reminding us it's time to head to our first class.

"I'll walk over and refill my coffee. You come up to me and say it."

He rolls his eyes at me. "Fine."

"Wait," Riley says. "I'm going to get coffee with her. I gotta hear this."

Riley and I wander up to the coffee thermoses, refill our cups, and then turn to walk to class.

Dallas saunters up next to me. He's wearing a very cute smile. It's the smile I noticed the first day, when I decided to go sit by him. He stops and lays his hand gently on my forearm.

I stop walking and give him a confused look.

He grins at me and says, "I just have to ask. Did you have Lucky Charms for breakfast this morning?"

"Uh, no. Why?"

"Cuz you look magically delicious."

I can't help it. I grin back at him and laugh. Because if I didn't have a boyfriend, I would totally fall for that.

"I didn't have Lucky Charms," I say, "but now I wish I would have. You should say that to Katie today. It'd probably melt her panties off."

Riley hits Dallas on the back as he walks off to his first class. "I thought that was pretty lame."

"Only because you didn't think of it first." They both laugh, then Riley turns to me. "So I hear you asked Ariela to go shopping with you. Now Dallas and I will be stuck here alone."

"Why don't you go to Columbia with Dawson?"

"Dawson is going to Columbia?" He raises his eyebrows at me.

"Yeah."

"And you're okay with that?"

"Uh, I think so. Should I not be okay with that?"

"Camden is . . . well, he's trouble."

"Trouble, how?"

"I know what goes on there. Cam knows a lot of girls. *Gets* a lot of girls."

I squint my eyes trying to follow. Then I realize what he's not saying and my eyes get big. "You think he's going to cheat on me?"

"Cam is an awesome brother, but he can be a dick. All I ever wanted was to be like him." He sighs. "Part of why I got kicked out of school."

"You need to tell me what happened."

"I was told to never speak of it again," he says seriously.

"By who?"

"The dean."

"Oh. So you can't tell me?"

"Maybe some other time." He laughs. "It's a pretty epic story, really. I can't believe I'm sitting here saying all this. What the hell did you do to me?"

"What I did to you?"

"Yeah, I'm turning into Dawson. Pussy whipped but getting no pussy."

I smile at him. "You like Ariela. She's going to be so excited tonight. I can't wait."

"It was cool of you to ask her to go shopping with you. I'd like it if you were friends."

"I know. That's why I asked. So you really think your brother is going to cheat on me? He's, um, not really in the same situation as you."

Riley punches my shoulder. "He's whipped, all right."

I nod my head. "I meant the other part."

"Unfortunately, he's been rubbing that part in. Not details. Just how hot you make him, that kind of thing. Although he's not very excited about you doing the play. I heard you got called back to read with Jake and Logan."

"I did. Jake and I have good chemistry on stage and Logan seems to kind of hate me, which, really, is perfect for the part. He's going to pretend to like me just to screw things up for his brother. Getting a callback is exciting, but I still don't know if I'll get the part."

WINNING RUNS IN THE FAMILY.
HISTORY

DURING HISTORY, OUR classroom is paged and I'm called to the office.

Everyone in class goes, *Ooooohhhh*. Like I did something I'm about to get in trouble for.

As I put my notebook into my bag, my mind starts to go crazy thinking about what I've possibly done wrong.

I've never gotten in trouble at school.

Except Aiden causing me to be late those two times.

Do they know Dawson sneaks into my room? Do they know we party at Hawthorne House after curfew? Do they know I smoke at the Cave?

I get to the office and say to the secretary, "I'm Keatyn Monroe. You called me out of class?"

Peyton steps out from behind a cubicle. "Oh, that was me. I need your help on some of this after party stuff. I didn't think you would mind getting out of class."

I smile at the secretary, trying to assure her that I wasn't the least bit nervous.

Peyton loops her arm through mine and says loudly, "We're going to my dorm so that we can make some phone calls in peace."

As we walk by the big trophy cases out front, she stops and points at some photos. "These are all the past Homecoming Kings and Queens. Isn't that cool? I love looking at the dresses and hairstyles and how they've changed over the years."

I study the photos, going back to the early 40s. "They are very cool. I like this dress especially." I point to the winner from four years ago. She's wearing a gorgeous but simply cut pale pink gown. "Clarke?" I look at her closer. "Is she related to Whitney?"

Peyton nods. "That's her older sister, Winnie Clarke. Isn't she gorgeous? She was captain of the dance team too." She points at two other photos a couple years further back. "And these are her brothers."

"So winning runs in the family?"

"Yeah. Part of why she acts like she's entitled to win."

"I love her sister's gown. Is Whitney's that pretty?"

Peyton laughs. "I guess that all depends on what you consider pretty. Come on. We better get going."

AS SOON AS we walk out of the building, she says, "I lied. The event coordinator is handling most of the after party stuff. I thought maybe we could go to my room and look at dresses online. The dress is a big part of the tradition. Did you notice how all the dresses were very subtle? Very classy?"

"Yeah, and I read the flyer with all the rules regarding the dress."

"Everyone who was nominated is either a cheerleader or a dancer. We'll change into our dresses right before halftime, but Whitney will wear hers for the entire game. Want to see a picture of Whitney's dress?"

"Sure," I say. I'm sure it's going to be gorgeous.

We get to her room and she pulls up a photo of Whitney's dress on her laptop. "So this is hers. What do you think of it?"

I look at the dress. It's a strapless nude-colored gown with a high slit up one leg. The entire bodice down to just above the knee is encrusted with very large multi-colored pastel jewels. Past the knee, the jewels are sprinkled sparsely down the nude colored mesh.

"Wow. It's, um, pretty bold. It looks more like a pageant dress to me. But it's hard to tell until you see it on."

"It's way over the top. Especially when you consider the way they want us to look. Wait 'til you see mine."

She clicks the mouse and up pops a photo of Peyton in a fully beaded gown. I can't help it. I start laughing. "You look like you should be turning letters on a game show, not wearing a Homecoming crown!"

She giggles with me. "That's why I'm so excited to go shopping with you. I want a dress that's me. This is not me. And it weighs about ten pounds."

"I think that's why Whitney's choice is such a shock. She dresses so conservatively. I'm surprised she would buy something like that."

"She said she wants to stand out."

"You stand out when a dress enhances your beauty. You have to wear the dress. The dress can't wear you. That's why so many people choose their Academy Awards dresses wrong. They look at the dress's beauty, not their beauty in the dress."

Peyton gives me a mega-watt smile. One that is identical to her brother's.

"Exactly. That's *exactly* what I want."

She clicks around and shows me some dresses she's found online. Shows me a list of stores she'd like to go to.

I show her the dress that I ordered last night online.

"Oh, Keatyn, that dress is so you. It's traditional, but the red is just a little more watermelon and the cutouts on the bodice are a really unique detail. It's really pretty."

"Thanks. It's a brand I've worn before, so I have a pretty good idea of how it will fit. I think it's the one, but I'm going to look this weekend to see if I find anything better. And I need some cute outfits for our dress up days."

Peyton continues to click around on her computer. I decide to be brave and just ask what I've been wondering since the day Whitney called us glitter whores. "So what does Whitney have on you anyway?"

"What do you mean?"

"I just get the feeling that she's holding something over your head."

She shakes her head. "I can't tell you. It's horrible. I'm so ashamed of myself."

"At my old school, my best friend was a girl like Whitney. She threatened to tell everyone that my relationship with my perfect boyfriend was a sham because we hadn't had sex yet."

"You didn't want people to know you were a virgin? Why not?"

"Because we dated for a year and a half. Everyone thought we were doing it. She even thought we were until I slipped and told her one day. You shouldn't care, Peyton. If you don't care, then she can't hurt you. She loses her power over you."

"What she has on me is *way* worse."

"Tell me. Get it off your chest. I promise you'll feel better."

She squints her eyes at me and sizes me up. "You swear to god that you will never tell anyone?"

I raise an eyebrow at her. "I'll do better than that. I'll pinkie swear." I hold my pinkie up and let her grab it.

"Okay," she says. "So, not long after Cam and I broke up . . ." Her chest heaves.

I can tell she's all torn up about this. Maybe it is worse.

"No, I . . . I'm sorry. I can't tell you."

"Tell me. I promise I won't be shocked."

She blurts out, "I slept with a teacher."

My eyes get huge. I can't hide my shock. "I'm sorry. I am shocked. Who?"

She sighs big. "Coach Kline."

"The hot Assistant Boys' Soccer coach?"

She nods.

"How did that happen?"

"After Cam slept with Whitney and never called, we started dating. We dated for well over a year. Even survived a summer apart. We broke up in October of my sophomore year. I was devastated and it didn't help that there were stressful things going on at home. So I was crying on the soccer field one day after practice. Coach Kline was nice. He listened. That's how it started."

"Started? So it wasn't a one-time thing?"

"No. It lasted a few months. We didn't sleep together right away. We were sort of friends first. He was single back then and fresh out of college. He's an alum. Was a soccer stand out when he was here as a student. Played soccer in college. He did his student teaching here and when they offered him a coaching position, he jumped at it. Since then, he's gotten his Masters and gotten married. He was only twenty-two at the time. And it just went further. I never regretted it."

"How did Whitney find out?"

"We were roommates. She thought I was lying to her about something, so she followed me one night. Even took pictures of us, um, together."

"Oh my gosh."

"She threatened to tell the school. Said I was going to get expelled. She hated me because of Cam. I know, in retrospect, he probably would've gotten fired and I wouldn't have been in trouble. Clearly, I was underage when it happened. But I didn't want to upset my parents. And now, if she showed the pictures, it would ruin his marriage, get him fired, and definitely get me expelled."

"Were you more popular than her? Back then?"

She shrugs and wipes a tear from her eye. "Maybe. I didn't really think of it that way. I made dance team and she didn't. But I didn't think she really cared. She didn't seem to want to get involved in any activities. I signed up for everything. Figured if I stayed busy, I wouldn't have to think about stuff."

"The other day in the locker room, when you threw away the shoes . . ."

"Wasn't that great? It felt so freeing. And she always makes snide comments about our dance outfits. I think it's because she's jealous."

"If she tried out and didn't make it, I'm sure she is. Did she try out the next year?"

"No. Ever since, she acts like she's too good for it." Peyton snickers. "Really, it's that she's just not a very good dancer."

BETTER THAN NAKED CHESTS?

FRENCH

ALTHOUGH PEYTON WANTS to skip the rest of the day, I tell her that I need to get to French.

"My brother has really started enjoying French," she teases.

"He doesn't enjoy it. He just likes it better because he's not so close to failing anymore. Takes some of the pressure off."

She looks at the clock. "You better scoot, then. I think I'm going to stay here. Maybe take a nap."

"Sounds good. I'll see you before the game."

I SLIDE INTO my desk just before the tardy bell rings.

From behind me, Aiden says, "Congrats on the play. I told you you'd get the part."

I flip around. "What do you mean?"

"Didn't you hear the cast announcement at lunch?"

"No! I skipped lunch. I was helping your sister with some Social Committee stuff. Well, sorta."

"You're playing the part of the Cheerleader Bachelorette."

I let out a loud shrill. "Ahhhh!"

Miss Praline goes, "Keatyn?"

I flip back around. "I can't help it. I'm so excited!"

Aiden explains, "She just found out she got the role she wanted in the school play."

"Well, that's nice, Miss Monroe. Congratulations."

"I'm excited for you, Keatyn," Annie says. "But I'm even more excited for tomorrow."

I grab her arm. "Oh, I didn't tell you about tonight, did I? Riley is going to ask Ariela right before the game. We're writing *Homecoming?* on a football and he's going to pass it to her during warm ups."

"Oh, that's so cute!"

"And she'll be able to keep the football. I kind of wish I had something to keep."

"Me too," Annie says. "Although I do have a screen shot of him asking me. And Maggie took pictures."

I think about Aiden's Homecoming stars.

I spin around to ask him. "What ever happened with your stars, Aiden? I keep thinking I'll see someone post them on Facebook."

"What stars?" Annie asks.

Aiden ignores Annie and says in a stern voice, "I don't want to talk about it."

I turn back around.

Why doesn't he want to talk about it?

Oh my gosh. Is he embarrassed because she said no?

And who in their right mind would have said no?

I think about what Shark said in detention that day. What was it? Something about Aiden and the dream girl. Or waiting for the dream girl.

Who is this dream girl and what the hell is her problem?

Is she blind?

I sneak a peek at Aiden.

His head is down. But I can see his arms. His lightly bronzed skin. His blond hair, which he's been pushing over to the side instead of spiking up because it needs to be cut. He's doodling on his notebook, causing the muscle in his forearm to flex the same way it did when he trapped me against the wall the other night. When he said, *Date us both.*

Is that what he wanted to do? Date both me and the Homecoming girl?

Ugghh. Riley was right. He is so the player.

But my curiosity gets the best of me, so I write him a note.

Why don't you want to talk about it?

Maybe I'm embarrassed about it.

Awww. Aiden . . . did she say no?

Not exactly. It just didn't work out.

I'm sorry.

What would you have said?

Like if I didn't have a boyfriend or a date already?

Yes, hypothetically. If someone asked you like that, would you have liked it?

I close my eyes and think about lying next to him. His pinkie just touching mine.

If you would have laid next to her on the bed, touched her pinkie, and asked, I think it would have been perfect.

Better than naked chests?

Different than naked chests. The stars were romantic and they must have taken freaking FOREVER to hang up.

They were a pain in the ass. Kinda lke the girl.

I probably shouldn't tell you this, but Shark told me in detention that you have a crush on someone that doesn't like you back. He said you've been waiting on the dream girl. I'm sorry it's not working out the way you want it to. It sucks to have a crush on someone and not have them like you back.

You know how that feels? That surprises me.

Yes, I know how it feels. I crushed on someone for almost two whole years before anything happened between us. Why does that surprise you?

Was it the Keats guy?

Yeah. We were friends before we dated. So don't give up on her. You know, like if you aren't too mad about the stars and stuff. My step dad says sometimes true love takes a bit. So if she really is your dream girl, you shouldn't give up.

But I thought the Keats guy was my dream guy.

He isn't.

Or, at least, he isn't right now. He loved me, but not. If that even makes sense.

What didn't he love about you? You seem fairly lovable. I mean, when you're not annoying.

We're getting off topic here. I'm supposed to be helping you with your girl problems.

And I told you that I don't want to talk about it. So stop asking.

You could tell me who she is. Then maybe I could help.

I don't think you could help. But maybe if I knew what happened with you and the Keats guy, I could avoid making the same mistakes with her.

I hate to break it to you, but if you asked her out and she

said no, she maybe shouldn't be your dream girl.

Like, sometimes you think they are the dream.

But then they get mad at you for buying Italian leather in Italy. But how could they? I mean, it's ITALY!!

And they get mad at you for dancing on top of a bar or with guys at a club.

But sometimes you can't help yourself.

Cuz you like to have fun.

And sometimes when they don't want to have fun with you, they sit around and pout. that should probably tell you that it isn't going to work unless they change.

But if you have to change for someone, then you are not still you, and that's bad too. You have to be careful not to lose yourself in the process.

I think . . .

Really, I'm rambling and I shouldn't have offered to help. I don't think I know what true love is. Or how to spot it. Every time I think I know, I'm proven wrong. Maybe that's what happened to you. You were just wrong about it.

Love is a tricky bitch.

Do you know about the greek goddess, Aphrodite?

She's the goddess of love, right?

Or, maybe, seduction. I think she's tricky, mostly. She teases us with the idea of love. She and Disney probably have a deal. Get young girls to watch princess movies. Get them to believe in fairytale endings. Then when they grow up, they will have unrealistic expectations of what true love is about.

I mean, seriously, do I really think some guy is going to ride up on a white horse and rescue me and we'll fall in love and have little hottie babies and it will be all magical and amazing?

Actually, yes, I do.

It worked. That is what I want. That's really what EVERY girl wants.

But then there's Aphrodite. She gets you to fall in love. Tricks you with sex and seduction. Then she names your baby AWFUL. Or she makes you believe in soul mates. But then she sleeps with someone else. She lets guys quote you poetry, which makes you all swoony, but then you find out that they don't really mean it. They just want to sleep with you.

And then they're good in bed. And sweet. But you know the other shoe is gonna drop. So you are afraid to say it.

To tell someone that you love them.

But then you do.

Because you believe in love.

Cuz, hell, I don't even know why. Because you just do. I mean who doesn't want to believe that their soul mate is out there. Their other half. The person that will love every annoying thing about them.

But, really, it's probably mostly bullshit.

Just for the record, your lips were my bliss.

See.

Case in point why love sucks. You were playing me. Telling me sweet stuff when you were really in love with someone else. You're lucky I'm even willing to try and be friends. I should hate you.

Actually, sometimes, I kinda do.

Sometimes, I kinda hate you too.

And that is what might save our friendship. We don't have to worry about love getting in the way.

You love someone else (even though you probably shouldn't) and I'm in love with someone else.

(Even though you probably shouldn't.)

By the way, you haven't tutored me all week.

I know. I'm not sure I can tonight either.

He whispers in my ear. "You better be there, or I'll quit Social Committee."

"So quit. I'm tired of you telling me that. If you don't want to be there, then just quit."

He leans up a little closer and sighs, his breath warming the side of my face. "I need you. Please?"

I turn around to tell him I'll try, but when I do my cheek smashes straight into his lips.

"You want me to kiss you, all you have to do is ask. You don't have to try and be all sneaky about it."

I whip my head forward, flipping my hair in his stupid face. "Kissing you is the *last* thing I want to do," I mutter.

"In your life?"

"What?"

"Are you telling me that will be your dying wish? *It's the last thing I want to do. Have his lips on mine. Then I can die happy*," he says dramatically.

"You really should've tried out for the play. Drama king."

"I'm not a drama king."

"Ha! Everything about you is drama." I turn back around and smirk at him. "Big production. But no one is buying the tickets."

"And you're the little production that gets out of hand. Turns into a massive time and money pit. Then goes straight to DVD."

I think about something sad and let tears come to my eyes. "That's harsh." I dab the corner of my eye for effect. Hang my head down a little.

I'm so sad.

His face completely softens. I can tell he feels bad.

"I was just teasing. I already told you that you'd get amazing reviews and I . . ."

I slowly let my face break into a wide shit-eating grin.

"Seriously? You can bring on the fake tears that easily?"

I shrug a shoulder. "It's a gift."

A GOOD SEND OFF.

3:30PM

WE DON'T HAVE dance practice, since there's a game tonight, so I drag Dawson to his room to kiss him.

Actually, I'm thinking about doing more than kissing him. His parents are coming for the game and he's going back home with them, so I won't get to see him later. And he's going to be hanging out with his brother and lots of other girls.

I'm thinking he needs a good send off. And I have the perfect thing for that.

I reach down and skim my hand across the front of his pants.

Dawson gives my body a squeeze. "I'm not sure that's a good idea."

"You don't want me?" I pout.

Shit. Maybe Riley is right. Maybe I should be worried.

He pushes himself against me, so I can feel that his body does want me.

"I do want you, but you'll wear me out. I need to be fresh for this game. St. Thomas is a big rival, and I thought you had to tutor Aiden?"

"I thought you were jealous of Aiden?"

"Well, that was before. When I thought he liked you."

"And now you think he doesn't?"

"It's pretty obvious that he doesn't. He could've taken advantage of what happened last weekend. Instead, he told Riley about it. So that Riley would tell me. I was wrong to be jealous. He's obviously not into you, so I'm fine with you tutoring him. I mean, we do need him. He's our starting kicker and since Cole got hurt, he's starting at receiver too. We don't want him to get kicked off the team because he's failing."

"I know, but . . ." I make a sad face. Now I am feeling jealous. I don't want to sound like a whiny, jealous girlfriend. But still. "Will your brother encourage you to cheat on me? Riley says he will. Says I should be nervous," I blurt out.

Dawson smiles at me and pulls me down on his bed. "Is that what this is all about?"

"Kinda, yes."

"You're going to New York with a bunch of girls. Are you going to be looking for guys? I suspect you could pick up a guy any time you wanted."

"You're silly. Guys really don't pay that much attention to me."

He gives me a look. "I'm not buying that."

"At my old school, my best friend used to tell me I was good bait. Apparently, I'm easy to talk to. Which meant I'd become their friend, and she'd sleep with them."

"Was she not as pretty as you?"

"She was very pretty, but more like Whitney. Not very approachable."

"So she was a big bitch?"

I can't help but laugh. "Kinda, yeah."

He grabs both of my hands and looks at me seriously. "Keatie, I love you. I'm not looking for other girls. I just want to hang out with my brother. It's weird not having him here every day."

"Are you closer to him than you are with Riley?"

"Riley and I are getting closer, but he wasn't here the last two years. It was me and Cam."

"That makes sense." I sigh. "I guess I better go."

He leans in to give me what I assume is a good-bye kiss. But it's better than that. His lips press hard against mine and he pulls me up onto his lap.

"I am leaving right after the game," he says in between kisses.

"I'm wearing the leopard print bra," I whisper as I kiss down his neck. "And, I have a little surprise for you."

"Then it's settled. You're not going anywhere."

IF I ONLY HAD A BRAIN.
5:30PM

DAWSON AND I walk hand in hand down to the field house. He gives me a fiery good-bye kiss, smacks my ass, and walks into the boys' locker room to get ready for the game.

I head to the dance room and see Aiden and Peyton walking toward me.

Shit.

I forgot to text Aiden about not doing tutoring.

Peyton gives me a radiant smile.

Aiden raises his eyebrows at me and frowns. "So you're not dead."

Peyton smacks him on the shoulder. "Be nice."

"She ditched me."

"I did ditch him. I'm sorry. I, um . . . I had something else I needed to do, and I kinda forgot to text you."

Peyton giggles. "Was that thing you *needed to do* Dawson?"

My mouth hangs open. I don't know what to say. "Um . . ."

Aiden shakes his head at me in disgust.

Or hate, maybe.

"He's going home with his parents after the game, so I won't get to see him tonight. I just, we just, I wanted to say goodbye. And he . . . "

Aiden seems to recover from his hate quickly because a little smile starts playing on his lips. It's the smile that makes a girl feel weak at the knees.

Not my knees.

Just probably girls in general.

"That's understandable," he says. "So then we'll have to do it tonight."

"You have a game."

"After the game. After curfew."

"Everyone is going to the Cave tonight."

"Everyone but us. We'll be in my room studying."

"No. No, we won't."

"Will Dawson get jealous?"

"No, he has nothing to be jealous of, but I don't want anyone to get the wrong idea. I love Dawson."

Aiden tilts his head at me in question. I can tell he's dying to know if I told Dawson yet.

"Yes, Aiden. I told Dawson I love him. Yes, I was confused for a while about love. That happens after you go through a break up. It's normal to question it and become more cynical of love because you don't want to get hurt again. But Dawson's not going to hurt me."

"Awww," Peyton says. I didn't realize she was still here. Aiden has been staring at me with so much intensity. And, apparently, using some of that godly power.

The one that makes you feel like the scarecrow in *The Wizard of Oz.*

If I only had a brain.

"When did you tell him?" she asks.

I get that gooey feeling. That feeling like I'm being hugged by Dawson. I hug myself and gush, "It was the other night. I told him I hearted him. He asked if that was close to loving him. I hadn't said it because I was scared to. But he makes me happy, and I wanted him to know it."

"I love that feeling," Peyton gushes back. "It's so dream—"

Aiden interrupts her. "I'll let you ladies finish your love fest here. I have to get in the locker room." Then he gazes deep into my eyes and says, "I know where we can go. I'll be outside your window at one. We'll study then go party with everyone."

"Really?"

He shrugs. "What? You think you're the only one with plans?"

HAS HE TRIED?

11:30PM

KATIE AND I are in our room packing for New York.

"Wasn't the way Riley asked Ariela so adorable?" she gushes.

"It was. I was a little nervous though. He whipped that football at her pretty hard. Can you imagine if it would have hit her in the face? It could have gone horribly wrong. Of course, when we were coming up with the idea, I didn't think of that. As soon as he threw it, I started thinking about all the bad things that could happen. It hitting her in the face. Someone else catching it."

"Well, she caught it. And the look on her face when she read it. You could tell she was really surprised."

"I loved how they both ran toward each other and kissed in the middle of the field."

"Now I wish I had made Dallas ask me. Do you think he would've come up with something cute?"

"Probably. How's that going? We haven't really talked about it. You kissed, right?"

She grins. "Of course we've kissed. I'm not Annie."

"That's kind of mean."

"Oh, I didn't mean it that way. I just meant I won't wait. He's too cute."

"What do you mean by *you won't wait*?"

"I'm going to attack him tonight at the party."

"Don't you think that's rushing it a little? You've only hung out with him twice, and you aren't going out yet."

"Did you wait until Dawson asked you out?"

I sigh. "That's not really the point. I just think if you like him, you might want to wait. Let him try before you attack him. Has he tried?"

"Not really." She giggles. "He's obsessed with my boobs. But we've done more than kiss."

"Hands more or mouths more?"

"Just hands, but tonight I plan on changing that."

I'm a little worried about this. My poor baby Dallas is going to get attacked tonight, and I feel like I should protect him or something. Part of me wants to tell her to keep her slutty mouth off him.

"So what are you packing to wear shopping?"

"I think this," I say, setting my grey Frye boots on my bed along with a funky pair of silver sequined shorts.

"I swear, you are the only person I know that could mix sequins and cowboy boots and get away with it."

I laugh as I pull more clothes out of my closet. A bright peach silk J. Crew pintuck-front blouse, a slightly gaudy silver rhinestone necklace, and a little Louis Vuitton Eva bag.

"Have you checked the weather?" I ask.

"I think it might be chilly in the morning, but it's supposed to be sunny."

"I better wear a jacket then," I say, grabbing a gabardine Burberry trench coat with fun black leather sleeves. And even though it might rain, I throw in a pair of big black sunglasses.

Her phone buzzes with a text. She looks down, smiles, and turns her back on me.

Um, hello? Weren't we in the middle of a conversation here?

I FINISH PACKING then say to her, "So I'm going to sleep for a little before the party."

She gives me a barely perceptible nod of her head as she laughs to herself and furiously texts.

My own phone buzzes.

> ***Dawson:*** *I'm still in the car with my parents. Bor-ing. But before the game was really fun ;)*

Me: *Which part was really fun?*

Dawson: *The gummy lifesaver part.*

Me: *Who knew they the stretched like that.*

Dawson: *You knew.*

Me: *Only because I overheard a couple of the girls from dance talking about it. I've never tried anything like that before.*

Dawson: *Me either. It was sweet.*

Me: *It did make it sweeter. LMAO.*

Dawson: *It's just really cool that you wanted to try it with me. I love you. Seriously. Love you.*

Me: *I love you too.*

Dawson: *Jake says everyone is partying at the Cave tonight. You going?*

Me: *Yeah, later. I have to help Aiden with French first, since I ditched him today for gummy lifesavers and won't be here all weekend. We have an oral test on Monday. But he has plans and I'm going to the party, so I'm sure we'll get through it fast.*

Dawson: *Oral test? You better not be tutoring him with gummy lifesavers.*

Me: *You're bad. And, no. Definitely nothing like that for Aiden. I miss you already.*

Dawson: *Ugg. My mom says I need to put my phone away and talk to them. Which means they are going to grill me about you, Riley, Ariela, what Cam has been up to, blah, blah.*

Me: *I miss my parents. Talk to them. They're dropping you off at Cam's tonight, right?*

Dawson: *Yeah, we're going to a party.*

Me: *I'm jealous.*

Dawson: *I'll probably be texting you the whole time. I love you.*

Me: *I heart you.*

WHERE'S THE HAREM?
1AM

IT SEEMS LIKE I just shut my eyes and all of a sudden Katie's phone alarm is going off.

She pops out of bed, pulls her jeans on, and practically dives out the window. "I'll see you at the Cave, okay?"

"Sure," I say. I peek at my clock, see it's a few minutes to one, and try to figure out what I want to wear. Dawson won't be here to keep me warm, so I throw on a long-sleeved Free People thermal shirt and some Rag & Bone jean shorts. I look at the Golden Goose boots that Cush gave me. They'd be perfect with this outfit.

I haven't worn them since he told me his mom bought them. I've been sort of mad at them.

I pick the boots up and run my hand across the leather.

It's not their fault that Cush lied. It really doesn't matter how they became mine, what matters is what I thought. That these boots are everything I want to be.

I put the boots down on the floor and slide my feet into them.

Perfect.

I hear a little knock on my window and know it's Aiden.

I climb out the window, laughing at how easily I glide out now. How different my life is now than when school started.

My boots should hit the ground about now, but instead I find myself sliding down Aiden's body as he catches me.

"What are you doing?" I say madly. I don't want to be in his stupid arms.

"Just catching you," he says sweetly.

It's really hard to be mad at someone that looks the way he does. Tonight, with the moonlight shining down on him, he almost looks angelic.

Asshole.

I try to push out of his arms, but he holds me tightly. "You can let go now," I say.

He drops me to the ground and looks down at my feet. "You're wearing boots."

"I wear boots all the time."

"Not *those* boots. You haven't worn those since the day we met."

How does he even know that?

I roll my eyes. "I've been sort of mad at them."

He tilts his head to the side and squints his eyes at me. "Mad at your boots? You can't be mad at *those* boots."

"I'm not anymore. We made up."

"Well, that's good to hear. Let's get French done so we can go party."

His hand curves across the small of my back.

Electricity shoots straight up my spine, causing me to arch my back and jump away from him.

"You're awfully jumpy tonight."

"Stop touching me then," I state a little too emphatically.

He stops touching me and leads me to the chapel, which is apparently open all night. I think I knew that, but had forgotten it.

We study in a very business-like fashion. Our test on Monday has a speaking portion, so mostly we work on his word enunciation.

"I think I've got it. I'll keep working on it this weekend, but at least I know the proper way to say everything now." He looks at his phone, which is loaded with texts. From girls. And Logan and Nick. And girls. "I better get going."

"Um, okay. Yeah, me too," I say, glancing at my phone like there's something important in it. All my friends begging for me to get there. Unfortunately, there are no texts from anyone.

My friends suck.

WHEN WE GET to the clearing known as the Cave, Aiden says, "Thanks for helping me. Have a good night."

I watch him go over to where Nick and Logan are standing. A cheerleader that I don't really know wraps her arms around Aiden's neck in a greeting.

I study her. Wondering if that's what Aiden's dream girl looks like.

She's petite, with long dark hair, and a sweet smile. Her eyes are small and just a little too close together, but other than that she has a nicely proportioned face. And a body. A killer body. That kind of curvy body that boys love and I couldn't get with the best plastic surgeon in all of Beverly Hills.

I look around.

All my friends are paired off. Which explains their lack of texts. Annie is sitting on a log with Ace. Heads together. Holding hands. Deep in conversation. Maggie is making out with Parker up against a tree. Katie isn't really visible because Dallas is lying on top of her, groping her shirt.

Jake has his arm wrapped around Whitney. She's smoking a cigarette and he's drinking whiskey straight out of a bottle.

My eyes flit back to Aiden and the girl.

"S'up, girly," Shark says, wandering over to stand next to me.

He appears to be a little tipsy, but his eyes follow mine straight to Aiden.

"Is she the dream girl?" I ask him.

"Chelsea? No."

"She seems to like him."

Shark laughs. "*All* the girls like him."

I watch as another girl bounces up to Aiden, shoves her boobs out, and hands him a shot. They click glasses and slam the shots together. Then she starts dancing in front of him. Grabbing his hands and trying to get him to dance with her.

"It appears that they do," I say, realizing I've never seen this side of Aiden. He's flirting. Laughing. Drinking. Doing shots. He even does a little arm shimmy, which gets the girls all worked up.

He, Nick, and Logan are literally surrounded by girls.

Weird.

"So who do you think will be Homecoming Queen? I'm having a tough time with the odds," Shark admits.

"Why?"

"Because history suggests that Whitney will win. Every other Clarke has won. But there are other factors."

"What factors?"

"My personal opinion is supposed to stay out of the odds. I always look at the facts. But the fact is, I don't care for Whitney much. I'd rather see Mariah or Peyton win. Also, the freshman class is large this year, and I have no idea how they will vote. One would think based on Whitney's lack of activities, it would give Peyton and Mariah an advantage."

"Can I tell you a secret?"

He leans his head close to mine. "Will it affect the odds?" He pulls out a flask, takes a swig, and hands it to me.

I nod my head as I take a swig. When the alcohol hits my throat, I want to spit it out. It burns all the way down to my stomach. "What is this?"

"Everclear. Hundred proof. Fastest way to get drunk."

"Are you trying to get drunk fast?"

He gives me a wide smirk. "No, but I have been known to share with an attractive female or two."

I laugh. "I see. Trying to get the girl drunk fast."

"So, tell me the secret."

"Ninety percent of the freshman class voted for me for Student Council. I never would have gotten on it otherwise. And I was thinking . . ."

"Of swaying their vote?"

I grin at him. "Yeah. But I don't want anyone to know. I want to sway quietly."

"An underground campaign. Excellent."

"Something like that. Whitney hates me. And I'm not doing it to be mean to her, but I just think a person that is more involved in school activities should win."

"So Peyton or Mariah?"

"I'll vote for Peyton, and I hope she wins."

Shark and I sit down on a newly vacated log. The couple that was sitting here has wandered off, hand in hand.

It makes me miss Dawson.

Directly across the circle of logs, right in my line of sight, is Aiden. Logan sitting on his left. Two girls on each side of them and three girls sitting in front of them in the dirt. Logan appears to be telling a story, and Aiden is occasionally interjecting a comment and laughing.

Aiden's blond hair is practically glowing in the moonlight. The shadows playing across his face make him look angular and more mature. And when he smiles, it's like a god reached down and touched the forest with light.

Shark pulls out a joint and lights it up as Peyton sits down next to him. "What's up, girlie?" Shark says to her.

"I hope you're sharing," she replies.

He nods, takes a hit, and passes it to her. She takes a big hit, holding it in her lungs for a long time, then slowly breathes out and hands it to me. "Whitney's pissed at me."

"Why?" I ask, as I pass the joint back to Shark.

"Because I'm going with you this weekend. And I didn't even mention a new dress. She would have come unglued."

"What did you tell her?"

"That we're shopping for dress-up days for the dance team." She takes another deep hit. "Ah, much better."

Aiden walks over and sits down next to his sister. Shark hands him another joint. As he sucks in, the stubble on the side of his face becomes more noticeable. All that light scruff.

I can sort of understand why the girls were literally sitting at his feet.

A girl leans down in front of Shark and whispers drunkenly, *Let's hook up.* He stands up, tells us, *Duty calls*, and leaves with the girl.

Peyton gives Aiden what appears to be some sort of godly telepathic message. They nod at each other and she says, "There's Brad. I need to talk to him."

Leaving me sitting alone with Aiden.

"Where's the harem?" I ask, slightly sarcastically, as my phone vibrates.

Dawson: *I lobe you*

Me: *I love you too.*

Dawson: *I druk.*

Me: *You're drunk? Where are you?*

Dawson: *no shoes./'*
Me: *Where are you?*
Dawson: *gurl bed partzy*

I feel like someone just stabbed me. My cell phone drops out of my hands.

AIDEN PICKS MY phone up, reads it, shakes his head, and hands it back to me.

"Um . . ." I look to Aiden, hoping he'll say something reassuring. That all the awful thoughts I'm having about Dawson cheating couldn't possibly be true.

But he doesn't. He just looks at me. With those green eyes. Unfortunately, there's no confidence in them, only sympathy.

He feels bad for me because he thinks Dawson is cheating on me.

And something else. Something that I always see when he looks at me. It's like his eyes speak to me. Trying to get me to understand something. Something that resonates deep inside me.

But something that I don't understand. It's like being spoken to in a foreign language.

I don't have a clue what it means.

But I do know what to do.

Me: *Your brother is "druk," can't find his shoes, and is in a "gurl's bed at a partzy."*
Riley: *Shit.*
Me: *Yeah.*

Aiden says, "Are you okay?"

"Not really. Have fun with the harem. I'm heading back to my room."

"I'll walk you. The harem will wait."

I shake my head. "No, I'm fine." Tears start leaking out of my eyes. I don't want Aiden to see them, so I turn around and run. Run through the trees. Run to my dorm window. When I get there, I close my eyes, lean against the side of the building, and start to slide down into the grass.

Aiden is right there. He pins me against the brick wall, moves his leg between mine, and pushes his chest tightly against me.

He looks down at me, taking in my lips like he always does right before he kisses me.

But he doesn't kiss me.

He shakes his head, wraps his arms around me, and hugs me.

Just hugs me.

Which really makes me start sobbing. "I'm never, ever telling a guy I love him again. It's like I'm love cursed."

He nuzzles his face into my hair and whispers soothingly, "You're not love cursed. You just aren't . . ."

"Just aren't what?"

I feel his chest move deeply in and out, sighing against me. "Maybe he's just drunk at the party. If he was hooking up, I doubt he'd stop to text you."

"I think the hooking up is over and now he can't find his shoes."

"So you don't trust him?"

"What do you mean?"

"I mean, when he left, did you trust him?"

"I did. He told me over and over not to worry. To trust him. That he loves me."

"If he really loves you, he won't cheat on you. Even if he's drunk. You should have faith in the people you love. Maybe if you did, they wouldn't let you down."

I pull out of the hug and turn my back on him. "I'm going to cry alone in my room now. Thanks for your kind words," I say sarcastically. But then I swing around madly. "So it's my fault if he cheats?! That sounds like the kind of zen bullshit the Keats guy would tell me. I didn't expect it from you. But I should have. It fits your whole player thing. The whole it's-never-my-fault, take-no-responsibility-for-your-actions-because-it's-easier-to-blame-fate, or cosmic forces, or someone else, than it is to admit that you just suck. Good night."

He runs his hands down the sides of my arms and for reasons I don't understand, it calms me.

"Boots, I didn't mean it that way. I meant that . . ." He pushes his hand through his hair, causing the ends to stick up a little. "Maybe the guy you're with isn't worthy of your love."

"Yeah, maybe."

My phone starts buzzing and buzzing.

"Who is it?" Aiden asks.

"It's Riley," I reply as I answer the phone. "Hey, Riley."

"Where are you?"

"About to go in my room."

"Cam wants to talk to you. I've got him on conference with me. Say hi, Cam."

Cam says, in a voice that is almost identical to Dawson's minus the sweetness, "Don't be mad at him."

"He's texting me from a girl's bed!"

"Yeah, a bed that he's in alone."

"No offense, Cam, but Riley told me about you. How you didn't think Dawson should have a girlfriend. I get it. You're a player. You want to have fun and not be tied down."

He laughs. "Actually, I'd love to be tied down." I hear him yell out to whoever is at the party. "Anyone got any rope? I want to be tied up."

"I said tied *down*."

"Close enough," he says with another laugh.

"It's been great talking to you. Tell your brother when he sobers up not to bother calling me."

"And you need to cool your panties. He didn't hook up with anyone. In fact, he sucks as a wingman now."

"What do you mean?"

"He won't shut up about you. It's hard to pick up girls when one of us is all panty whipped and talking about his amazingly hot girlfriend. So I did what I had to do. Got him drunk. Put him to bed."

I let out an audible sigh and get tears of relief in my eyes. "He's really alone?"

"Yes. He's crazy about you. I'm not gonna let him screw that up. At least not until I meet you. I gotta go. Just got a taker on the rope."

Riley lets out a loud laugh then says to me, "You okay?"

"Do you think Cam's telling the truth and not just covering for him?"

"Yes, I do."

"Then, yes, I'm okay. Thanks, Riley."

Aiden looks at me expectantly.

"His brother said he's a bad wingman. That he kept talking about me in front of the girls. So he got him drunk and put him to bed."

Aiden crosses his arms in front of his broad chest and stiffens up his jaw. "Well, that's great."

"I'm going to bed now," I say as I climb in my window. Once inside, I stick my head back out. "Thanks for following me. Checking on me. Trying to make me feel better. I appreciate it, Aiden."

"Can I ask you a question?"

I give him a sassy grin. "You just did. But yes. Ask away."

"What you said today in French. Do you think true love is bullshit or do you believe in it?"

I look up at the almost full moon shining over his head and sigh. "I really *want* to believe in it."

Aiden turns around and looks up at the moon. "The moon is really pretty tonight, isn't it?" He turns back around and gives me the kind of smile that almost makes me believe it could be true. I think gods have that effect on people. They give them hope. "Don't let my sister go crazy shopping tomorrow."

I laugh. "I won't."

"Night, Boots."

Saturday, October 1st

IT DOES FEEL GOOD.

8:30AM

I'M ON THE train with all the girls. Ariela is funny. One minute she's telling us how Riley drives her nuts, the next minute how crazy she is about him.

"I still can't believe I'm dating a junior! I didn't even date juniors when I was a freshman!"

She turns to me. "Why does Riley call you baby?"

"I don't know. It's like his nickname for me. He's called me it pretty much since we met."

"It makes me crazy. He doesn't have a nickname for me." Her pretty face pouts.

"He likes you a lot. It shouldn't matter what he calls anyone else. I mean, you know his reputation, right?"

"Well sure, he's a player. Why do you think I'm making him wait for sex?"

Maggie deadpans, "Cuz you want it to be special." Annie says it at the exact same time, only she says it in her dreamy way.

We all laugh. Katie says, "Do you think I should do it with Dallas?"

Annie goes, "It's way too soon." Then she turns to Maggie and says, "Sorry, but I think it is."

"We almost did last night."

"You did?" Annie screeches. "Why?"

"Cuz it feels good," Maggie replies.

Annie looks at her like she's crazy.

Peyton high fives Maggie and says, "It does feel good."

Maggie, Peyton, and Ariela go on to discuss which sexual positions are their favorites while Annie is shaking her head. I'm laughing at them when I get a text from Dawson.

Dawson: *I don't even know what to say. I'm being a chicken and texting you. I'm sorry. I swore to you that I wouldn't cheat and then . . .*

My heart is back in my throat again. Did Cam lie to me? Is Dawson confessing?

Me: *And then . . . what?*

Dawson: *I read what I texted you last night.*

Me: *You were drunk and in a girl's bed. I cried.*

Dawson: *I'm so sorry, Keatie. I don't even remember what happened.*

Me: *Somehow that doesn't make me feel better.*

Dawson: *Are we broke up? I looked at facebook and you didn't change your status.*

Me: *You must remember something. Flirting. Kissing. That's usually how it starts.*

Dawson: *But I don't. I didn't kiss anyone. And I was telling them all about you. About how amazing you are.*

Me: *Is that a Johnson brother rule? If you don't remember it, it didn't happen.*

Dawson: *I don't know what happened.*

Me: *But you think you did something? Why do you think that?*

Dawson: *My texts last night. And I just woke up. In a girl's bed.*

Me: *You alone in that bed?*

Dawson: *Yes.*

Me: *Have you talked to your brother yet?*

Dawson: *No.*

Me: *I talked to him last night.*

Dawson: *Oh. Shit. Why?*

Me: *Because I got your texts and was very upset. I told Riley. Riley called Cam.*

Dawson: *Fuck. You hate me now, don't you? I'm so sorry, Keatie, really. I would never do that to you on purpose. Like Cam kept giving me shots and we were playing pool and he was flirting with this one chick. I was giving him shit about just wanting to hook up. I was telling them how amazing a relationship can be. He told me I was a bad wingman and to shut the fuck up. Playing pool is the last thing I remember.*

Me: *It's hard to trust someone who gets so drunk they can't remember what they did or who they may have been with. Because you know eventually they will screw up. Cam told me you didn't hook up with anyone. That he got you drunk and then put you to bed. But he's your brother. He would lie for you. So I'm not sure what to think.*

Dawson: *Thank God. I was sitting here thinking I'd lost you.*

Me: *Maybe you already have, Dawson. I'm not sure what to believe at this point. You told me you missed your brother. I stupidly assumed you went there to hang out with him. Not just to party. I'm on the train going to shop. You and Cam have fun this weekend.*

Dawson: *You're mad.*

Me: *Tell you what. Tonight, I'll party. Go to a club. Meet up with a bunch of guys I don't know. Then I'll text you about how I'm so drunk. In some guy's bed. And how I can't find my shoes. We'll see how that makes you feel. And if you trust me after.*

Dawson: *</3*

I know I'm kind of being a bitch right now. But I can't just let him get away with it. He's a big boy. He could have said no to the shots. So I'm not texting him back for a little while.

Screw him. I'm going to enjoy shopping with my friends.

I text Riley.

Me: *Do you really think Camden told me the truth? I was relieved to hear it last night. But now I'm kind of upset again and don't know what to believe. Dawson texted me. He doesn't remember and assumes he hooked up with someone based on the texts he sent me. Says the last thing he remembers is Camden "making" him do shots and them playing pool. Please don't lie for them to protect my feelings. I really like Dawson. You know that I do. But I'd rather know the truth.*

Riley: *Cam might be a jerk, but he's not a liar.*

Me: *It's his brother.*

Riley: *Yeah, but you have to understand him. If Dawson got drunk and hooked up, Cam would be proud of him. He might have lied to you, but he wouldn't have lied to me. He had no reason to. He doesn't know how close we are.*

Me: *Just so you know, I love you. I don't care what happens with your brother, I'll always love you. And Dallas. Speaking of Dallas. Katie told me she attacked him last night!*

Riley: *I love you too :) and he fended her off. Barely. LOL. Do you think it's weird or cool that he's still a virgin?*

Me: *It's kinda cool, really. That he has done a lot but wanted to wait to do it with someone special. Was your first time with someone special?*

Riley: *Ha. No. Hamptons. Summer before 8th grade. I was drunk. She was horny and, thankfully, much older than me. Our parents were out of town. Cam threw a big party. All I really remember is her long dark hair kept getting in my mouth. And I felt like I was going to puke.*

Me: *That's pretty young.*

Riley: *Yeah, probably. That and my getting kicked out freshman year are part of why they've tried to shelter Braxton a little more. Why they won't let him come to the beach when they aren't there. He's trying to talk them into letting him be with us all next summer.*

Me: *I can't wait to meet him Homecoming weekend.*

Riley: *He can't wait to come here Homecoming weekend. Thinks he's going to hook up with someone. LOL. He's a little shit. But funny as hell.*

Me: *So . . . I shouldn't be mad at Dawson?*

Riley: *I'd be mad, but I don't think you should break up with him.*

Me: *Okay, thanks.*

Riley: *You gonna help Ariela find a boner-worthy dress?*

Me: *You are so bad. You know she's purposefully making you wait.*

Riley: *I know. But it's fun. We had fun last night. Just making out is really fun. I think I tend to skip it because I want to get to the good stuff. But kissing is good stuff. At least it is with her.*

Me: *You're getting all mushy.*

AN EASTBROOKE GIRL.
10:30AM

I INTERRUPT THE girls' conversation, which has moved on to what kind of dresses they hope to find. "I got a car and driver for us, so that we wouldn't have to worry about getting cabs, our luggage, or packages. Do you want to go to the loft now or should we start shopping?"

"Shopping!" everyone yells.

At the first dress shop, I'm helping Annie look for a pretty pink dress for the dance.

"How are you and Ace? You haven't really said anything."

"I'm feeling a little guilty myself . . ."

"No! You had sex with him? I thought you were going to wait!"

"Oh, no. I just mean I let him, like . . ." She hems and haws, then kicks her foot into the ground. "I let him put his hand down my pants."

"Oh, really? And?"

"I really liked it. I think that's why I feel guilty. He also asked me out."

"He did?! Why didn't you tell us?"

"Do you think he only asked me because I let him?"

"Did you do anything else to him? Like more than you've done before?"

"No, why?"

"He asked you out because he likes you, not because you let him touch you. I'm so happy for you. Are you happy? I can't believe *you*, of all people, haven't put this on Facebook yet!"

"I know, weird, huh?"

"You can see why sometimes I want to keep things private, can't you?"

I spot a gorgeous pink dress that is perfect for Annie. It's got a sleeveless pink lace top, pink ribbon waist, and a flirty pleated skirt.

"Oh, look at this one! You have to try this on!"

"Yeah, I do. I love it. It's sexy, but not too revealing."

I flip it around. "But look at the back!" The back has a large triangular-shaped cutout that is sexy, but not blatant.

She hops up and down and claps. "I love that." She grabs it from my hand and runs to the dressing room.

I follow her back as Maggie walks out in a simple black gown.

"Oh, Maggie, I like that one," Ariela says.

I look at it critically as she asks, "What do you think, Keatyn?"

"Honestly?"

"Yes, honestly. I want to look amazing."

"I'd say the top doesn't fit you properly. It's too loose. I think you would be constantly pulling it up. And the way it's gathered here," I point to her hip, "makes your hips look bigger than they are. It doesn't flatter your hot body. I also think I'd like to see you in something besides black with your skin tone."

"How about this one?" Peyton asks, holding out a strapless tiered dress in a deep navy blue.

"I like that one better! Try it on!"

Annie comes out in her pink dress. She's already twirling and clearly in love with it. "I'm getting this. Do you think I should get this?" She grabs the skirt and twirls again. "I feel beautiful. For the first time in my life, I actually feel beautiful."

"Then you should definitely get it," Ariela says, walking out in another dress.

"Speaking of beautiful. That dress is like a dream," Peyton says to Ariela, who is wearing a soft coral strapless gown with a thick band of silver beading sparkling at the waist.

Ariela looks good in anything she puts on, but this dress just isn't her style. And based on the way she is looking at it in the mirror—shoulders shrugged and nose scrunched up—tells me she doesn't like it either. "I don't think this one is me. Do you want to try it on?"

"Yes!" Peyton practically screams.

Katie comes out in another dress that she's rejecting. She's in kind of foul mood. "What's wrong?" I ask her.

She plops down next to me in a tight red dress that barely contains her boobs. "Dallas doesn't want me."

"Why do you think that?"

She purses her lips and pushes her hair behind one ear. "Last night. Things were fun. Like really fun. And I wanted to. And—I'm embarrassed to even say it—I tried. And he said no. Guys never say no."

"Sometimes they do," I say gently. "I think he really likes you. Maybe he wants it to be special the first time you do it. Like not just some romp in the bushes, you know?"

She lets out a sigh so big it causes one of her boobs to completely pop out of the dress. She looks down and laughs. "Probably not this dress, huh? So do you really think that's it?"

"What did he tell you?"

"He didn't explain. Just sort of moved away. Said he was tired. Stopped things pretty abruptly."

"Why are you trying to go so fast with him? You've only been dating him, sort of, for like three days."

"I'm tired of being a good girl all the time. I'm ready to get some experience, and I like Dallas. I really like him. I've crushed on him since school started."

Maggie comes out in the navy dress at the same time Peyton walks out in the coral one. They both look stunning.

"Wow! You both look amazing!" Katie says.

"I can't believe I found a dress so fast!" Peyton exclaims. "This is the one. It's conservative, like they expect us to be, but I adore the bling at the waist. I feel like a goddess."

"You look like one too," I tell her. And she does. The color of it with her blonde hair and green eyes is amazing.

She smiles and literally lights up the room.

Maggie stands in front of the mirror. "So you all like this one?"

"It's very different from Peyton's but it's amazing on you. The layers are flirty and fun, but the fit—the way it hugs your body, all the way down—makes it sexy. You look incredible."

She cracks a naughty smile. "I think Parker will like it."

"I think *all* the guys will like it," Annie says.

"We did good here," I say. "Maggie, Annie, and Peyton all found dresses. Katie and Ariela, what do you think? Next store?"

They both nod in agreement.

WE GO TO three more stores and try on a bunch more dresses.

Katie finds a shimmering black and gold sequined dress. I find a long, fitted gown that glides down my body like liquid gold. It would be great for a party back home, but after looking at the photos of the past Homecoming Court dresses and listening to everyone talk about the tradition, I really want to wear something appropriate.

I also find an adorable strapless burgundy gown with the cutest flouncy skirt. I buy it to save for another occasion, just because it is so damn cute, but the burgundy would have totally clashed with all the red in the stadium.

It's weird.

I want to look amazing in my dress but, for the first time in my life, it feels okay to want to blend in. To be part of something bigger than me. I get Whitney's wanting to stand out. I never want to look like anyone but me. But what I really want is for the alumni to look at me and say, *There's an Eastbrooke girl.*

I look at my friends, who are *oohing* and *ahhing* over Ariela in a black gown with a soft flowing skirt, sweetheart neckline, and a beaded bodice, and realize that I'm really glad to be here.

Even with things a little up in the air with Dawson right now.

Even though I miss my family.

I feel happy.

I feel like I've made friends. Friends who are supportive of each other. Friends who seem to like me for me. Not because of what I wear or who my mom is. They just like me.

And it feels really good.

Dawson texts me just as we're about to go shoe shopping.

Dawson: *I know you're shopping and won't answer if I call, but please don't be mad at me. I'm sorry. Cam said he talked to you last night. That he told you the truth.*

Me: *He did. But he's your brother. You can't tell me he wouldn't lie for you.*

Dawson: *Yeah, I guess.*

Me: *The good news for you is that I trust Riley and he says it's true.*

Dawson: *So you're not mad?*

Me: *When I got your texts last night, I was really upset, Dawson. I think maybe you have some major sucking up to do.*

Dawson: *I'm good at sucking . . .*

Me: *Yes, I know. I gotta go. Shoes are calling. I heart you.*

Dawson: *I heart you more.*

Now that everyone has their dresses, we're at a department store looking at jewelry, handbags, and shoes.

Katie, Maggie, and Annie rush over to Peyton and me. "I just heard one for the sales girls say that Abby Johnston is here. In THIS VERY STORE! Can you believe that?"

"Um, no, actually, I can't." My mom is here? Could that be true? Garrett did say she was taking a trip.

"We're all going down to the cosmetics department. That's where she's supposed to be. We're going to go stalk her and see if we can get a picture with her."

Shit. I can't go see her.

But I want to see her.

God, I want to see her.

They all take off, but Annie turns back around to look at me. I'm still standing here, frozen in my spot.

"Aren't you coming?"

"Um, you guys go. I lived in LA. Seeing a celebrity isn't that big of deal to me. I'm gonna go back and get that clutch I saw earlier. I think it would be perfect with my dress for the dance. I'll meet up with you later."

She runs off and I slink over to the second floor balcony, where I can see down to the cosmetics and perfume counters. I spot Mom right away. There are two men, Ryan and Craig, in black suits trailing closely behind her. James is not with her, which is surprising. He almost always accompanies Mom when Tommy doesn't. It makes Tommy worry less.

Which means Mom made James stay with the girls. Which means she's worried about them.

Which makes me worry.

I watch her stop to try on some perfume. She smiles graciously and takes a photo with a fan. I see my friends wandering through the cosmetics counters.

I pull my phone out and call her.

She puts her phone up to her ear just as Annie and Katie approach her. I watch her hold up a finger to them as she answers.

"Whatever you do, Mom, do not say my name out loud. I go to school with the girls who are standing in front of you. They want your autograph."

"You're here?"

"Yes. I'm hiding behind some clothes on the second floor balcony. I want to see you. Go ahead and sign the autographs. Annie is a huge fan. Then go upstairs to the lingerie department on the fifth floor, grab a couple things to try on, and I'll be waiting in a dressing room."

"Sounds good," she says and hangs up.

I slowly back away from the balcony and almost knock over a rack.

"Can I help you?" a sales clerk asks me.

I jump. Look guilty. "Um, no." I look at the escalators and decide I'd be better off going the back way. "Where's the elevator?"

She points a finger toward the back of the store.

"Thank you."

I quickly walk to the elevator and take it to the fifth floor. I grab the first four items I see and ask for a fitting room.

I shut the door and drop to the little stool.

I look at my hands. They're shaking. I'm so excited and nervous to see Mom.

Pretty soon, I hear Ryan speaking. "*Yes ma'am, that's fine.*"

"Keatyn?" Mom whispers.

I swing open the fitting room door. She rushes into the room, pulls me into a tight hug, and I immediately start crying.

She smells so good. Like lavender, honeysuckle, and the ocean.

We hug each other tightly and cry for a while before either one of us speaks.

Finally, Mom gently pushes me away and looks at me. "God, I've missed you. And look at you. You look grown up. Your outfit is adorable. You put it together yourself, didn't you?"

I smile and wipe tears from my eyes.

"You were always better at fashion than me. I can't put anything together without Kym. So you're just here shopping with your friends?"

"Yeah. I got chosen for Homecoming Court, so I needed a dress."

"Oh, honey, that's great! I'm so proud of you! So, you're doing well?"

"Yeah, I'm doing well. I actually really like school."

"Does that have something to do with a certain boy?"

I grin, just thinking about him. "Yeah, it probably does. But all of it's good. I've made some great friends. So why are you here in New York?"

"I'm doing a couple morning shows tomorrow and a couple interviews today. Pre-release buzz for *To Maddie with Love.*"

"How are the girls? I miss them so much."

She holds up her phone and scrolls through pictures of the girls. I start crying harder. I've only been gone a month, but I can already tell they've grown.

But then she stops on one that causes me to start laughing through my tears.

It's Gracie. She's apparently moved on to cold weather gear from her usual swimsuits, princess gowns, and angel wings. She's got on fuzzy multi-colored striped tights, ladybug rain boots, the pink tie-dyed tutu I was wearing the first time I met Tommy, and a long-sleeved T-shirt with pink hearts. Her hair is in pigtails and she's holding a chalkboard with an arrow on it. The arrow is pointing to an adorable fluffy Golden Retriever puppy. The chalkboard has the words, *Bad dog* written next to the arrow. It's so funny because the dog looks like an angel and you wonder if the dog should be holding a sign pointing to Gracie that says, *Bad girl.*

We hear Ryan cough. Then he says, "Abby, we need to get going. You have that interview with Vogue."

"I can cancel it," Mom says.

"No, it's okay, Mom. My friends are going to wonder where I am."

I hug her one more time.

"I love you, Mom."

She smooths down the back of my hair and says, "I love you too. You should probably stay in here for a few minutes. Give me a head start so no one sees us together. I know people don't recognize you, but if we were together, they might figure it out. There are a swarm of photographers out front."

I SIT DOWN and waste ten minutes on Facebook. See Annie's newsfeed photo of the girls with my mom.

I walk out of the fitting room, go through the lingerie department, and down the escalators. I'm just stepping on the escalator to the first floor when my phone buzzes.

> ***Annie:*** *Meet us on the second floor back by the dresses. Abby came off the elevator and was surrounded fans. We're trying to get another picture.*

Shit. Mom's not gone yet.

I'm halfway down the escalator when all of a sudden I see Vincent step onto the up escalator.

My heart starts pounding.

I look around, trying to quickly assess the situation.

Trying to remember everything Garrett taught me.

Mom and her security are upstairs. I could go up there. But then my friends would know. Vincent would follow me. It'd be a mess.

Vincent is messing with his phone. His head is down and I pray that he doesn't look up.

But just as I'm getting ready to pass him, he does.

Our eyes meet and his widen in shock. His look of shock is quickly replaced with a scary smirk.

He reaches out and tries to grab my hand, but I quickly pull it away.

He leaps up, hops across the escalator, and is now jogging down the stairs after me, yelling, "Abby, wait!"

Why is he calling me Abby?

As I get to the first level, I can see out the front door. Mom was right. There are a mess of photographers waiting for her.

A plan starts to form in my mind.

Can I use them to get away?

It's the only thing I can think of.

I slip my big black sunglasses off the top of my head and down over my eyes.

I run fast out the front door as Vincent yells out again, practically on cue, "Abby, please wait!"

The cameras start flashing. I rush through them toward the street. They let me through then turn their backs to the store, huddling together.

Which blocks Vincent's way.

The paparazzi.

I haven't been photographed by them for a long time. They only seem to want pictures of cute little kids, not the gangly pre-teen that I used to be.

What used to sort of scare me when I was little seems very comforting right now.

They are protecting me from Vincent.

I put my hand in front of my face as I hear Vincent yell out again. "Abby!"

I turn around and see that he's working his way through the crowd.

The driver that I hired for the day is parked in the parking garage. There's no time to call him.

I spy a black town car idling at the curb. I dart toward it and open the door.

As I'm getting in, I hear one of the camera men say, "That's not Abby, dude. It's just some chick in a wig pretending to be. They do that sometimes. Send out a fake. A decoy."

I run my hand through my soft hair wondering how he could have mistaken it for a nasty wig.

I must need a deep conditioning.

The driver yells at me. "I think you've got the wrong car."

Vincent breaks through the crowd and lunges toward the car as I slam the door shut and yell, "Go!"

Vincent grabs for the door handle just as I slam down the lock.

He stops and stares at me through the dark glass.

The driver is telling me to get out of his car. Telling me he's not going anywhere.

Vincent smirks again and lunges for the front passenger door.

I scream at the driver, "Go! Go! Go! Please just go!" I lean over the top of the passenger seat and slam down the lock.

The driver quickly pulls into traffic and says to me, "I got it. And in case you didn't notice, we're going."

I didn't realize I was still screaming.

"So where are we going?" he asks. Then he starts rambling. "You know, I could get fired for this. Who was the suit? Did you steal something from the store? I'm not going to get in trouble for transporting a thief, am I?"

I take a deep breath and slip off my sunglasses.

"Whoa," he says under his breath.

"What?"

He shakes his head and talks to me in the mirror. "Nothing, but, um, I think now we are being chased by a cab."

I turn around and see a cab riding our ass. See Vincent in the front passenger seat, pointing toward me.

"Can you lose him?"

He rolls his eyes at me and starts talking to himself. "Can I lose him, she asks? Can I lose him?"

There's a little space in traffic up ahead of us, so he stomps on the pedal, which causes me to be thrown back in my seat.

"Buckle up, buttercup," he says, as he cranks up the radio and yells over the noise. "This is just like in the movies. I'm like that dude from *Trinity*, what's his name?"

"Tommy Stevens," I say with a grin. I turn around and see the cab weaving in and out of traffic. "I think they're still after us."

We had pulled away from them, but now we're stuck at a light.

There are lots of people walking in front of us in the crosswalk. We can't go anywhere.

The cab stops just two cars behind us.

Shit.

I run scenarios through my brain. What will I do if they wreck us? What will I do if he has a gun and starts shooting? What will I do if aliens crash down in front of us?

I'm ridiculous. I have no idea what I'm going to do.

I close my eyes and try to think of a plan.

"Um, I think the dude just got out of the cab," the driver tells me.

"What?!" I say, my eyes opening as I rip off my seatbelt and turn to look out the back window.

Holy shit.

Vincent has gotten out of the cab in the middle of New York City traffic and is slowly walking toward me.

Not running like you would think he would be.

Or maybe everything just feels like it's moving in slow motion.

"He's getting closer!" I yell.

"Don't worry. I've got this," the driver says. "The light is going to turn green just about . . . now."

I'm jostled as the driver cuts across traffic, but my eyes never leave Vincent.

Our eyes are locked on each other even though I know he can't possibly see me through the tinted glass.

He knows I'm looking straight at him. I can feel it.

He mouths *Abby* then slowly puts his index finger up to his lips and kisses it. Then his hand forms a gun and he shoots the kiss at me.

I want to scream.

I put my hand over my mouth and shudder instead.

Vincent just did what Cush did to me that day at his soccer tournament when he scored. I remember thinking how adorable it was. How he stopped in front of everyone and shot me a kiss. There were no photos of me that day in the batch he sent after he tried to kidnap me, but now I know that he was there then too.

He was everywhere.

I cross my arms in front of me, grab my shoulders, and give myself a hug.

"I'm sure we lost them," the driver says, breaking my thoughts. "Even if he gets back in the cab, they will cut over at the next block. But I doubled back the way we came from."

"Back to the store?"

"Yeah. I have to pick up my ride."

I realize I've been holding my breath and let it out in a *whoosh.*

"So what's the deal? You don't look like a thief."

"I'm not a thief."

"So why's that guy after you?"

"Uh, bad breakup?" I say with a laugh.

But then I keep laughing. Uncontrollably laughing. Then I start laughing and crying at the same time. This guy's gonna think I'm a lunatic. Probably will turn me over to Vincent himself.

I pull myself together. "I'm sorry. Thanks for getting away from him. You're like my hero."

He shrugs his shoulders in an aw-shucks way. "It's okay. So, what do you do?"

"I'm a dancer," I say wondering where the hell that lie came from.

He gives me a lascivious grin. "Oh, really? Exotic?"

"No, I'm a Rockette."

He nods his head at me. "Damn, that's cool." He makes another turn and I can see we are back on the street in front of the store. I notice the cameras are gone, which means so is Mom.

I sigh with relief. Not only did I lose Vincent, Vincent lost Mom. He had to have been following her.

I get a call from Garrett.

"Are you okay?" he shouts.

"Yes. I think so."

"Your mother just called me in a panic. Call her. Then call me back."

I call her. "Mom!"

"The photographers told me that my decoy and the guy running after her out of the store yelling *Abby* didn't work. Tell me that wasn't you. And *please* tell me the guy running after you wasn't Vincent!"

"It was him, but it's okay. We lost him. I'm fine."

"We?"

I smile at my driver. "What's your name?"

"Allan," he says.

I say into the phone, "Allan just drove better than Tommy Stevens did in that car chase in *Trinity.*"

Allan beams at me.

Mom laughs uncomfortably, so I say, "I gotta go. Be safe."

I hang up and say to the driver, "Do you think you could take me down to that coffee shop?"

I'm a little nervous about going back in the store, just in case Vincent would think to go back there.

"Sure," he says.

I open my wallet. I have no cash.

Shit. I never have cash. "I want to pay you something, but I don't have any cash."

He shakes his head. "You don't owe me anything. That was the most fun I've had in a long time. Unless, of course, you can get me a part in Tommy Stevens' next movie. That's the only thing that could top this." He pauses. "Speaking of that, you do kinda resemble Abby Johnston. Did that guy mistake you for her?"

"Sorta. He has a thing for her. Thought I looked like her. Used to call me Abby. He's a little off his rocker. One of those rich guys that thinks he can have anything he lays his eyes on."

"But he couldn't get you?"

"Not today, thanks to you."

He studies my face again. "Yeah, I don't see it. Like when you had your sunglasses on, you kinda resembled her, but as soon as you took them off, it's easy to see your eyes are very different."

"Do you have a card, Allan?"

"Sure." He pulls a card out and hands it to me.

I read it. "*Allan Broadmore, actor.* Thanks."

His phone buzzes with a text. "Obviously, not a full-time actor. That's my boss. I've gotta get back there."

"Thanks, Allan."

"I didn't catch your name."

"It's Maggie."

"Fun times, Maggie. Maybe I'll come see your show sometime."

"That'd be cool. I'll be the one, um . . . kicking."

I GET OUT of the car and stand outside the coffee shop.

There's a text from Annie and the girls asking where I am. I text back and ask them to meet me here.

I take a photo of Allan's card and send it to Tommy with a text.

> ***Me:*** *Please call this guy and give him a job in your current endeavor. He has excellent driving skills. When you call him, tell him Maggie the Rockette suggested him.*

Tom: *That's kind of a weird request, even for you.*

Me: *He may have just saved my life.*

Tom: *Hang on, your mom's calling me.*

I close my eyes and take a deep breath, trying to slow down the adrenaline coursing through my body.

Then I say a prayer. *Thank you for letting me get away. Please keep my mom safe. My family safe.*

My phone buzzes.

I open my eyes and look down at it. It's Tommy.

"Hey," I say.

"We're bringing you home. This isn't working."

"No, you aren't. I'm sorry, but you're not."

"We can make you."

"How? I'm emancipated, and I have my own money."

"Don't get smart with me."

"Well, you try getting chased through the streets of New York City by a psycho and see what kind of mood you're in."

Tommy laughs just a little. "You know, I did that in *Trinity*."

"Yeah, I know. I didn't mean to snap at you. I love you and Mom, but I love my sisters more. Vincent called me Abby today. He's different. Worse, I think. Mom's not safe either. You worry about them, and I'll take care of me."

I start to get tears in my eyes as I see my friends walking down the street toward me.

Tommy says, "We've got to do something."

"I agree, but you'll have to excuse me now, my friends are almost here and I have to go pretend to be a normal teenager."

Garrett is calling me back, but I don't answer.

I can't deal with him right now. I can't deal with any of them right now.

I have to act normal.

I'm normal.

A normal Eastbrooke girl shopping in New York City with her friends.

Just breathe, Keatyn. It will be okay.

"Hey," Peyton says. "You missed out on all the excitement."

I laugh.

I actually, really laugh.

They have no idea the excitement I just had.

"I need some coffee," I say.

What a stupid excuse.

"I need coffee too," Maggie says. "So what's up next?"

"We need cute pajamas for PJ day. I know a great lingerie store. Should we go there next?"

"That sounds fun!" Katie says. "I'm thinking I need some new lingerie too."

"What for?" Maggie asks, nudging Katie with her elbow. "You planning to attack Dallas?"

Katie smirks. "Nope. I'm just going to look so hot that he won't be able to resist me."

After we all get coffees, I call our driver and we head to the lingerie store.

We all pick out fun pajamas to wear for PJ day.

"Let's have a lingerie party tonight," I suggest. "We'll drink wine and wear something fabulously sophisticated."

WE HAVE A great time giggling and trying on silky chemises, robes, camisoles, gowns, all sorts of stuff. Annie buys a gorgeous long silky gown.

She says, "Who cares if I didn't make Court. I'd rather buy a gown like this. I feel like a movie star."

We shop until we can't shop anymore then head to my loft.

When I walk in my front door, I instantly feel safe.

At home.

While the girls check out the place and claim their bedrooms, I walk into my closet, sit on my chair, and finish my prayer.

Please let this be over soon.

HOT TUB NAKED.
7PM

WE ALL FRESHEN up our makeup, put on our lingerie, and do some shots. By eight, we're all a bit tipsy and feel like partying.

"This loft is amazing. We should be having a party," Maggie says.

"Maggie, we *are* having a party," Annie scolds.

Ariela and Katie agree. "Do we know anyone in the city we could invite over?"

I can think of two boys who happen to be in the city right now, one of whom has some very important sucking up to do. "Let's invite some boys."

"Which boys?" Katie asks.

"Our Homecoming dates. Just our Homecoming dates. But we need to make it fun."

Maggie mutters, "All we have to say is we're half naked and drinking wine in a killer loft by ourselves. Get your asses here."

I laugh. "Well sure, that would work, but let's make it fun."

"Wait!" Annie says. "If we invite them to come and then they stay, that would mean we'd have to sleep with them."

"Sleep with them here, yes. Have sex with them, no. It's not any different than hanging out in their room at school."

"What if he sees me in the morning and it scares him away?" Annie asks.

"You're gorgeous, Annie. You're not going to scare him away."

"So what are we gonna say?" Peyton asks me.

I type something in my phone and send it to each girl. "Read what I just sent you and tell me what you think."

Me: *Mission: Impossible.*

Your mission, should you choose to accept it, is to dance with lingerie-clad girls, drink excessively, eat decadent food, hot tub naked, and party all night long. If you can handle this mission, please reply immediately to get the address, then get your sexy ass here. This message is for your eyes only. Do NOT bring your friends. This is a VERY private party.

P.S. This message will self-destruct in five seconds.

"That's awesome!" Katie squeals. "So we'll invite Dallas for me, Parker for Maggie, Riley for Ariela, Ace for Annie, Dawson for you. But what about Peyton? Do you have a date for Homecoming?"

"I have a date, but I don't want anyone to know who it is. So if I invite him tonight, you have to promise not to tell anyone at school."

"Deal," the girls all say.

"Should we send a picture of all of us, holding drinks in our lingerie?" Katie asks.

"No. We want them to be surprised when they get here," Maggie tells her while I type the proper boys' names in and send the text.

"Okay, I'm sending it."

DALLAS IS THE first to reply.

Dallas: *I am getting my ass on a train.*

Riley: *Dallas and I are getting our asses on a train.*

Parker: *I'm so there.*

Ace: *Does Annie know about this? Is she really in lingerie?*

Me: *Yes, she does. And yes, she is.*

Ace: *On my way :) Did she tell you that we're going out?*

Me: *She did :)*

Ace: *Tell her to check her phone. I just made it Facebook official.*

Me: *Awww, she'll love that. I'll tell her.*

"Annie, Ace says you need to check your phone. He did something he wants you to see."

She looks confused, grabs her phone, presses a few buttons, and then screams, "He MADE IT FACEBOOK OFFICIAL!!!"

"Made what Facebook official?"

She grins hugely. "He asked me to be his girlfriend last night. He just put it on his profile."

The girls all scream excitedly.

"I think that calls for another shot," Peyton says with a grin as she pours another round.

"Ace, Riley, Dallas, and Parker replied. They're getting their asses on the train."

WE DRINK, LAUGH, giggle, and dance. The boys, minus Dawson and Camden, all arrive about a couple hours later

They look hilarious. Dressed in camouflage and with black marks under their eyes. Like they're going on an actual undercover mission.

And they like the lingerie.

I immediately show them the bar, make each boy do a body shot off his girl, and get the music cranked up. Then the boys do a few more shots to catch up.

Peyton and I are at the bar, eating chips, when our phones buzz at the exact same time.

"Cam," she says.

"Dawson," I laugh.

I answer the phone, buzz them up, then go greet them. When I open the door, Dawson is standing there holding a big bouquet of flowers and wearing a sheepish grin.

Cam swats him on the back of the head and rolls his eyes. "So whipped." Then he looks me over from head to toe. Taking in my sheer orange sherbet and bright pink two-tone chemise. "This is a great loft. You're a keeper."

"I'm a keeper because of real estate?"

"No. You're a keeper because of your ass, but I was told to be polite."

I break out into a wide smile.

I like him already. I can see why everyone thinks Camden is so hot. He's tall, dark haired, and has a chiseled face. He's taller than Dawson, with a leaner build. More like Riley.

He walks by me, smacks my ass in the exact same way Dawson does, grabs Peyton, and heads to the bar.

"Flowers, huh?" I say to Dawson. "You must have done something bad."

"Well, my dad says flowers get you laid, but jewelry gets you out of jail."

"So you're just looking to get laid?"

He gives me his sexy-ass grin. But his eyes say something different. "I made you cry, Keatie. I don't ever want to make you cry."

I set the flowers down on the bench and give him a hot kiss.

"Can we just do it right here?" he asks, pointing to the bench.

"I thought you had some sucking up to do?"

"Speaking of that." He reaches in his pocket and pulls out a huge handful of big ring gummy Lifesavers. "I brought party favors. Thought I'd share the magic."

"You liked it that much?"

"Keatie, I loved it."

"I love you. Thank you for the flowers."

"I love you too. I have another surprise for you later."

"I can't wait. But for now, let's go get you a drink."

WE PLAY POOL, dance, drink, and have fun.

I dance crazily around Dallas and Riley. Ever since that night at the Cave, the three of us often crank up the music in their room and just dance around like maniacs. One of our favorite songs is playing, so we naturally congregate together.

After dancing, people start to pair off.

Ace and Annie sit on the couch talking and holding hands. Peyton and Camden are naked in the hot tub. Riley and Ariela have wandered upstairs to "watch a movie" on the big sectional couch, and Maggie and Parker have already claimed one of the bedrooms as their own.

Katie, Dallas, Dawson, and me are playing pool. It's boys against girls and since Katie and I both suck, we're using different techniques to distract the boys.

After a couple games of me suggestively leaning over the pool table, Dawson drags me to my room, locks the door, and attacks me.

It's literally a throw-me-on-the-bed, rip-off-my-panties, wham-bam-thank-you-ma'am kind of thing.

"Was that my special treat? No offense, but I get that all the time," I tease.

He's slightly out of breath. "I just had to get that out of the way." He pulls on the strap of my nightie. "I almost brought you in here after you, Peyton, and Maggie were grinding on each other. That was fucking hot enough, but the way you were leaning across the pool table, I couldn't take it any longer."

"So tell me about this surprise."

"Shouldn't I just show you?"

I run my finger lightly down the front of his chest. "I don't know, maybe."

He gets off the bed, grabs my hand, and pulls me into my bathroom.

He stops in the center of the room, pushes the spaghetti straps off my shoulders, and watches with delight as my nightie slithers down to the floor.

He grabs a couple towels off the rack, lays them across the floor, and motions for me to lie down. He steals one of my makeup brushes off the counter, turns on the tub, and holds the brush under the water.

Then he puts the brush directly in the center of my cleavage and slowly moves it in an arc over the top of my right boob then down my side.

I giggle as the brush tickles my skin.

He opens a little bottle and sprinkles it on top of the water line he just created.

"Is that glitter?" I ask, looking at the hot pink sparkle.

He shakes his head and starts working very intently. Brushing water on me then sprinkling it with the glitter.

Just having the brush tickle my skin is enough to make me super hot again.

"It's not glitter. It's sugar glitter." He dips his finger into one of the little bottles and holds it in front of my mouth. I slowly suck the glitter off.

"Mhmmm, that's good."

I look down my body and see a large multi-colored sugar heart. The tops of the heart curve out from my cleavage, wrap around my boobs, and meet at a point between my legs.

"That's quite artistic. If I wasn't naked, I'd want to take a picture of it."

"I'm glad you like it. Now, for the fun part. I get to lick it all off." He puts his hands under my butt, lifts it up in the air, and starts licking the point of the heart.

I find myself wishing the point went down just a teensy bit farther.

His tongue works its way up my body, licking sugar, but causing most of it to fall off onto the towels. He licks some, but then seems to get distracted, stopping to kiss and suck my skin. He only makes it about a quarter of the way up the heart before he's hot and ready for round two.

I can't say the hard marble feels that great on my back, but I've drank enough not to care.

When he finally collapses next to me, he says, "Sorry, that sugar was making me feel kinda sick. I think I'm still hung over from last night."

I laugh out loud. "Ha! Serves you right. Hangovers are your body's way of telling you that you're an idiot."

"You're mean," he says with a laugh as he rubs his knees. "Can we get on the bed? This marble is killing my knees."

"Yeah, let me wash the sugar off real quick and I'll meet you there."

He leans up on his elbow and gives me a sexy grin. "I think I might like to watch that."

I give him a little smack. "You're such a horn dog."

"And you love it."

I nod my head and smile to myself, because he's right, I do love it.

I turn the shower faucet to hot and step inside my shower, which is glass on three sides.

I decide since he didn't go through with all the licking that I will mess with him just a bit.

I give him a grin, stick my tongue out, and run my finger down it while I stare at him.

Then I look down at the spot in my cleavage, where the heart starts. I press my wet finger onto the sugar. Some of it attaches to my finger and the rest sprinkles down the front of me.

I hold eye contact with him while I put my finger back in my mouth and suck the pink sugar off.

Then I return my finger to my chest, tracing the top of the heart over my swell of my breast, causing Dawson to lick his lips.

I trace the heart further down around the side, put my finger in my mouth, and close my eyes as I suck the sugar off.

I've only cleaned off about another of quarter of the heart when Dawson and his raging hard on join me in the shower.

He presses his lips hard against mine as he pushes me through the stream of water and up against the shower wall. In one swift motion he picks me up, cupping his hands under my ass, and frantically pushes inside me.

After a very steamy shower, we dry off, and then collapse into bed.

Before we fall asleep, he pulls me into his chest, kisses the top of my head, and whispers, "I love you."

Sunday, October 2nd

I'M NOT KINKY ENOUGH?

8AM

DALLAS AND I are the first ones up. I'm toasting us English muffins when he says, "So last night was interesting."

"What do you mean?"

"Katie and I did it."

"Did it! You had sex? I thought you wanted to wait?"

"I thought she'd *make* me wait. We haven't even been dating for a week."

"So what happened?"

"Did you see the way she looked? That hot little thing she was wearing? It was all silky and her boobs were just like, *Bam*! But even then, I was going to wait."

"And?"

"And she decided to convince me otherwise." He blushes.

"You're blushing. How did she convince you?"

"She put Dawson's party favors to good use. But it didn't go well."

"Why not? Because it was your first time or because you were kind of drunk?"

"No, it's just that she was sucking the, uh, lifesaver, pretty enthusiastically. When I was close, she stopped and we did. And so as soon as we did, I did."

"Believe it or not, I actually followed that. So it was over fast?"

"Very fast. I was sort of embarrassed, but she didn't care. She came back out here, grabbed us a bottle of vodka, poured me another shot, and said that we needed to do it again." He sits up straighter. "I obliged."

"Still, you could have said no."

"Why would I want to do that?"

I put on a pout. "What about me?"

He grins. "We got high. We kissed. We're not friends with ben-e-fits. We're friends who hit-and-kiss. Ha! Get it? That rhymes."

"You're hilarious. But you didn't answer my question."

"No offense, but you're sorta straight."

"I'm not kinky enough? And you think Katie is? She's hasn't even done it much. And neither have you, for that matter."

"I didn't mean it that way. I just meant, like, your body. I prefer shorter, curvier figures. That's what I'm attracted to."

"I'm straight and unattractive. Great."

"Straight, yes. Unattractive, no. You're hot. Just not my type. Seems like you're pretty happy being Dawson's type though."

I smile big. "That's true. Last night, he did things to me that were so hot."

"You're gonna have to tell me about them, so I can make Katie hot."

"Seems like that's not a problem." I glance at the clock. "We better get everyone up. We have to be back at school soon to work on the dance float."

YOU'LL CAUSE A RIOT.
2PM

I SPEND MOST of the day working on the dance team's float for the Homecoming parade. A group of alumni dancers really do all the planning and designing of the float. Basically we're just here to be worker bees. I flit around like a good bee should and do what I'm told.

Maggie and I are sitting on the ground, legs crossed, stringing fake red and yellow flowers onto streamers to make garlands for the sides of the float.

Maggie goes, "So I know that I'm in lust with Parker right now. And I know that you are in love with Dawson, but I think we should take a moment to admire the magnificence that is right in front of us." She nods her head toward Aiden and sighs. "Look at the way he's swinging that hammer. He's so intense. And those biceps. Totally jacked. Can't you picture him building you a gazebo or something?" She scrutinizes me. "Come on, say something. Gush with me."

"He's good with a hammer," I say, knowing I sound totally lame.

"I'd let him hammer me, any time," she says with a naughty grin.

"Maggie!" I giggle.

"What?" she says as we both lean our heads to one side to get a better view. "You know you'd let him hammer you too."

"I would not! I love Dawson. Oh, look. He's starting to sweat."

"I don't see sweat."

"Yeah, look at the back of his neck, right below his hairline. There are little beads of sweat. He must be hot."

Maggie fans herself. "You're not a kidding, he's hot. Oh. My. God. He's taking off his shirt!"

I lower my head and try not to watch, but he catches my eye with those damn tractor beams of his just as he pulls his shirt over his head.

He tosses it to the ground, gives me a little grin, looks down at his chest, and then looks back at me with one of those freaking smiles. The same smile he was flashing to numerous girls at the Cave the other night.

I think he just can't help it. It's just in his godly blood to make girls swoon.

"Would you look at that?" Maggie continues. "It's like he's perfect. Hey, help me out here. Look at him carefully and see if you can find anything that isn't perfect."

"I'm not going to sit here and stare at him. He already has a big enough head as it is."

She giggles. "I've heard that he is big."

"Big? Like, down there?"

"Yes, down *there*. What are you, ten?"

"Where did you hear that?"

"Well, he's been with quite a few girls. They talk, you know. About his package."

"Which girls? No. Wait. I don't want to know. I couldn't care less." I bite the corner of my lip and try to focus on the garland I'm supposed to be making. But then I look around and realize Aiden and I are the only ones getting any work done. Half the dance team and most of the alumni have stopped what they're doing and are all drooling in his direction.

I feel a little bad for him.

Being objectified and all.

"This is ridiculous, Maggie. I'm going to tell him to put his shirt back on."

She gives me an evil eye. "Don't you dare. You'll cause a riot."

"Still, I'm going over there." I get up and walk toward Aiden. He is hammering nails.

I said that already, didn't I?

I lean down to talk to him just as he stands up straight, which means his abs are now staring at me.

Hello, sexy, perfect abs.

Hi, amazing deep V-line.

Howdy, . . ."

"You need something?" he says, bending over at the waist and taking my view away.

"What?" I'm feeling just a bit dazed. Must be all the spray glue fumes. "Oh, I was going to say that you're doing a great job. With the hammer. With the, uh, hammering. Like, you seem to be pretty good at hammering. Uh, I mean pounding. Or, um, nailing." I shake my head. "You know, whatever it's called."

Why does every word I say suddenly sound perverted?

Aiden tosses the hammer into the air. It spins in a circle then drops back into his hand. "I like to hammer things."

I gulp.

Damn Maggie for turning basic carpentry all sexual.

Aiden pulls a drill gun out of the little tool belt that he's wearing and holds it up. "I'm good at screwing too." He laughs. "That didn't come out quite right. I meant that I'm good with a screw gun. I'm good with lots of power tools."

My mind immediately goes to his tool. His godly, powerful tool.

I glance down at his crotch before I can think better of it.

He catches me, leans in, and whispers to me, "I'm good at all kinds of screwing."

I blush.

I'm blushing.

I know I'm blushing.

"That's just gross," I say, trying to recover, while peeling my eyes off Aiden's body.

He sets the hammer down to reach up and wipe the sweat off the back of his neck.

When he does this, it causes the muscles on his entire right side to flex. I hear an audible gasp from a woman near me, whose face looks permanently surprised from way too much Botox.

Aiden ignores her or maybe he's so used to it he doesn't even notice. He whispers to me, "Trust me. When we do it, it will so not be gross. It will be amazing. Best you'll ever have."

"We are never doing it. And you need to put your shirt back on."

"Why? I'm hot."

"Because you're going to cause one of the old alumni women to have a stroke or something. And that would sort of ruin the Homecoming festivities."

He takes a step toward me. His naked chest almost touching mine and trapping me between him and the float.

"I think I'll leave it off, just for you. You can think about us naked. Hammering. Nailing. Pounding. Screwing." He gives me a totally naughty and completely adorable smirk.

"I will be thinking no such things."

"Oh, yeah, you will. It will be all you think about for the rest of the day."

NO TWO ARE EVER THE SAME.
5:35PM

I'M ON MY way to meet Aiden, the dirty carpenter, in the library, but the sunset is so gorgeous that I have to stop, sit on the bench, and admire it. I close my eyes and pretend that I'm on my deck in Malibu. Mom and Tommy are sitting next to me. We're having a glass of wine and talking about our day. My little sisters run out in their pajamas to give us good night kisses.

When I open my eyes, Aiden sits down next to me.

At least he put his shirt back on.

"How come you're sitting out here?"

"I was just looking at the sunset. Thinking about home."

He looks at the sky. "It is gorgeous. Sunsets are like fingerprints. No two are ever the same."

"It sounds like you've watched a few."

"Sunsets remind me of home too." He looks sad for just a second then changes the subject. "So I hear you helped my sister find the perfect dress."

I study Aiden's face. Even though he's trying to act happy about the dress, the way his jaw is set makes me think he isn't thrilled about it. Maybe he uses his godly telepathy on me, because I suddenly understand why. "You're not thrilled she asked Camden, are you?"

"I'm just really surprised she would ask him after all he put her through. They used to date, you know? And he broke up with her right when she needed him the most."

I squint my eyes at him. "I know they dated, but I didn't know the break up was bad. I got the impression they're still pretty, uh, close."

Close being a bit of an understatement.

Seeing as they were naked in my hot tub.

Aiden shakes his head. "They might be now, but not back then. That's why I ended up coming to school here. I had no desire to live away from my family. But Peyton wasn't doing well, so I came here to take care of her. Which was a tough decision because I had been helping take care of my mom."

"Your mom. Why?"

"She had cancer."

"Oh, wow. I'm sorry."

"It sucked. Cancer sucks."

"Is your mom, um, like, is she okay?"

Aiden brightens. "She is. Her having cancer definitely changed our lives, though. We lived in Atlanta when we found out. They didn't give her long to live and the thought of losing her really affected my dad. He realized how short life can be. He told us that love is the most important thing in life. As part of her treatment, Mom made a list of all the things she wanted to do when she beat cancer. One of the things on her list was something my parents always said they wanted to do when they retired. Buy a vineyard in Napa Valley. Dad decided not to wait until Mom beat cancer to do it. Within a month, he had sold his business and our house in Atlanta, and he had bought her a vineyard. They made Peyton and me make lists too. Peyton was having a hard time with it all. She was mad. Mad that Mom had cancer. Mad that Dad made us leave all our friends. On her list she wrote that she wanted to go to boarding school. I don't think she really meant it, but they thought she did, so they sent her here Freshman year."

I realize now why Peyton turned to the teacher after she and Cam broke up. Why she was more worried about upsetting her parents than telling the truth. It must have been terrible to have Whitney hold something like that over her head. Much worse than my being a stupid virgin.

I was really, really shallow.

Aiden continues. "I loved California. I could play soccer pretty much year round. I had made some friends. Liked school. But then one night she called me bawling, and I decided she needed me more than Mom. When I got here, Peyton still looked perfect on the outside, but on the inside, she was hurting."

"Because of the breakup?"

"Because of everything, I think. So when Cam broke her heart, he changed my life too."

"It was really sweet of you, Aiden." Now I understand why Aiden seems more mature than most boys his age. He's lived a lot already. We kind of have that in common. We came here for reasons other than ourselves. "So do you wish you weren't here?"

"Not at all. Even though I came to take care of her, I ended up loving it. With us being only a year apart, people used to think we were twins. We did everything together. I liked us being back together, if that makes sense. I made Varsity soccer right away and the girls seemed to like me."

I laugh. "That's cuz you're hot." Shit. I didn't mean that. Why did I say that?

"You think I'm hot, huh?" he says with an easy grin.

"I mean, not me, but I've heard that a lot of girls think that."

He raises an eyebrow at me.

I roll my eyes at him and laugh. "Fine. I think you are a nice looking boy."

He stares at me for a beat then looks back out at the sunset. "One of my favorite things about Napa is watching the sun set. We'd sit outside, have a glass of wine, and talk. Mom said that no matter how bad a day she'd had, the sunset was comforting because it meant she'd made it through another one."

"Your mom must be amazing."

"She is. And that's why I like sunsets. They're, like, hopeful."

"My family used to do the same thing. Watch the sunset together. Only we had a house on the beach. How is your mom doing?"

"For now, the cancer is in remission and she and dad are working through their lists. Traveling all over the world." He gets a pained expression on his face. "She decided though that if it comes back, she won't fight it. She won't go through chemo again."

"That's got to be hard on you. My dad died when I was eight."

He reaches out and touches my pinkie with his. "I'm sorry."

We both sort of sigh, lost in our own thoughts, look out at the sun, and don't say anything else until it slips below the horizon.

ROUGH TO HANDLE.

10:35PM

KATIE AND I are getting ready for bed when Garrett calls me.

"I just wanted to let you know that your mom cut her trip short and is safely back in Vancouver."

"Why did she cut her trip short?"

Garrett sighs. "You told me that you want to know everything, right? Even if it's rough to handle?"

"Yes."

"When she woke up this morning, there was an envelope pushed under her hotel room door."

"And what was in it?"

"A photo of you. From that day on the beach when you let him take your picture. You were blowing a kiss."

I shudder remembering the kiss he shot me yesterday and know that the photo was not really meant for Mom.

Is was meant for me.

I try to sound unaffected. "He already sent us that picture."

"Yes, honey, but this one was different."

"How so?"

"It was stabbed numerous times with a very sharp object. All that was left intact was your face."

My stomach lurches and all I manage to say is, "Oh."

Katie says to me, "Hey, I'm gonna hop in the shower."

I nod to her, wait for the shower to turn on, and then say to Garrett, "Poor Mom."

"Poor Mom? Poor you, if he finds you. You need to tell me everything that happened on Saturday."

I give him the run down.

"So it was a completely chance encounter?"

"Yes. You told me Mom was planning a trip, but you didn't tell me where she was going. I had no idea."

"I didn't tell you because I was afraid you'd try to see her."

"I'm sorry about the Brooklyn thing, Garrett. I wouldn't have gone to see her. You know what was really weird though? He didn't call me Keatyn. He called me Abby. He's never called me Abby before."

"He's getting worse. More out of touch with reality."

"Did he leave when Mom did? Are you following him?"

"We were. We tracked down his hotel. He might be out of touch with reality, but he's still not making any mistakes. He didn't stay at the same hotel as your mom and he had what appeared to be a business dinner tonight. Since neither you or your mom are in the city, I saw no need to continue surveillance. He's scheduled on a flight to LA tomorrow night at seven. We'll make sure he's on it."

"Even though I know I'm safe here, I'll feel better when he's back in California."

"You and me both."

YOU NEED TO CHILL.
1:30AM

EVERYONE IS STILL in a party mood and looking forward to this week, so we all meet up at the Cave.

I'm sitting between Jake and Dawson, sharing a joint and getting chewed out by Jake.

"So you invited Peyton but not Whitney on your little shopping trip? How is that any different from what she did to you?"

"For one, I didn't take her boyfriend with me and lie to him. For two, Peyton invited herself. And for three, my loft only sleeps so many people. So, I couldn't have invited Whitney because she doesn't really go anywhere without Rachel and the minions. I mean, do they follow you into the bedroom?"

Jake squints his eyes at me. "That's mean."

I roll my eyes at him. "It's different, Jake. I didn't purposely exclude her. I didn't invite everyone else in front of her and then tell her she wasn't worthy of going."

"Dude," Dawson says to Jake. "You need to relax. We're supposed to be partying."

I look at Jake. "Are you mad because you think I excluded Whitney or because I didn't invite you to the Mission: Impossible party?"

"The party sounds like it was a lot of fun."

I feel bad. "Maybe we could all hang out sometime."

Dawson giggles. "Fuck that. I'm not hanging out with her."

"Dawson, be nice!"

"What do you expect, Jake? Keatie is right. Whitney wouldn't have gone even if she was invited."

"Maybe not, but I would have."

"It was a couples' thing that wasn't planned in advance. It was completely off the cuff. We were supposed to have a girls' weekend. Shop, drink wine, watch romance movies. Then we started doing shots and felt like a party. We only invited our Homecoming dates." He keeps staring at me. "Next time I'll invite you. Okay?"

"Thank you. And we need to talk about Homecoming. What are you planning?"

Dawson looks at me. "We haven't really talked about the details, but I've made a few plans." He leans over and kisses me. It's a sexy kiss, full of tongue.

"We were talking about planning Homecoming?" Jake says, interrupting us.

"We're just doing what everyone is," I say. "The day's festivities. Dinner. The Dance. Coronation. Then changing and going to the club."

"Are you riding one of the buses to the club?"

I nod my head yes at the same time that Dawson shakes his head no. "We have to go to the after party, Dawson. You'll love my outfit."

"I love everything you wear." Then he says under his breath, "And everything you don't."

I kiss him again. Smoking makes me want to kiss. So I kiss him.

He pulls me over onto his lap and I kiss him some more.

Jake gets a frustrated tone in his voice and interrupts us again. "So how are you getting to the club?"

Dawson pulls his lips away from mine. "I got a limo for Keatie and me. Just the two of us." He grins at me. "I also got us a hotel room."

I run my fingers through his hair and snuggle up closer to his chest. "Really? That sounds fun. I like just the two of us."

Jake lets out an audible sigh.

"What?" Dawson says to him.

"It's hard to carry on a conversation when you keep making out."

"Fine. Keatie, stop attacking me."

I giggle, then do just that. Attack his neck with kisses while he tries to carry on a conversation with Jake.

"What are your plans, Jake?"

"I just thought we'd party together. It's our senior year. We've gone to every Homecoming together."

"We will be partying together. At the dance. The after party. You and Whitney are welcome to come in the limo with us to the club if you want. We're stopping at the hotel first. Changing. Which might take awhile. Going to the after party. Then back to the hotel. I booked it for two nights, so we wouldn't have to check out at noon. We'll crash. Get room service. Enjoy some private time. Then head back to school after dinner. Did you book a room?"

"No. Whitney is taking care of all of it."

I can tell that Jake is bummed. I stop kissing Dawson's neck. "What about dinner? We could sit together."

"Whitney already has planned the seating arrangements too."

"Do you get to plan anything?"

"Sure, from the list she gave me."

"She likes to plan," Dawson says.

"Yeah, well sometimes it takes the fun out of it."

I hand Jake the joint. "Here. I think you need this."

Monday, October 3rd

I THOUGHT YOU'D NEVER ASK.

8:20AM

I'M IN HISTORY class with Riley when I get called to the office. I smile, grab my bag, and figure that Peyton got me out of class again.

When I get to the office though, I don't see her.

Instead the Dean's secretary says, "Miss Monroe, the dean will see you now."

The dean will see me now? Why does the dean want to see me?

What did I do!?

I walk into his office.

Be calm, Keatyn. Don't look guilty.

The dean looks up from his desk. "Sit down, Miss Monroe. There's something we need to discuss."

"Yes, sir," I say as I fidget with the zipper on my handbag.

"This is a delicate situation," he tells me. He's got a little bead of sweat on the upper corner of his forehead, where his hairline just barely recedes.

Is he nervous?

"We pride ourselves on security here at Eastbrooke, but it appears that someone was in our office last night. We believe that your file was accessed."

My eyes get huge, my thoughts immediately racing to the rehabs that were broken into. To Vincent being in New York City.

Vincent tracked me from New York.

He had me followed, and I didn't know it.

He knows I'm here.

But if he knows I'm here, if he broke in last night, why didn't he come and get me last night while I was sleeping?

Didn't Garrett say Vincent was too smart to do it himself? That he probably hired someone.

Does that mean he's on his way?

I clear my throat. It's obvious that the dean expects me to respond. "Were there other files accessed?"

Please say yes.

"It appears to have been just yours."

I try not to panic.

I need to know what Vincent knows. "What exactly is in my file?"

"The basics. Your school transcripts. Current class schedule. Parking pass. Dorm assignment. And, well, the financial arrangements regarding your tuition."

That's why he broke in. He knows I'm here, but he needs to know what dorm I'm in. Tonight, he's coming to get me. Or maybe he's waiting for me inside my car. Hiding in the backseat, waiting for me to drive off, then he'll overtake me. Or maybe he wanted me to know he found me. Maybe he'll make me wait. Make me crazy with wonder as to when he's coming. Maybe he's playing with me. Garrett said that stalking is all about control.

What am I going to do? Where am I going to go? I just started building a new life here.

"Thank you for letting me know, sir. Is there anything else?"

"No, we just needed to make you aware of the situation. Particularly since your financial data may have been compromised."

"Thanks," I say.

He has no idea. He's worried about money. About getting sued.

I'm worried about someone grabbing me and never being seen again. I grab the locket around my neck and pray that whatever they installed in it actually works.

I think I'm going to need it.

"You should probably take a few minutes to check your account and then head back to class," the dean says as he shoos me out of the relative safety of his office.

My mind is reeling.

I imagine Vincent waiting for me outside.

I remember Garrett telling me to go where people are.

I can't go to my dorm room. He could be there. I can't go to class. He knows my schedule. I have to be unpredictable. I have to do something he couldn't have planned on.

I stand outside the school office, trying to think.

"Earth to Keatyn."

"What?" Riley is standing in front of me. Big, strong Riley. The boy who said I'd need protecting.

"Did you get in trouble?"

"What? Oh, uh, no."

He wraps his arm around me. "Then what's wrong? You're shaking. Is your family okay?"

My eyes get tears in them. I don't know what to do.

Riley sees that I'm about to start crying.

"Come on, let's go talk." He tries to drag me down the hall.

"No! Wait!" I yell.

"Why? Tell me what's got you so upset."

"Just give me a minute!"

Think, Keatyn. Don't stay in this building. Don't go to the dorm. Your car is out. *Lots of people.*

But then I think about the crazy people that come into classrooms with guns. No classrooms. I need to hide.

I remember Garrett telling me that Hawthorne House was next to my dorm. That it housed most of the school's athletes. That I should go there if I was ever in trouble.

"Can we go to your room?"

Riley grins and raises an eyebrow at me sexily. "Baby, I thought you'd never ask."

I don't laugh at his joke. "I, uh, don't want anyone to know. Can we sneak down there? Go the back way or something?"

"It's gonna be a secret affair, huh? You want me to tie you up?"

My face goes a shade whiter. I think about what was in the van. Imagine being tied up in the back of it.

Riley looks at me closely. "Okay, you're scaring me."

"I'm sorry. I just . . ." I can't even come up with a lie. I'm stuck in one spot. I thought if he ever came and got me, found me, I'd be all badass and fight him, but I'm not a badass. I'm a scared, freaked-out mess.

I'm paralyzed with fear.

Snap out of it and make a decision, Keatyn.

I look at Riley. He's got on a hoodie over the tie-dyed shirt he's wearing for 70s day today. "Can I have your jacket?"

He pulls it off and hands it to me. I put it on and pull the hood up over my head. I look over and see the big Lost and Found box. There are a pair of Cougar Athletics sweatpants lying right on the top. I grab them and pull them on over my skirt and fringed cowboy boots.

"What are you doing? You're acting very strange. Are you on something?"

"What? No. I'm . . . I, uh, just thought that I shouldn't walk in your dorm looking like a girl. It's a disguise."

"When we get there, you are going to tell me what the hell is going on."

I nod my head and pull on his arm. The second bell already rang for the next period, so the hallways are empty. I peek around a corner to look outside. To survey the area. To see if Vincent or any other stranger is lurking there.

"Let's sneak down by the trees."

"No way. If we look like we're doing something wrong, we'll get caught. We're walking straight down the pathway to the dorms. If anyone asks what we're doing, we'll say getting a paper out of my room, for class."

I'm beyond logic but that sounds good. "Give me your sunglasses."

"A hoodie, sweats, and sunglasses. Are you afraid Dawson will find out? I swear, I'll never tell."

He's trying to make me laugh, I know.

But it's not working.

WE SAFELY GET to his dorm room without running into anyone.

I shut the door, slump against it, then slide down to the floor.

Riley kneels down next to me. "Okay. Tell me what the hell is going on."

"Just give me a minute, okay? I need to think."

I open the file copy the dean gave me and look through it. Look for any link between me and my old life.

A school I didn't go to. A fake transcript from a fake school but with my actual classes and grades.

A fake mailing address for my fake parents in France.

My schedule. My activities. My parking pass.

The account that my tuition comes out of from the bank in Atlanta.

Nothing to connect me to my old life.

Except the picture on my school ID. If he saw that, he'd know it's me.

I look up at Riley and tell him as much of the truth as I can. "Someone was in the school office last night and accessed my file. Only my file."

"Why are you so upset about that? Jeez, I thought someone died or something."

I think about me being the one to die.

"I just feel a bit violated, I guess. Why would someone do that?"

Please let there be a viable alternative to Vincent.

"Maybe it was just a prank?" Riley guesses.

I shake my head. "Why?"

He snaps his finger. "Maybe it was Whitney. Jake said that she was pissed about Peyton going shopping with you. About her weekend."

"Whitney? Why would she do that?"

"Because she's a bitch and she hates you. Maybe she was looking for dirt." He grabs my printout. "Any dirt in here? Did you get kicked out of your last school? Do you have an illegitimate child? An affair with a teacher? Been to rehab?"

I listen to him rattle off all the fake life ideas my family came up with.

"Riley?"

"What?"

I throw my arms around him and hug him tightly. "Thanks for being my friend."

He hugs me back, which causes me to start crying.

"Are you on the rag? What's with all the tears?"

"I'm not sure." I laugh.

He starts reading my file. "Wow. This *is* scandalous."

"What is?" What did I miss?

"You got a B. Seriously?" He scans the pages. "You've only had one B in your life?"

I shrug. "Yeah."

"Brains and beauty. It's a deadly combination. No wonder my brother is crazy about you."

"Do you see anything else that might come back to haunt me?"

"Well, you should probably call your bank and check your account. I bet that's why the dean was freaking out. They have your whole account number on here. They aren't supposed to do that."

I nod at him. I know just the banker to call.

"You're right. Let me call my financial guy real quick."

I get out my cell and press Garrett's number.

He answers. "Are you okay?"

"For the moment, yes. But I just got called to the dean's office. Someone accessed my personal information last night. *Only my* information."

Garrett is quiet. I wonder if the call dropped. "Are you still there?"

"Yes. I'm thinking. This sounds a lot like the rehabs."

"That's what I thought."

I internally panic. Even Garrett thinks it's him.

I let out a little cry.

Riley looks at me with concern. "What happened? Is your account okay? Is their fraud on it?"

"Who are you with?" Garrett asks.

"A friend. My file has my full bank account number in it."

"I'm putting you on hold. Give me just a second. Do you feel safe right now?"

"Yes, and I'll wait." I point to the phone and tell Riley, "I'm on hold."

"Tell me what's really going on."

Should I tell him? Can I trust him?

What I need to do is leave school. Now.

Get on a train to nowhere.

Run.

Garrett comes back on the line. "Your school has excellent security measures in place. Did he say the school was breeched or just the office?"

"Just the office, I think."

"Keatyn, take a deep breath. Calm down for a minute. I'm almost positive that this was not Vincent."

I turn to Riley. "Riley, will you excuse me, please?"

I walk out his door and down the hall.

"He was in New York City, Garrett. What if I didn't lose him? What if I just thought I did? What if he followed me here? What if he didn't know where to find me on campus and broke into the office to find out my dorm number. And what if he's just waiting for me?"

"The timing is troubling and no security system is infallible. That and the rehabs getting broken into is too much of a coincidence to ignore. I'm sending a car for you. I want you out of there until we can locate Vincent. Until we're certain it wasn't him."

"How long will that take?"

"About an hour."

"An hour? Are you fucking kidding me? What happened to *We'll send in the cavalry*? I thought if something happened to me, there'd be people here right away." All of a sudden, it hits me. "There is no cavalry. You're relying on the necklace, aren't you?"

"Yes."

"Don't bother sending a car. I'm going off campus, and I'm leaving the damn necklace here."

"Keatyn, don't. Don't do anything stupid . . ."

"I'm not. I'm doing something smart. I'm getting the hell out of here."

I hang up, go back to Riley's room, take off my necklace, and lay it on his dresser.

Riley grabs me. "I want the truth. You're shaking and scared to death. I can see it in your eyes."

"The truth is I need to leave campus. *Now.*"

He shakes his head. "No way I'm letting you drive. I don't know what's going on, but you are in no shape to drive." He gets on his cell. "Hey, Mom, can you call school and tell them I'm headed off campus? Yeah, everything's fine. I just need to help out a friend. Tell them I have a dentist appointment. Thanks, Mom." He nods at me and grabs his keys. "Let's go."

I get outside the dorm and feel completely exposed. Like I'm naked at the Super Bowl.

"Run!" I yell.

He grabs my hand and we sprint to his car. I dive into the backseat.

"I'm not checking out," I tell him. "I don't want anyone to know I'm gone."

He starts his car, drives down to the entrance, checks out, and drives through the gates.

"Where do you want to go?" he asks.

I want to go see my mom and Tommy, I think.

Which causes an idea to pop into my head. "The movies," I say. "Let's go see a movie."

I'll hide out in the dark all day then call Garrett later to find out if Vincent got on his flight home.

I decide to text him.

Me: *I'm sorry I yelled at you but I assumed that if I needed help it would be there instantly. I know logically that's not feasible. Please don't call my mom. I don't want to worry her. I left school with a friend. I didn't sign out, so they don't know I'm gone. I'm sure I'll get in trouble later for skipping, but that's the least of my worries. Please let me know if Vincent gets on his flight.*

Garrett: *I'm glad you left. I sent a man to his hotel and he's not there. It also appears that he did not spend the night.*

Me: *So he could have been here? He still might be here.*

Garrett: *Yes. Where are you?*

Me: *I'm going to the movies. Not the theaters by school. We're driving to anoth-*

er town in my friend's car. Mine is still at school. I hid in the backseat, so if anyone was watching, they wouldn't have seen me.

Garrett: *I'm very impressed with your quick thinking. I'll keep you updated.*

About twenty minutes later, Riley stops the car and says, "In case you're wondering, we weren't followed."

I climb into the front passenger seat, but leave his sunglasses on and the hood up.

He looks at me seriously. "Let's go inside. Then you're going to tell me what has you so scared."

I BUY TICKETS to Mom and Tommy's latest release. We go inside the theater, but since the movie doesn't start for almost an hour, we sit on a bench out front.

"Okay," he says.

I blow out a breath of air. "Remember my meltdown that day in my room?"

"Yeah."

"My parents moving to France wasn't the only reason I came here."

"You did mention something about a guy."

"I had a relationship, um, go bad."

"Go bad? Like abusive? You don't seem like you would put up with that shit."

I shake my head. God, I hate lying to him.

Close to the truth, Keatyn. Close to the truth.

"I would never stay with a guy who hurt me. This was, um—look, you have to promise, swear to me, that you won't tell anyone this—not even your brother."

"I swear, baby." He holds out his pinkie.

I laugh. Take it in mine and swear.

"Tell me."

I close my eyes and think. About Vincent. About his grabbing my arm on the escalator. How I got away from him. How I know he's found me.

But I have to tell him something. I may not ever be able to go back to school.

I may have to just up and leave like I did at home. I wouldn't get to see Dawson anymore. Or Riley. Or my friends.

I'd be alone again.

I can't help it. My body involuntarily shudders and tears start streaming down my face.

Riley wraps his strong arm around me, pulls me into his chest, and whispers, "You'll feel better if you tell me. I need to know if I'm going to help you."

I can't look at him. I keep my head buried in his chest and start talking. "My mom has this, um, ex-boyfriend. And he sorta was stalking me."

"Stalking you?"

"Yes. Following me around when I didn't know it. Coming to my soccer games. Showing up at restaurants I was at. He was even taking pictures of me." Even though I'm lying about who Vincent is, I'm telling him a lot of the truth. And it feels good—like it did that day with Aiden in the chapel, so I keep going. "He was older, good looking, and he flirted with me. When I met him, I didn't know he was, um, my mom's ex-boyfriend." I sit up and take a deep breath. This part isn't a lie and it's the part I'm most embarrassed about. "I was flattered by his attention. I was so stupid, Riley. I always thought I was a good judge of character but I'm not."

"Did he hurt you?"

"He tried to kidnap me at my seventeenth birthday party. It was supposed to be this magical night. You should have seen my shoes. And my dress. He showed up. I think he caused a commotion. Then he grabbed me. I tried to fight, but he was strong. He was dragging me toward an exit." I suck in a big breath of air. "He was opening the exit door when I got away. There was a van outside the exit that he was taking me to. Inside the van they found zip ties and drugs. He was going to. To . . . I don't know for sure, but people think that it wouldn't have ended well for me."

"Was he arrested?"

"For about two seconds. There was no proof he did anything wrong. The van was a stolen rental. It was my word against his. And my word didn't mean much since I invited him to the party because I didn't know. After they released him, he sent some pictures he had been taking of me to my mom. He wanted her to know that he could hurt me anytime he wanted. At one point, he even put a note in my little sister's backpack. That's how close he got to her. I left mostly to keep them safe."

"Even if they couldn't prove the attempted kidnapping, stalking is illegal. Why isn't he in jail?"

"Stalking is really hard to prove and it didn't help that I thought we were friends. I had dinner with him one night. Let him videotape me on the beach. We couldn't even get a restraining order. My family moved to France. I came here."

"So that's why you didn't have a Facebook and why you only had like four numbers in your phone?"

"Yes. I just had to leave. Only a few people know what happened. There were rumors at my old school that my parents sent me to rehab. Not long after, the three rehab facilities—where people said I'd gone—were broken into. Their files accessed."

Riley's eyes get big. "And here, your file was accessed. Wow."

"That's why I'm freaking out. I know he's found me."

Riley shakes his head. "No. It's not him. If it was, he would have broken into your dorm last night and surprised you."

"You're probably right. I don't think he would have waited. But maybe he needed time to plan. Maybe he wasn't sure I was there. Maybe he sent someone to break in. Either way, now he knows."

"I keep going back to Whitney. I'm telling you, that girl is evil. I think she was looking for dirt."

"I'm not worried about her. Hell, I used to be her. Kinda. At my old school."

"You were Queen Bitch?"

"No. That job was taken by my best friend. But I could be mean sometimes. I got caught up in the whole popularity thing and I really didn't like the person I was becoming. I swore to myself that when I came here that I wouldn't be popular. That I would never sit at the popular table in the cafeteria."

"And my brother has been dragging you straight to that table, hasn't he?"

"Yeah, but I've realized it's not the table that matters. Just because I sit there, doesn't mean I have to be like Whitney."

"You are *nothing* like her. So follow along with my reasoning here. We have major security at school. If this guy broke into the office, he had to get on the campus first. Our campus is extremely secure. If someone broke in, got past the guards, the whole school would have been on lockdown. That's why I think it was done by someone who was already at school."

What he says actually makes sense, but I'm not convinced. "I hope you're right."

"Come on, our movie is about to start. Let's get some popcorn."

We eat popcorn and I get to spend a couple of hours with my mom and Tommy.

SCREWED OUR WAY AROUND SCHOOL. 5PM

Dawson: *Where are you? I heard you get called to the office. Is everything okay?*

I have similar texts from most of my friends.

"What am I going to tell them, Riley?"

"Maybe you should tell them the truth."

"You won't tell me the truth about Homecoming and why you got kicked out of school."

"That's cuz it's embarrassing. Epic, but embarrassing."

"It's been two years."

He give me a big dramatic sigh and then says, "Fine, I'll tell you. So, freshman year, I come to school thinking I'm the shit. I'd had sex a few times that summer and felt like I was joining my brothers for what was going to be four years full of nothing but girls and sports. So Homecoming weekend rolls around. By this time, I've been with two older girls at school, which has done nothing but up my cockiness.

You know, the Cave has traditionally been a place that only juniors and seniors get to go to. I talked Cam into letting me come to a party with him. He handed me a flask and told me to find someone to share it with. I shared it with this gorgeous junior. Maybe it was the combination of the fact that I was pretty big for my age and the alcohol we'd shared, but I had her convinced that I was Cam and Dawson's older brother and a college freshman. That even though I had gone to a different school, my parents made me come to support my brothers.

She bought that and proceeded to tell me how she hated that her dad came to Homecoming. How she hated him showing her his old stomping grounds and telling her long, boring stories. She also mentioned she hated her dad, although I forget why. Then she told me she had the perfect revenge. She dragged me to every place he took her that night. The bleachers at the football stadium where he played in the band was the first place we had sex.

There were about four more places, many of which I only vaguely remember. Which is a surprise because I remember thinking she needed to shut the fuck up about her dad because dads are sort of like cock-blocking.

We drank more, lost our clothes, and screwed our way around school.

One of the things her dad was the most proud of was the alumni band float.

He always helped plan it. Came in early to work on it. Had even designed that year's and would be riding on it.

All I remember is her being really pissed at that point. About her telling me this was the place she wanted to defile. How awesome it would be to watch her dad ride on the float we'd done so many dirty things on. That's all I remember until I was woken up that morning by her father, who had come down with some other band alumni to make some last minute adjustments to the float."

Riley laughs.

"We were both completely naked and passed out on the float. The float was half trashed and I was in a whole lot of trouble. They threw us each a coat and dragged us to the dean's office."

"Talk about a walk of shame," I say with a giggle.

He nods at me and continues. "I was somewhere between still drunk and majorly hung over. And if getting caught wasn't already embarrassing enough, our parents sat in while the dean questioned us. By this time, most of our clothes had been recovered and turned in by various people. Granted, in retrospect, the girl was obviously pretty messed up and had some serious daddy issues but I was drunk and horny enough not to consider that at that time.

"She started crying. Thinking she'd get out of it that way. She told them all how I got her drunk and took advantage of her. When they seemed skeptical, she pulled out what she thought was her get out of jail free card. She told them that I was a nineteen-year-old college freshman and that she was underage. That I forced her. The dean stopped and looked at me. Sized me up. Glanced back at my dad. My dad and the dean were in the same graduating class, and I think they have plenty of their own stories because the dean sort of smirked at the girl when he informed her that I was actually a freshman at Eastbrooke.

"She just started going psycho. Yelling at her dad. Screaming at the dean. At me. She tried to attack her dad.

"My parents dragged me out of the room and told me they were extremely disappointed.

"My mom marched off, but Dad slapped me on the back and said, You know you're going to be expelled.

"I was like, *Really?*

"And then he told me that was the best story he's ever heard and how he hated her dad's pompous ass."

I've been trying to hold in the laughter, but I can't anymore.

"See, you're laughing."

"Because it's funny. My story isn't funny-embarrassing it's more scary-embarrassing."

"At the time, it was pretty embarrassing. Can you imagine sitting in the dean's office hung over as fuck, listening to the dean explain in detail your being naked on a float. I couldn't even find my pants. I was half frozen."

"I'm glad you told me your story, but I really don't want to tell people mine. Maybe in a few years when it's not so fresh. And if I'm still alive."

"You really think he wants to kill you?"

"I think he will keep me for a while. But eventually, yes, I think he would."

"So we've seen three movies and I've eaten two tubs full of popcorn, two boxes of candy, and three slushes. Do you think we can go back?"

I check my phone for the time. It's after six o'clock. Vincent's flight doesn't leave until seven, but he should be there by now.

I text Garrett.

Me: *Any word?*

Garrett: *He's at the airport.*

Me: *Oh, good. That's a relief.*

Garrett: *I'll let you know when he's on the plane.*

"Am I going to get in trouble at school for skipping?"

"I think if you do, you should say you were upset about what the dean told you. That you left to handle some financial stuff. To check your account or something."

"That's a good idea. Can we go in the mall for a bit before we go back?"

"Are you dragging me to the shoe department?"

"We can go wherever you want. Do you want to look at clothes for you?"

"Not really. Let's go with the shoes. They seem to make you happy."

"That they do."

I try on a bunch of shoes, buy a couple new pairs, and am paying for them when I get a text from Garrett.

Garrett: *He boarded the plane and we watched them close the doors and pull away from the gate. I really don't think he knows where you are, Keatyn. If he did, he wouldn't be going back to LA.*

Me: *That makes me feel a little better. But you said he's a planner. What if he went back there to plan? What if he knows you're watching him?*

Garrett: *What do you think?*

Me: *I don't think he would wait.*

Garrett: *Me either, but still be cautious. Pay attention to your surroundings. Listen to your gut. If you feel danger, get somewhere safe. Just like you did this* *time. And please put the locket back on.*

Me: *I will.*

I grab my packages and we head back to school.

When Riley drops me off at my dorm, he tells me, "I'm sleeping in your room for the next few nights, just to be safe."

"I think I'll be fine. He might have hired someone to break in, but I think the rest of it, he'll want to do himself. And he just got on a plane back to LA."

"Still, I'm sleeping in there."

"Riley, he's strong."

"Doesn't matter. I'd have the element of surprise. He wouldn't expect a guy to be in there. What are we going to tell Katie?"

"We don't have to say anything to Katie. That girl sleeps like a rock. Dawson has come over a couple times and she never even knows he's been here."

WHEN RILEY SNEAKS in my room a bit after midnight, he lays down on my fluffy rug.

"Riley, just come up here and sleep with me. I feel bad you're on the floor."

"Don't feel bad. I love this rug. I just want to keep petting it, and I so want to do Ariela on this rug. That's how you can pay me back. Lend me the rug."

Tuesday, October 4th

TOTAL DIVA.

6AM

EVEN WITH RILEY in the room, I don't sleep well.

I keep having dreams about Vincent. Him being in my room. Me screaming. How I'm screaming as loud as I possibly can, and even though there are people all around me, none of them can hear me.

When six o'clock rolls around, I get up feeling happy to have survived the night.

Luckily, it's Pajama Day, so I don't have to do much with my hair. I just put it in a messy bun, throw on the pink and black polka dot camisole and short set, a black slouchy sweater with a big pink heart on it, a pair of black sweater thigh highs, a great pair of Valentino ruffled lace-up biker boots, and I'm out the door.

I even have time to grab a latte before the Social Committee meeting.

I'm in line for coffee when Peyton cuts in next t0 me. "Will you please get me a hot chocolate?"

"Sure. You look really pretty today," I say, taking in the long silky gown and matching fur heels she bought this weekend. Her hair is smooth and straight and she's even wearing a long strand of pearls. "Total diva."

"Whitney is going to be pissed when she sees me. All of them are wearing silk pajamas. You know, like the kind your mom wears."

"Were you supposed to wear them too?"

"Well, it was suggested that we all wear them."

"Are they wearing heels with them?"

"We'll find out as soon as we get to the meeting. You look adorable, by the way. I love how you combine stuff that doesn't seem like it would go together and make it look so good."

I laugh. "This was all together at the store."

"The pajamas, yes, but they didn't have them with the thigh highs and the motorcycle boots."

I look down at myself. "That's true. I don't know. I just have weird taste."

"Well, it works. Oh, there's my brother."

"Do you want something?" I ask him right before I order.

"Naw, I'm good," he says, holding up a bottle of water.

"Your T-shirt is awfully tight," I tease, taking in his Lorenzini blue and white striped sleep pants, extremely fitted white T-shirt—that I know the girls will be going crazy over—and a pair of driving shoes that are so cool, Tommy would die for them.

"Those might be the coolest driving shoes I've ever seen," I say, commenting on the color-washed, tie-dyed shoes he's wearing. "My step dad would love them. What brand are they?"

"Alberto Moretti Arfango," he replies. "I found them online at Barneys. Had to have them."

"You are seriously a man after my own heart."

Aiden gives me that stupid grin. Like I just admitted my undying love or something.

I roll my eyes at him and head to our meeting.

AFTER THE MEETING, I'm leaving the building when Aiden runs up from behind me. "Where are you going?"

"I have to go get my stitches out."

"Are you going by yourself?"

"Uh, yeah. Everyone says that it doesn't hurt."

"I'm coming with you."

"No, you're not. I'm fine." I study his face. "Is it gonna hurt?"

"Sometimes they come out easily. Other times they sort of grow into your skin and it hurts a bit."

I wince thinking about the possible pain. "I'm kind of a baby when it comes to stuff like this."

"Really? You always seem so tough."

"Emotionally, maybe I'm kinda tough, but with physical pain, I'm a wimp. I don't know how I'm ever going to have kids."

He gives me an intense look.

"What?"

"I was just thinking you'd be a great mom. Lots of fun."

I smile. "I adore my little sisters. I think I'll love being a mom. Pregnancy and birth, that's another story."

"Pleasure and pain."

"Kinda like love in general. It can be really great or just a great big pain."

Aiden nods his head agreeing with me.

"I was fine before, but now you have me all nervous."

"I make you nervous?" he asks, moving closer to me in a way that makes me feel a completely different kind of nervous.

Because, hello, I have a boyfriend.

Who I love.

Get that tight-fitting T-shirt away from me.

"What's with you lately? It's like your goal in life is to pin me against the wall. I'm not going to fall for your little tricks, *friend*."

"What little tricks?" he asks innocently.

"*Hammering. Nailing. Screwing.* Give me a break. Your tight white T-shirt may leave most of the girls at school panting, but it doesn't work on me."

"And why's that?"

"Because I think there's a lot more to a person that their looks. And I really don't like you all that much."

"Bullshit. You're afraid to like me."

"Afraid to like you?" I roll my eyes at him. "Is this a new experience for you? A girl that doesn't fall into bed with you."

"I'm not like that."

"Please. I've heard enough from Maggie to know that's *exactly* what you're like. I'm just not interested in a guy that's a player. I've been burnt by that kind of guy. I've been lied to by that kind of guy. That's part of what I love about Dawson. He's not a player."

"Except for his summer in whoredom."

"You've heard about that?"

"Hard not to when he bragged about it all during football camp. All the girls. All the parties. All the meaningless sex."

"He was just on the rebound after Whitney. She broke his heart. He had fun. Big deal. Everyone has rebound sex." I remember Aiden telling me that Dawson was just a rebound, so I quickly add, "I mean, it's something guys do. Girls just cry."

He shakes his head at me. "And what about the party? When he was pawing your shirt? He's still rebounding. So are you for that matter."

"You don't know anything."

"Keatie," I hear Dawson call from behind us. "Wait up."

Aiden and I turn around as Dawson catches up to me. "I'm coming with you to get your stitches out. My hand has recovered. We should be good."

I laugh at him. "I'll try not to kill your hand this time. Jake told me this is the easy part. Although Aiden says it might hurt a little."

"Aiden's right. Sometimes it hurts a little. And with today being a special day and all, I couldn't let you go alone." He throws his arm around my shoulder and pulls me in for a hug. He turns to Aiden. "You going to see the nurse too?"

The tops of Aiden's cheeks turn slightly pink. "Yeah, I've, uh, got a sore throat. Wanted to get it checked out. Don't want to be sick for the big game."

Dawson slaps him across the back. "Good plan. We don't want to disappoint all the alumni. Dean would be pissed off for a week. And you know what happens when he gets pissed off."

Aiden nods in agreement, but I say, "What happens?"

"He just gets all pissy, which causes the teachers to get pissy, which causes our dorm advisors to pay more attention than we'd like. But we're lucky we have Aiden. Everyone thinks he's a good boy. That's why we always party in his room."

Aiden grins back at Dawson, but there's something there. Something fleeting in his eyes.

AFTER A SURPRISINGLY pain-free removal of the stitches, Dawson says, "You did good. Let's go celebrate."

"We're going to celebrate getting my stitches out?"

He holds up the passes the nurse gave us. "Did you notice how I distracted her with questions when she was filling these out?"

"You were asking a bunch of dumb questions."

"Yeah, she's not a good multi-tasker. See this line where she's supposed to write what time we left? She didn't fill it out. That means we can go have some fun. And we need to have fun this week. When you start play practice next week, you won't have any time for me."

"I like fun," I say. "And I'll make time."

"You know what today is, right?"

"Tuesday?"

"Yeah, what else?"

"Pajama day?"

"Try again."

"Uh, Taco Tuesday?"

"It's our anniversary."

"We have an anniversary? We haven't even been going out for a full week yet."

He grins. He's got his school blazer off and the sleeves of his oxford rolled up. He looks so damn sexy.

"Yep." He pulls my waist into his. "It's been a month since our first time."

"Our first time. As in when we had sex in the Hamptons?"

"That's a night worth remembering, don't you think?"

"Is it bad that we're celebrating our sexual anniversary?"

"I don't think so. It's when we got together."

"True."

"So I have plans for you after Taco Tuesday, but since we have some extra time now, we might as well take advantage of it."

"How are we going to celebrate this anniversary?"

"Exactly the way it started."

HE PULLS ME inside his dorm and pushes me against the door, kissing me. He drops his jacket and backpack on the common room sofa then pushes me against the wall in the hallway. He's kissing me with that same intensity he did that first night. That night I knew there was no way I could resist him.

We work our way down the long hall. His hands are feeling their way across what's underneath my sweater.

After seriously making out down the hall, we finally make it to his room.

He pulls my sweater off and takes in my little pink knit camisole set.

"Very cute," he says.

"Take it off me. There might be something underneath that shouldn't be categorized as cute."

He gets a naughty grin on his face and slowly pulls up my cami, revealing a sexy black lace Agent Provocateur push-up bra.

He licks his lips, kisses my cleavage, then slowly pulls down my shorts to reveal the teeny matching briefs.

He stands back and looks at me. Then he literally leaps on top of me, pinning me to the bed.

"You always ruin my plans," he says, as he strips his own clothes off.

"What's that supposed to mean?"

As he pulls off my panties, he says, "I always think I'm going to be able to go slow. I can't go slow with you." He covers my mouth with his and quickly proves his point.

A SHORT WHILE later, we're dressed and heading to class.

"We'll go to Taco Tuesday tonight, but we're leaving early. Gonna do some more celebrating."

"Where are we going?"

"Back to our lake."

As in the lake where we parked and did it standing up against his car.

Dawson is like a sexual buffet. I never know what to expect, what's going to be next in line. But I definitely want to keep going back for more.

LOOKING LIKE A SLUT.

LUNCH

DAWSON AND I are in line getting lunch. Whitney and Peyton are ahead of us and Peyton is getting chewed out.

"What is your problem lately? You go on one trip with Dawson's little plaything and come back looking like a slut. Did she help you pick out those furry heels?" Whitney asks, scowling at Peyton.

I give Dawson a look. Like, what a bitch.

Dawson winks at me, walks past me, and smacks Peyton on the butt. "Looking pretty sexy there, Arrington."

Peyton jumps slightly from the smack, but her face breaks out in a wide grin. A smirk, really, directed at Whitney.

Whitney doesn't bite though. "My point, exactly."

"Whitney, I don't tell you how to dress. Why would you think you could tell me?"

"Because the five of us have dressed alike for every spirit day for the past three years, maybe?"

Peyton shrugs. "Well, if you were on the dance team, you'd understand. Sometimes you get tired of dressing like everyone else."

Oh. Damn. She just slammed Whitney for not making the dance team.

Peyton's bitch is totally coming out.

But I'm worried about her because I know what happens when you go up against a Queen.

You become just as big of a bitch as she is.

I want to tell Peyton it's not worth the fight. Just do your own thing.

Then Damian's song starts playing in my head. *Just do your own thing, do it up big, rocket to the moon, now everybody sing.*

I think maybe I need to get Peyton to listen to that song.

I get my food then go to our table.

"That was sweet of you," I whisper to Dawson as I set my tray down.

"So you have to help me win Mr. Eastbrooke," he replies.

"What's that?"

"It's a contest we have every year. The competition is held during the pep rally on Friday. Each boys' sport chooses a junior or senior to represent their team. I got picked to represent the football team. It's a big deal."

"What do you have to do?"

"Dress up like a girl."

I laugh. "Seriously? And you *want* to do that?"

"Of course. It's awesome. So you have to make me look pretty. I'll need makeup, a wig, heels, and an outfit. We all walk out in heels and wave at the crowd. Then we have to do either a dance or a cheer."

Bryce adds, "Everyone votes by clapping for their favorite."

"Hmmm. I just can't picture you as a girl."

He runs his finger down my arm. "Just think. You can grind all up against me and pretend I'm a girl. Only when you take me home, I'll have a little surprise for you under my skirt."

"I can handle the clothes. Do you want me to help you with a dance too?"

"No. Honestly, even though it's always an option, no one ever dances. A cheer is a lot easier to learn. Riley said Ariela could teach me one."

I finish up my lunch quickly, then tell Dawson I have some stuff I need to do. What I need to do is work my way around the freshman tables and start suggesting they vote for Peyton.

HE'S SWEET?

5:30PM

I'M JUST FINISHING up tutoring Aiden in the library when Dawson texts me.

Dawson: *I'm STARVING and ready to start celebrating ;)*

Me: *I'm about done. Be there soon. Heart you.*

"So I have to get going. A bunch of us are going out for Taco Tuesday."

"I'm going to Taco Tuesday," Aiden says. "Riley invited me, but he said it was a guy thing."

"I'm the only girl that goes, usually. Well, so far, anyway. Dawson and I won't stay all that long though. He wants to go celebrate."

Shit. I shouldn't have said that. Now he's going to ask what we are celebrating. *How* we're going to celebrate.

"I heard him say something about a special day this morning. What are you celebrating?"

"Um, just our anniversary."

"Yeah, but anniversary of what? You haven't even been going out a week."

"It's been a month since I stayed with him in the Hamptons. That was when we got together. Like, I was done with the Keats guy, and then I sorta started seeing Dawson."

"And this anniversary of when you sort of started seeing each other, was this your idea or Dawson's?"

"He remembered it, if that's what you mean."

"That doesn't sound like something a guy would remember."

"He's sweet?"

"Lots of people said you had sex with him that weekend."

"People speculate lots of things, doesn't mean they're true."

"That would be the kind of anniversary a guy would remember."

"Or, he's just adorably sweet?"

"I can't believe you had sex so soon."

"I never said I did."

"I know you did though. It makes so much more sense now."

"What makes sense?"

He just shakes his head at me.

"Okay, whatever. I have to go. I guess I'll see you at dinner."

WE'RE DEFINITELY NOT.
6:30PM

I STOP AT my dorm and quickly freshen up. I don't want to wear my pajama shorts to dinner, so I grab a skirt, throw it on, and then run down to meet Dawson at his car.

"There you are," he says, eyeing my skirt then pulling me in for a kiss. "Damn, Keatie, you looked sexy today, but tonight you just look hot. Does this zipper work?" he asks, referring to the one that runs down the front of my black Valentino biker mini.

AT TACO TUESDAY, the boys are all talking about the Homecoming game. How they have to win. About how it sucks having their parents here. About how they have to help Aiden move the keg to the basement tonight because the dorm advisors are doing room checks tomorrow to make sure they look presentable for Homecoming.

Then they start talking about sex. One of the guys brags about doing it with one of the cheerleaders, and I'm slightly horrified at the intimate details he shares.

I'm so glad Dawson isn't like that.

I'm also listening closely to what Aiden talks about. To see if he's the type to kiss and tell.

Dallas tells everyone about the big ring gummy lifesavers Dawson brought to the party.

"That's a dance team girl trick," Logan says, grinning straight at me.

"Yeah, I remember hearing that," I say in a noncommittal way. Mostly I say it that way because Aiden is staring at me.

Nick pats Aiden on the back and says, "And last year the cheerleaders were on a fruit rollup kick, remember that, Aiden?"

Aiden gives him a little smile back and repeats my words. "Yeah, I remember hearing that."

"Hearing that? More like *lived that,"* Nick says with a mischievous grin.

So cheerleaders are Aiden's thing.

Jake says, "What about mints? Altoids. Red hots."

"All this blow job talk is making me incredibly horny," Dawson whispers, snuggling up to me.

"You're always incredibly horny," I tease.

He runs his hand down my thigh. Then up my thigh and inching closer to going under my leather skirt.

I grab his hand. Hold it firmly in a respectable spot. He looks at me, grins, and laughs.

"What's so funny?" Riley asks him.

"Nothing, we just need to go study, so we're gonna head out . . . "

Riley interrupts. "You don't need to make up a lame ass excuse. I think we all know."

"Oh, well, okay."

I just wave.

I'm feeling a bit sleazy leaving with Dawson early, knowing they all know what we're going to do.

But in my head, I tell myself we'll just talk, kiss some.

Yes, it's our anniversary, of sorts, but that doesn't mean we have to.

We already did it earlier today.

We're not.

We're definitely not.

When we get to his car, he pushes me up against the door and gives me a hot kiss.

"I'll never forget how excited I was when you showed up at the Hamptons, in that bikini. I felt so lucky and happy. And that night. God, that night was amazing. Really. Of course that was probably pretty obvious. Like, how much I wanted you. And then it was so good. Every time is *so* good. It's been the best month of my life."

I slink away from him and get in the car, so he doesn't attack me right here.

But what he said totally makes me melt, so I lean over, unzip his pants, and slide my hand inside while he drives to the lake.

Wednesday, October 5th

THE PEOPLE THAT YOU LOVE.

LUNCH

I OFFERED TO go help Dawson work on his cheer, but he doesn't want me to see it until Friday. So I sit down between Riley and Ace, who has stopped sitting at Whitney's table and started sitting here with Annie.

Annie shoves a tabloid magazine in front of my face. "Look at this! Abby is having an affair with her bodyguard. The hot one that was with her on Saturday."

I read the headline.

Abby and the Hot Bodyguard's Secret Affair.

Underneath that is a large photo of Mom and Ryan. Mom's head is down and Ryan's hand is on her back, guiding her. It's not unusual for Ryan to do that when there are a lot of people around. He's trained to keep her close. To shield her if necessary. Off to the side is a photo of Tommy. He's wearing a ball cap and sunglasses and his head is down. The photo is not a new one. He's wearing a shirt that I know he gave to charity over a year ago. The little headline above it says, *Friends Say Tommy Distraught Over Affair.*

"You shouldn't believe everything you read in these kinds of magazines," I tell Annie.

But even though I know it's not true, I'm worried.

I leave lunch, get to French early, and text Mom.

Me: *Saw what the tabloids are saying. Are you doing okay?*

Mom: *Of course, we are. Our publicist was going to release a statement that it's false, but sometimes when you do that people assume you're trying to cover it up.*

Me: *So it's better to not say anything? Does it upset you?*

Mom: *Of course, it's upsetting when people say stuff about you that's not true. But it's part of the business. Don't worry about the tabloids. Remember, the only people you should care about what they think, are the people you love.*

Me: *That's good advice. I love you, Mom. I have to go. The bell just rang.*

Mom: *We all love you too.*

Aiden sits down behind me. He's dressed for Western Day in a way that reminds me of my grandpa. He's got on a soft cotton western shirt with pearl snap buttons, Rag & Bone jeans, and a pair of brown leather cowboy boots. The boots are scuffed and well-worn. I can picture him riding a horse around their vineyard, wearing the boots, stopping to have a glass of wine.

"Guess what?" he says.

"You like my boots?" I say, holding up my feet to show off my faded red boots.

"I do like your boots. They look cute with the lace dress."

"Thank you. I noticed your boots are worn. They your favorite pair?"

"Actually, they are. I wear them nonstop when I'm back home. But that's not what I was going to tell you."

"What were you going to tell me?"

"I'm going to be competing against your boyfriend for Mr. Eastbrooke."

"Really?"

"Yep. Got picked by the soccer team."

"You'll probably make a good looking girl. You and Peyton look a lot alike. So are you going to dance for everyone? Finally show them how good you are?"

He shakes his head. "No. Guys never dance. They all do a cheer."

"And I thought you weren't like all the other guys?" I tease.

"I told you. No one has ever seen me dance like that. Everyone would think it's weird."

"I wouldn't think it was weird. I'd think it was awesome. Besides, the only people you should care what they think are the people that you love."

"And those people will be seeing me do a cheer."

I think about the cheerleader comment from last night. About how Nick said "lived it." How cheerleaders must be his thing.

The dream girl must be a cheerleader.

That's probably the real reason he wants to a cheer. So he can ask her to teach him.

"Whatever. I'm just saying, you dance like you can, you'll win."

"Have you ever seen a Mr. Eastbrooke competition?"

"No."

"Then you don't know if I'd win or not. And you promised you wouldn't tell anyone about how I can dance."

I shrug my shoulder. "You're secret is safe with me. But you break out the dance moves you have and your competition does a stupid cheer, you'll win. Common sense tells me that."

He rolls his eyes. "It's not the dance that wins, it's how you look."

"Okay. Good luck."

Thursday, October 6th

A LITTLE SKIMPY.

1:30PM

I DON'T ATTEND very many classes today. No one does, really. We all get out of class for different reasons. Some get called back to their dorms by their dorm advisors to make their rooms spotless for the alumni tours. Others are finishing up the floats for the parade. Others get out of class to take pictures for the yearbook. Most of the band goes off to practice marching.

Today is officially Sports Day, so I'm wearing Dawson's football jersey, a red sequined skirt, and tall white athletic socks with stripes of red sequins at the top.

I take Dawson to the drama department to find him a wig and do a test drive on his makeup for Mr. Eastbrooke.

"Here, try this," I say, putting a pirate hat on his head.

He does a Captain Morgan pose then grabs me. "Ahoy, my little matey. Want me to show you my *sword*?"

I kiss his neck and then giggle. "Stop that. We need to be serious about this if you want to win."

He grabs a teeny little costume off a rack. "You should put this on, be my little cowgirl."

"You'll actually get to see me in that costume in the play. I'm a cheerleader for a professional football team."

He narrows his eyes at me.

"Don't be mad. It's a little skimpy, but it's a short scene."

"I'll make you a deal. Borrow it and wear it for me in my room, and I won't give you shit about the play."

"Hmmm. Deal."

I rummage through a cabinet and pull out a long blonde wig and a shorter brunette one. "Which way do you want to go, blonde or brunette?"

He puts the blonde wig on his head. "Blondes have more fun. You're fun."

I look at the blonde wig on him. "Um, they maybe do, but I don't think you're very convincing as a blonde. Is the goal for you to look pretty or funny?"

"Pretty. Do you want to see my cheer?"

He leaves the blonde wig on and starts a cheer. "Be Aggressive. B-E Aggressive. B-E-A-G-G-R-E-S-S-I-V-E. BE AGGRESSIVE." He uses a high-pitched voice that sounds hysterical coming from such a buff guy. "Gooooo Cougarssss!"

I can't help but laugh.

"You totally butchered that cheer."

"Yeah, I need a little more work on the motions. I can remember football plays, but these stupid arm motions are just confusing."

"Do you want me to help you? I know that cheer."

"Maybe you can come teach me in my room. I'd probably learn it better if we were naked."

"If you were naked, there wouldn't be any cheering going on."

"You cheer me on sometimes. *Go, Dawes!*"

I smack his shoulder. "Shut up. You should hear yourself." I grab the blonde wig off his head, motion for him to sit down, and put on the darker one.

I swivel the chair around so that he can see himself in the mirror. "See, you look more convincing with dark hair. Wait until I do your makeup."

He looks at himself. "I look like my mother."

I use a sponge to put a little foundation over the dark stubble on his cheeks. "You're going to have to shave for sure," I tell him as I add some blush and a little bit of bronzer.

I'm getting ready to add some eye shadow next. "Close your eyes. I want you to be surprised at how you look."

"Maybe you should blindfold me," he says, grabbing me and pulling me onto his lap facing him.

"That might be fun too." I wrap my arms around his neck and give him a deep kiss.

Which turns into a deeper kiss.

Which turns into a full-blown make out session.

"It's really hot that I'm kissing you while you're wearing my team jersey. I wish that's all you had on."

"Mhhmm," I say as he moves my hair off my shoulder and attacks my neck. "You talked me into it."

We rush to his dorm room, lock his door, and I quickly remove everything but the jersey.

He sits in his desk chair and pulls me onto his lap.

We're in the middle of our fun, when there's a knock on his door. A voice calls out, "Dawson, honey, it's Mom. Are you in there?"

"Shit," Dawson whispers.

I jump off him as he quickly pulls on his pants.

I grab my skirt off the floor and put it back on, but I can't find my dance briefs. Fortunately they are not black and lacy.

"Just a second, Mom," he yells out. I grab my purse, run into his bathroom, and spread my makeup out.

But then I look at him walking toward the door, his shorts sticking out in a way that I doubt his mother wants to see.

"Dawson!" I point at his shorts and toss him a towel to hold in front of himself.

"Hey, Mom" he says at the door. "Come in. Keatyn and I were just trying some makeup for the Mr. Eastbrooke contest."

I lean my head out of the bathroom. "Hi, Mr. and Mrs. Johnson."

I walk out and get air kisses from his mom. Then I grab the dark wig off the bed and, of course, there are my briefs—which I ignore—and put it on Dawson's head. "What do you think of your son as a girl? I haven't done his eyes or lipstick yet. Would you like to help?"

"Oh, I'd love that!" she squeals. "I got to dress your father up for Mr. Eastbrooke about a million years ago. Of course we weren't dating back then."

Dawson's dad sits down on the very chair Dawson was just sitting in. I notice him eyeing my briefs lying on the bed. A big grin forms on his face.

I walk over, grab them, and toss them to Dawson. "Don't forget you were going to see if you can fit into these. If not, I'll see if I can find a bigger pair."

He catches them and tries to put them on over his shorts. It's not working so well.

"No, silly. They're never going to fit like that. There's too much fabric." I turn to his mom. "What did you make him wear under his skirt?"

"He was on the swim team, so he wore one of those little Speedos."

"Oh, that would work much better." I take the briefs out of his hand and shove them into my purse. "That way you won't stretch mine all out."

I glance at the clock. "It's almost three. I have to get to the dance locker room and get ready for the parade." I turn to his mom and say, "If I leave my makeup, could you finish his eyes and then take a picture of it?"

"Of course, dear," she replies.

Dawson gives me an evil eye. I know he doesn't want to stay here with his parents. I give him a quick kiss on the cheek and tell him I'll see him later.

A BLOWOUT.

3:30PM

THE PARADE IS a blast. We perform a dance routine at four different spots on the route, but mostly I just ride on the float and throw bubblegum and Blow Pops into the crowd.

Our float's theme is *Homecoming: It's Gonna Be A Blowout.*

Get it? Bubblegum. Blowout. Beating the other team.

Of course, as the dance team suspected, the guys all loved this year's theme and are hoping to get more than bubble gum if they win.

Peyton tried to tell the alumni dancers that she didn't think it was a good theme, but they loved it and wouldn't listen.

They loved the play on words between the blow and the bubblegum.

When Peyton said, *But a blowout?* The alumni in charge said, *Yes, dear, we're a well-educated bunch. Everyone will know that we are referring to beating the other team badly, not getting our hair done.*

So I'm thinking maybe when you get old and you hear the word blow, you don't automatically think blowjob anymore?

I'm not sure.

But I do know that Shark has been having a field day. There have been numerous bets placed between girls and boys based on the game's score that have *nothing* to do with money changing hands.

After the parade, he walks up to me and comments on the sucker in my mouth. "There is just something so sexy about a girl licking a lollipop."

"Oh, it's not just a lollipop. It's a *Blow Pop*. Imagine how exciting it will be when I get to the surprise inside."

Shark snickers. "Were you not just dying laughing the entire time? I followed your float down the whole parade route just to watch the old guys drool." He hands me his ever-present flask.

"You're drinking already?"

"The parents have just arrived and I'm beyond horny. What do you think?"

"Dawson's parents about walked in on us in his dorm room today."

"My parents did walk in on me and Shelley today, although we were just kissing. I'm not sure if they were proud or pissed. Hard to tell. Mom's had so much plastic surgery she has a permanent smile."

"So how are the odds looking for Queen?"

"The odds are in Peyton's favor. Does Whitney know that you've been chatting up the Freshmen?"

"I hope not. She'd really hate me. I'm not doing it to be mean; you know that right?"

"I know that," he says as he hands me back the flask. "Here, have another drink."

My cell phone rings. "It's Dawson," I tell Shark.

"Hey, Dawes."

"Come meet me in Riley's room. The Johnson boys are wishing Riley luck before the JV game, and my little brother, Braxton, wants to meet you."

I tell Shark I have to go.

I WALK INTO Riley's room to find Camden, Riley, Dawson, and a little Dawson clone who must be Braxton, involved in a loud conversation.

Cam says to Braxton, "I heard you got caught by Mom with two girls in your room, who were only wearing their underwear."

"Bro," Braxton says, "I was this close to a threesome." He holds his thumb and finger an inch apart. "Damn giggly girls. Mom heard. Came storming the fuck in. Now, I'm fucking grounded for a whole month. Which is fucking shit cuz Dad was grinning at me the whole time Mom yelled at me. Then he asked me how old they were. They were 16. So shit, ya know."

"Brax, Keatyn is here now. You need to watch your mouth," Riley scolds.

Braxton cocks his head at me. "What? You've never heard the word fuck? Funny, cuz I'm pretty sure I heard my brother implying that Mom and Dad interrupted you doing just that."

I'm not easily shocked. But my mouth flops open. Braxton continues. "Just wait until this summer. You gonna be there?"

"Uh, I don't know."

"Well, you can be sure of this. My brothers are gonna be wishing they were me. I was ready this year, but my fucking parents thought I was too young. But this summer, I'm up to bat. Fucking Whoredom, here I come. Girls all think I'm 17."

"I'd know you're not," I say.

"How's that? Everyone says I look really old for my age."

"You might look older than you are, but you cuss too much. You sound like a kid who just learned how. Makes you sound like the eighth grader that you are."

His studies my face. "Are you fucking with me?"

"Nope. I'm serious."

He nods his head. Smiles at me, just like Riley does, and shakes his head. "I'm gonna like you. Since these douches haven't invited you yet, you come stay with us this summer. As long as you want. You can be my wingman."

"Your wingman?"

"Yep, I have my arm around a hot older chick at the beach, all the other hotties are gonna want me. Proven fact. Girls always want what they can't have."

"Now that sounded very mature. And as long as it's okay with Riley and Dawson, I'll be there. Nice to meet you. I have to get to dance. We're having a pizza party with some of the alumni before the game."

Riley says, "I'll walk with you. I've got to get to the locker room too."

ON THE WAY there, he asks me about tonight. "So Braxton is spending the night with me and Dallas. I'm worried about sneaking to your room."

"It's been three days, Riley. I think you're right. It must not have been him."

"But what if he was waiting for Homecoming? There are going to be a lot of people coming and going this weekend. It's kind of a security nightmare. Caterers. Foodservice. Delivery trucks. Rental companies. Alumni. Families. If you didn't belong here and wanted to get in, this would be when you'd try to do it."

I sigh. "Shit. I didn't think of that. You're right. Maybe I just won't sleep?"

"That won't work. Maybe you could go stay with Dawson? No, I have a better idea. I'll send Braxton to stay with him. It might mess up some of your fun, but it's worth it, right?"

"Yeah, it is. Thanks, Riley. I know it's a pain for you to have to get up every night, sneak out, and then sleep on my floor."

"Your rug and I are having a hot affair."

"I think I'm going to give you that rug when this is over."

"If we get through Homecoming weekend then I think you're safe."

I CAN'T EAT anything at the pizza party because I'm feeling a little sick.

Riley brought up an extremely good point about security this weekend.

It makes me worry about Katie. What if Vincent did come in my room?

What if I screamed and she woke up? What would he do to her?

And what about this weekend? All these people here? What would he do? How would he try and take me? Would he cause a commotion like he did at my party?

Or would he try to catch me when I'm alone?

I'm deep in thought when I get a text from Aiden.

Aiden: *Quick. Come outside.*

Me: *I don't think I can.*

Aiden: *Make up an excuse. Trust me, it's worth it.*

I make up a lame excuse in my head, but don't end up having to use it. I just slip out unnoticed.

Aiden is waiting for me outside the dance room.

He tells me to close my eyes.

Once we're outside the doors, he puts his hands on top of my shoulders and turns me so that I'm facing another direction. Down toward the football field, I think.

He leans his face over my shoulder. His lips lightly touch my ear as he whispers, "Open."

I open my eyes and see a brilliant sunset. It's gorgeous. Today was cloudy, kind of dreary, the sky threatening rain. Now the bottoms of those puffy clouds are multiple shades of pink, gold, and blue all radiating out from a red ball of fire low in the sky.

"It's beautiful," I whisper.

"Yeah, I thought so too. I'm glad you like it."

I turn away from the sunset to face Aiden. The view in this direction is just as brilliant. The colors of the sunset are bouncing off Aiden's green eyes.

I turn back around and look at the sunset again, remembering what Aiden told me about his mom.

I say a quick thank you that I made it through another day. That I'm still here.

I start to get tears in my eyes.

Aiden has no idea how much seeing this sunset helped me. How it calmed me down from freaking out about Vincent.

For some reason, this sunset gives me hope that I'll win.

Somehow, I have to win.

"Thank you. I was having a rough day. Showing me this sunset helped put it all in perspective."

"Do you want to talk about it?"

I shake my head. "Remember the stuff we talked about in the chapel?"

"Is your friend having more trouble?"

"Yeah, she had a scare, I guess you could say. Something weird happened recently and she thinks he might have discovered where she is. But he hasn't come for her yet. Like, to get her. So she's waiting. And waiting is scary."

"I bet."

"But the sun just set on another day of her being safe. So that's a good thing."

Aiden touches my arm. "I'm glad I could help."

"You always help," I say before I think better of it.

Aiden smiles at me and gives my arm a little squeeze. "What have I told you before?"

"When I need you, you'll be there?"

"I mean it."

"I know, it's just that . . ."

"You have a boyfriend."

"Yes."

"Doesn't matter. I'm still here. Besides you helped me yesterday."

"I did?"

"Yeah, in French. What you said about only caring about what the people you love think. It was something I needed to hear."

I smile big. "Really, I actually helped you?"

"Yeah, you did."

"Thanks. I, um, better get back in there."

I walk towards the door to the field house, but glance back to look at Aiden bathed in the light of the setting sun, and I can't help but wonder what he's going to do for the person he loves.

Friday, October 7th

A LITTLE TAIL.

6:27AM

TODAY IS SCHOOL Spirit Day. Everyone is dressed in lots of red and yellow. As I get in line for coffee and a muffin, I realize that our Cougar Kitty outfits really stand out. I've got on a black spandex tank and a flirty black dance skirt with a leopard tail attached to the back. I straightened my hair, teased it up big, added the ears headband, and then drew kitty whiskers on my face with black eyeliner.

Someone pulls on my tail and says, "Here, kitty, kitty."

I turn around and see Dallas and Riley grinning at me. They are wearing their red football jerseys and each have a red E painted on their cheek.

Riley says, "I was hoping to get a little tail at Homecoming."

Dallas laughs and adds, "That, or some pussy."

"Oh my gosh, you guys. Grow up."

Dallas gives me a once over. "I'm digging the outfits for today. You all dressed that way?"

"Yes, we are. Including Katie, your new obsession. I swear, if it weren't for classes, I don't think I'd have seen you this week."

Dallas grins. "We're having fun. It's new."

Whitney walks by, gives me a completely different kind of once over and says, "From glitter whores to kitty whores."

I suck in a deep breath.

"Don't let her bait you, baby," Riley says. "She's just jealous she doesn't look as hot as you. For god's sake, she's wearing a turtleneck."

I laugh. "And pearls."

"What are the cheerleaders wearing today? Ariela gonna be dressed as a kitty too?"

"No, they're wearing their sporty warm ups today."

"Phew," Riley says, while fake wiping his brow. "That's good. I don't think I could have resisted the temptation. No offense, but guys are going to be having some kitty fantasies today. I'm just saying."

CATCALLS.
PEP RALLY

THE DANCE TEAM does a fun skit for the pep rally and, later, performs a dance.

There are lots of cheers, speeches, and honoring of alumni, but you can tell everyone is waiting for what is sure to be the highlight of the afternoon.

The Mr. Eastbrooke contest.

I helped Dawson get ready and his face looks pretty good. His cheer still kinda sucks, but I don't think he cares. It sounds like it's almost more of a popularity contest anyway.

Maggie and I roar with laughter when he sashays his way across the gym. He can't zip up the cheerleading skirt that he's wearing, so it's gaping open in the back, and he's completely stretching out Ariela's cheerleading sweater with a hugely stuffed bra that his mom bought him. He says it's the boobs that will win, not his cheer.

He sticks his fake chest out, puts his hand on his hip, puckers up his bright red lips, and blows kisses to the crowd. Everyone claps.

Then he does his cheer. "Be Aggressive . . ."

When he finishes the cheer, he attempts a cheerleading jump.

The jump is pretty good, but causes one of his fake boobs to fall out of the sweater.

Of course, everyone laughs and cheers about that.

The dean calls up the next candidate and so goes on the annihilation of all that is sacred to cheerleaders. It's hilarious. I can see why everyone looks forward to the contest.

Aiden is up last. He looks a lot like Peyton, and if it weren't for his manly build and the stubble on his face, he'd make a pretty girl. He's got on a long blonde wig but, unlike all the other contestants who have worn cheerleader costumes, he's wearing a version of the kitty costume I have on today.

All the way down to the tail.

Some of the guys make catcalls. Haha. Get it? *Cat*calls?

Anyway, people are whistling and yelling out his name.

I expect a cheerleader to walk out with him like Ariela walked out with Dawson, but instead, Peyton walks out. She brushes his hair down and then turns to speak to the crowd. "And our last contestant in the Mr. Eastbrooke contest is Aiden Arrington." She shakes her head and smiles at her brother. "I hope you are ready for this!"

She points her arm over to Shark, who flips on loud dance music.

Oh. My. Gosh.

Is he going to dance?

He said he never would.

I watch Peyton go sit in the stands next to a man and woman who must be her parents. Both her face and Aiden's look a lot their mother, but their dad is equally attractive. Actually, that's not true. Aiden's dad is hot. Aiden may have gotten his pretty face and green eyes from his mom, but everything else is all dad. The strong jawline, the color of stubble on his cheeks, the broad shoulders tapering down to a lean torso. Even the little freckle on his cheek.

Aiden picks up a pair of pompoms and starts doing one of our dance routines.

And although I shouldn't be, I'm quite shocked at how good he is.

Like, he is a really good dancer. Not quite as good as Sander was, but clearly good enough to blow away the other contestants.

The crowd goes nuts, cheering, screaming.

Maggie keeps hitting me on the arm. "Oh my god, are you watching this?"

"I think everyone is watching this."

"Who knew he could dance like that. I told you. I don't think there's anything that boy can't do."

He can't speak French worth a shit, I think to myself.

"Why doesn't he dance like that all the time?"

"I don't know," I reply.

"Oh my gosh! He just did the booty shake. Like, he did it pretty good. Gosh, he is sexy. Justin Timberlake better watch out. I wonder if he can sing too?"

"Have you always been such a big fan of his?"

"Everyone has always been a big fan of his. I don't know. He's always been hot but this year there's just something more mature about him. He's gotten totally sexy."

"Hmm."

By the time Aiden finishes, the entire gymnasium, including Maggie and me, are on our feet giving him a standing ovation.

Peyton runs out onto the court and gives her brother a big hug as the dean announces, "By unanimous decision, Aiden Arrington is this year's Mr. Eastbrooke."

The soccer team rushes onto the floor and jumps around him.

I glance over at Aiden's mom. She's in tears but beaming with pride. Which causes me to get tears in my eyes.

Because I know why he did it.

Why he risked making a fool of himself in front the whole school. He wanted to make his mom, the person he loves, happy.

I feel like I just watched him grow up a little.

They put the silly princess crown on his head and a red glittered sash around his chest.

"This concludes the pep rally, so everyone head out to the alumni tailgate," the dean announces.

Everyone files out of the gymnasium, but I'm stuck in my spot.

I still have tears in my eyes as I watch Aiden in the crowd.

I find myself walking over to congratulate him.

There's lots of girls giving him hugs and kisses on the cheek. Guys patting him on the back and giving him fist bumps. But he sees me sort of standing here waiting and moves out of the crowd toward me.

I can't keep the tears out of my eyes.

I don't know why what he did is affecting me so much. I think it's the combination of seeing his mom. Knowing what she's gone through. What their family has gone through. And probably a lot of me wishing my own mom could be here today. To see me perform. To beam with pride as I take the field at halftime as part of the Homecoming Court in a beautiful dress and shoes that I picked out completely by myself.

I want to make my parents proud too.

He stands in front of me and wipes a tear from my cheek. "Why are you crying?"

"I'm just really proud of you, Aiden. You should have seen your mom. She teared up and beamed when you won. I just think it's really cool that you risked making a fool of yourself for her. You did it for her, right?"

"I did it for all the people that I love. Did you love it?"

"Everyone loved it. You got a freaking standing ovation."

"That's not what I asked. Did *you* love it?"

I take a deep breath, so that I won't start crying. "I loved it, Aiden. I really loved it."

I get the grin. The grin that grows into the megawatt, brighter-than-the-sunset smile. "I want you to meet my parents," he says. He takes ahold of my elbow and guides me through the crowd that is still trying to congratulate him.

"Mom, Dad, this is Keatyn Monroe. She's the girl I told you about."

Told them about?

Shit. What did he tell them? That he hates me most of the time?

That I'm a freaking soccer-ball-stealing, boot-wearing, French-speaking lunatic?

Aiden's mom holds out her hand. As we shake, Aiden's dad says, "We understand Aiden's French has improved because of you."

Tutoring. Thank god. He just told them I'm his tutor.

I smile. "Yes, but we still have a long way to go. Especially if he's going to get to our goal of a B."

Aiden's mom smiles. "We heard you're taking him to France to celebrate when that happens."

I look at Aiden. My eyes search his for answers. He told his parents that?

He gives me a sly grin.

"He sort of tricked me into agreeing to that," I say honestly.

His mother laughs. "He's had that gift since he was a little boy. He smiles that dang smile and looks at you with those big green eyes and he can get away with anything."

"Mom!" Aiden says, laughing. "Don't give away all my secrets."

"Oh, that one I already know," I say with a laugh of my own. I like his mom already.

Peyton interjects, "Yeah, he never got into trouble. He'd always make Mom laugh or he'd kiss her on the nose and get out of it. It never worked for me."

Peyton's dad laughs. "Give us a break. You may not know how to work your Mom, but you have your daddy wrapped around your little finger."

Peyton beams and gives her dad a hug.

Aiden says, "Well, I supposed I better get out of this makeup and ready for the game."

"Oh, I have to get going too. It was nice to meet you both."

Aiden and I turn and walk away in the same direction. "Your parents are great."

He nods. "Yeah, they are. I'm lucky. Everyone has been complaining about their families coming. I couldn't wait to see mine. I bet it's hard not having yours here. Hey, who is going to walk you onto the field?"

"It is, but my uncle is coming."

We get to the boys' locker room and as he heads through the door I sort of whisper, "Good luck, Aiden."

He hears me, stops, does a one-eighty, and comes back to me. He pulls up the sleeve of the black leotard he's wearing. On his arm is a marker drawn four-leaf clover.

"That looks like . . ."

"Points for dances, Round 3? I had someone draw it to match your note. I needed some of that luck today."

He still has my note? Of course, I still have the real clover he gave me. It's pressed between the pages of my Keats poetry book.

"Why did you need luck?"

"Probably because I risked making a fool out of myself. I'm glad I did it though. It was exhilarating. Is that how you felt when you went running down the field and kicked the soccer ball in the middle of our game?"

I laugh. "Yeah, kinda."

"That was really brave. New girl. New school. To take that chance."

"Maybe, but what you did was braver. Changing people's perception of you is a lot harder than making a first impression."

"Well, since I'm feeling lucky. What do you say? Points for Dances, Round 4?"

"I can't do that, but . . ." I reach out and trace the outline of the four-leaf clover. "I do wish you and the team lots of luck."

IT SEEMS KIND OF MEAN.
6PM

I GO TO the dance room, change into my game outfit, and get ready for the fun surprise we have for the alumni tailgate. I get a text from Garrett letting me know that he's here. I text him back and let him know where to meet up with me.

I know he's not my family. I know that he's being paid a lot to help me, but I also know that Garrett runs a very large and successful security firm. I know that he's taken a special interest in my case. I know that he cares.

I spot him. He's looking really handsome in his charcoal pinstriped suit. I never really paid much attention, but Garrett is really quite good looking. And, apparently, Miss Praline has already noticed this. She is totally chatting him up.

"Do you know Melissa?" Garrett asks me.

"*Melissa* and I do know each other. She is also Miss Praline, my French teacher."

Garrett grabs her hand, kisses it, and starts speaking to her in French.

He's so flirting with her.

And she is totally swooning.

It's really, really cute.

"Um, Miss Praline," I say, as I pat Garrett on the back. "My uncle, Garrett, really doesn't know anyone. Do you think he could sit with you during the game? I have to go now and do a dance thing, and I'll be out on the field during the game."

Garrett grins at me and Miss Praline gets all flustered. "Well, um, of course, I wouldn't want your, uh, uncle, to get lost or anything."

Ha! I doubt Garrett ever gets lost. He probably has a full recon poster of the school's building plans on his cell phone.

"That would be great." I give my uncle a hug, then point and say, "We'll meet right over there to line up when there are two minutes left in the half."

"Sounds good. I'm looking forward to it."

THERE'S A WIDE pathway running down the parking lot and tailgaters are set up on both sides of it. I get a text from Peyton telling us to take our positions.

I walk casually over to a tent and pretend to be interested in what they are doing.

Someone turns up a great song. Which is my cue. I walk out into the pathway and start doing a line dance to the music. I'm the only one out here, so people are turning to stare.

After a few lines of the song, Peyton and Maggie come out to dance with me.

Pair by pair, dancers join in the dance, and pretty soon a lot of the alumni dancers join in too, then some of the crowd.

By the end of the song, the pathway is full of people dancing with us.

After the flash mob, Peyton runs up to me, flushed and beaming. "That was so much fun. You did a great job starting it."

"A great job making a fool out of myself, you mean?"

"Speaking of fools, what did you think of Aiden's dance?"

"It was really good. So, does Whitney know about Cam or your dress yet?"

"Are you kidding? I made sure to parade him in front of her the second he arrived. I know she's mad, but it's not like she can say anything about it. And no, she doesn't know about my dress. I want that to be a surprise."

"That seems kind of mean, Peyton. I think you should tell her."

"I don't think it's any of her business what I wear."

"That's true, but—"

She holds her hand up. "No. I don't want to hear it. I'm going to do what I want to do."

"Yeah, but . . ."

"I'm not listening."

I really want to tell her that this is going to blow up in her face. That someone will end up getting hurt in the crossfire. That her boyfriend will get drugged. That she'll turn into a bitch. That her secret will come out.

But I know she won't listen.

Maybe it's a lesson you have to learn on your own.

EXCITEMENT IN THE AIR.
HALFTIME

AT HALFTIME, I change into my formal gown, then meet Garrett just outside the field house. We gather with the other Court members waiting for the processional. The game has been going in our favor. We're up by fourteen already and you can feel the excitement in the air.

Except for here.

Here, there is tension.

Peyton is happily sashaying around in her new dress, but you can feel the tension between her and Whitney. You can see the glares Whitney gives her and you can tell that Peyton is pretending not to care.

Whitney is standing next to her perfect-looking parents.

Where there is even more tension.

I think it's safe to say that Whitney's mother does not approve of her dress. She keeps looking at it and scowling.

I have to hand it to Whitney though. She has her head held high and a smile plastered on her face.

I didn't think she could pull off a dress covered with jewels, but she so is. She looks amazing and I can see why she fell in love with the dress. It makes the rest of our gowns look plain in comparison.

Dawson grabs me from behind, kisses my neck, and whispers, "You look hot." Then he gets in line with his own parents.

I forget about Whitney and Peyton and just stare at him. He looks so sexy in his football uniform and my mind can't help but wander back to wearing that jersey and nothing else yesterday. Although, in my daydream we are *not* interrupted by his parents.

Garrett is reading emails from his phone. He coughs and a troubled look crosses his face.

"What's wrong?" I ask.

"I just got some news."

I instantly panic. "Bad news?"

"I'm not sure yet. We had an interview scheduled next week with a guy regarding Vincent and, possibly, your case. Now he's dead."

"Dead?" I croak out.

The band director, who is in charge of leading us all out onto the field, yells out, "Okay, line up by class starting with the freshmen. We're about ready to go out."

We're supposed to follow the band director out onto the field. Then, as our class is called, we'll walk down the sideline, then turn and go up through the 50-yard line toward the home crowd.

"Yes," Garrett replies. "He was apparently killed in a random mugging."

Random mugging. Where have I heard that before?

He continues. "His family doesn't think it was random. They think he was murdered. And, I mean, they're right . . ." He stops to listen to the stadium announcer who starts talking about the Homecoming Court tradition over the loudspeaker.

The band director yells out, "As soon as he says *freshmen*, all freshmen proceed on your route."

And this year's Freshmen Court is . . .

Garrett whispers to me, "The guy was huge. I can't imagine anyone trying to mug him."

"What did he have to do with Vincent? How did Vincent know him?"

"He had an appointment with him a few weeks ago."

"And this year's Sophomore Court is . . .

"Was he a doctor?"

Garrett looks at me and shakes his head. "No, he was a tattoo artist. He did Vincent's chaos tattoo."

"All right, juniors, walk down to the fifty-yard line and hold," the band director instructs us.

Garrett and I walk to the fifty-yard line. I hear someone shouting my name from the Visitor's section, which I'm now standing in front of. I look up and see Braxton waving at me.

I smile and give him a little wave back, but there's something gnawing at the back of my brain.

"We had hoped Vincent might have said something about the tattoo that would help our case. Like maybe he mentioned why he was getting the same tattoo as you. Or something like that." He shakes his head. "It was a long shot."

And this year's Junior Court is . . .

I remember the tattoo artist who Brooklyn brought in to do our tattoos. How big he was. "Tell me he wasn't covered in tattoos and looked like Santa Claus."

I take a step forward to walk onto the field, but Garrett doesn't come with me.

He's firmly holding his stance and my elbow.

"How do you know that?"

The band director yells, "Miss Monroe, go, please."

I pull Garrett down the center of the field, putting on a big smile that completely masks the sick feeling in my stomach.

"Because Brooklyn hired a guy who looked like that to do our tattoos. Everyone called him Tiny."

"That's the guy who is dead," Garrett says.

Keatyn Monroe.

As I accept a bouquet of flowers, the student section yells, "MON—R-O-A-R!"

I plaster a fake smile on my face and wave to the crowd.

Then it hits me. Where I heard it.

"Garrett," I say out of the side of my mouth, while still keeping a smile plastered on my face. "Vincent's mom and stepdad were killed in a random mugging."

Garrett says, "This is quite disturbing."

"Yeah, it is."

And this year's Senior Court is . . .

We all turn to watch Dawson, Jake, Brad, Whitney, Peyton, and Mariah walk down the fifty-yard line toward us.

Garrett holds my arm tight. "Are you okay? You've got a smile on your face, but I can feel you shaking."

"I'm fine. I'll be fine. But I'll be better if you can prove Vincent killed him.

Then he can go to jail and I'll be free."

"Do you need me for anything else after this?"

"No, this was the big deal," I say, looking down at the designer dress and shoes I've had on for a total of twenty minutes. "Kinda silly, isn't it? Like, in perspective."

"Yeah, it kinda is. As soon as this is over, I'm catching a plane to LA."

"I think that's a very good idea."

A NEW JERSEY HOUSEWIFE.

HALFTIME

GARRETT IMMEDIATELY LEAVES for the airport and I work my way through the halftime crowd. I have to change back into my dance costume for the rest of the game.

Whitney is surrounded by her family. I hear her mother say, "What in the world are you wearing?"

Whitney stands up straight. "A dress."

"If you had some feathers, you could be a Vegas showgirl."

Her sister laughs. "Expect she can't dance."

Oh, wow. That was a low blow.

"First you lose Dawson and then you wear a dress like that. Are you trying to lose?"

"Everyone already voted, Mother. They didn't vote based on me not wearing my sister's hand-me-down gown."

"You know, you'll be the only one in the family that hasn't won. What a let down," her mother replies.

"This dress was very expensive," Whitney counters.

"Well, there's no accounting for taste. You look like a New Jersey housewife."

I actually feel sorry for Whitney, especially when I see the tears shining in her eyes. The ones she refuses to let fall.

I make a beeline toward her. "Whitney," I say, grabbing her arm. "Will you come with me to the dance locker room? There's an issue that I need your help with."

"What kind of issue could she possibly help with?" her sister asks in a tone dripping with bitch.

I look straight at Whitney's mom and ignore her bitch sister. "Mrs. Clarke, do you mind if I steal her away?" I roll my eyes dramatically. "We're having an issue with the security for the after party and since Whitney runs the Social Committee, I feel it's best that she handle it."

Her mother looks at me shrewdly. "Your dress is very pretty."

I smile sweetly at her. I am an adorable, respectful young woman.

One who wants to rip this woman's eyes out.

"Thank you." I look down at it and scrunch up my nose. "Although it doesn't compare to Whitney's. I'm so jealous of her bold choice. She looks amazing, don't you think? You must be so proud. I mean, Homecoming Court is nice and all, but it's nothing compared to Social Committee. There isn't a more respected position at school. Did she tell you how we're doing themed weekends? They will be a learning experience, incorporate the entire student and faculty population, and raise funds for some great causes. We're all so excited."

Winnie is looking at Whitney like she's an alien, but her mother turns to her. "Whitney, darling, you didn't tell us about all the amazing things you are doing."

Whitney says with no trace of a smile, "You didn't ask."

The tension is thick, so I start moving her. "Nice meeting you all," I say, as I pull her through the crowd.

When we get to the door, she asks, "Why did you just do that?"

"Your family sucks. And I meant what I said about your dress."

She looks wistfully at her dress. "Peyton had a beaded one. We were both supposed to look different. But then she went shopping with you."

"You sister is just jealous. She could never pull off a dress like that. You can tell by her wardrobe tonight that she prefers to blend in. You took a chance. I give it two thumbs up."

"Really?"

I laugh. "Well, I'm not the most conservative person around here, and you hate how I dress, so you can take my compliment with a grain of salt."

"If only I could have a shot of tequila with it," she chuckles.

I wrap my arm around her neck. "I'm pretty sure I know a guy that can help with that."

"Shark!" I yell out.

He saunters over. "S'up ladies?"

"Shark, you're tipsy."

"My parents are here for the next forty-some hours—not that I'm counting—and it's just so wonderful to hear them tell me what a failure I am."

"Wanna share with Whitney? I think she's counting down the hours too."

He holds out his flask. "Rocking dress," he says, while staring directly at her cleavage.

Whitney blushes.

I've never seen her blush.

She raises his flask in the air. "Here's to being a disappointment to our parents."

"You two enjoy," I say. "I gotta go change back into my dance costume."

"From glitter whores to kitty whores?" she says with a laugh. It's her typical slam, but she says it in a nicer way. Like we're sharing an inside joke.

"Yeah, something like that."

I'M LATE GETTING to the dance room, so I quickly change back into my dance costume.

Everyone is already back out on the field. I can see their dresses all lined up on the rack. I should hurry and get out there too, but I need a minute.

I sit down, close my eyes, and take a deep breath.

When I open them, I roll the waistband of my skirt down, look at my tattoo, and remember Tiny.

As much as I wish we could find something on Vincent, I pray that Tiny's death had nothing to do with me.

I stand up, pull my phone out of my locker, and call my mom.

Tommy answers with, "What's shaking, baby?"

"I just called to tell you and Mom that I'm thankful I have such a supportive family. That I appreciate all you and Mom have done for me."

"Well, we love you. Um, have you done something we won't love and are buttering us up?"

"No. It's Homecoming, so everyone's parents are here and a lot of the kids are miserable. I was thinking how I would love to have you around. I'm lucky to have parents like you and I probably don't tell you that enough. And I'm sorry that I talked back to you last week. I was sort of under some stress."

"I know you were. It's killing your mom and me not to be there to share Homecoming with you. But I hope you know how very proud we are."

"I know. Thanks."

"Heard you invited *Uncle* Garrett."

"Yes. He walked me on the field and then just left to catch a flight for LA."

I don't tell him about Tiny. Probably because I really don't want them to know.

"Tell Mom I love her and kiss the girls for me."

"You got it."

Saturday, October 8th

A RICH HISTORY.

11AM

AT THE WOMEN'S Tea, Peyton and I are bored to tears, so we start contemplating our escape.

"Let's go find the boys at the golf tournament," I suggest.

Whitney walks up to me. She had been sitting at a table with her mother and sister, along with Rachel's family. "Keatyn, may I speak to you for a moment?"

"Um, sure, what's up?"

"Jake is throwing a bit of a fit. He wants to spend part of Homecoming with his friends. Rachel is going to the dance with Bryce and the other girls have respectable dates, but he's insisting that he wants to be with Dawson. They've gone to every Homecoming together."

"Yeah, they told me that."

She gives me a cool smile. "He also says that I should give you a chance."

"Jake seems to take friendship seriously."

"He does. So I'm compromising. It's obviously going to be a bit awkward, since Dawson and I have such a rich history. I'm sure that must bother you."

I shrug my shoulders. "Not really. We have a very different relationship than what you had."

"How would you even know what we had?" she snarls. Her true bitchy self coming back out.

"Because he told me about it. Before we dated, we were friends. We were both hurting from breakups and that's sort of how we bonded, I guess."

"And what makes him different now?" She doesn't have the bitchy look anymore and I can tell that she sincerely wants to know how Dawson has changed.

"Probably his time spent trying to make you mad. He's more experienced now, in lots of ways."

There's a little wrinkle between her eyes. She quickly puts on a happy face and says, "Well, I'd like you and Dawson to sit with us at dinner."

"Oh. That we can't do. But Dawson got us a limo. We're going to the hotel to change and then to the after party. Jake thought it would be fun if we went together. Partied a little."

"Will there be champagne?"

"I'd say that's a given."

She shakes her head. "I think I'll need it."

I can tell she can't believe she's agreeing to it. I'm not sure if she's doing it because she actually likes Jake or if she's afraid he'll dump her if she doesn't.

I give her a big smile. "Who knows, Whitney, we might actually have fun."

PEYTON TELLS HER mom that we have to head out to take care of some last minute details for Social Committee.

She takes me to a golf cart that all of the Senior Prefects have for the weekend to ferry people around. We hop in and ride down to the school's nine-hole golf course.

On the way, I ask about Aiden. "So who's your brother taking to the dance?"

"He doesn't have a date."

"Really, why not?"

She shrugs. "I'm not sure. He always has a date. I asked him about it and got some vague response. He and Logan are going stag. But lots of girls are going stag too, so they'll have plenty of fun."

"Uh, yeah. I'm sure they will."

We pull up to the golf shack and find Camden with his arm wrapped around a leggy brunette.

"Ugh," Peyton says. "That's Samantha. She's why Cam and I broke up in the first place. I hate Homecoming week. I can't wait to get the hell out of here and go to college."

"Where do you want to go?"

"My parents want us both to go to Yale, but I'm hoping to get into Stanford."

"Really? I'd love to go to either Stanford or Pepperdine. But I like it here too. I think Yale would be cool. Dawson wants to go to Columbia."

"So he can party with Cam?"

"Yeah, probably."

"Have you two talked about that? Like, what you'll do if you're still together then?"

I shake my head. "No. We've only been together for a week. College is the last thing on my mind." Really, I'm just praying I stay alive long enough to be able to choose a college.

"Watch this," she says as she hops off the cart.

She walks straight up to Camden and slides her arms around his waist. Clearly staking out her territory.

"S'up, girls?" Cam says and gives Peyton a kiss.

Score one for Peyton.

The Samantha chick says, "Cam, you didn't tell me you were here with Peyton."

Cam fires back, "You didn't ask."

"Who are you here with?" Peyton asks her politely.

"Oh, um, just my parents."

"Cool," she says with a smirk. Then she tugs cutely on Cam's shirt, sliding her hands underneath it. "Come have some beer with me and Keatyn."

He eyes me. "That's actually a good idea. Keatyn, you and I need to talk."

"Oh, do we?" I say.

"See ya, Sam," he calls out as he puts one arm around me and the other around Peyton and leads us to the beer garden.

"I can't be seen drinking a beer here!" Peyton tells Cam.

"Oh, live a little. Fine. I'll get you a soda. Then we'll spike it. What about you, missy?" he asks me.

"I'll have a beer." Peyton gives me a little scowl. "What? I'm not a Prefect." As Cam sets a red cup in front of me, I ask, "Where's Dawson?"

"Out golfing with Dad and Braxton. Riley left to sneak Ariela out of the tea."

I grin. "They are so cute together."

Cam rolls his eyes.

"What?" Peyton asks. "You don't think they're cute together?"

"He's stranded on second base."

"Yeah, and he's happy there. So don't give him any shit about it."

"What's your deal?"

"My deal?"

"Yeah, you come here a nobody and now you're Miss Popularity."

I roll my eyes. "I'm not Miss Popularity at all."

"So why Dawson then?"

"First off, I'm not like Whitney. Dawson and I ended up together because we had something in common and we got to be friends."

"Really?" Peyton says.

"Yeah. I hated him when I first met him. He was a jerk to Riley. Slung his arm around me and said Riley was a cheap imitation of the real thing."

Cam busts out in laughter. "Oh, that's classic. What a great line."

"No! It's a horrible line. I thought he was a jerk. Then he gave me the worst kiss ever."

"My brother gave a bad kiss? Damn, he's going to ruin our reputation."

"Yeah, well, he's made up for it."

"So I hear," Cam says.

"What's that supposed to mean?"

"Don't worry. He won't tell me anything. But he's too freaking happy for it not to be amazing. So, I guess I'll let you stay."

I laugh. "Gee, thanks. I'm so honored."

He clinks my glass and looks at me seriously. "You should be."

AFTER A COUPLE beers, Dawson, Braxton, and "Daddy" Johnson come off the course. Peyton told me that all the girls call Mr. Johnson "Daddy Johnson" because he's really good looking.

I will admit the four of them all together do make a pretty nice picture. All dark hair, dark eyes, muscles, and cocky attitudes.

Braxton rushes over to us, clearly trying to win some kind of race. He sits on my lap and says, "Baby, we need to talk."

I can't help but laugh at him. "And what do we need to talk about? The fact that you're small enough to sit on my lap?"

Camden says with a snort, "If Riley was the cheap imitation of the real thing, then Brax is the pocket-sized version."

Braxton hops off my lap and says proudly, "Ain't nothing about a Johnson that's small."

Camden high-fives him just as Dawson and Mr. Johnson join us.

"Is he bragging about winning already?" Mr. Johnson asks. "Because you should know he's a cheater."

"I didn't make up the silly scramble rules. And Dawson has obviously been spending too much time with this one." He tilts his head in my direction. "And not enough time on the course."

Dawson sits down next to me and gives me a sweet kiss. "At least I have something better to do than chase my own balls around."

Braxton does a little huff and folds his arms across his chest. He's ready to spout off a comeback.

Probably a dirty one, because his dad says, "Don't even say it, Braxton. You need to mind your manners in front of the ladies."

"Did you decide to ditch the tea?" Dawson asks.

"Yeah, it was really boring," Peyton replies. "So I made Keatyn sneak out with me."

The boys all talk about their golfing. The best shots. What little contests they think they might win. I'm listening to their conversation when I catch Braxton typing into my phone.

I grab it from him. "What are you doing?"

"Putting myself in as a contact. You need to text me tonight with the party info. My brothers tell me nothing is going on after curfew tonight. But I don't believe them."

"Everyone is going to the after party. At least everyone I know."

"Can you get me in? I'm a good dancer." He stands up and does a couple dance moves.

"I wish I could. The security for the event is really tight. It's the first time the school has allowed something like this, so each student has to show their student ID to get their wristband. You have to have the wristband to get on the bus and into the event."

I can tell Braxton's brain is in motion. "So I just need to get a school ID and a wristband and I'm in? That should be easy."

"Don't you dare, Braxton," his dad says. "We don't need you getting kicked out before you ever get in. You want to come here next year, don't you?"

He hangs his head in defeat. "Yeah."

"Then behave."

He raises his head and smiles. "Can I have beer instead?"

His dad and brothers just roll their eyes and continue their conversation. Braxton sends me a text.

Braxton F*cking Johnson: *You need to hook me up with a wristband. I know you set up the security. Dawson was bragging about it. He was bragging about some other things too.*

Me: *Dawson never brags about other things and, sorry, but no.*

I change his name to something a little more normal.

Braxton: *My life sucks. I've been here for three days and haven't got laid.*

Me: *You're a little young for that, I think.*

Braxton: *I'm not. I'm ready. I'm SO ready. Hook me up. There was a party last night and you didn't invite me. I was hurt.*

Me: *I didn't go to a party last night. Neither did Dawson.*

Braxton: *I know that Riley snuck out.*

Shit. How does he know that?

Me: *Where did you hear that?*

Braxton: *Dallas.*

Me: *Probably went to see Ariela.*

Braxton: *Nope. I asked.*

Me: *I don't know then.*

Braxton: *He calls you baby. He doesn't call his girlfriend, baby. What's up with you two?*

Me: *He's my friend. Tell you what. You're coming back for the Prospective Student weekend, right?*

Braxton: *Hell, yeah, I am.*

Me: *Be a good boy and don't get in trouble for Homecoming and I'll take you to a party then.*

Braxton: *You swear?*

Me: *No, I'd say that you're the one who does all the swearing.*

Braxton: *Fucking right, I am.*

"I have to go," I say, checking the time on my phone.

"I'll walk you," Dawson says.

"You'll *what* her?" Braxton says really loudly.

"WALK," their dad says to Braxton. "Get your mind out of the gutter, son."

As we walk away, Dawson is laughing. "I like my brother's idea better."

"Really? I never would have guessed that," I say with a smirk. "You want me to look good tonight, right?"

"Of course."

"Then I need to go get my nails done."

"I have a few errands I need to run myself."

"What kind of errands?"

"Champagne kinds of errands."

"Yum."

When we get to my dorm, he gives me a steamy kiss and says goodbye.

I go into my room, grab my handbag and keys, then text Annie, Maggie, and Katie.

> **Me:** *Ready to head to the salon?*
>
> **Annie:** *Still at the boring tea. Where are you?*
>
> **Me:** *Coming to rescue you. I'll pull my car up. You run out. LOL It's okay to leave for our appointments. We have to look beautiful for tonight.*

As I walk to my car, I'm suddenly very aware that there are a lot of people milling about that I don't know.

Riley's words about how it would be the perfect time to sneak on campus start running through my mind. I feel very paranoid as I walk to my car.

Twice, I see someone with Vincent's build and hair color and have a momentary freak out.

When I get close to my car, I carefully look behind me and around me.

I peek under my car and then walk along it, making sure no one is hiding in the cargo area. Then I hit the unlock button, jump quickly into the car, and lock it back up.

I'm probably just being silly, because I really do feel safe here.

Didn't Garrett tell me to listen to my gut? And to that little voice inside my head that lets me know when I'm in danger?

I take a deep breath and clear my head.

I don't feel danger, so I start my car and go pick up the girls.

NOT THE JEALOUS TYPE.

8:30PM

AFTER DINNER, THE walls on each side of the banquet hall are slid open to reveal the dance floor.

I enjoy being appropriately held in Dawson's arms all night. It's strange being in his arms for such a long period of time without attacking each other.

Although it doesn't stop him from whispering all the things he'd like to be doing right now.

Or what he wants to do later.

Or trying to talk me into a quick visit to his dorm, or the bathroom.

Or anywhere, really.

At a little before eleven, the Homecoming Court is assembled for our procession and then the announcement of the King and Queen.

We walk to the middle of the stage when our names are called and then line up on the stage.

The Dean thanks the Homecoming Court and gives a short speech about exemplary students, all aimed at the alumni and parents as opposed to the students.

Then he opens an envelope and says, "And this year's Homecoming King is Dawson Johnson!"

I let out a somewhat dignified *whoop* as the crowd cheers.

Last year's Homecoming Queen, the leggy Samantha that Camden was flirting with at the golf tournament, walks across the stage, places a crown on Dawson's head, and gives him a kiss on the cheek.

The dean is handed another envelope and slowly opens it.

He smiles and says, "And this year's Homecoming Queen is Peyton Arrington!"

Peyton gets teary-eyed and walks to the center of the stage. Dawson holds out his elbow for her and they smile for the flashing cameras. Camden, who I didn't realize was last year's King, walks out onto the stage, grabs Peyton, and dips her back for a sexy kiss on the lips.

All the students hoot and whistle.

He pulls her back upright then places a tiara on her head.

I think ahead to next year. How cool it would be to have Dawson come back, place a crown on my head, and dip me back and kiss me?

I look out into the crowd and realize that I survived the dance. The dance was really the part I was most worried about. It felt a lot like my birthday party. People all around.

I tried to act normal, but I stuck as close to Dawson as I could.

I catch him smiling at me. He looks so handsome. He's wearing a soft tan dress shirt that is just slightly darker than the nude color under my dress, a black suit with a tan pinstripe, a black tie, and shiny black wingtips.

I watch the assistant dean place a bouquet of red and yellow roses in Peyton's arms.

Peyton beams and her smile lights up the stage.

But another brightness catches my eye. Aiden is smiling at his sister. I can tell he's so proud. And he looks extremely handsome standing there. He's wearing a grey Armani suit, the palest of blue shirts, an artistic gray and blue striped tie, and by far the coolest shoes of the night. I had seen them earlier and hadn't noticed. They just looked like basic black Prada dress shoes, but up here in the bright light you can see the perforated pattern on them and the bright blue undertones.

He catches me looking at him and gives me a little wink. At least, I think he's winking at me. There's no one behind me and I don't think he was winking at Ariela or Maggie, who are standing beside me. I give him a little smile back.

Music starts playing again and Dawson and Peyton descend from the stage for the Royal Dance.

I glance at Whitney. There's no mistaking the venom in her glare.

She's pissed.

Pissed she isn't out there dancing with Dawson.

Pissed her perfectly scripted life hasn't gone according to plan.

About halfway through the dance, Dawson and Peyton break apart. Dawson dances with his mom and Peyton with her dad.

I picture myself dancing like that with Tommy.

But if I danced with Tommy, that would mean the truth about who I am would have to come out.

Vincent would have to be in jail.

And if he was, would I come back?

Would everyone hate me for lying?

Or would I go back to my old school?

My old life?

Everyone claps, breaking me out of my reverie, and indicating the end of the song.

Dawson comes up to the stage and holds his hand out to help me descend the stairs.

I'm happily swaying in his arms when Whitney says, "May I cut in? For old time's sake?"

Jake holds out his arm to me, so I politely let her dance with Dawson.

Dawson looks stiff, but she looks happy.

She doesn't look like a scheming bitch when she dances with him.

And, while I'm not the jealous type, I'm practically giddy when Dawson ends their dance halfway through and takes me back in his arms.

LIKE A RED SOLO CUP.

11:15PM

DAWSON AND I walk down to the dorms, so we can pick up our bags to take to the hotel. Then we stop off at the student center, show our school IDs, and get our wristbands.

The school was really concerned about students inviting friends to come to the event, so, for liability reasons, we had to devise a way to make sure the party stayed closed.

The rule is: no wristband = no entrance. No exceptions.

Whitney and Jake meet us at the limo. Jake gives me a hug and whispers, "Thank you. But, beware: she's in a pissy mood after not winning."

Dawson had taken his crown off and put it on me at the dance. I realize I'm still wearing it, so I pull it off my head and tuck it into Dawson's duffle bag. I don't want to make her feel worse.

"Champagne is in order, I think," I say to Jake.

He opens one of the bottles he brought along and pours some in a flute for Whitney.

She doesn't even bother to wait for a toast. She just drains it.

Jake refills her glass and then grabs another flute.

"Oh, here," I say to Jake and hand him two red Solo cups. "Put ours in here."

"Very classy," Whitney sneers.

"It has nothing to do with class, Whitney. I'll never drink out of limo glasses. They don't wash them. Just sort of Windex them off between uses. Way to many germs for me. Besides, nothing says party like a red Solo cup."

"Maybe your kind of parties."

"Yes, my kind of parties. Shots. Dancing on the bar. You know, fun stuff."

Jake asks Dawson for a red cup, fills his glass, and toasts, "No more parents. No more alums. Watch out club. Here we come."

"Whooh!" I yell, and take a sip.

Dawson pulls me into his arms. "Are you going to dance on the bar tonight? That sounds hot."

"Definitely."

Dawson is all over me in the limo.

"I can't wait to help take this off," he says, touching the bow on my shoulder.

Jake puts his arm around Whitney and as hard as she's trying to pretend things are perfect, she looks like she's ready to cry.

And I'm sure it doesn't help that I'm sitting here getting mauled by her King.

I grab Dawson's hand and place it on my thigh, keeping my hand firmly on top of it.

Jake says, "So, tell us about the after party."

"Although, at first, I wasn't supportive of the idea," Whitney admits. "After spending the last three days with my family, I'm looking very forward to cutting loose."

Jake grins and promptly refills her flute. She chugs it and then leans into Jake, clearly a little more relaxed.

WHEN WE GET to the hotel, Jake asks Whitney, "How long do you need to change?"

"Maybe fifteen minutes."

Jake says to us, "Okay, so we'll meet back here at 11:45."

As we walk into the lobby, Dawson puts a shoulder into Jake's. "I'm gonna need a little more time than that. Let's shoot for 12:30."

"But the party starts a midnight," Whitney pouts.

Dawson shrugs his shoulder. "The party won't start until we get there. That's how it's always been."

Whitney beams at him.

As we walk to our room, I say to Dawson, "You gave Whitney a nice compliment."

"Yeah, Jake hasn't quite learned how to deal with her yet."

"But you know," I say, not quite able to conceal the hurt in my voice.

He rolls his eyes at me. "We dated for a long time. She needs her ego stroked. Always has. That's why she and Jake won't work long term. He's too stubborn."

My stomach drops. Does he want her back? Does he want to stroke her ego?

He continues. "I'm so glad you're not like that. And, besides, it was worth it. I'm going to need every bit of that hour with you."

"Oh really, why?"

He opens the door to our room and says, "This is why."

He barely gets the door shut before he's got me pinned against it and is untying the bow at my shoulder.

The front of the dress falls down to reveal my nude-colored strapless bra.

"This needs to go," he says, unhooking it and flinging it on the floor. I push his suit jacket off his shoulders as he bends down to kiss my chest. He tries to push the rest of the dress down off my hips, but it's very fitted and has a zipper.

"There's a zipper," I moan as he sucks his way across my chest.

He fumbles with the zipper, gets it undone, and pushes it and my panties to the floor.

He picks me up and carries me to the couch, quickly undoing his own zipper.

"God, that dress has been driving me crazy."

Then he's moving like we have two minutes instead of an hour.

I THROW ON a hotel robe, carefully darken my eye makeup, and add more blush. Then I hide in the bathroom and get dressed for the after party. I want to surprise him with the full look.

I walk out into the living room. Dawson has changed into a pair of dark jeans, leather loafers, and a black shirt with silver stripes. He looks so incredibly hot.

"Whoa," he says, grabbing my hands and taking in my metallic crepe strapless dress. "Now that's a dress. What there is of it."

He smacks my ass and tells me we better get downstairs.

Whitney and Jake are waiting in the lobby. Whitney looks perfect, not a strand of hair out of place. Completely different from the messy pony I'm wearing. But when you dance, you sweat, and there's nothing attractive about wet hair.

Whitney's club clothes, well, they aren't really club clothes. She's wearing a simple red silk dress with a black cardigan over it. She looks like she should be going to brunch at the country club.

I grab her hand, drag her back to the elevator, and tell them we'll be back in five minutes.

"Let go of me," she says.

I smile. "Nope, it's time for you to embrace your inner slut."

"I don't want to look like a slut."

"You're going to a crazy club, not the country club. You definitely want to look a little slutty."

I pull her into our hotel suite. Of course, she takes in the articles of clothing strewn about.

"You ever think about cleaning up after yourself?"

I ignore her comment and lead her to a barstool. I pour her a glass of champagne from the bottle we didn't finish. "Drink. Don't move."

"You know, you're kind of bossy."

I grab my makeup bag and plop it into the counter.

"You have gorgeous eyes. We're going to play them up a little." I do up her eyes, starting with a white sparkly color in the corners, going to a deep rose in the middle and ending in an intense charcoal. I smudge a little of the charcoal under the bottom outer edges then add a thick swoop of a charcoal liquid liner with flecks of silver glitter. Then I find my reddest lip stain, carefully brush it onto her lips, and add some High Beam gloss.

"Okay, take off the cardigan."

She takes off the cardigan to reveal the simple red dress and a pair of sparkly silver pumps. I grab my bag, which still has the black leather skirt I wore the other night in it. After our time at the lake, I just had thrown the little PJ shorts back on.

I'm trying to figure out what she's going to wear for a top, when I spy a pair of scissors.

"Here, try this on," I say, handing her the leather skirt.

She looks at the skirt like it's a piece of trash. "Just because we want to look slutty doesn't mean we have to be cheap."

I flash the Saint Laurent label at her.

She tilts her head, studying me and the skirt. Like she's trying to decide if she should go for it or not. Finally, she takes it and slips it on under her dress. She holds the dress up and looks in the mirror. Then she spins around, scrutinizing the back. "My ass looks amazing in this skirt."

"It does. And watch this." I bend down and unzip the zipper that runs up the front middle of the skirt, giving her a nice slit leading straight to her crotch.

She studies her eyes in the mirror. "I can't believe I'm saying this, but I love what you did to my eyes."

"Good, cuz you may freak about what I'm about to do next." I hold up the scissors. "May I?"

She looks down at her dress, which I want to turn into a top.

She grabs the bottle of champagne, takes a big swig, and says, "What the hell."

I carefully cut from the hem of the dress straight up to her bellybutton. Then I cut around the waistband of the skirt so that the new top will just graze it. When she puts her arms up to dance, her flat stomach will be nicely exposed.

She hands me the bottle and says, "Take a drink."

I take a sip while she looks at herself in the mirror.

"Let's go shorter."

I cut up an inch higher all the way around. "You look hot," I tell her.

"And you . . . I still hate you, but maybe not as much as I used to."

I smile, knowing that's a compliment.

"Come on, let's go knock Jake's socks off."

Jake's response is more than expected and he's all over her in the limo.

When we get to the club, I'm shocked to see that the dance floor isn't packed yet.

I grab Whitney, round up Peyton and Maggie, and lead them up to the center stage.

"Girls, it's time to get this party started."

Whitney gets a panicked look in her eye. I know she's not a great dancer.

"Don't worry," I tell her. "Just move a little and let your hands glide across the other girls' bodies. Drives the guys crazy."

The DJ sees us coming up to dance and cranks up one of my favorite songs.

I grab Maggie and grind up against her. Peyton does the same to Whitney and pretty soon we're in a line, butt to butt, and lost in the music.

I lose track of how many songs we dance to but when I look out, I'm excited to see that the dance floor is now packed.

I see Katie, yell at her, hold my hand out, and pull her up onto the platform. Dallas takes my hand as I climb down. He's already hypnotized by Katie's boobs bouncing up and down in her teeny top.

I find Dawson and Jake and pull them both onto the dance floor.

"Jake, go get Whitney."

He laughs and says, "I'm just enjoying the show."

Dawson pulls me close and runs his hands all over me. We dance for at least an hour before Dawson says he needs some water. "That champagne gave me a headache. They serving food?"

"Yeah, there's snacks upstairs. Want to get something?"

"Definitely."

We go upstairs and find Aiden, Nick, and Logan chowing down. It's a little quieter up here. There's a balcony that's probably packed on a regular night, but our school isn't big enough for that. So this is a great spot to sit and watch everyone dance below.

"You go get food. I'll get water," Dawson says.

I'm waiting in the short food line when Aiden gets in line behind me.

"Hey," I say to him. "Are you guys having fun?"

"We were having fun watching you dance on the stage. Although some of the things they were saying about my sister were a bit inappropriate."

"Do you like watching girls grind on each other?"

"I like it better when we grind on each other. Don't forget you promised me a dance."

"I won't."

"Great shoes by the way."

"You noticed my shoes?"

"Yeah. The stones on the heels were catching the light when you were dancing. It looked really cool. Peyton asked me to take some pictures. Wanna see?"

He holds up his phone and scrolls to a picture of us dancing. There is light dancing all around my feet.

"Oh, that is cool. Will you send me that?"

"Sure. So did you do that to Whitney?"

I laugh. "Yeah. She got the Barbie Goes Clubbing makeover."

"I'm surprised."

"That I'm nice to people?"

"That you're nice to her after what she did to you."

"Honestly, I mostly did it for Jake. He's my friend. And if that means Whitney won't hate me as much, all the better."

"Just when I thought I had you all figured out, you surprise me again."

I load up a plate with bacon and other breakfast foods.

"Was it a good surprise?"

His eyes bore into mine.

He nods, then smiles and steals a piece of bacon off my plate, popping it into his mouth. "This is good. We did good with the party, don't you think?"

I look around. "Yeah, Aiden, we did good."

I finish filling our plates with some fruit, a couple muffins, fried hashbrown patties, and French toast sticks. I don't even think about the calories. I know I'll burn them off dancing.

Dawson laughs about how much I eat of the kind of junk food I usually avoid.

"We're gonna burn it off dancing."

He pulls my hand up to his lips and kisses the back of it. "I can think of some funner ways for us to burn calories."

THE PARTY STARTS out fun, but as the night rolls on, the drama grows.

We take a break from dancing and Whitney runs to the restroom.

She comes marching back out with a pissed look on her face. Rachel and the minions are behind her and they all look to be in tears.

"Those backstabbing bitches," she rants. "They all practically jumped me in the bathroom and bitched me out for dancing with you. For coming in the limo with you."

"Well, I am practically your sworn enemy. You've confused them. They don't know who the hell to like."

Whitney breaks out in laughter. "They couldn't find their ways out of a paper bag without me."

"I don't know what you said to them, but they're all crying."

"They're all drunk. Which is something I am not." She reaches in Jake's pocket, grabs his flask, and drinks whatever was left.

Then she looks at Dawson. He takes the flask out of his pocket and hands it to her. The three of them do multiple shots.

Once it's finished, Jake and Dawson go on a hunt for more alcohol.

I sip on my water for a few minutes and then go back out to dance.

Maggie is dancing with Parker, Nick, Logan, and Aiden, so I join them. Hard to believe that two of the hottest guys at school don't have dates.

Aiden tells me it's time for our dance and pulls me into his arms.

I pull out of his arms and dance with a more respectable distance between us but, really, we're all sort of grinding on each other.

For the first time all night, they play a slow song. Aiden pushes his leg between mine and moves his hips against me. I feel the fog in my brain start to collect. Like it always does when I'm near him.

But, no.

I can't.

"I told you, I can't dance with you like that anymore."

He grins at me. "Can't blame a guy for trying."

I gave him a sad smile. I had fun dancing with him. I don't know what kind of game he's trying to play. Maybe it's just that gods are used to getting their way. Or maybe not getting a Homecoming date bruised his ego.

"What?" he says when he sees my pout.

I shake my head. "I'm just disappointed that you'd say that. But it shouldn't be a surprise. Have fun tonight, Aiden."

I STOP AT the dessert table, grab a cheesecake square, then go sit down with Whitney.

"The boys still aren't back," she slurs.

I can tell that the alcohol she was chugging early is starting to affect her.

While I'm eating my cheesecake, I notice that Whitney is watching Peyton and Camden, who are doing some very dirty dancing right in front of us.

Jake and Dawson finally make it back to our table. Jake is stumbling a bit.

"Where have you been?" Whitney yells at him.

He goes to sit down, misses the chair, and falls flat on his ass.

Dawson drags him to his feet and helps him sit on the barstool.

"Are you okay?"

"I'm fine. Mission accomplished," he says. He slides a flask under the table to her. She openly chugs from it.

I give Dawson a kiss. I can tell he's a little tipsy and I'm happy he's not drunk like Jake.

I hand him my bottle of water.

He takes a swig and says, "We're heading back to the hotel now. I just called the driver."

"That sounds like a good idea."

"Jake and Whitney both drunk is going to get ugly. I don't want them to ruin our night. I've had the best night with you."

I give him another kiss. "I've had the best night with you too."

He grabs my hand and says, "Come on, Jake. Let's go."

As we head out the door, Peyton and Camden follow us.

"Hey, bro, can we hitch a ride back to the hotel?"

"Yeah, sure," Dawson says.

We all pile into the limo.

Whitney is swaying just sitting still. She's looking from Dawson to Jake to Camden and it sort of reminds me of when I was standing in my entryway with Sander, Brooklyn, and Cush and wondering what in the world made me think having them all in one place was a good idea.

I guess at least she's drunk.

Jake has his arm sloppily wrapped around her.

She whispers to Jake, but she's drunk, so we all hear exactly what she says to him.

And I probably won't be repeating it.

She tries to give both Dawson and Camden one of those looks that tell a guy he doesn't know what he's missing, but they just laugh at her.

She ignores them, pushes Jake into a corner of the limo, and starts making out with him.

Dawson pulls me a little closer and says quietly, "I ordered us room service. It will be there when we get back."

"Yum. What did you order?"

"Chocolate covered strawberries to go with the rest of our champagne and . . ."

"URRGGGG," goes Whitney, and then proceeds to puke all over the floor of the limo, somehow, thankfully, managing not to get a drop on my leather skirt.

Got to give the girl points for that.

She wipes her mouth on Jake's jacket then lies across the back seat of the limo and starts crying.

Jake slides away from her, holding his hand up to his mouth. Then he starts gagging.

I quickly reach over to roll down the window just as Camden gags and adds to the pile of puke on the floor.

Jake sticks his head out of the window like a dog.

Peyton leans over to me and says, "Is this awesome or what?"

Sunday, October 9th

TIGGER WITH BOOBS.

1PM

DAWSON AND I wake up late in the afternoon.

"I'm starving," he says, as his stomach growls.

"Me too."

We grab the menu, decide what we want, and he orders it.

When he sets down the phone, he attacks my neck and says something about how we have twenty-five minutes to kill.

WHILE WE'RE EATING, I hear my phone buzz.

I dig around the room, find my bag, and check my messages.

Katie: *Where the HELL ARE YOU!!! I HAVE to talk to you about last night!!!!!!!*

Dallas: *Katie was making out with Tyrese last night after you left. Like we were dancing together, having fun. I come back and she's making out with him. We're done.*

Me: *Dallas! Are you okay? Are you upset?*

Dallas: *I'm more pissed than anything. Really, I feel used.*

Me: *Because you lost your virginity to her and she didn't really love you?*

Dallas: *Ha! No. I'm pissed because I spent a bunch of money on her and then she does that. Although, really, we had no long-term potential. She's way too high strung for me. It was like dating Tigger with boobs.*

Me: *OMG. She totally does bounce around like Tigger. Still, I'm sorry.*

Dallas: *I'll survive. It's not like we were going out. I'm still talking to other girls.*

Me: *Good. I'll see you later.*

Me: *Dawson and I are in our hotel room. Where are you?*

Katie: *I'm at the dorm.*

Me: *Dallas told me you got drunk and were making out with Tyrese?*

Katie: *I think maybe it was more than making out. A lot more. I think we had sex. What if I get pregnant????!!!*

Me: *Oh, wow. Why do you think you had sex? Do you remember it?*

Katie: *Kind of. I remember thinking we were going to and then that's it. I'm so embarrassed. And I'm FREAKING out. I think he was drunk too. What if we didn't use anything?*

Me: *CALM down. It will be okay. Are you okay? Do you want me to come home?*

Katie: *No. But do you think maybe you could talk to him? I've been throwing up and I look like shit. Annie is here, but she doesn't know what to do. She's taking good care of me but, you know, she's never done anything, so she doesn't really know how I feel.*

Me: *Did he take advantage of you?*

Katie: *I wanted to leave with him. Would I have if I wasn't drunk? No.*

Dawson sees me frowning. "What's going on?"

"Katie hooked up with Tyrese last night. Well, this morning, I guess, after the party. But she was really drunk and isn't sure what happened. She's freaking out because she's pretty sure they had sex. Katie's not on the pill or anything, so if they did it and didn't use protection . . ."

"She's been getting drunk a lot. It's getting annoying."

"I know. I talked to her about it. What should we do? Should I just call him and ask him if they did?"

He pops another French fry in his mouth, chews it while thinking, then says, "Let me."

I give him a kiss on the cheek. "You are so adorably sweet. You know that, right?"

"I don't think I do," he teases. "Why don't you show me?"

"Text Tyrese, then I will probably be needing a shower."

"I was thinking we could stay here until almost curfew. Do all sorts of fun stuff. Enjoy the privacy."

"That sounds like the perfect day. Room service and you."

I lean back on the bed and stretch out like a cat while Dawson is texting.

"They did hook up. Twice. He says they may have used a condom the first time but not the second. He was drunk too."

"That's bad."

He shakes his head. "It's definitely not good. You know, he's gotten at least two other girls pregnant."

"I didn't know that."

"He's not at all careful."

I start to text Katie then put my phone down on the bed. "I can't tell her this over a text."

He studies my face for a second. "Tell her we're heading there."

"You are seriously the sweetest boy I have ever met," I tell him as we're packing up.

He sets his bag on the bed and pulls me into his arms. "I love you. And she's your friend. You need to be there for her."

"I know, but a lot of guys would say it's her problem and to stay in bed with them."

"Oh, trust me, I thought about it. But I know you won't be able to stop worrying about her. And it's not like we can't come back here if we want. Or go to my room."

ON THE SHORT drive back to school, I text Katie.

> ***Me:*** *Dawson and I are on our way.*
>
> ***Katie:*** *OMG!! I look horrible!*
>
> ***Me:*** *He won't care.*
>
> ***Katie:*** *We did, didn't we?*
>
> ***Me:*** *Yeah.*

Dawson sits on Katie's bed and tells her what he knows.

Katie starts bawling, so Dawson pulls her into a hug.

I sit on my bed with Annie and swoon. Is he seriously not the sweetest boy ever?

I look at Annie.

She looks shell-shocked and I can tell what's going on in her mind.

She mutters, "I'm never, ever having sex in high school."

I grab her hand. "You've been an awesome friend to Katie. Thank you for that."

"I don't know what to do. I have no experience with stuff like this. What do we do? Just wait and pray she's not pregnant?"

"Um, no. Hell no. We need to get her that Plan B pill."

"What's that?"

"The morning after pill?"

"Oh, I've heard of that. I guess I never really knew what it was for."

"Basically, if your birth control fails, you can take it. But I'm pretty sure you have to be eighteen to get it without a prescription."

"So we have to tell someone?"

"That or she has to call her doctor for a prescription."

"She's not gonna wanna do that."

"No, I wouldn't think so. Do you think boys can get it?" I ask, looking at Dawson, my eighteen-year-old boyfriend.

"Let me look online," Annie says as she taps away on her phone.

"What's it say?"

"It says that she needs to take it right away. They say the sooner the better but there's a 72-hour window. Some things I'm reading say 17, others say 18. So I'm not sure. But definitely anyone, boy or girl, can get it if they're over 18."

I go sit down next to Dawson and Katie. She's calmed down some. "Okay, so the first thing we need to worry about is pregnancy. You need to take the Plan B pill. Like right away."

"I'm not calling my doctor. He's friends with my parents!"

"Well, if you were eighteen, you wouldn't need a prescription but since . . ."

Dawson interrupts me. "I'm eighteen. I'll go."

Like I said, the sweetest boy ever. And if I wasn't sure before, I am now.

I am in love with Dawson.

Katie gives me a huge hug, then starts crying again. "I feel so bad. So guilty. So slutty. So *stupid.*"

"It'll be okay," I say, praying that it will be.

Dawson grabs my hand. "Ride into town with me?"

As we're walking back out to his car, I ask, "Shouldn't we make Tyrese do this? Shouldn't he have to take some responsibility? I feel like we should make him. But I don't want to embarrass Katie by involving him."

"Tyrese is a friend. He's fun to party with, but he isn't respectful of women. To him, they are all hoes. I know for a fact that he won't help. He got a girl from the dance team pregnant last year. Hers was one of the spots you tried out for. We're better off taking care of it ourselves."

Monday, October 10th

PUTTING IT OUT THERE.

7:55AM

IT'S THE TYPICAL Monday morning after a big dance. Half the people who went together don't ever want to go out with that person again and the other half are all lovey-dovey.

Riley is clearly in the lovey half.

"I think I'm gonna ask Ariela to be my girlfriend. What do you think?"

"I think if you want to be exclusive, that's a good idea. Are you talking to anyone else?"

"No! I stopped talking to other girls when I started talking to her. Is she still talking to other guys?"

"Um, I think so."

"Who!?"

"Remember when you first asked her to hang out and she was still talking to a guy from home?"

"Yeah. Has she hung out with him?"

"No. But I know they still text each other."

"That kind of pisses me off."

"I don't think it should. Have you told her she's the only one you're talking to?"

"No."

"Then I don't think you can be mad. Just talk to her."

"Now I don't want to."

"Don't be a brat. You survived Homecoming and don't hate each other."

"What Katie did to Dallas was pretty shitty."

"Yeah, it was. How's he doing?"

"Well, he was still talking to other girls. So he hung out with one of them last night. And one of them is a girl that's in your math class, so next period should be interesting. Do you think Mr. Miremadi would notice if I sat in there, just to watch the fireworks?"

"He never takes roll and none of us ever sit in the same seat. He probably wouldn't notice."

"He doesn't in our class either, and I have math the following period anyway. If he says anything, I'll say I got confused."

"Let's sit in the back. I want to try and stay out of that mess. I feel bad since I set them up."

"And then she took poor Dallas' virginity."

"I know. And now I'm afraid he's going to feel heartbroken and used."

Riley laughs out loud. The teacher gives him the evil eye and he tries to stop, but he can't.

"What's so funny?"

"Guys generally don't feel that way about sex. We're not girls," he whispers.

WE HAVE TO stop talking while our history teacher gives his lecture. He stops a few minutes before the bell is due to ring and allows us to talk quietly.

Riley says, "Speaking of Homecoming. We made it through without any kind of incident."

"I know. I'm feeling better about it. You're right. It couldn't have been him. No way he'd wait this long. You can stop sleeping on my floor."

"Does that mean I get the rug?"

"We'll see."

The bell rings, so we gather up our stuff and file out of class. Riley follows me into math, where we take seats in the back.

Katie walks in later, but doesn't seem to notice us. She sits up front next to Jordan, who she was sort of seeing before Homecoming. I suspect that she was nervous about seeing Dallas and sat next to the first friendly face she saw.

A few minutes later, Dallas strolls in with his arm wrapped around a girl. Not the casual my-arm-is-wrapped-around-her-shoulder but the tight-we-can't-get-close-enough-around-the-waist version.

Our teacher isn't in the classroom yet. He usually wanders in with his third cup of coffee of the day right before the bell rings.

Dallas acts like he's totally into the girl. She giggles at him and even gives him a kiss before they sit down next to each other.

I glance at Katie. She's pretending not to watch, but I can tell she is because there are tears shimmering in her eyes.

"I feel bad for Katie," I whisper to Riley.

"I think she deserves it."

"Tyrese took advantage of her."

"Maybe it will teach her a lesson. She's always drunk. What does she expect? And when she's drunk, she's pretty forward. I didn't tell you this, but she was all over me one night. A girl who keeps putting it out there like that shouldn't be surprised when someone takes her up on it."

"Yeah, I guess that's true. She was really freaked out yesterday though."

"Dawson told me."

"He was so sweet. Like, the way he helped her. I think I fell a little more in love with him."

"Weren't you already in love with him?"

"Yeah, but I don't doubt my feelings anymore."

"So, what should we do about those two? Think it will just blow over?"

"I'm not sure. I think I'll text her.

Me: *You doing okay? He's just trying to hurt you because you hurt him.*

Katie: *I know. Where are you?*

Me: *Me and Riley are way in the back. I didn't want to look like I was taking sides. Riley was hoping for fireworks.*

Katie: *Maybe I should give him some.*

Me: *Katie, don't. It won't help. Jordan looked like he was being nice to you.*

Katie: *So I shouldn't yell at Dallas that he sucked in bed?*

Me: *Did he?*

Katie: *No. He was sweet. It reminded me of my old boyfriend. A little awkward, but sweet. Like he didn't seem very experienced.*

I show Riley her text. "Should I tell her?"

He nods his head yes.

Me: *You were his first. He's been with other girls and done stuff, but he was waiting to do it with someone special.*

Katie: *He thought I was special?*

Me: *Yeah.*

Katie: *Fuck my life.*

THROWN UNDER THE BUS. LUNCH

DAWSON IS BEING adorable and feeding me pieces of a juicy orange.

I guess Riley's not the only one in the lovey-dovey half. I feel blissfully happy.

"You're so cute," I whisper to him as Rachel and the minions set their trays on the lunch table.

"You need to take your trays and go sit somewhere else," Whitney says to them. "You're not welcome here anymore. You're not going to talk shit about me and then sit at my table."

Rachel stands there frozen. She's not sure what to do.

"Wait. Why do we have to leave?" Minion #1 says. "It's not our fault Rachel's a bad friend."

Rachel looks at her in disbelief. She can't believe she's being thrown under the bus.

"Who did you vote for?" Whitney asks the girl.

"You," Minion #1 says.

"And you?" Whitney asks Minion #2.

She glances at Rachel, gives her sorry eyes, then looks straight at Whitney and lies through her teeth. "You, of course."

Whitney nods at her, like a Queen does to barely acknowledge people.

"And what about you?" she asks Minion #3.

Minion #3 hangs her head and whispers, "Peyton."

I have a new respect for Minion #3. You gotta give the girl credit for telling the truth.

Whitney has a fiery look in her eye.

"Aren't you going to ask me why?" the girl asks in an innocent voice.

Whitney plays along. "Why?"

"Because Rachel told me to."

Or not.

Wow. This table is like a snake pit.

"The three of you may stay at the table," Whitney announces. "Rachel, you can go now."

Rachel looks at the minions for support. Any kind of support.

None of them will even make eye contact.

So she turns to Peyton.

Peyton glances at Whitney. A silent agreement passes between their eyes. Probably the secret threat.

Rachel says to Peyton, "I voted for you. Do *you* want me to leave? Whitney doesn't own this table."

Peyton takes a deep breath and sits up straighter. "She doesn't own this table, but you shouldn't have talked trash about her. Friends don't do that to each other." Then she puts on her bitch face and says, "Bye."

Rachel is desperate. She points at me and says, "So Keatyn, the girl we all hate, gets to stay? But I have to go?"

"Yes," Whitney says coolly. "That should be a good indication of my disappointment in you."

The minions don't dare look up. They are staring down at their lunches, but not moving to eat them.

"You are the biggest bitch," Rachel says.

"Better than being a backstabber," Whitney replies flatly.

Rachel balls up her fists and goes, "Ohhh." Then she looks at the other girls and says, "We don't want to sit here anyway. Let's go."

The girls don't move.

They know better.

The girls give Rachel a little head shake, letting her know they have no intention of going anywhere.

Rachel leaves her tray on the table and runs out of the lunchroom crying.

I think about going after her. Telling her that Whitney's acceptance shouldn't matter. The only thing that should matter is what you think of yourself.

But since she called me *Keatyn, the girl we all hate*, I'm thinking I'm not the best person to deliver that message.

FOLLOW MY SCRIPT.
DRAMA

DURING DRAMA CLASS, our teacher goes over the rehearsal schedule.

"We want a great production, so we expect everyone to attend all rehearsals. If, for some reason, you feel you cannot meet this schedule, please let me know today and we will recast your part. Tonight, we'll have costume fittings for anyone who will be on stage. The rest of you will be painting sets, so dress accordingly. Normally, Mondays will be our day off. This week, we'll practice Tuesday, Wednesday, and Thursday evenings. Then you get this weekend off, as we're hosting the district Choir Competition. Here's the calendar."

WHILE I'M WALKING from drama to the field house for soccer, I call my mom, hoping I'll get lucky and catch her during lunch break.

"Hey, honey! How are you?"

"I'm good. Just on my way to soccer practice. Is everything okay there?"

"Yes, it's good. Although Tommy filmed some stunt scenes and is pretty banged up. Bruised a couple ribs."

"He needs to stop doing so many of his own stunts."

"I have recommended that, but you know how stubborn he is. He doesn't want to hear it. Although, we're off this weekend and he did say all he wants to do is lie on the couch, watch football, and spend time with the girls."

"That sounds like a great weekend."

"I think so too. Hey, so we hired that Allan guy."

"For the movie?"

"Actually, no. To be our driver. Garrett wanted us to stop having one of the guards do double duty. Garrett is sending him to a special driving school. He starts in a couple weeks."

"Is he excited?"

"Thrilled. He seems like a really nice guy. He told Tommy about a particular car chase through Manhattan. I'm so thankful you ended up in his car."

"Me too."

"Hey, Gracie is here with me today. Would you like to talk to her?"

"Oh my gosh, yes!"

I hear Mom move about. Then some clunking around of the phone.

"Kiki! Kiki! Kiki!"

"Hi, Gracie! How are you?"

"I want to be on TV but Mommy won't let me."

"What do you want to do on TV?"

"Wear makeup."

"Just wear makeup?"

"Sing too."

"Are you being a good girl?"

"I got new pink glitter shoes because I'm a good girl."

"I bet they are really pretty," I say as the bell rings. "I have to go, Gracie. I love you."

"Gracie loves Good Kiki too."

"I'm Good Kiki?"

"Yes. You are my Good Kiki and puppy Kiki is Bad Kiki."

I laugh as I hear Mom take the phone from her. "She wants to be on TV. She's been acting out shows in front of the television. It's hysterical because she tries to play every single part in the movie."

"I bet that's cute."

"It is and she's surprisingly good. She memorizes the lines and plays everyone. She reminds me of you."

"I have to get to class, Mom. I love you guys."

"We love you too. Take care of yourself."

I HANG UP the phone and want to cry. I want to see them so badly.

An idea pops in my head. Mom said they were going to be home all weekend.

And I'm off this weekend.

I know what I'm going to do!

I'm going to Vancouver.

And, I'm going to ask Dawson to come with me.

I'm crazy about him and I feel so bad that I've lied to him about things.

And I don't want to lie anymore.

I want to tell him the truth.

He's been so amazing. He was patient with me. Gave me the key to his heart. Ditched Whitney's weekend. Asked me to Homecoming in front of everyone. And then yesterday, he was so sweet to Katie.

And never once has he tried to change me. He loves me just the way I am.

So I'm going to do it.

I'll use my fractional jet membership to get a private flight there.

On the plane, I'll tell him the truth.

My real name. About the stalker. About my parents.

All of it.

He'll be surprised. Shocked, probably. And maybe a little mad at first.

But it will be fine.

He will understand. We'll kiss.

It will do nothing but strengthen our bond.

And then he'll meet my family.

My mom will understand why I first called him Gorgeous.

He and Tommy will bond over football.

My little sisters will love him.

And best of all, since no one knows I'm coming, Vincent will have no way of knowing that I'm there.

We won't leave the house all weekend, so I won't have to worry about being followed back to school.

For once, my life is going to follow my script.

And I can't wait!

A MUTUAL ATTACKING.
5:40PM

"DAWSON, SINCE WE don't have a football game Friday and this will be my only weekend off from play practice for a while, I think we should go away."

He kisses up my stomach then looks at me with a pleased grin. "We going back to the love shack?"

"Are you referring to my gorgeous, expansive New York City loft as *the love shack?"*

"Yes, I am. And I am definitely up for another weekend of sin." He pushes his hips into mine and laughs. "Get it? I'm *up* for it."

"Yes, I get that you are perpetually horny. However, I want to go somewhere else because . . ."

Dawson kisses my chest and moves his hand up my thigh.

I let out a contented little sigh.

When he leans his hips into mine again, I decide we can discuss this later. I clutch his back, raise my hips toward his, and start pushing off his shorts.

AFTERWARD, I'M GETTING dressed. I don't feel like putting my school uniform back on, so I steal a pair of his sweats.

He grabs me and pulls me back on the bed.

"Aren't you ruled by your stomach? It's almost six."

"I think I'm ruled by you. I'm pretty sure I could go without food, but I can't go with out you."

"We've done it, like, every day."

"I know, it's awesome. I love you."

"You love sleeping with me."

"That hardly qualifies as sleeping, Keatie. That was f—"

I interrupt him. "Don't say it."

"You seem weird tonight. Is it because of what happened with Katie? You know I'm not anything like him."

"I know you're not. You're adorable." I kiss his cheek sweetly. "I was trying to talk about going away this weekend when you attacked me."

"I attacked you? You attacked me!" He holds his hands up like he's being arrested. "I swear, I just wanted to kiss. You were the one that pulled off my shorts!"

I laugh and give him a kiss. "Fine. It was a mutual attacking. So, I was wondering if maybe you'd like to meet my family. They're going to be in Vancouver this weekend and I just thought . . ."

He runs his hand across my cheek. "Keatie, I'd love to meet your family."

"Really? That makes me happy."

"Making you happy is my favorite thing to do," he says adorably.

I give him a deep kiss and say, "I love you, Dawson. I really do."

"Good. Now let's go eat."

GIRLS LOVE IT.
7PM

AFTER DINNER, I head to the auditorium for my costume fittings. I have four different outfits to wear in the play, which means I'll get called four different times.

Aiden agreed to meet me here for tutoring and I find him sitting in the back row.

I pull a little present out of my bag. It looks so cute. I took white paper and stamped black Eiffel Towers all over it and then tied it with a pink and black striped ribbon.

"What's this?" he asks when I hand it to him.

"It's sort of to congratulate you for applying yourself in French. I ordered it after you passed your first test and it just came in. Open it."

He tilts his head and eyes me. "It's not going to explode or anything, is it?"

"Very funny."

He pulls the ribbon off the package, rips the paper off, and reads the book's cover. "Dirty French: Everyday Slang from What's Up? To F—Off. Very nice." He flips through the pages and nods his head. "I can see that this will come in quite handy."

"What do you mean by that?"

He holds open a page that lists numerous ways to ask for sex in French.

"You're not supposed to use it to get girls to sleep with you," I huff. "I didn't even know all that was in there. I got it because that day in class . . ." Shit. Now I feel stupid for getting it for him. I thought he'd get a kick out of it, not use it to pick up girls.

He touches my arm and finishes my sentence. "When we were talking about cussing in French. I love it. Thank you."

Keatyn Monroe.

"Shoot, I have to go try on my first costume. Here's my homework, if you want to work on it. I shouldn't be too long. Are you sure you have time to wait?"

"I'm sure," he says. "I'll start working."

AFTER I FINISH the first fitting, I sit back down next to Aiden. His head is down and he's writing in his French workbook. He's taken his school blazer off and has rolled up his oxford's long sleeves.

The four-leaf clover he showed me before the Homecoming game is still on his forearm.

I touch it and say, "Won't come off, huh?"

"I haven't tried to get it off. I'm hoping it will help me get lucky."

I rip my French notebook away from him. I didn't mean to pull it away quite so hard but the thought of him using my four-leaf clover to get lucky with a girl pisses me off for some reason.

I look at him with disgust.

"Figures you'd twist its use for something like that."

He gives me a little smirk. "Between the lucky four-leaf clover and this dirty French book, I should be set. Girls love it when you speak to them in French. They think it's such a sexy language."

"French is a sexy language when you don't butcher it."

"Most girls don't know any better. Why do you think I took French to begin with?"

"That's why?" I am appalled.

He chuckles at me. "It is."

"Give me the book back," I say, holding out my hand.

"Nope. In fact, I learned a couple things while you were gone.

"And what's that?"

"*Rouler des pelles.*"

"French kissing?"

"Yeah, isn't that kind of funny? They don't call it French. And the word for kiss is *baiser.*"

"That's because it's slang. Translated literally it means *rolling shovels*. Open your mouth."

He looks at me funny, but complies.

I laugh. "So you do have a tongue."

"What's that supposed to mean?"

"I don't know. I'm just surprised that you chose French kissing as your first slang word when you don't do it."

"I French kiss. I just didn't kiss you like that. What's that got to do with rolling shovels?"

I stick my tongue out at him. "See the shape?" I draw the outline of my tongue with my finger.

"I guess it is sort of shaped like a shovel."

I make my tongue do a version of the wave. Rolling it up and down.

"You have a talented tongue," he says with a laugh.

"You have no idea," I say with a smirk. I'm going to add, *And you'll never find out*, but I'm interrupted.

Keatyn Monroe.

"I have to go."

I GET MY second costume fitted then go sit back down. Aiden is still here with the book in his hand.

"I found a few more words you might like. If you're cool with it."

"I hung out with French surfers half the summer. I don't think you're going to shock me."

"*T'exploser.*"

"Pound."

"*Tringler.*"

"Screw."

"Hammer wasn't in here."

"You want to hear one that cracks me up?"

"Yeah."

"*Enfourner mon pain.*"

"Bake my bread?"

Keatyn Monroe.

I laugh. "Think about it. I'll be back."

AFTER MY THIRD fitting, Aiden is smiling at me and holding up the book. "That one was in here. It means, *Put it in your box*. But it literally means, *Put my baguette in the oven*."

"I know. The guys we hung out with in France this summer used that one a lot. It just cracked me up that were comparing themselves to a baguette."

"Well, they are long and hard."

I can't help but smirk and laugh at him. "Yeah, exactly. Learn anything else?"

"*La chatte*."

"Pussy. It sounds prettier in French, don't you think? Like, not as dirty."

Aiden bursts out laughing.

"What?"

"I could so make a comment about dirty pussy, but I will refrain."

I smack his shoulder. "Gross, Aiden. How about *la touffe?*"

"Oh, I saw that one." He scans through a page. I see he's already written in the book. Marked it all up.

"Muff."

"Yeah, but translated, it means, *the tuft*."

"I can see why you need to know the slang. I mean think of all the normal words we use that aren't sexual, but said right, have that meaning."

"Like your hammering, pounding, nailing, screwing?"

"Exactly. That's just basic carpentry."

Keatyn Monroe.

"SAVED THE BEST costume for last, huh?" Aiden says to me when I'm finished with my last fitting.

"Figures you would like the cheerleading costume, seeing as it's pretty skimpy."

"*T'es super sexy comme ca*."

"I looked super sexy like that, huh?"

"Well, all your costumes for the play are nice. Do you like them?"

"Yeah. The ball gown for the big dance is kind of lame."

"You don't like the ball gown?"

"Let's just say it's not what I would wear."

"What would you wear?"

I know my answer right away. It's the dress that I pictured in a dream.

"I had this dream once that I wrote down. The dress in it was gorgeous. The most gorgeous dress I've ever seen. That's the dress I'd want to wear."

He grins at me. "Tell me about it. And the dress."

"Okay, so you fade in on a beach that's bathed in moonlight. A young prince is riding down the beach on a white stallion. A girl is also on the beach. She's wearing a gorgeous pink strapless gown with a corseted waist. The skirt of the dress is layer upon layer of pale pink ruffles. Her hair is half-up, the rest is cascading in curls onto her shoulders. A tall, dark man dressed in a black suit has ahold of the princess' wrist and is dragging her up the beach to the dragon's lair. The Princess yells, *Help!* The Dark Man says, *No one is going to hear you scream.* But the Prince does hear her scream. He turns his horse around and gallops toward the noise. He sees the girl. And instantly falls in love. He'd do anything to protect her. He jumps off his steed and pulls out his sword. Fights the Dark Man to the death. Then he turns his attention toward the princess, who was knocked to the ground in the scuffle. The Princess turns to face her rescuer and she recognizes his handsome face. That's it. It's just a short scene."

"It's amazing. So who was the Prince? How did she know him?"

I shake my head. "I don't know yet. It came from a dream I had. When I dreamed it, I felt that she knew him. That she recognized him. But I didn't see his face in my dream."

"You need to figure it out. Finish the story."

"Yeah, maybe. Hey, so I'm done." I glance at my phone. "I'm going to see Dawson for a little bit before curfew."

THREE SLUTTY GIRLS.
10:45PM

I STOP OFF to give Dawson a goodnight kiss after my fittings. Well, a couple kisses, then head to my dorm before curfew.

I'm studying my lines when I get a text from his little brother.

Braxton: *I stopped cussing for Lent.*

Me: *It's not Lent.*

Braxton: *Haha. I know. So, my brothers suck.*

Me: *Do I dare ask why?*

Braxton: *Dirty girl. They suck cuz they won't help me with girls. I think they're afraid I will learn too well and they won't have a shot when I'm around.*

Me: *I think you might be right about that.*

Braxton: *Tell me what girls want.*

Me: *I think that depends on the girl. Also depends what kind of girl you want.*

Braxton: *Right now, I'd like a trio of slutty girls. All naked together in my room with nothing to do but me.*

Me: *Let's try to deal with reality.*

Braxton: *I was. I originally wanted a harem.*

Me: *Fine. Three slutty girls it is.*

Braxton: *Actually, what I need is experience.*

Me: *Dallas told me a really fun pickup line a while ago. It totally would have worked on me. And you're funny. You could probably pull it off.*

Braxton: *What was it?*

Me: *He goes, "Did you have Lucky Charms this morning?" And I was like, "No, why?" And he said, "Cuz you look magically delicious."*

Braxton: *That's brilliant.*

Me: *He also used to have the Psychic Panty Network. He'd guess the color of a girl's panties. He was shocked by how many girls offered to prove he was wrong. Some even donated their panties. That's when he started Panties for the Poor. That didn't last very long though. Then he started trying to guess cup size. He got talked to by the school about that. (Sexual harassment, or something.) Now he's on to pickup lines.*

Braxton: *Tell him I totally worship him. And text me his next pickup line.*

Tuesday, October 11th

ARRESTED OR HOSPITALIZED.

7AM

I HATE GETTING up at the crack of dawn for Social Committee meetings, but I always try to dress especially cute for them. It puts me in a better mood.

Today I have a sweet and innocent look. I'm wearing the longer navy pleated skirt, a white Burberry stretch cotton tie-neck blouse, and my red cardigan. With it, an amazing pair of navy Prada gold-studded platform sandals, a gold Proenza Schouler suede bag, and a preppy Juicy Couture red and navy striped headband with a golden crest.

Brad stands up in front of us and says, "Well, I think it's safe to say that the Homecoming after party was a huge success. The staff loved not having to worry about or chaperone us. No one was arrested or hospitalized. And the students all seemed to have a blast. I know I did."

Everyone starts talking about the party. About how much fun they had.

Finally, Brad raises his hand in the air. "Because of its success, people are expecting big things from our first themed weekend. I'm a little worried about it being held in conjunction with the Prospective Student Weekend. We're going to have to keep things very clean, but still make it fun. Peyton, you want to share what we've got roughed out so far."

"Sure," Peyton says while she consults the notes on her laptop. "Saturday day will mostly be the Olympic-style competitions. Logan is working with the athletic department to organize all that. We'll have some fun, easy games that everyone can participate in. Some events for teams." She turns to Logan. "Logan?"

"Well, I think games that everyone can play is fun, but if we want to go authentic, there should also be a competition for our elite male athletes."

"You do know that the original elite male athletes competed in the nude?" I say to Logan.

Not that I've researched that sort of thing.

Logan gives me a dirty look.

"What? You're the one that wants it to be *authentic*. I'm just trying to help."

Whitney, surprisingly, takes up my cause. "We'll clean it up and make them compete shirtless. And they must wear white all weekend so they are easily identifiable as the elite Olympians."

Logan looks to Brad for help.

Peyton decides to add her two cents worth. "It would impress the female half of the prospective students and give the male half something to aspire to. What kind of competitions will you have?"

Logan goes on. "In Greek history, it's said that the Olympics were started to entertain the newborn Zeus. They had wrestling, jumping, and running competitions. I think we should focus on those."

"Oh," I say. "And the winner will be declared an Olympian god, and we will wear togas to the feast in his honor and celebrate with Greek food, song, dance, and, hopefully, a little mead."

"That sounds like a plan," Peyton says, entering the details in her laptop, which signifies to us all it's a done deal. "What about Friday night?"

"This is sort of off the wall," I admit. "But what if we watched the sing-along version of *Mama Mia*?"

Sheila, who has the lead of the Queen Mother in the school play, practically squeals. "That would be so much fun." She looks at the guys. "If you get to be Greek gods, we should get to have some fun too."

"The new students would just be getting here and I think it would be sort of a fun icebreaker, since it'd be interactive."

Brad says, "Done. Let's go get some coffee."

I MEET UP with Riley and Dallas for breakfast. Apparently Camden told Dawson that he was losing tone. So he's been on a morning protein shake kick, since, well, yesterday. As much as he likes a huge breakfast of bacon and eggs, I doubt it will last long. Plus, his brother was totally giving him shit. His tone looks very fine to me.

Dallas finishes up his breakfast and says, "When Katie and I had our little fling, I starting slacking in testing pickup lines. It's time to dust them off and get them back out there.

"When you and Katie had your little fling, I hardly saw you. I missed you."

He smiles at me. "I missed you guys too." He laughs. "Okay, that's sort of a lie. I was having fun, but I should have made time for you."

I nod, agreeing with him "So what pickup line is up for today?"

"I'm not sure, but, Kiki, have you always been so cute?"

I look at him kind of funny, wondering what that has to do with anything. "Uh . . ."

"Or did it take practice?" he finishes.

I break out in laughter. "Oh, that's really cute." I smile at him. "Get it? Cute?"

Riley rolls his eyes at us. "You're both so incredibly lame." He picks up his coffee cup and holds it out in front of us. "Want to hear a secret?"

"I do. Is it Homecoming gossip?"

"I grind so fine, I'm practically coffee," he says with a straight face, then busts out a grin.

"That is so lame. That has to be a Camden line."

Riley laughs then says, "Wait a minute. Why is Dallas' pickup line cute and mine's not?"

"When Dallas does them, like the magically delicious line and this one too, he's giving me a compliment. In yours, you are giving yourself a compliment. Unless the guy is really hot and I'm looking to get picked up, I would probably flip you off, laugh in your face, or suggest you and your hand have their own party."

"At least my hand never tells me no," Riley says sort of seriously. Which causes Dallas to start laughing again.

"Dude, it's like we've switched roles. You were the player and now, thankfully, I am."

My eyes get big. "Dallas?! Did you have sex with someone else? Do I need to have a talk with you? Who else have you played with?"

"Cool your panties. No, I haven't slept with anyone else. But I am working on it, so you can skip the sex talk."

"How about a responsible sex talk? You know that you need to be responsible, right?"

"Thanks, Mom, but I know to wrap it up."

"Dallas, it's not a present. I'm serious about this."

Dallas slaps Riley on the back as the bell rings. "I'm going to use Riley's condoms before they dry rot."

Riley shakes his head. "That is so not cool."

WET AND WEARING A TOWEL.
5:45PM

I WAS SNEAKY during drama today. I mentioned to the Costume Director that I have some really cool silver sequined ribbon that would look great across the bottom of the cheerleading skirt I'll wear when I meet The Good Prince and offered to sew it on.

I'll sew it on later tonight but, for now, I have the costume on under a pair of Dawson's sweats and a big sweatshirt.

He told me if I wore the skimpy thing to his room, he wouldn't give me shit about the play. And with practices starting tonight, I want to make sure he's fully supportive.

But, before I surprise him, I stop at Riley's room to give him the fluffy rug. I ordered a new one last night. Everyone loves sitting on it and I think the rug is half the reason we always seem to congregate in Katie's and my room.

But Riley earned it.

He and Dallas aren't in there, so I spread it out in the space between their beds and head to Dawson's room.

"DAWSON?" I'M NOT sure why I'm calling out to an empty room, but his bathroom door opens immediately.

"Just got out of the shower."

He's wrapped in nothing but a damp white towel and it's clear he hasn't actually dried off yet. There are still beads of water sliding down his muscular chest. One is running straight down the center of his body, through his thick ab muscles and toward the towel.

I quickly move closer to him. My hand drawn to the bead of water. I catch it before it hits the towel, then run my fingertip back up its path.

"You should be wet and wearing a towel every time I stop by."

"And you have way too many clothes on," he replies with a grin.

I look down at his baggy sweats. "There's kind of a reason for that."

I run and lock his door, then stand in front of his bed, and strip the sweats off. Showing him the skimpy cowboy-style cheerleader costume.

He grins at me, drops his towel to the floor, and practically leaps across the room, knocking both of us onto his bed.

"You have play practice every night this week, don't you?"

"Yeah, and you promised not to give me shit about it if I wore this for you."

I move out from under him.

I stand in front of the bed, to give him a good view of the costume, then slide off my underwear and toss them on his desk.

"That's even better. You gonna do a cheer for me?"

"That's the plan."

"I like the plan." He rolls onto his side and puts his arm under his head. "Go team! Go."

I do a half cheer, half dance thing. Making sure that the skirt flips up a lot in the process.

Since he's lying there naked, it's pretty easy to tell that he's enjoying it.

He jumps up off the bed and unties the little center tie that holds the top together.

I take off the rest of the costume and lay it carefully across his chair.

"Come here, my little cowgirl," he says as he pulls me back on the bed.

SHUT UP AND LOOK PRETTY.
7PM

I'M FIRST UP at play practice tonight. We're practicing the scene right before the Queen Mother tells her sons, the Good Prince and the Bad Prince, that the first one of them to marry will win the throne. She will also tell them about the reality-show-style contest and how it will all conclude with a rose ceremony at a ball in the Royal Gardens.

I'm cheering at a football game where the Good Prince, Jake, is enthralled by my dancing. After the game he gets someone to introduce us. It's a fun scene. We have one of those instant, amazing connections. Sparks. Witty banter. Then he boldly asks me for a date.

We run through it a few times before Jake gets the lines right during the instant connection part. "That's what I'm looking for," our director says. "Okay, next up. Good Prince, Bad Prince, and Queen Mother."

I GO BACK to the spot where Aiden is waiting for me. He agreed to meet me here for tutoring during the play, which should work well. It means I'm able to spend time with Dawson after football practice and then go to dinner with him.

Aiden says, "Maybe we should have a ball at my Royal Vineyard."

"Did I miss the part where you told me you're really a Prince?" I tease.

He gives me an easy laugh. The deep laugh he does when he's entertained. "Afraid not. But it would be cool to do something like that at our house. I can't wait to live there again."

"Really? What do you want to do? Like, don't you want to go to college?"

"Yeah, I do. I'd like to play soccer in college. Get my degree. Maybe see about getting drafted into the Major Soccer League. It'd be cool to play pro for a bit."

"You seem like you're good enough."

"I don't know. A lot depends on how you do in college and if you stay healthy."

"Then what? Do you know what you'll major in? What kind of job you want?"

Aiden leans back in his chair and crosses his feet on the top of the seat in front of him. "I'll probably major in business. But I'll get my trust fund soon and if I live reasonably, I'd never have to get a job. But I want to work."

"Doing what?"

"Don't laugh, okay?" he says seriously.

"I won't."

"I'd like to produce and sell my own wine."

"Why would I laugh about that? That's totally cool."

"What about you? Still thinking about acting? I can't believe you had your lines memorized for that first scene already."

"I have almost *all* my lines completely memorized, not just the first scene. And yes, I still think I'd like to act. Not very many actresses make it big though, so I'd have my work cut out for me."

Especially if I don't use my mom's name to get auditions.

Not that it matters. I couldn't be on a big screen anyway with Vincent still looking for me.

"So do you dream of winning an Academy Award?"

"Not really. I know it's a big deal, but I'd rather be in big blockbuster-type hits. Movies that really entertain people."

"Like the *Trinity* series. Those movies are badass, but they will probably never win those types of awards."

"Exactly. I'd like to be in moves like that. And romantic comedies. Not the all serious cry-me-a-river roles. Like *The Notebook*."

"You don't like *The Notebook*?"

"I love it. It's just not what I want to play."

"You can cry on command."

I laugh again. "Yeah, that's true. But I write scripts too. Maybe I'll do that instead."

"You write scripts?"

"I used to. I was a weird kid. Instead of writing stories and poems, I wrote screenplays."

"What made you want to do that?"

Uh, crap. What did?

"I got to go on one of those backstage type tours for school. Someone's dad worked for a production company. They let us sit in a live studio audience. I came home and told my mom I wanted to write a fairytale movie, so she helped me look up how format a script."

"I think that's really cool. You said that you used to write them. Does that mean you don't anymore?"

"I stopped writing them when I came here."

"Why?"

"I decided to start living life without a script, I guess you could say. I was kinda lame. I thought I could get my life to follow a script. Like I could write the script for the perfect life and then live it."

"But that didn't work?"

"Not really. For scripts to work, everyone has to a have a copy and know their lines."

"Tell me about one of them."

"I told you one last night. The one with the dress in it."

Cheerleader, Good Prince, Bad Prince. You're up.

"I've got to go. I'll talk to you later, Aiden."

I GO BACK on stage. This is the scene where my character and The Good Prince—although at this point, I don't know that he's a prince—share an amazing date. Because the play itself is a comedy spoof, we have one of those only-in-the-movie dates where you're together all day and do like a million different things. In the play, they all happen very quickly and it's pretty funny for the audience because as Jake and I are onstage, the background behind us quickly scrolls through different settings. In the last one, we are on a beach in the moonlight and share our first kiss. It's supposed to be a magical true love kiss. One that the Bad Prince sees. The Queen Mother has already told the princes about the contest. And although I'm not a contestant yet, the Bad Prince schemes to make me one, so that I will find out that my true love didn't tell me the truth about being a prince, which will make me question our love.

Jake whispers to me before we start. "Are we supposed to do the kiss?"

"I don't know. Just listen for the director. Seems like mostly he's been working on line delivery and where he wants us on the stage. If he doesn't tell us to stop, keep going."

I close my eyes for a second and become her. The girl with big dreams. The girl who believes that fairytale love does exist.

Jake and I run through our lines, moving across the stage on our fantasy date, and then coming to stand center stage, where a large moon is dropped down behind us. It's really cheesy and pretty funny that we share our kiss with this huge golden moon literally directly behind us.

Jake and I turn to face each other.

His hands are down by his sides, so I gently take them in mine. I slowly lean in toward him until our lips barely touch.

"And, stop there," the director says. "What you did, Keatyn. How you held his hands. That was perfect and it looked beautiful in front of the moon. Jake, your body position was a little off. I'd like to see you both lean in at the same time."

I come down from the stage feeling practically giddy. Like a girl that did just fall in love. Only I'm in love with this play. With the process. I feel fulfilled and at home up there.

Maybe someday.

I look at the moon that is being pulled back toward the ceiling and start to make a wish on it.

No, wait.

I'm not going to wish on it this time. I'm going to make it a promise.

If I get my life back . . .

No, when I get my life back, I'm not going to let anything stop me. Not fear of embarrassing my mom. Not fear of failure. Not fear of what people might think. I'm going to audition for as many movies as I possibly can. I'm going to live my dream.

I HEAD BACK to my spot. I still need to study for a vocabulary quiz and do a couple pages of math.

I'm surprised that Aiden is still here.

"Why are you still here? Don't you have stuff to do?"

"We weren't done with our conversation."

"What conversation?"

"You were going to tell me about the scripts you wrote."

"No, I wasn't."

"Come on. Tell me about one."

"I already did."

"So tell me about a different one."

I hesitate. No one really knows about the scripts that I write except for Damian, and Brooklyn a little. It's something I've sort of kept hidden. Kind of like my acting ambition.

But I know Aiden won't quit bugging me unless I tell him something.

"Fine. I'll tell you about a script I worked on this summer. It's one that could be made into an actual movie someday. It's not a silly script I wrote to try and plan my life."

"So will its premiere be the one I'm your arm candy for?"

I smile at him. "Hmmm, probably not," I say, but then I decide what the heck, I feel like dreaming big tonight. "You will be my arm candy when I walk my first red carpet as an actress. I'll have a role in a big blockbuster action film."

"You gonna be a Bond girl?"

That makes me laugh. "I don't know. That'd be fun, although it seems like they usually die, don't they? I don't want to die."

"Okay, so an action film where you don't die. You the star?"

"Probably not for my first film. That wouldn't be very realistic now, would it?"

"So I'm *realistic* arm candy?"

I roll my eyes and smile at him. "For someone who is supposed to be arm candy, you're awfully worried about yourself. This is supposed to be my night."

Aiden leans back in his chair and just stares at me for a minute. His mouth starts to move, like he's going to say something, but he stops himself. Finally, he says, "If we're being realistic, we both know that I wouldn't be your arm candy."

"Oh," I say and immediately lower my head.

Aiden doesn't want to be my hypothetical arm candy?

For some reason that sort of bothers me.

Hypothetically.

He pushes my chin up with his finger and looks into my eyes. "A night like that would be magical. You'd want to share it with someone you love."

"That's exactly why I don't write scripts for my own life anymore. You promised you'd be my arm candy. I wrote the script in my head, and now you're backing out." I reach into my bag and grab a pencil and my English notebook. "I have to do some homework."

"No."

"No, what?"

"No, we're not done talking."

"Yeah, we are." I tap my notebook with my pencil. "I have homework."

He runs his hand through his hair and sighs. Then he gets up, gathers his books, and leaves.

I STRUGGLE THROUGH my homework, my mind still trying to figure out why Aiden doesn't want to be my hypothetical arm candy.

But then I decide I don't care. I'll cast someone else.

Dawson is hot; he'd make great arm candy. Of course, I don't know if he'd want to be arm candy or not. Riley would though. He'd be the perfect eye candy, really. He's cocky and would love it.

But, unfortunately, Aiden is right. I'd rather share my dream night with my dream guy. I don't just want arm candy.

But the odds of that happening are slim. Why do you think so many people take their mom to the Oscars? They've been working hard, filming all over the place, and don't have time for love.

I shake my head. This line of thought is silly.

I'll recast.

I'm walking my dream red carpet with Mom and Tommy. With my family. Not with some guy that can't just shut up and look pretty.

MY PHONE VIBRATES with a text that makes me smile.

> **Dawson:** *I miss you.*
>
> **Me:** *I miss you too.*
>
> **Dawson:** *How's practice going?*
>
> **Me:** *It's good. You should come sometime. I sit around a lot waiting for my scenes. I have all of my homework done. What have you been doing?*
>
> **Dawson:** *Well, I was supposed to go play racquetball with Bryce. But after dinner I came back to my room, thinking I'd just lie down for a minute. LOL I just woke up.*
>
> **Me:** *Did your cheerleader wear you out?*
>
> **Dawson:** *She did ;) Is she coming back tonight?*
>
> **Me:** *She isn't, but I'd like to. I need a goodnight kiss.*
>
> **Dawson:** *I'll be waiting. <3*

REHASHING IT.

10PM

WHEN I GET back to my dorm, I find Annie, Katie, and Maggie sitting on our bare floor.

"Where did the rug go?"

"Oh, I donated it to a worthy cause, but don't worry. I ordered us a new one. What's going on in here?"

"We're talking about Homecoming," Annie says.

"Rehashing it, really," Maggie corrects her.

"Did you end up having fun with Parker, Maggie? He seemed to like when we were up there dancing together."

"He did, but we're not going anywhere. It's really more of a friends with benefits thing."

Annie huffs. "Why would you settle for that? Don't you want him to ask you out?"

"No. I don't. We've been there. Done that. And it didn't go well. We fought constantly. Now we never fight."

"You just have sex," Annie states.

"That's not true. What's true is that when he starts to piss me off, I just leave or tell him to stop it. I didn't do that when we dated because I didn't want to mess up our relationship. I have more control now. Besides, it's not like we have any long-term potential. So this works for us."

"What will happen if he starts hanging out with someone else?" Annie counters.

"More power to him. I like him and his friends are fun to hang out with."

"I've had bad cramps for the last two days. My body is making me pay."

I lean over and give her a hug. "I'm sorry you don't feel well. Have you talked to Tyrese at all?"

"No, he's avoiding me like the plague. Like, we almost ran into each other in the hall and he literally turned around and walked the other way."

I decide a change of topic might be good. "Are you and Ace good, Annie?"

"We're perfect. He was such a gentleman and I loved getting to meet his mom. It was a dreamy weekend." She smiles and her cheeks flush. "And he loved the back of my dress. He kept putting his hand on my naked skin while we were dancing. It was hot."

Maggie's eyes get huge. "It was hot?"

"Yes, it was. Just because he makes me hot doesn't mean we are going to do anything. Some people can restrain themselves," she says, very judgmentally. She instantly puts her hand up to her mouth. "Oh, Katie, I'm sorry, I didn't mean that. I just meant . . ."

"It's okay, Annie," Katie says. "You better get going. It's almost curfew."

"Oh," Annie says, looking at the clock. "I guess you're right."

JUMPING OUT OF THE BUSHES.
MIDNIGHT

KATIE IS FAST asleep.

I'm sewing the sequined trim onto the cheerleading costume.

My phone vibrates.

Riley: *Cave tonight?*

Me: *I probably shouldn't.*

Riley: *Me and Ariela are over.*

Me: *WTF??!! Why???!!!! What happened?*

Riley: *I'll tell you at the Cave.*

Me: *Tell me now.*

Riley: *Dallas is coming. We'll discuss then.*

At one o'clock, I pull on a pair of sweat pants, grab a jacket, and sneak out of my room.

Riley jumps out of the bushes just as I crawl out of the window. He covers my mouth with his hand and muffles my scared scream.

"Shhh," he says.

"Don't jump out of the bushes at people and they won't scream. Where's Dallas?"

"He's already there. Even though we made it through Homecoming and I'm sure everything is fine, I didn't want you to walk by yourself."

"Aww, thanks, Riley."

We get to the Cave and find Dallas already smoking. We sit down next to him and Riley spreads a blanket out over our legs. It's starting to get chilly at night.

"So what happened?" I immediately ask.

"Smoke first. Questions later," Riley replies. I can tell he's upset.

Dallas says, "We're still keeping the rug."

"What's this got to do with the rug?"

"Everything," Riley says with a sigh. He hands me the joint and starts talking. "So, tonight, Ariela came to my room. I mean, we had a great time at Homecoming. A really great time. I didn't get a hotel room because I didn't want her to think that I expected sex. But then you gave me the rug."

"And?"

"And she came to my room tonight . . ." he hesitates.

"And?" I say again.

"And we were kissing on the rug. She liked it. Loved it. Commented about how soft it is. Then I sort of blurted out how I want to do her on it. How I've been thinking about it. Then I made a move."

"And she got pissed?"

"Yeah. Said she wants to be more than just sex. Of course, then I got pissed and asked if she was still talking to that guy from home. She said yes. I told her I haven't been talking to anyone since we started talking. Then I got more pissed. Told her I'd been going slower than I've ever gone in my life and I was sick of it. It went downhill from there."

I put my arm around his shoulder. "I'm sorry."

Dallas puts his arm around my shoulder. "What about me?"

"What about you kissing a girl in front of the whole math class? Are you even upset? Did you do that just to get back at her?"

"I was hurt at first. I've never been completely ditched like that. Then I was pissed. Then I just wanted to get even."

"Because she hurt you."

"Yeah, I guess." I give him a big hug. He wraps me in a hug and rubs his hands down my back. "I'm very, *very* hurt. I need you to help cheer me up, sweetie."

I wiggle out of his grip. "You're so full of shit," I say with a laugh.

He laughs too. "Fine. I don't really give a shit."

"I give a shit," Riley says pathetically. "For the first time in my life, I really give a shit. And it sucks."

"So are you going to try and win her back?"

"Nope. She wants to talk to other guys behind my back, then I'm going to be talking to other girls in front of her."

"You're going to try and make her jealous?"

"No. I'm done with her. I was really, excruciatingly, patient with her. I did everything I could to make her feel special. And if she's going to be pissed at me because I got hot and tried something, fuck her. A simple no would have sufficed."

Dallas says, "All right. You need to chill." Then he passes him back the joint.

Wednesday, October 12th

NEVER WEARING PLAID AGAIN.

10AM

PEYTON GRABS ME after math class and holds up a note. "What's that?"

"It's a pass. You, me, and Whitney are going on a field trip."

"A field trip with Whitney? Why?"

"We need to go to the party rental company's warehouse and look at props for Greek weekend. The drama department has a few columns, but they are too busy with the play to do anything custom for us. The art department is going to do some large canvas pencil drawings of classic statutes. Their teacher is giving them extra credit for it, so we should have that to line the walls of the banquet, but we need more."

"That sounds fun."

"Good. Now go change out of your uniform into something cute. I'm not wearing this plaid skirt in public."

"Oh, really? I just got a cute dress that I ordered online. I'm excited to wear it."

"What's it like?"

"It's a Thakoon mini. It has the cutest quilted leather sleeveless top and then a plaid straight skirt on the bottom. I'll probably wear it with a pair of black Burberry riding boots."

"The bottom is plaid?" Peyton asks, scrunching up her nose. "Don't you get sick of plaid? I swear, when I leave here I'm never wearing plaid again."

"I guess I haven't been here long enough to be sick of it."

"Fine, so go change and meet us outside your dorm in ten minutes."

WE GO TO the rental store and find a few more props.

"So, we headed back to school now?" I ask.

Whitney turns to look at me sitting in the backseat of Peyton's car. "We are going to the spa."

"But won't we get in trouble?"

"The spa is decorated with columns and has a Romanesque feel to it. We'll be immersing ourselves in the culture and brainstorming. It's strictly business," Peyton says with a laugh.

I laugh when we get to the spa. It has a total of two columns that flank the entrance to the hot tub. I look over a menu and sign up for a lavender bath. That's one thing I really miss from home. My bathtub. I soaked it in all the time to relax. My loft has a great bathtub, but I've yet to take a bath in it because Dawson prefers showers.

"We're getting massages and spa pedicures together," Peyton tells us. "I already booked those."

I nod even though I don't need a pedicure, since I just got one right before the dance. I don't want to rock the boat. Since Homecoming, things seem strained between Peyton and Whitney.

But, since they banished Rachel, Whitney's down a minion.

I'm just hoping she's not looking for a replacement.

No one really talks during the massages, which is fine with me.

Then I get to go soak in a fragrant bath for almost an hour.

I ask one of the spa helpers, who I could tell didn't speak much English, for a glass of white wine.

Needless to say, she did not ask me for ID, since I was naked in the tub, and I was thrilled when she walked back in with a glass of chilled Chardonnay.

I lean back in the tub, take a sip, and totally relax.

I'm not sure what I think of Whitney, but her idea of coming here was perfection.

AFTER MY BATH, I throw on my robe and meet the girls for our pedicures.

Whitney politely asks, "How was your bath?"

"It was amazing. They really need to install bathtubs at school."

She laughs. "I totally agree. So, Keatyn, Peyton seems to think you and I should get to know each other better. That was the whole point of today's little outing."

I smile at Peyton. She wears a pained expression, which lets me know for sure that this was not her idea at all. She's trying to pull away from Whitney, not get closer. I have a sneaking suspicion that this is one of those keep-your-friends-close-and-your-enemies-closer kind of things. Even though I was nice to her at Homecoming and appreciate her being civil, I doubt we'll ever be BFFs.

But, then again, maybe I should be nice and give her a chance.

"I'd like that," I say to Whitney. "Tell me about yourself."

"Well, you already know that I'm Dawson's ex and pretty much everyone at school loves me."

"Loves you or fears you?"

"Same difference," Whitney replies haughtily, with a wave of her hand. "And, let's face it, even you like sitting at my table."

Peyton rolls her eyes but doesn't contradict her.

"I like sitting with Dawson."

"Whatever. So, I think you know enough about me. I'm sure you made Dawson tell you all about us."

"Most of what he told me wasn't very happy. You hurt him. It hurts to have your heart broken."

"He told you that I broke his heart?"

"Yeah, he did. We talked about you at the Cave one night."

"Was that the night he was trying to make me jealous by flirting with you?"

"It was the next night after the dance. Everyone else was partying at Hawthorne, but we both ended up at the Cave. He told me he couldn't be your friend."

She scrunches up her nose. "Interesting. So that's how you got together. Did you sleep with him that night?"

I let out a loud laugh. "Not even close. He kissed me once and that was only to prove to me that he wasn't a bad kisser."

"Dawson is an amazing kisser."

"Well, not when he's drunk and you're not expecting it."

Peyton laughs. "I remember that. He stood up, which knocked Mariah off his lap, and walked straight across the room and kissed you. I actually thought it was kind of romantic."

"Trying to make your ex-girlfriend jealous is not romantic," Whitney and I both say at the exact same time.

We look at each other and laugh. "So, you lived in L.A. What do you think of Connecticut?"

"It's definitely different here. But I like it."

"Does that mean we're not getting rid of you anytime soon?"

I chuckle. Gosh, she reminds me of Vanessa. It almost makes me like her.

You have to appreciate that kind of confidence. "Afraid not."

Peyton smiles at me and touches my arm. "I'm glad you're staying. I know we're going to be good friends. Especially since we're in so much together. Dance Team, Soccer, Literary Club, and Student Council."

I study Peyton. She seems sincere, but I get the feeling she's listing all her activities for Whitney's benefit. She didn't mention Social Committee. She's trying to make Whitney feel left out.

"Don't forget Social Committee," I tell Peyton.

"Oh, yeah, I forgot about that."

Whitney glares at her. "Kind of hard to forget about it when that's why we're here."

"Are you feeling inspired for Greek weekend yet?" I laugh, trying to dissolve the tension.

"No, but I really want to go there now."

"Have you been there, Keatyn? I hear its coastline is very different from the French Riviera where your parents live."

Her comment makes me pause. How does she know where my parents live? I've never been that specific.

Then it hits me.

The school file. It had my parents' fake address in it.

"I have been to Greece, and you're right, Whitney, is does look different."

"So, you've traveled a lot?" Peyton asks me.

"Yes, quite a lot. I was homeschooled for most of my life because of my mom's job."

"Oh, really?" Whitney asks. "What does your mom do?"

"She's retired now but, before that, she worked in oil and gas." Oh my gosh. Where do these lies come from?

It's really kind of sad how good I'm getting at lying.

Whitney laughs, "She retired when she hit the lottery?"

I sigh. Just when I was thinking Whitney wasn't half bad, she reminds me what a bitch she is. "Yeah, something like that," I mutter.

AFTER LETTING OUR toes dry completely in the sauna, we decide it's time to head back to school. Whitney wants to get back in time to have dinner with Jake, and I haven't seen Dawson all day.

The three of us are standing at the counter to check out. For some reason, they put all of our charges together rather than separating them.

I get my credit card out of my bag and toss it onto the counter at the same time Whitney does the same with hers.

We both say, "I'll get it."

Whitney looks at me then down at our cards. My black one next to her platinum one.

I could give a crap what color anyone's credit card is, but obviously Whitney cares.

She gives me a puzzled look.

I shrug my shoulder, give her a smirk, and don't hide the sarcasm in my voice when I say, "Lottery."

A SILLY WASTE OF TIME.
7:50PM

I FLOAT INTO rehearsal feeling relaxed.

"I've changed my mind," Aiden says when he sits down next to me.

"About what?"

"About being your arm candy. If you need arm candy, I'll be there."

I can't stop from smiling. "Thank you."

"You like getting your way, don't you?"

"Um, yeah. Who doesn't?"

He laughs at me and then says, "You also need to finish telling me about that script you wrote. When did you write it?"

"I spent most of last summer in Europe and I had a lot of free time. The script is about a girl who makes a wish."

"Like, one of those movies where two people make the same wish at the same time and when they wake up they've switched bodies?"

"No. It's more like her wish sets other events in motion. Events that make her think she's on the verge of having everything she's ever dreamed of. But then it all comes crashing down."

"How so?"

"She finally gets the boy she wanted. Some guy offers her the lead role in a movie. It seems like her life is getting perfect, but it's not. The boy is selfish and doesn't really love her. And the guy that wants to make the movie with her is, um . . ."

"Sleazy?"

"Yeah, he's sleazy. And the boy who doesn't really love her moves away. She decides to move away too. Like, for a fresh start."

"And then what? Wait, let me guess. When she moves away, she meets a guy? The dream guy she should really be with?"

"I'm not sure. I haven't finished it yet. I stopped writing when I came here."

"Why?"

"Sometimes it seems like a silly waste of time."

"That sounds like something someone told you, not what you feel."

"The boy who moved away. When they were together, sometimes he'd catch her writing. He kind of thought it was dumb."

"Wait. Are we talking about the script or your real life?"

"The script. I think I'm going to make her parents be famous. Maybe actors themselves. Or screenwriters, or directors. I haven't figured that part out yet, exactly, but I do know that she's going to be afraid to follow in their footsteps."

"I could relate to that. My dad used to talk about me taking over his business. It was all about investments and it seemed really boring. I've liked being outside since I was a kid and when we moved to Napa, I felt like I was home. I could ride my horse, play in the dirt, kick a soccer ball around all day and not come in until it was dark. And then I fell in love with the whole growing process. I love the lifestyle. It fits me. Now, if my dad leaves me the Napa place, I will happily take it over. And in the meantime, I want to make a wine for charity."

"The wine you want to make will be for charity?"

"Yeah, like all the profits will go to good causes. Like, cancer research, maybe. Helping the homeless."

I study Aiden for a moment. The god continues to surprise me. "That'd be really cool," I tell him.

Because it would be.

I PULL MY phone out of my bag and check my texts. I have one from Braxton.

Braxton: *Magically delicious got me a date.*

Me: *Really? A date?*

Braxton: *Okay, not a date. She's coming over to help me study. Tonight. In like five minutes. I'm a little nervous.*

Me: *Why?*

Braxton: *She's seventeen. And slutty.*

Me: *I thought you were grounded. And do you really want a slutty girl?*

Braxton: *I got the grounding lifted with my exemplary behavior at Homecoming. And I can't decide.*

Me: *I think you should find a nice girl your own age. Don't rush it. Kiss. Enjoy it. Seriously, kissing is my all-time favorite thing. The more you practice, the better you are at it. I think you should focus on that. Not sex.*

Braxton: *We'll see. Got any new lines?*

Me: *Yes. "Have you always been so cute? Or did it take practice?"*

Braxton: *That's kind of lame.*

Me: *Not as lame as Riley's was. His was "I grind so fine, I'm practically coffee."*

Braxton: *That one is AWESOME!! I'm totally using that.*

Me: *NO! You want to make it all about the girl. Riley's made him sound like an arrogant jerk. Dallas' made me laugh. I think that's the key to a successful pickup line. When you make a girl laugh, you break the ice, and lower her guard. You seem like you would be fun to hang out with. Are there some cute girls in your classes?*

Braxton: *There's one that's really pretty. She's almost as tall as me. Long dark hair. Big brown eyes with the longest eyelashes ever. I heard she's going to Eastbrooke's Prospective Student Weekend.*

Me: *You should ask her on a date. Take her to a movie. Buy her popcorn. Hold her hand. Kiss her goodnight.*

Braxton: *I'll think about it.*

Thursday, October 13th

REVOKED.

LUNCH

TYRESE DECIDES TO grace our table with his presence today.

I start to get up when he sits down. "I'm not sitting next to him," I tell Dawson when he grabs my arm.

"Stay. I'll tell him to leave." He turns to Tyrese. "What you did to Keatyn's friend was not cool."

Tyrese holds up his hands. "She was all over me, bro. What else was I going to do? I was drunk."

"Why don't you go sit somewhere else. You haven't sat here most of the year anyway."

Tyrese looks at him, like he can't believe Dawson chose me over his friend. "If that's the way you want it," he says, picking up his tray and walking away.

Minion #2 says directly to Whitney, "What the hell is going on here?"

Minion #3 agrees. "That's what I'd like to know. Yesterday, you and Peyton take Keatyn with you to the spa instead of us."

"You're not on Social Committee," Whitney says.

"And now, today, the tramp is in charge of our seating arrangements?"

My eyes widen in shock. "Are you calling me a tramp?"

Minion #2 puffs her chest out. "Yes, I am."

"Then you should go with sit with Tyrese," I tell her flatly. I'm not going to get all pissed off. It's what she wants.

"I'm not going anywhere. I've been sitting at this table for the past . . ."

Peyton interrupts and shakes a finger at them. "You've been sitting at this table for the past two years because Whitney and I allowed you to. That status has been revoked. Effective immediately. Why don't you take your jealous little selves and go sit with Rachel."

They both stare at Peyton in confusion. Like she spoke to them in a different language.

"Both of you, go," Peyton says. Then she looks at Minion #1.

Minion #1 doesn't even give her the chance to speak. "I don't think Keatyn is a tramp. I think she's very nice."

Her two friends stomp their way over to sit with Rachel at the end of a table full of awkward sophomore boys.

Jake laughs. "They're dropping like flies. Pretty soon it'll be just me and you, Monroe."

"I'm not going anywhere," Whitney says with an air of superiority.

"I'm just teasing, baby," he replies.

ALL HOT AND SWEATY.
6:50PM

AFTER DINNER, DAWSON walks me to rehearsal and kisses me up against the side of the building.

"You know, you could come sit inside with me. I'm only up on stage when my scenes are up. The whole rest of the time I'm just sitting around doing homework."

"A bunch of guys are having a pickup basketball game tonight. You could skip and come watch. I'll be all hot and sweaty." He leans down and kisses up my neck. "Or you could just come to my room and get me all hot and sweaty yourself."

"Hmmm, I'm pretty sure I got you all hot and sweaty before dinner."

He runs his fingers through my hair and kisses my cheek. "You own me. You know that, right? Totally and completely own me."

"You're my sex slave," I tease.

"I could skip the game. We could lie around naked in my room for the next three hours."

"We couldn't lie in your room for three hours naked and you know it. We'd get caught."

"Hmm, maybe. So this weekend, when we visit your parents. Are we going to have some time alone?"

"After we put them to bed, I'm sure I'll be sneaking you into my room.

Then you can have me naked all night long."

My phone beeps. "Shit, Dawson, it's after seven. I'm supposed to be in there!"

I start to pull away from him, but he pulls me back in for one more long, steamy kiss.

"I love you," he tells me, then holds the door to the auditorium open for me.

I RUN INTO the auditorium, set my bag down, and am immediately called onto the stage.

I do a scene where all the bachelorettes are getting ready for the contest together. In this scene, the audience sees the true personality of each contestant. The contestants are pretty clichéd. The sweet girl (me), the slutty girl, the stuck up debutante, and the girl from the wrong side of the tracks. I nail my lines, not having to refer to my script once.

Then I walk off the stage and look for Aiden so we can do our French homework.

He's in his usual spot in the back.

When I sit down next to him he says, "So, I'm doing a survey for health class. I'm going to need you to answer a few questions for me."

"About what?"

He leans close to me. Does that thing where he lets his lips just barely touch my ear and says in French, "Sexe."

I pull away and roll my eyes at him. "Why doesn't that surprise me?"

He rubs his hand across his seemingly perpetual stubble. "Of course, all your answers will be kept in confidence."

"Do you ever shave anymore?"

He leans back toward me and rubs his stubble up the side of my face. It's a total Cush move. One that makes me smile remembering how I told him I had Cushburn. Aiden misinterprets my smile as confirmation that I like what he just did.

"Girls say they love stubble. For specific reasons," he says with all sorts of swagger and confidence in his voice, leaving me no doubt that's exactly what girls have been telling him. And probably why he hasn't shaved.

I pull my hair behind my ear, fully exposing my cheek. "Is my cheek red?"

He studies it for a second, then replies, "No."

"That's because you have a baby face with soft stubble. It does make you look older, though." And hotter too, if that's even possible, but I don't tell him that. "Girls like rough stubble." I give him a smirk and then add, "For those specific reasons."

He closes his eyes and takes a deep breath. Kind of like my mom does when she's about ready to lose it and is trying not to.

"So, let's start with the questions. How old were you when you lost your virginity?"

"Wow. That's kind of personal."

"The questions are about sex. They're all personal."

"I was sixteen. How old were you?"

"I'm not answering the survey."

"Neither am I, if you don't answer my question."

He sighs again. "I was fifteen, if you must know. Next question. How long had you been dating the guy you lost your virginity to?"

"Uh." I think back. I dated Cush for, what was it, a day? I can't answer that question. I'd sound like a slut. "No comment."

He tilts his head at me. "That's not an answer."

I grab his little notebook, write No Comment on it, and hand it back to him. "It is now."

"How long?" he asks again sternly.

"I didn't expect to do it with him, okay? It just kind of happened."

"Kind of happened?"

"Yes. It was spontaneous."

"So it was just a hookup?'

I scowl at him. "No, it wasn't just a hookup."

"You're used to getting what you want when you want it."

"No! I don't get what I want." I put on my pout face. Just so he knows that I'm serious about it.

Aiden flicks my pouty bottom lip with his finger. "Come on. Look at you. You flash that little pout and boys fall at your feet."

"They do not!"

"Okay, how long did you date Dawson before you had sex?"

"One. That is not one of your questions. And, two. It's none of your business."

"Fine. How about the Keats guy?"

"That one I will answer. I knew him for almost two years before we did."

"That wasn't the question. Once you got together, how long did you wait?"

Shit. He made me wait. All of about 8 days.

"Eight days."

"And the virginity friend?"

"That doesn't matter. I dated a guy for a year and a half before him and we never did it!"

"Was he gay?"

Shit! How the hell did he guess that? Has the stubble on his face added to his power? Has he mastered mind reading?

I try to clear my mind of all thoughts.

He grins at me. "I can tell by your face the answer is yes."

"No, he just wanted to wait until he was married."

"Bullshit."

"Fine. He may have been gay but I didn't know it."

Aiden bumps my elbow with his. "I bet that drove you nuts. Did you try and get him to?"

"Yes. And it sucked. Being turned down after a year of dating someone sucks."

"What did you do to try and seduce him?"

"Lingerie."

Aiden leans his chin on his hand on top of the armrest separating us. "What did it look like?"

I push his elbow off the armrest, completely catching him off guard and causing his chin to drop down.

Cheerleader Bachelorette. Bad Prince. You're up.

I give him a smirk, set my homework on the floor, and go up on stage.

THE BAD PRINCE, Logan, and I run through our lines. He tells me that he's a prince and about the contest. What he fails to tell me is that he has a brother who happens to be the guy I had the most amazing date ever with. He tells me it will be good for my career. That reality shows are all scripted anyway. That even if I'm not chosen to be the princess, I'll get lots of jobs from the show. I decide to do it. Then he kisses me. And, tonight, Logan actually takes me completely by surprise and kisses me. Wraps his arm around my waist, pulls me in tight, and lays a fat kiss on my lips.

I manage to stay in character. And my character likes his kiss. He's handsome, and, come on, he's a freaking prince! Of course I'm going to be fine with a kiss. Even though it's not a true love kiss—but, then again, the true love kiss guy still hasn't called.

"Ok," the director says. "Let's try that kiss again. Keatyn, I think I'd like to see a little more body language from you. This guy is a prince. I'd like you to lean your body into him. We want this kiss to be very different, visually, from the sweet kiss you had with the Good Prince."

I nod my head. "Got it."

Logan says his last line. Then he grabs my waist. This time, I don't fight it. I push my body into his, slide my hand around the back of his neck, and pull his face toward mine as I kiss him.

"Yes! I like that! That will really make the audience question your intentions. Is she a scheming slut or the sweet true love girl? Love it."

"Thanks," I say to the director. To Logan, who still doesn't really seem to like me much, I ask, "What do you think?"

He grins at me for the first time ever and replies, "I think we could do better than that with a little more practice."

I WALK OFF the stage and sit back down in my seat. Aiden isn't here, but his backpack is sitting on the floor. I'm still trying to figure out what Logan meant by that. Does he really want to practice for the play's sake?

I will admit, he makes a really good Bad Prince. The girls in makeup decided to add a dark henna tattoo across his back for the play. And we all know that he has a damn good back. Honestly, the way the makeup girls were giggling, I think the tattoo is as much for them as it is for the audience. Either way, the audience will get to see his shirtless back when he gets down and dirty with the slutty bachelorette in a hot tub scene. She is the one who just wants him for his money.

AIDEN SITS BACK down next to me.

"Where were you?"

"I've been surveying some of the other cast members and talking to Logan."

"Learn anything exciting?"

"Not yet. You need to finish telling me about trying to seduce the gay guy."

"What else is there to tell? It didn't work. But he was a great boyfriend. Never looked at another girl. Treated me like a princess. And he was my favorite person to shop with."

"You haven't shopped with me yet. And don't worry, I'm definitely not gay."

"I liked the shoes you had on at the dance. They were different. You'd be fun to dress."

"What do you mean?"

"I don't know. You kind of look like a life-sized Ken doll. All blond and lean. You wear clothes well."

"Thank you. I think when the play is over and you have a free weekend, we should go shopping together."

"We could stay at my loft. I have extra bedrooms."

"I heard about your loft."

"From who?"

"Peyton."

"What did she say?"

"She said it's you. Over the top cool but completely casual and comfortable. She said you must have the coolest parents ever."

I smile. What she said almost makes me want to cry.

Aiden studies me. "Your eyes are all shiny. Did I say something wrong?"

"No, that's just exactly how I hoped it would be."

"Being here without your family is hard on you, isn't it?"

"Yeah, but at the same time it's like I'm able to grow up. Like I've had to grow up. Do things on my own. I picked the place out completely by myself, bought it, and had it furnished."

"You bought it? Not your parents?"

I lean closer to him and speak softly. "No one knows this. But when my parents moved it created some problems. Like, they couldn't just sign school notes every day."

"That's understandable."

"So I had to get emancipated. Legally, I'm an adult. And my grandpa gave me my trust fund early. The loft was one of my first purchases."

"Peyton said that place had to cost $20 million."

I raise my eyebrows and shrug my shoulders. "It's a really nice trust fund. But I haven't gone crazy. My car and the loft are the only things I've bought. And Grandpa always told me real estate is a good investment."

"You respect your grandpa. Is he the one that gave you the boots you wore the day you did your speech?"

"Yeah, he is. He lives on a simple ranch. Lots of land and a nice home, but compared to his net worth, very simple."

"That's how the place in Napa is. Lots of land. The house is big. But it's very causal and comfortable."

"I love places like that."

"You're an interesting girl. Like, the more I find out about you, the more I want to know. And I need to know more in order to finish the sex survey."

"I'm pretty sure we're done with the sex survey."

"No, we're not. There are questions you didn't respond to." He flips back a couple pages in his notebook. "Okay, so the Keats guy you knew for two years, but once you got together, you waited eight days. What about the virginity guy?"

I close my eyes. "A day. But there were extenuating circumstances."

"Such as?"

I hang my head. "The Keats guy upset me. And . . ."

Aiden's hand brushes my knee as he leans across me.

I look up at him. I expect to see judgmental eyes, but I don't. They are soft and caring. Like he wants to know.

"And what?" he says gently.

"I was tired of waiting for love." I sigh big. "The Keats guy and I got together. Like, we kissed. We hung out. It felt different. He quoted me poetry and I was so happy. Then there was this camping trip I was supposed to go on with him and his friends. They left without me. I thought he was hooking up with other girls. That was the first time he sort of broke my heart."

"And the second time he broke your heart, was that Labor Day Weekend?"

"That was the third time."

"Is that why you slept with Dawson in the Hamptons?"

"I never said I slept with Dawson in the Hamptons."

"Who did you sleep with the second time he broke your heart?

"No one."

"What'd he do?"

"He wouldn't dance with me at my birthday party."

Aiden shakes his head. "What a douche. Why would you even give a guy like that a third chance?"

I blow out a big breath of air. "Love."

Aiden puts down his notebook. "Want to know the findings of my survey?"

"Uh, sure. When you figure it out."

"I already have. I think I learned it last year, but after interviewing a lot of people, I've confirmed it."

I nod my head at him, telling him to go on.

"Sex doesn't equal love."

I think about my sweet, sexy ass Dawson and say, "I agree with you on that point, but sometimes, if you're really lucky, sex can lead to love." I grab my phone and say, "Excuse me," to Aiden.

"Hey," I say when Dawson answers.

"Hey, yourself. You about done with practice?"

"It's not really over yet, but I don't think they are going to get to my next scene, so I'm going to sneak out of here. I need some real kisses. Not fake play kisses."

THE FIRST THING out of Dawson's mouth when I get to his room is, "Just how many fake kisses did you get tonight?"

"Just one. But the director didn't like it, so he made us do it again. Differently."

"Who did you kiss?"

"The Bad Prince."

Dawson pulls me onto his bed and kisses me. "I can be bad."

"I'm pretty sure we couldn't do your kind of bad in front of an audience." I run my hand through the back of his hair and down his back. Then I just wrap my arms around him and hug him. Tightly.

He pulls me closer to his chest and hugs me back. "What's this for?"

"I love you, Dawson. I did this survey thing tonight about sex and the person's conclusion was that sex doesn't equal love, but I told him that sometimes, if you're really lucky, sex can lead to love. I feel really lucky to be with you. I can't tell you how excited I am for you to meet my family. For us to spend the weekend with them. I'm sorry that I waited so long to tell you that I love you. I was just scared. I'm not scared anymore. I totally and completely am in love with you."

He buries his head in my chest and gives me another hug. "I love you too, Keatie. I know we did things a little bit backward, but it worked for us. You made me believe in love again."

I get tears in my eyes because he makes me so happy. "You made me believe in love too."

He kisses me. Just kisses me. Over and over again until I have to leave to make curfew.

AN EMERGENCY LANDING.
11PM

AFTER I GET to my room, I dig through my clothes and pack for our trip. We'll be leaving at six, which doesn't give me much time to shower and get ready after dance practice.

I pack mostly casual clothes. Yoga pants and sweatshirts for hanging out with the girls. A cute sweater dress and boots to wear for dinner Saturday night. A sexy bra and panties for Dawson's enjoyment. A skirt, tights, sweater and boots to wear back home.

I'm so excited I can hardly stand it. My little sisters are going to be so surprised. Mom and Tommy will be happy. And I'll even get to meet Kiki, my namesake dog.

I fall into bed, close my eyes, and imagine how good it will feel to hug my family again.

I WAKE A few hours later in a cold sweat. I was on the plane with Dawson. I told him everything and he was super supportive and understanding, but then the captain announced that we were making an emergency landing. Vincent walked out of the cockpit dressed as a pilot. He pulled a gun out of his pocket and shot Dawson. I started screaming.

Friday, October 14th

EFFORTLESS.

DRAMA

JUST AS THE bell rings for the end of drama class, my teacher says, "Miss Monroe, could you stay for a moment, please?"

"Sure," I say.

He walks up to the stage and sits on it.

"We called you on stage at 9:45 last night to do a scene and you weren't here."

"Oh, I'm sorry. I left a little early because I didn't think you'd get to any more of my scenes."

"You have a lot of raw talent. Acting seems to be effortless for you. But you need to understand that acting is a business. It's long hours, hard work, and commitment."

I'm tempted to tell him that I know exactly what is required of an actor. I've seen it. Lived it.

I'm also tempted to tell him that I quit. It pisses me off that he has the nerve to suggest I'm not committed.

I'm the only one who has all her freaking lines memorized!

And it sucks not seeing Dawson every night from seven until ten. That's really our only free time all day. And I'm not sure a stupid school play is worth it.

"I'm thinking about quitting," I blurt out.

"That would be upsetting. You have star potential and I'd hate to see you waste it because of a boy."

"It's not just because of a boy," I lie.

"Tell you what," he says. "Take this weekend to think about it. I'll expect an answer from you on Tuesday."

SECOND-GUESS MYSELF.
5:30PM

I'M SITTING ON Dawson's bed trying not to second-guess myself.

But my drama teacher pissed me off and that stupid dream left me rattled.

So, now I'm worried about, well, everything.

How will Dawson take the truth?

Will he understand? Will he be mad?

Will he freak out about Vincent? Will it make him treat me differently?

Will Tommy and Mom get pissed at me for showing up?

And the fact that Dawson still isn't packed is making me even more stressed.

Our car will be here in ten minutes.

He's standing in his mess of a closet, not really doing anything, just staring at it.

I'm about to start pulling clothes out of it and packing for him when his phone buzzes.

I glance at it.

Whitney: *Baby, please.*

I instantly can't breathe.

I want to look at the rest of their texts. I want to know what else she said. I could be sneaky and read them. He wouldn't notice. But I decide on a direct approach instead.

"Dawson."

"Yeah?"

"You just got a text from Whitney."

He walks out of the closet looking pale. "Uh, I, um . . . we're just talking."

"Just talking does not say, *Baby please*. I get it. We did it. Our image makeover was successful and now she wants you back, right?"

He stands stick still. "Yeah, I guess."

Tears start to prickle my eyes. "When were you going to tell me?"

He still doesn't move. "She just started texting me. I wasn't sure what to tell you." He finally moves, grabs his phone off the desk, and hands it to me. "Just read it."

Whitney: *When we danced for old time's sake at Homecoming, you can't deny that we both felt something. You and I together is how it was always supposed to be. That's why you stopped dancing with me so suddenly, because you felt it, right?*

Dawson: *I stopped dancing with you because I didn't want to hurt Keatyn.*

Whitney: *I'm sorry I broke up with you.*

Dawson: *Thanks for saying it, but it's too late.*

Whitney: *It's never too late. I'm really sorry, baby. If I could take it all back, I would. Don't go out of town with her this weekend. Stay here with me. We can hang out and see what happens. I promise I'll make it all up to you.*

Whitney: *Baby, please.*

I want to tell Dawson that she is a lying bitch who slept with his brother. But I don't want that to be the reason he chooses me.

I want him to choose me because he loves me.

"Is that really true? Is that why you stopped dancing with her?"

"She said, *Peyton never would've won if we were still together*. And I said, *Yeah, you're right, but then you dumped me for some college asshole*. That's when I got pissed and walked away."

"And now she's begging?"

"Yeah."

"And that was what you wanted all along."

"Yeah."

"Is that all we were? You took my idea of making her want you? Was it all about making her jealous?"

"No, it wasn't. Keatie, I do love you. I meant everything I've ever said to you."

I hold up my hand. "Don't, okay. Don't lie."

"I've never lied to you about anything."

"This week when I was at rehearsal. Were you talking to her then, too?"

"No. This completely caught me off guard. And I want to meet your parents but . . ."

"But why bother?"

"No. Just give me a minute. I just need a minute to think."

"You don't need a minute to think, Dawson. You've already decided. You're not packed. That says it all."

"I just . . . try to understand." He puts his hand to his forehead and rubs it across his temple. "It's what I wanted for so long."

I nod, holding back the tears, and calmly walk past him to the bathroom.

When I open the door, Jake is standing naked in front of the sink. He shoves a towel in front of himself and yells, "Keatyn, what the hell?"

"You and Whitney are still going out, right?"

He looks at me like I'm an idiot. "Yeah, I'm getting ready to go pick her up."

"You should maybe look at this first." I hand him Dawson's phone.

He reads the texts and his eyes get big. "That bitch."

"Yes, she is," I say as I walk back into Dawson's room.

"So, congratulations, you're finally getting what you dreamed of." I take the key from around my neck, drop it into his hand, and say, "I understand perfectly."

Then I walk out his door and hope the drama of giving him back the key to his heart will make him think. Will make him realize her doesn't want her.

I stand outside his door for a minute, expecting him to come running out to say, I'm sorry. I didn't mean it. I don't want her. I love you.

But he doesn't.

I wait for a few more minutes.

I picture him tossing the key on his dresser and happily calling Whitney to tell her yes.

And it starts to sink in.

We're over.

I start to tear up as I walk down the hall in a daze because I can't believe it.

Can't believe he would do that.

Aiden walks by me. "Boots, are you okay?"

I look at his green eyes and shake my head. Because I'm not okay. But I say, "I'm fine," and walk quickly past him.

Then I start running. I don't even think about where to go. I run straight to Dallas and Riley's room and pound on their door.

The minute Riley opens it, I lose it. I dive my head into his chest and start bawling.

"Aw, shit," he says. "Am I gonna have to kick my brother's ass?"

I nod my head and keep crying. Then I start babbling about Whitney, and her text, and how he never loved me. How no one ever really loves me.

He wraps me in a tight hug and pats my back to comfort me.

Dallas walks in saying, "I just ran into Jake. Keatyn and Dawson just broke . . ." He sees me and stops talking.

"Up," I say, finishing his sentence. "We were supposed to leave for the airport in a few minutes."

My phone buzzes with a text.

I hold it tight to my chest and pray it's Dawson.

That he's sorry. That he's stupid. That he realizes he made a mistake. That he doesn't want her.

That he loves me.

Only me.

For the first time in my life, I'm a little disappointed to see a text from Damian.

D: *I don't care what plans you have for this weekend. Change them. One of the Moran Films' jets is sitting at an airport near you waiting for your arrival. (Don't tell Dad. I worked it all out with Margie, his assistant.) The crew is "waiting to pick up guests who won a contest." I didn't want anyone you knew from the past on the plane, so there is just a pilot and co-pilot. Bring the guy who treats you too well, bring some friends. Whatever you want. Just get your ass here. We'll tell your friends we know each other from grade school. Which is true.*

Me: *You have NO idea how perfect your timing is. Just broke up with the guy who was treating me too well. His ex texted him and said baby please and now he wants her back. I was supposed to take him on a trip this weekend. To meet my parents.*

D: *I can't believe your parents were okay with that.*

Me: *I was going to surprise them all. I figured if no one but me knew I was coming, V couldn't know. He said he loved me, Damian. I believed him. I was going to tell him everything. I'm an idiot.*

D: *Guess my ass-kicking list just got longer.*

Me: *Are you talking about my ass? Because I'm stupid to believe boys when they say they love me?*

D: *We'll see :) Bring something hot for the club. Don't worry about a place to stay.*

Me: *I love you. Seriously.*

D: *Are you gonna cry on me?*

Me: *Shut up. Me and my tears will see you soon.*

I look up at Riley as he says, "Good news?"

"Do you two have any plans this weekend?"

"Not really," Dallas says. "Unless you consider trying to avoid Ariela and Katie plans."

I smile. All three of us are single. "Sounds like the perfect time for us to get the hell out of here and have some fun." I hold up my phone. "That was my friend."

Riley shakes his head. "I was hoping it was my brother, coming to his senses."

I shake my head as tears flood my eyes again. "No, my friend is going to be performing at a club in Miami. He invited us to come."

"We just gonna go to the airport and catch a flight?" Dallas asks.

"I have that taken care of."

Dallas grins at me. "Sound like me and Riles here need to pack quick."

"I need to repack. I was taking Dawson . . ." I stop myself and try not to start crying again. "I packed for colder weather. Now all I need is a couple bikinis, a hot outfit for the club, and maybe something to wear to dinner." I smile at them. I'm so glad they are coming with me. "Meet me at my dorm in five. A car is coming to pick us up."

I RUN BACK to my dorm with my head down. I don't want anyone to see me. I'm sure I'm a mess.

I make it back into my room without having to talk to anyone, kick my suitcase, grab a different bag, and toss some clothes into it.

Jake texts me.

Jake: *I'm so fucking pissed.*

Me: *I told you this would happen.*

Jake: *Funny thing is, I thought I was using her.*

Me: *Yeah :(*

Jake: *I cheated on her. I felt bad about it.*

Me: *I know you did. Please don't tell her even though you are mad. It would be bad for the girl.*

Jake: *Are you okay? Dawson's an idiot if you ask me. He's gonna realize what a big mistake he made.*

Me: *Doubtful.*

Jake: *Wanna hook up? Piss them both off?*

Me: *I'm pretty sure your moral code points just north of sleazy.*

Jake: *<3 That may be the best compliment anyone ever gave me, Monroe. I'm touched.*

Me: *I'm going out of town but when I get back, let's party.*

Jake: *You sure you're okay?*

Me: *Not really, but I'll live.*

My phone rings. I want to ignore it, but I see it's school security. I answer, ask them to send up the car, and meet Dallas and Riley out front.

LOOKING GOOD IS THE BEST REVENGE.

6:15PM

WE PILE INTO the town car and head to the airport.

On the way there, Dawson calls three times. I don't bother answering, so he texts me.

> **Dawson:** *I keep trying to call you. You need to let me explain.*
>
> **Me:** *You weren't packed. You don't need to explain. Have fun with Whitney. And don't text me again.*

When we get to the executive airport, the town car pulls out onto the tarmac, and we hop out, grab our bags, and board the plane.

"Miss Monroe? I'm Captain Cummings. Were you informed of our situation for the flight down?"

I shake his hand. "Situation?"

"We're running without a staff for this flight. I was told you could handle seating and serving yourself?"

I smile. "I think we can handle that."

"Excellent," he says. "My co-pilot and I will do our pre-flight check and then we'll announce when you should take your seats. Please help yourself to the galley. It's fully stocked."

He shuts the cockpit door as Riley whistles and runs his hand across the leather couch. "This is nice."

Dallas is already at the bar. "Miss Monroe," he says to me. "You look like you could use a drink."

"I think we all need a drink," Riley says.

Dallas pours us three shots of top shelf tequila. I start to down mine but Dallas says, "Not so fast there, Kiki." He holds his glass up and sings. "Here's to the three best friends anyone could have."

"Shouldn't we be the two best friends?"

"I'm including myself. There's three of us."

"I love you guys," Riley says.

Which makes me start crying again. His voice sounds like Dawson's.

And it doesn't help that my phone keeps vibrating.

I look down and see I have eight missed calls and a couple texts.

> **Dawson:** *Keatie, please.*

Me: *"Baby, please" might have worked for her. Keatie, please, is NOT going to work for you.*

I slam my phone down. "Riley, please call your brother and tell him to stop calling and texting me. It's stressing me out," I cry. "I can't take it."

He grabs his phone as Dallas hands us each another shot. I down it quickly.

Riley calls Dawson. "Hey, bro. Just thought I'd let you know that me and Dallas are headed out of town with Keatyn for the weekend. Please quit calling her. She's not going to answer."

"Um, yeah, very. What the hell did you expect?"

"Yeah, well you know how I feel about her. And that makes you an asshole in my book."

"Yep."

I interrupt Riley. "Wait! I do want to talk to him."

Riley hands me his phone and I say, "Why do you keep calling me?"

He replies, "Keatie, I'm sorry. I just wanted it for so long. And now she's offering and I just feel like I need to see. Please don't be mad at me."

"Don't be mad at you? Are you fucking kidding me? This is what you wanted all along. Congratulations. Now you've got it. You won."

"Will you stop saying that? Yes, it's what I wanted, but when you walked out that door, I felt like part of me died."

"I'm actually glad to hear that. Bye."

I immediately get on Facebook and do something I usually don't care about. I change my Facebook status from *In a Relationship* to *Single.*

Then I put as my status, *Gonna party all weekend with my two favorite boys* and tag Riley and Dallas.

Dallas sees it. "Hey, you tagged me. Sweet. I'm gonna change mine too. Read it."

I scroll down my newsfeed and read, "*Dallas McMahon is fly like a G6.* Cute."

Riley holds out his phone, so I can see his new status.

Riley Johnson: *My brother's an asshole. Team Kiki all the way!*

Dallas laughs. "I have to like that status."

My phone buzzes with a Facebook notification. "Oh, wow."

"What?" both Riley and Dallas say.

"Aiden just liked my status. The single status."

"Well, of course he would," Riley says. "He likes you."

"He does not."

"He also liked my team Kiki status."

Riley's phone keeps buzzing and buzzing.

"Damn, baby, lots of people are team Kiki. We all love you."

"Thanks Riles," I say, then I grab a blanket, put my head on his lap, and try to sleep.

But, of course, I can't. I lie here instead and think about Dawson. How could I have been so wrong? How can you go from crazy happy and *You own me* to *I just need to see.* I think about Brooklyn. About Cush. About how I thought I was being so smart by waiting until I knew I loved Dawson to tell him. How I waited until I was sure he loved me. And how I even waited for a while after that. I waited until after he asked me to Homecoming. Until I knew I felt it. Until I really trusted him. I was going to tell him everything tonight. I am an idiot.

I guess I do doze off because Riley wakes me up. "Baby, I gotta pee."

"Oh, sorry," I say, sitting up.

"Besides," Dallas says, "how can you sleep? We are in a freaking amazing jet. I'm living a rap video."

"So where is the Cristal and all the hot girls?" Riley asks.

I smile. "Well, your crew is kinda small, but no one really likes you, so that's no surprise."

"There isn't Cristal, but I saw a few bottles of Dom," Dallas says with a grin.

"Pop it," I say.

When Riley comes out of the bathroom, Dallas tells him, "Let's make a video."

"A video?" I ask.

"Yeah, my own personal rap star video."

I pour myself another shot, slam it, and decide to have some fun. "Hang on."

I grab my bag, run in the bathroom, and redo my makeup. Heavy eyes. Red lips. I tease my hair out with my hands, flip my head upside down, and hairspray it, making it big and slutty looking. Then I put on one of my bikini tops, a pair of daisy dukes, and my highest platforms. I pull my thong up so you can see it just above my low-cut shorts. Mom always says, Looking good is the best revenge.

And I'm about to get some revenge.

Riley whistles, "Damn, baby."

I look at the boys. They are both still in some version of their uniforms. I make Riley take off his shirt and tie, then throw the tie back on, so that it's on his naked chest. Then I have him put his navy blazer back on. "Sunglasses?" I ask.

He gets a pair of Aviators out of his backpack and puts them on.

I stand back and look at him.

Perfect.

Next I grab Dallas, spike his hair up with some gel, strip him down to his boxers, then put his shirt back on, leaving it all unbuttoned. Then I throw his loosely done tie back around his neck. He grabs a pair of Ray Bans out of his bag and puts them on. He looks at himself in the small mirror above the bar.

"Oh, yeah," he croons. "Let's make a video." He plugs his iPhone into the speakers, sets it to repeat, and cranks up the volume.

I start by shaking the bottle of Dom.

Riley videos the bottle.

Me popping it.

Then Dallas holds the bottle as champagne shoots suggestively into my mouth.

Dallas swigs from the bottle, and I start dancing up against him.

I also figure, *What the hell.* It's not like we've never kissed, so I grab him and make out with him a little.

Dallas videos Riley rapping.

Then some shots of me sitting in Riley's lap.

I grab a pilot's hat and jacket from the closet, make Riley change into them, and then sit him in one of the Captain's chairs. It's not the cockpit, but we can pretend.

Dallas videos me walking up to Pilot Riley, straddling him, and playfully putting his pilot's hat on my head.

Riley pretends to fly a plane, while I'm pretending to, uh, fly him.

I give him a lap dance of sorts.

Then we all get up and dance. Riley holds the camera out away from us all grinding together. Drinking champagne. Being naughty.

Looking like we're ready to have a wild threesome.

I pull on Riley's tie, pulling him toward me.

Kiss Dallas again.

Then kiss Riley on the cheek.

All of us singing.

Riley adds some pan shots of the inside of the plane then decides he wants a few shots of me by myself.

Me with a new bottle of champagne.

Me in sunglasses dancing.

Me doing a slutty dance in front of the kitchen counter.

Some of just my ass.

Then Dallas pulling me into the bathroom, like we're joining the Mile High Club.

I get behind the camera and film the boys together, pretending like they are trying to get me to come with them.

Then us all doing shots.

Finally Riley says, "I think I have enough," then pulls out his Mac, uploads all of the video, and starts editing it.

By the time we start our descent into Miami, I'm tipsy and the video is complete.

Naughty, fun, and complete.

We watch it one more time and laugh hysterically.

"Dawes is gonna come unglued," he says with a naughty grin.

"He probably won't even see it. He's probably all enthralled by Whitney."

"Whitney is nothing like you, Keatyn," Riley tells me. "She's a cold-hearted bitch."

"You have no idea," I say. Shit. I shouldn't have said that. I immediately look guilty.

"What? What do you know?"

"I can't tell you."

"You can tell me and you will," Riley says very sternly.

I grab Dallas and whisper what I know into his ear. He looks at me and says, "Are you sure?"

"Yes, Peyton told me."

Dallas tells Riley what Whitney did. How she slept with his brother, and when she couldn't get him, settled for Dawson. How this was supposed to be their year.

"You can't tell Dawson," I say. "It would kill him. We talked one day about Peyton being pretty and he said he could never like her because she'd been with his brother. How that would be sick. He has no idea."

Riley shakes his head. "I can't believe Cam never told me."

"Dawson was a freshman when it happened, so maybe you were too young or something."

"He's had plenty of time since then. And why the hell didn't he tell Dawson? They didn't have sex for months after they started going out. He should have told him."

"Yeah, probably."

Riley leans over and kisses me on the cheek.

I'm half tempted to kiss him back.

Riley uploads the finished video to Facebook and his phone starts buzzing like crazy. "People are seeing the video and commenting!"

Dallas messes with his phone. "Holy shit, we have 67 views already!"

"Uh, oh," Riley groans.

"What?"

"My brother is not a happy camper. Look what he just texted me."

I look.

Dawson: *WHAT THE FUCK?*

"Reply!" I almost scream. "You have to reply. I want to know what he's gonna say."

Riley: *What?*

Dawson: *Saw the video. You're dead.*

Riley: *No, you're dumb. You should be here with Kiki, not kissing the bitch's ass.*

Dawson: *Are you showing our texts to Keatie?*

Riley: *No.*

Dawson: *I wanted her back for so long. Now finally she's begging me, saying baby please and all that shit. And I just feel like I need to see.*

Riley: *Then get off Facebook and go hang out with her. You finally got what you wanted. Enjoy your weekend, bro. I know I am :)*

Dawson: *You kissed her. I hate you.*

Riley: *Only on the cheek.*

Dawson: *FML*

Riley: *This is what you wanted, remember?*

Dawson: *Now I don't know what I want.*

Riley turns to me and Dallas, "What should I say?"

Dallas says, "Tell him you think he should watch the video again, then go hang out with Whitney."

Riley: *I think you should watch the video again, bro. Then go hang with Whitney.*

Dawson: *Can't watch the video again. Threw my laptop across the room. It's broken.*

Riley: *Borrow Jake's. Baby's already got over 100 hits, and it's only been online for about 10 minutes. Every guy at school is sitting around simultaneously thinking what a dumb fuck you are and thanking you for being one. I'm out.*

SURF THE CROWD WITH ME.
11:40PM

WE'RE DROPPED OFF at a beachfront mansion and are told that Mr. Moran is in flight and will be arriving late. To make ourselves at home.

When I go in the bathroom to pee, I realize I'm getting my period.

Seriously, Mother Nature? Do you really need to kick me while I'm down? But then again, *not* getting it would be way worse.

I'm exhausted, so I tell the boys I'm going to bed. I change into a pair of pajama shorts and a tank top and snuggle up under the covers.

I can't seem to sleep, though. I keep waking up then dozing off. Then waking up again.

THIS TIME I wake up because someone is bouncing on the bed.

"Hey, Keats," Damian says sweetly. "How's my girl?"

I jump into his arms and try not to cry. "God, I've missed you."

He gives me a squeeze then pushes me back and studies my face. "How are you doing, really?"

"I'm okay, sorta. I'm really glad to be here. To see you. How are you? You look tired. Too many late nights with groupies?"

He gives me a little grin then sprawls flat out across the bed. "Honestly, I'm exhausted. I had to fly commercial, and you know I can never sleep on a plane. I've been up for the last twenty-seven hours. So, tell me what happened."

I tell him all about Dawson. How crazy and amazing the physical side of it was. How that part was so different than it was with B. How I still haven't talked to B. About the music video we made on the way here.

"That I have to see. Pull it up."

I pull it up on my phone.

"Damn, girl. Did Dawson see this?"

"Yeah. He said he threw his laptop across the room."

"You are *so* going to be in our music video. You look very hot."

I smile. "Thank you. You don't think I looked silly?"

"Not at all. You looked like, well, like you became the part."

"Is that good?"

"It's very good. Have you ever thought about acting, Keats? I know you've always liked writing scripts, but I think you would be an amazing actress. You've always been able to shift seamlessly from one situation to the next and fit in. I think that's why you were having trouble at school. You can play any role you want and convince people that you are the surfer girl, the popular girl, the star's daughter, the rebel. You really don't let a lot of people see the real you."

"You've always seen it."

"Yeah, I know. I love you. All of the yous." He laughs at his own joke.

"Can I tell you a secret?"

"I don't know? Is it a good one?"

"This is hard for me to admit. I've always wanted to be an actress, but . . ."

"But your mom is good at it and you're afraid you'll fail?"

"Exactly. And be an embarrassment to the family or something. But, at school, no one knows. So I tried out for the school play. I mean, it's nothing big, but I got the part that I wanted. And it feels like I have a little part of my life back."

He studies my face. "Being off by yourself is good for you, isn't it?"

"In some ways, Damian, it's incredibly freeing. But I miss my family and I miss my friends."

"Do you really miss your friends? Like who do you miss?"

"I miss you. And even though I kinda hate B, I miss him. Surprisingly, I miss Vanessa and RiAnne. They may have been catty and superficial, but I knew what to expect from them. And Sander. He was always really good to me, and the best shopping partner ever. I've sort of been following news from his set. It sounds like the movie is close to being done. I admire him for having the guts to do what he did. To go for it. I'm proud of him."

"I'm proud of you."

"And what about you, Mr. Rock Star? Getting all famous."

"It's pretty cool, but it's tiring. I also understand what you used to talk about. How you played a role at school and sometimes it felt fake. I feel that way sometimes. Like people are all screaming my name and acting like they love me, but they don't even know me."

"I think that's okay. You can have two lives. The image you present to the world, and the you that you are at home. Mom told me the other day that it doesn't matter what everyone thinks. It only matters what the people you love think. I thought that was pretty good advice." My mind immediately goes to

Aiden. Telling me that he did the dance for the people he loves.

I suddenly feel exhausted.

"I'm really tired," I tell Damian.

"Me too."

"Will you sing me the song? Like a lullaby? Maybe you can put us both to sleep."

He holds his arm out so I can snuggle up on his shoulder.

Damian has been making me feel better since my dad died and lying on his chest makes me feel like no matter how bad things seem, it will all be okay.

He starts singing.

"She's the kind of girl
Everybody wants be.
But no one sees what's inside,
Or that she cries herself to sleep.

But I see, baby, yeah, I see.

She's Miss Popular
Floating with the crowd.
But it all feels so empty
That she wants to scream out loud.

But I see, baby, yeah, I see.

So forget about them,
Come surf the crowd with me . . ."

Saturday, October 15th

THE SINGLE BIGGEST REASON.

10:30AM

I DON'T KNOW when I fell asleep, but I do know that Damian singing to me was so comforting. I haven't felt that calm and relaxed since before I started dating Brooklyn.

I get up, go out into the kitchen, and find the ingredients to make Damian's favorite breakfast. Cinnamon French toast and bacon.

Dallas and Riley wake up to the smell and congregate in the kitchen. I take a piece of bacon into the bedroom and wave it under Damian's nose.

"Your ability to make French toast might be the single biggest reason why we have been friends for so long," he teases as he takes a big bite of the bacon. "Is that what I smell?"

"Yeah, do you want to get up yet, or do you want me to put it in the warming drawer for later?"

"What time is it?"

"Almost eleven."

He pops out of bed. "I better get up. We'll eat, then go out on the boat."

"Whose house is this? It's amazing."

"It's our record producer's. He said he hardly ever uses it. Comes to a few Heat games and throws parties a couple times a year, but that's about it."

I introduce Damian, my long time friend from grade school, to Riley and Dallas. They hit it off right away. We have fun out in the boat, then come back and sit in the hot tub on the deck overlooking the water.

Damian entertains us with all sorts of stories about touring with the band. The good, the bad, and the groupies. Dallas and Riley particularly love the stories about the groupies.

NOW WE MATCH.

11:15PM

WE GET TO the club and immediately go backstage, do some shots, get backstage wristbands, and get Damian set up to go. After that, he comes out and dances with us for a while.

About an hour later, it's time for him to go backstage to prepare for his performance.

"Hey, Riley, I'm going to run to the restroom before he comes on. I'll be right back."

I wait in line.

Forever.

No. Like, F-O-R-E-V-E-R.

I didn't have to go that bad when I got in line, but now I do.

Finally!

I pee.

Then I stop at the bar to get a bottle of water. After the shots we did backstage, I need some water.

I stand on the edge of the dance floor sipping my water and looking for Riley and Dallas. The dance floor is packed.

I'm scanning the crowd when I feel someone move in close behind me.

I'm pretty sure it's Riley. I start to turn around as he wraps his arms tightly around my waist.

"Come out, come out, wherever you are."

My heart stops.

I'm face to face with Vincent.

"Aren't you the tricky little minx?" he says. "I've been looking all over for you."

"How did you find me?"

"I followed the breadcrumbs. You toured with him this summer. I heard he was going to be here. Took a chance. So, where are they keeping you?"

"Here in Florida," I lie. "I'm in a witness protection program. So, you found me? You've found me a couple times before, but I keep getting away." I try to make my voice sound like I'm unaffected by him.

But I'm so affected.

I will my body not to tremble.

Don't let him know you're scared, Keatyn.

Vincent's still gripping my waist so tightly that I know it's going to leave a mark.

"You won't be getting away this time. So here's how it's gonna go down. First, we're going to dance. You want to be an actress; consider this your biggest role. You're going to dance with me like you were dancing with that boy at your birthday party."

I can't hide the surprise from my face.

Vincent nods, gripping my waist tighter. "Yes. I was watching. Even went to visit him in Oregon. He didn't know a thing. Not even your best friend, Vanessa, seems to know where they've been keeping you. She's quite the fun little distraction though. From what I understand, you left without saying goodbye to your friends."

"I just told you I'm in the witness protection program. Even my family doesn't know where I am." I put on a French accent and say, "I am a foreign exchange student named Michelle."

"You're not going to say goodbye to anyone tonight either. After we dance, you'll accompany me to my car and we're going home."

"Home?"

"Yes. We'll start filming immediately. I have everything prepared."

"And what if I scream? There are a lot of people here."

"I have a gun, Abby. If you even move wrong, I'll start shooting. And I'll start with your friend, Damian. He's scheduled to go onstage about now."

The music stops. Damian walks out onto the stage.

I can't let him kill Damian.

"My name's not Abby. I'm Keatyn. Don't you remember that? I'm Abby's daughter."

He just grins at me.

The kind of grin that makes my skin crawl.

"We're going to dance. Now."

He pulls me out onto the dance floor and pulls me into his arms.

I put my hands on his back but I can't move them.

I can't make them move. I don't want to touch him.

Anywhere.

He pulls me in close and runs his hands all over me. Down my back. Cupping my ass. Down the outsides of my thighs.

I feel like I'm going to throw up.

"It feels so good to finally have you in my arms. I heard we just missed each other at Long Beach."

"How do you know that?"

He grins. "I have my ways. And then we met again in New York City. Wasn't that something? Cat and mouse chase through the streets. We may have to add that to the movie. It was very exciting." He pauses. "You're not dancing with me like you did him. Move your hands," he commands.

My mind is going a thousand miles a minute. Don't make a scene here. Just do what he says. Then when he tries to get you out to his car, you can fight him.

Punch him.

Run.

Get the gun.

Something.

The gun. That's it.

I'll get the gun and use it on him.

Where could it be?

In the movies, they always tuck them in the small of their back. I swallow and move my hands. I close my eyes and try to pretend that he's anyone but Vincent.

I run my hands up the inside of his jacket, trying to make it feel sexy and not like a pat down.

"That's it, Abby," he says, smoothing the back of my hair. "God, that feels good."

Shit.

There is no gun in his waistband.

Shoulder harness?

I move my hands back to his chest, work my way up to his collarbone, then move under his arms and down his side.

He shoves his leg between mine, then moves his hands down my body. "I know what you're doing," he whispers.

Shit.

He knows.

"What am I doing?" I say, in my coyest and sexiest voice.

"You're trying to get me all turned on so I can't think straight."

Oh, thank god. He doesn't know I'm trying to find the gun.

"Is it working?" I purr.

He gives me a grin that if I didn't know how sick he is, would have made my heart flutter.

My heart is fluttering, but it's a bad way.

I'm going to have a heart attack way.

"I almost forgot," he says. "I did something just for you." He pushes me back just a little, flips over his hand, and shows me the chaos tattoo on his wrist. "Now we match."

"I heard about Tiny. How he died in a mugging gone bad. Suspiciously the same way your mother died."

Vincent smiles a sick smile. "I heard that too. You really have to be careful on the streets these days. Bad stuff can happen to anyone."

"Is that a threat?"

"No, Abby. It's a promise." He tucks his fingers under the waistband of my skirt and pushes it down slowly.

I know what he wants. He wants to see my tattoo.

I back away quickly, causing his hand to fall in front of him.

He grabs my arm and squeezes hard, pulls me back close, and gets in my face. "Don't even think about it. I want to see your tattoo. Now."

I hesitate.

"I said now."

I lean my back away from him and slide my skirt down a little further on my hips so that my tattoo is visible.

He puts his wrist against my skin.

Making our tattoos touch.

He keeps his hand in place but pulls the rest of my body back in closer.

"It's like our tattoos are making love," he says.

He pushes his hips further into mine so I can feel how this has aroused him.

I can barely choke back the bile in my throat.

I really feel like I'm going to puke.

Maybe that would be a good idea. If I puked, wouldn't someone come help me?

Or would he say that I'm sick and he is taking me home. No one would believe he was being anything other than helpful.

My chin is up by his shoulder so he can't see my face.

I allow myself a moment to be horrified.

To stop acting.

I shut my eyes tight. Breathe heavily and try to keep myself from crying.

"Keep doing that," Vincent says. "That way you're breathing. Having our tattoos touch is turning you on too, isn't it?"

I can't say anything.

I can't act anymore.

I cannot do this.

I just nod my head into his, so he thinks I am agreeing.

"Abby, god, this is amazing," he says, pulling me closer and rubbing his tattoo harder up and down against mine.

Gun.

Remember the gun.

Find the gun.

Get away.

I move my hands down his chest. To his front pants pockets.

He moans again. "Abby. Abby."

I still don't feel a gun.

Instead, I feel his erection.

Definitely not a gun.

That leaves his ankle. James always keeps a spare gun in an ankle holster.

I pull myself closer to Vincent and slide my foot down the side of his left leg.

I don't feel a holster.

That leaves his right leg. Which I should have checked first. He's right handed. Of course, it would be on the right side. A plan forms in my head. I'm going to find the gun. Shake into him or something. Drop it low. Get the gun. Tell him to get the fuck out of here and that if he touches my tattoo one more time, I'm going to shoot him.

But then I'd be the crazy person in the club with a gun.

I'd have to kill him, so he'd have no defense. So that he couldn't make up a story.

I have to kill him.

"What the—" Vincent says.

Vincent is shoved away from me and knocked to the ground in a blur.

Dallas grabs my hand and pulls me off the dance floor, with Riley right behind us.

"No!" I yell at Dallas. "I have to go back there. He has a gun."

"He said that? That he has a gun?" Dallas' face goes white and he looks scared.

"Yes, he said if I didn't do what he said that he'd start shooting people."

"Fuck," Dallas says. He pulls his phone out of his pocket and sends a text. Why he's doing that at a time like this, I have no idea. "I'm sorry," he says, "This is all my fault. I shouldn't have gotten you involved in this mess or put you in danger. Come on, we've got to leave."

He pulls my hand, bringing me and Riley with him.

I follow him, even though I have no idea how he could have put me in danger. I'm the one that's putting them in danger.

I listen for gunshots. I'm praying Vincent doesn't follow through with his promise to shoot Damian, who is still on stage singing.

I've got to warn him.

"I've got to go backstage first. I've got to tell Damian. He knows we came here with him. He threatened to shoot him."

Dallas looks like he's ready to cry. He runs his hand through his hair. "I'm sorry. This is all my fault."

I don't understand why he's rambling about it being his fault, but I do know I need to get to Damian.

Fast.

I run to the door leading backstage. Flash my backstage wristband to the guy standing in front of it.

I sprint through the hall, up the three black metal stairs leading to the stage, run across the stage and leap on Damian, bringing him and his guitar crashing to the ground.

Big guys dressed in black rush onto the stage, surrounding us and trying to pull me off Damian.

"What the hell did you do that for?" he whispers.

"He's here. Vincent is here. You've got to get off this stage."

The bouncers pull me off him and carry me off. They pull Damian to his feet, and he runs after me.

"Put her down," he says, once we're both safely offstage.

I can see the other backstage door from here. I see Vincent standing in front of it. He passes a wad of cash to the bouncer. The bouncer opens the door and lets him in. Riley and Dallas, who are both out of breath, come running up to us.

"We're leaving out the back. This way," Dallas says as he pulls me to the back exit.

I don't even have time to think. I just let him lead me. He seems to have a plan.

As we rush out into the back alley, I see three identical blacked out Suburbans. Men in dark suits pull me, Dallas, and Riley into one and Damian into another.

The trucks split up and we go flying down the street, slowing only to make numerous turns.

Dallas doesn't say anything, but I can tell he's as tense and scared as I am.

I put my shaking hand on his leg and start to say something. He gives me a slight headshake and moves his eyes toward the guys.

How did Dallas get these men here so fast? And just who are they?

After a fifteen minute drive full of turns and doubling back, we pull into an underground parking lot and are hustled to a nondescript elevator.

After a short ride, we enter a plush hallway to a huge Presidential suite with sweeping views of Biscayne Bay.

Dallas stops to give me hug and whispers in my ear. "They are going to want to debrief us. Just agree with me. I'll explain everything to you later. I'm so sorry that I put you in danger."

"But . . ."

"We'll talk later," he says firmly.

I nod as he leads me to a sofa, which I promptly collapse on.

I look out at the beach.

Try to pretend I'm back in Malibu and Vincent doesn't exist.

Two guys in suits sit down.

"Tell us what happened," one of them says to Dallas.

"I did what I was told to do if I ever felt threatened. An old guy had ahold of her on the dance floor and wouldn't let go. He grabbed her arm hard. At first, I thought it was just because she's pretty and turned him down or something. But I could tell he was threatening her. Riley and I decided to get her away from him. When we did, she told me he had a gun. That's when I texted."

The guy in the suit turns to me. "What did he say to you and did he threaten the Senator's son directly?"

"He told me he had a gun and that if I didn't dance with him he'd start shooting."

"But he never mentioned his name?"

I shake my head. What is going on here? Do they think Vincent was after Dallas? "No, he didn't say anything about Dallas. He only mentioned Damian, the guy you put in the other truck. He's my friend. That's why we were at the club in the first place. To hear him sing."

Another black-suited guy stands in front of us. "We'd still like to question him. I have a man in the club. Can you give us a physical description of the assailant?"

"He was white, dark haired, about six-two, and was wearing a dark jacket," Dallas replies.

"That's half the people at the club."

I could give them his name and a much better physical description, but I'm a little confused right now, because I think they think he was going to shoot Dallas, not me and Damian.

"Look, guys," Dallas says to the suits as he takes a calming breath. "I'm sorry for the hassle. It's the first time I've ever been in a situation like this and I panicked."

"Well, you're safe. That's all that matters," the suit says.

The other guy in the suit, who has been on his phone the whole time we've been talking, raises his head. "The senator will be calling you shortly. We've kept him abreast of the situation and we'll make sure you get safely back to school. You're free to retire, Miss Monroe."

I'm pretty sure I'm being dismissed.

"My friend, Damian, where did you take him?"

"We took him to where you were staying. He was not followed and is secure. We'll get your belongings brought here."

"Thank you," I say, because I can't come up with anything else.

I'm led to the door of a large bedroom. I walk in and collapse on the bed.

A FEW MINUTES later, Dallas and Riley walk in. Dallas grabs the bottle of champagne that was chilling in the corner. Probably waiting for the senator's arrival.

He pops it and pours us each a glass.

"So now that we're safe, I need to apologize to you," Dallas says as he climbs on the bed with me.

"Why would you apologize? You helped me."

"Because I've told you more than once not to lie to me, but I told you a lie."

"You did?"

He sighs and runs his hand through his short blond hair. "Yeah."

"What did you lie about?"

"I told you I got caught smoking weed and that I was an embarrassment to my dad."

"Yeah, I kinda thought your dad sounded like a dick."

"He's not. My dad is awesome."

"So why did you lie?"

Riley has been pacing the floor. "You lied too, Keatyn. About why you're here."

I lower my head. "Yeah."

"We'll talk about you next," Dallas says. "I need to get this off my chest."

He leans back on the pillows. I pull my feet under my legs and snuggle up next to him.

Riley turns from the window and leaps across the room and onto the bed. "How 'bout we all get naked and do something worth lying about?"

Dallas and I laugh.

Riley pulls me back into a hug. "You seem like you're doing better. Are you?"

I kiss his arm and nod.

Dallas says, "Okay, so I'm the youngest of five kids. I was the oops baby. I'm the same age as most of my brothers' and sisters' kids. They are all grown, married, and spread across the country." He pauses and sighs. "So, my dad was threatened by this extremist group. They specifically threatened our family. My mom and me. They were going to make me leave my normal school and go live in Washington with them, but I didn't want that." He rolls his eyes. "I threw a bit of a fit. So the drug thing was a lie. Dad let it be publicized. Said he was sending me to military school. That drugs are killing our youth, blah, blah, blah, and I went to Eastbrooke. To stay safe."

"I keep dangerous company," Riley says with a laugh. Then he looks at me seriously. "So that guy at the club. Is he the guy you told me about? Your mom's ex?"

"Um, yeah. He . . ." I don't know what to say. I want to tell them both the truth so badly. But I can't. Just yesterday, I was going to tell Dawson everything. I can't fully trust anyone. And even though I do trust these boys, I also know they are human. They could accidentally say something about Abby being my mom. If that happened, the whole school would find out in seconds. And I can't risk it.

My phone rings, startling me.

Shit. It's Garrett.

"I need to answer this," I say to the boys.

I try to act nonchalant. "Hey, what's up?"

"Keatyn."

"Yes?"

"Where the fuck are you and why aren't you wearing your necklace?"

"I'm out of town, but I think you already know that."

"Yes, I know that you're in Miami. I know that you went to see Damian. I know that you had a run in with Vincent. I know that you tackled Damian on stage and were whisked into black Suburbans by what might have been the Secret Service."

"That about covers it. I'm fine."

"I need to know what he said to you. Damian has already filled me in on the rest."

"I can't now," I say and hang up.

I get tears in my eyes. What could have happened to me is sinking in.

I'm gonna start crying.

I look at Riley. He's helped me so much. I'm not going to have another meltdown in front of him.

But it's coming.

"Uh, if you don't mind, I'm gonna go shower," I say, pointing toward the palatial bathroom.

"That's fine," Dallas says. "My dad is going to be here soon. He's here in Miami but he's out on a boat somewhere. They are choppering him in. He'll want to talk to me alone."

He chugs his champagne then goes back into the living room, shutting the door behind him.

"I'm just going to lie on the bed, drink champagne, and think about how bad-ass that was," Riley states. "I felt like I was in a spy movie or something."

I nod, walk into the bathroom, shut the doors, turn on the shower, strip off my clothes, and stand under the warm water.

I let the water fall and start crying.

I look at the tattoo. It's supposed to remind me of my first love, but now it feels violated and dirty.

I grab a washcloth and try to scrub it off.

I scrub and scrub and scrub.

When it won't come off, I sit on the shower floor, pull my knees up to my chest, drop my head to my knees, and let my emotions rack through me.

I cry about everything.

The way Dawson looked standing there in his closet.

How much I miss Damian.

The things Vincent said to me.

How he probably had Tiny killed.

How he's been following the breadcrumbs.

How he's not going to stop.

How I know it's just a matter of time before he shows up at school and gets me for real.

I suddenly realize the water has stopped running.

A towel is thrown across my body as Riley sits down next to me. "You're not gonna sit in here all by yourself and cry."

"Where's Dallas?"

"His dad is here. He's out with him. And your friend Damian called, so I answered for you. He wanted you to know that he's fine and that he's sorry about everything."

I grab Riley's shoulder, getting his shirt all wet, and cry into it until I have no more tears.

"I'm so glad you came with me, Riley. Otherwise, I'd have been here alone and I don't think I would've gotten away."

"What I don't understand is why he wants to kidnap you. For ransom or something?"

"No. He doesn't need money. He wants to make my mom pay for whatever he thinks she did. He wants to hurt her by hurting me. He also thinks I look like her when they, um, dated. When they were young. He even called me by her name tonight."

"That's just sick. But don't worry. You're safe now. Dallas and I will always make sure you're safe."

"Did you know about Dallas? Like what he told me?"

Riley nods. "Yeah. They did full background checks on everyone at the school. Specifically chose me to be his roommate. They liked the fact that I had some military training and that I'm not afraid to break rules when necessary. They briefed me on his situation and asked me not to tell anyone. That's why I was worried about you during Homecoming week. They told us with all the people coming and going we needed to be especially alert. Come on. Let's get you out of here. It's time to meet the senator."

WHILE RILEY GOES out into the living room, I brush out my wet hair and put on a big fluffy robe. Not what I would usually choose for meeting a parent, let alone a senator, but it's going to have to do. I threw my clothes from the club in the trash and I'm not putting them back on.

I'm getting ready to walk out when I hear my name.

A voice I don't recognize says, "Don't you think it's a little strange that this girl brings you to Miami and all of a sudden there's a threat? Who is this girl, anyway?"

"We don't know much about her, sir," another voice says. "She apparently was admitted to the school at the last minute."

"Don't you think that's a little odd? I want her background run now. I want to know everything about her."

Shit.

I call Garrett quickly.

"Um, I have a question. How solid is my backstory? Like if someone starting digging. Like, the government, maybe. What would they find?"

"It will stand up. I'm good at what I do."

"Okay, I won't worry then."

"Why don't you tell me what's going on."

I tell him about Dallas.

"You swore to me that you wouldn't go see a friend again."

"I know, but this was different. Brooklyn's event was public and planned. This wasn't. Damian said it was a surprise performance."

"Yeah, one that the club owners leaked all over the internet."

"I didn't know that. Damian didn't know that."

"He knows how the industry works. He's not stupid. He risked your life tonight."

"He's never done a surprise thing like this before. He'd never knowingly put me in danger."

Out in the living room, the same voice says, "Son, you need to start thinking with your head and not your dick. I don't believe in coincidences."

"They think it's my fault, Garrett. They think I may have set Dallas up to get kidnapped."

"Who is his dad?"

"He's a senator from Kentucky. Last name is McMahon."

"I know Senator McMahon quite well. Did security for his trip to Central America a few years back. When we were fighting the war on drugs instead of the war on terror. Let me talk to him."

"Garrett, no. I don't want Riley and Dallas to know who I am or the truth. I don't want to put them in danger."

"How did you explain the situation to them?"

"I told them that Vincent was my mom's ex-boyfriend. That he's been stalking me."

"That's a pretty good story. And don't worry about your background. I'll call the senator myself. I'm also working on a new plan for your security. We're going to be making some changes."

"Garrett, one other thing. When I talked to Vincent, he told me about how he's been following the breadcrumbs to find me. He never once mentioned anything about school. I'm positive he doesn't know where I am."

"Well, that's the best news I've heard all night."

He hangs up, so I walk out into the living room.

Even though he was just talking trash about me a few moments ago, the senator gets off the couch with an outstretched hand. He's tall and broad-shouldered with perfect white hair and eyes as blue as Dallas'.

I shake his hand just as his phone rings.

"Excuse me, I need to take this." He steps away from the living area.

"I heard what your dad was saying," I say to Dallas. "I would never want anyone to hurt you." I start getting tears in my eyes just thinking about someone hurting him or Riley.

He gives me a hug. "He's just watching out for me. What we went through was scary."

I nod my head into his chest, completely understanding.

The senator ends his call and sits on the couch again.

"So, Miss Monroe, I just spoke to our mutual friend."

"Yes, sir."

"I understand the situation now. We've decided to join forces."

I sort of squint my eyes at him. I'm pretty sure that whatever they are planning, we're not going to like. I'm pretty sure Garrett's ready to put me in solitary confinement on the moon right about now.

Dallas says, "Join forces?"

"Miss Monroe went to Eastbrooke at the last minute because she is in a similar situation. An old boyfriend of her mother's is stalking her."

I smile. Garrett lied. To a Senator. For me. I want to reach through the phone and kiss him.

Dallas says, "So you lied too?"

"Just about that," I say, but then I add, "mostly."

"It sounds like you kids had quite the scare, either way."

"I'm so sorry for all the trouble I caused."

The Senator puts his hand on top of mine and says, "I'd much rather you overreact and be wrong, than not react and be in danger. You kids can stay here in the suite, relax, and try to enjoy what's left of your weekend. We'll make sure you get back to school safely."

Sunday, October 16th

WE SHOULD PARTY.

11:30AM

WE SLEPT IN late, got up, ordered a huge breakfast, and ate it overlooking the bay.

I stay out on the deck because it's so incredibly peaceful.

Dallas and Riley yell at me to come inside. They're both sitting on the sofa drinking beers and laughing. Dallas has an iPad in his hand.

"What are you two laughing about?"

"We're watching our video. You know it has like 500 views already."

"It was really fun to make," Dallas says. "That plane was freaking sweet."

"You did a good job editing it. Really, Riley, you're very talented."

"Thanks, baby. So what are you gonna do about my brother?"

"What is there to do? He wanted her, not me. We're done."

"He's been posting stuff about you on his Facebook wall. I don't think he wants her. He wants you."

"I have to tutor Aiden when we get back. Then I guess I'll see what happens."

"Do you want me to ask him? I mean, I think you'd want to know before you get there."

"I kind of wish we could just stay here. You're right, though. I do want to know what happened."

AS WE'RE BEING driven to the airport, I text Jake.

> **Me:** *I'm heading back to school soon. Wondered what happened this weekend with Whitney and Dawson. Do you know?*

Jake: *They hung out on Saturday. I don't know if they did anything. Bryce said they seemed awkward. I avoided them. Hung out with some other people.*

Me: *So aren't they back together?*

Jake: *Don't think so. He told Ace he screwed up, and he was stupid for thinking he wanted her back. I think it was just sort of an ego trip. He had wanted her back for so long.*

Me: *Are you doing okay?*

Jake: *I'm doing very well actually.*

Me: *Okay, I'll see you later tonight. I think we should party.*

Jake: *Sounds good.*

Riley says, "I'm gonna text Dawson. See what he's thinking."

I lean over and watch him type.

Riley: *Headed back home. How did things turn out this weekend? You and W back together?*

Dawson: *This weekend sucked. And no, we're not.*

Riley: *My weekend was AWESOME!!! The best weekend of my life.*

"You're such a liar," I say to him. "This weekend was nothing but a clusterfuck."

"Maybe, but he doesn't need to know that."

Dawson: *Has Keatie read my Facebook statuses?*

Riley: *Nope.*

Dawson: *Things weren't the same with Whitney. Keatie has changed me and I didn't even realize it. I was so stupid. Has she said ANYTHING about me?*

Riley: *No. She forbid us to say your name.*

Dawson: *:(What should I do?*

Riley: *Try to talk to her I guess. You hurt her.*

Dawson: *I know. I'm going to try to fix it.*

"So what are you going to do? Will you take him back?"

"I don't think so. At least not for a while."

"Wanna make him suffer, huh?"

"No. That's not it at all. It's just that after what he did, I don't have much faith in him, or us, anymore."

I GET A text from Aiden.

Aiden: *Are you going to be back in time for tutoring?*

***Me:** Yeah. I can meet you in the library at 7. Will that work for you?*

***Aiden:** I'll make it work.*

I think about Aiden. About the mystery dream girl. About what Riley said about Aiden.

"Riley, why did you tell me Aiden's a player?"

"I heard that he dated and hooked up with a lot of different girls last year. This year, it's weird. He didn't even have a date for Homecoming."

Dallas says, "I'm pretty sure you're the only girl he's kissed this year."

"How many have you kissed?"

"A dozen, maybe. Are you thinking about Aiden?"

"Oh, no, of course not. I was just thinking that's sort of weird. For a guy that's a player."

"I could see you together," Riley says.

"Why?"

"I don't know. You just seem to sparkle around him. And he seems to affect you in a way no one else does. You're practically obsessed with him, but yet you say you hate him."

"I do hate him sometimes. I think we might end up being friends though. Sometimes he can be really sweet."

I GUESS I CAN RELATE.
7PM

I FIND AIDEN in the library, sitting at our table, and grinning at me.

"So . . . saw the video. Dawson had to be going crazy."

"I doubt it. He's into Whitney now."

"You looked very sexy in the video. I don't think I've ever seen that side of you. Well, maybe a little at the after party. Everyone has been talking about it all weekend. You have a lot of views."

"I don't care about the views. I just wanted Dawson to see it."

"He looked miserable this weekend. Even when I saw him with Whitney, he looked miserable. I can't believe I'm saying this, but he probably just liked the idea that she wanted him again."

"Whatever. I don't want to talk about it." But then I look at him. "What? Now you're pro-Dawson?"

"No. I just think it would suck to lose you. I guess I can relate."

"You've lost someone you cared about because you were stupid?"

"Yeah, you, I think. That night, with the Keats toast."

"I was fine with the Keats toast. It just caught me off guard, but then when I told you why it did, you completely changed. Got mad at me or something. Didn't talk to me. Made me feel like I'd done something wrong."

"You didn't do anything wrong. I was mad at myself. Kinda like Dawson feels, I think."

"Yeah, I don't think Dawson liked the video too much."

"I heard he smashed his computer. Remind me never to break up with you."

"You don't have to worry about that. We're never going out."

"Why's that?"

"I'm love cursed and I'm never going out with a boy again."

HELL, I PREDICTED IT.
8:30PM

SITTING ON THE brick wall outside my dorm, dealing with Dawson.

"Keatie," he pleads. "Please tell me we're not over. Give me another chance."

"Absolutely not."

He looks at me with puppy dog eyes, but then he gets that determined set to his jaw, and pulls me into a hug. "I'm sorry."

I try to stay stiff against the hug. I'm mad at him, but I also sort of understand. That doesn't mean that I don't hurt, or that I can forget, but I sort of understand.

Hell, I called it.

I knew it was going to happen. Screw the psychic panty hotline. Maybe I should become a relationship psychic. I foresaw the future. And, once again, I ignored the signs and fell for him anyway. I can't decide which one of us was stupider.

I soften in his arms and hug him back.

He looks miserable.

"Look, I forgive you. I understand what you did. Hell, I predicted it. I knew it would happen. Knew we'd get happy, and you'd become more attractive to her because of it. I planned your makeover. I was just as much at fault as you. I never should've believed you. But you made me feel amazing and loved and sexy, and I didn't listen to my head. I actually started to believe love could be a good thing."

"Keatie, I was stupid too. I don't know what I was thinking. You are so different, so much fun, and I feel like an equal with you."

His eyes look moist. Like he's on the verge of tears, which causes me to tear up. I try not to blink, so they won't come out, but I can't control them.

Dawson wipes away the tears from one side of my face and kisses the other side.

"I'm sorry. Please go out with me again." He pulls the key necklace out of his pocket and tries to give it to me.

"I don't want it, Dawson. Why don't you give it to Whitney?"

"No. I bought you the necklace because I love you. You do have the key to my heart. I just thought for a second someone else did. And she used to, but I think you changed the lock because she just didn't fit anymore."

And although what he says is sort of romantic, I'm not buying it.

"We're not getting back together."

He looks defeated again. I hate seeing him like this. It's the same look he had that night at the Cave, when I set out to make that gorgeous face smile again. And I did. But it wasn't enough.

"Please tell me we're not through."

"I can't say one way or another right now. I'm not trying to punish you or make you feel bad. I can see you feel bad already. But you know how parents always preach that there are consequences to the decisions we make? What you did hurt me, and I just can't forget it."

"Fine, don't forget it. Forgive me. Understand. I was completely blindsided when she broke up with me. Then I tried for six months to get her back and now, all of a sudden, what I wanted for so long is being offered. I think I just needed closure, maybe. You once told me that Whitney should have forgiven me. Why can't you?"

"That's when you were drunk and pawing at my chest. I wish you had been drunk when she texted you. But, no. You chose her, stone cold sober, as you were supposed to be getting ready to go on a trip with me. Ego or not, it says a lot about whether you really loved me. If this is going to go anywhere further, you're going to have to prove it to me. And, more importantly, you need to prove it to yourself."

"I'm sorry," he says again.

"You keep saying that. You're like a freaking broken record. You should tell yourself you're sorry. I thought things were good. You wanted to meet my family, we were having fun, you seemed happy, the sex was amazing, you told me I owned you, and then poof. A few texts from her, and I'm history. I can't forget that because you think you're sorry."

He hangs his head. "Shit. Everything you're saying is true." He pulls me close to him, holds my face like he does after sex, when he's the sweetest. Then he tries to kiss me.

"I can't do this. I gotta go." I tell him.

I run into my dorm and collapse in a heap on my bed. Then I decide I don't want to face my girlfriends yet. They will ask me a million questions that I don't know the answers to, so I sneak out the back door and over to Riley's room.

REVENGE SEX.
9:15PM

I'M LYING ON my side on Riley's bed. He's sitting on his wheeled desk chair, rolling around, unable to sit still.

"So, you talked to my brother and you're not back together, right?"

"Right. And I've been thinking."

"Oh, no."

"Shut up. Now is not the time to make fun of me!"

"Sorry," he says, as he throws a pencil toward me and winks.

"This is serious. Talk to me about hooking up."

"Well, see, there's your problem. Hooking up is not supposed to be serious. It's supposed to be fun."

"Well, I'm trying to decide which way I want to go. I'm leaning toward bad girl. Carefree. Emotionless. You know, a girl version of you."

"I'm not emotionless."

"I know that, but you can have meaningless sex. Well, maybe that's what I want. I'm tired of caring. When I was in detention, we made a list of the top five hotties at school. I think I'm gonna work my way down that list."

"Who else was on the list?"

"Jake, Aiden, Logan, and you."

"Really!? I was on the list? Who put me on the list?"

"Uh, I don't remember. So anyway, Logan is cute, but he kinda hates me. Which might make it difficult. Aiden is into some other girl. And then there's

Jake. I think he should be my first target. Plus it would have the added bonus of revenge."

"Baby."

"What?"

"You deserve more than that."

"Oh, I know, I just don't want it. I'm done with boys toying with my emotions."

"I don't think you should."

"Why?"

"Guys don't like sluts."

"You like sluts."

"Yeah, short term, but not long term."

"Exactly! I want short term. The shorter the better. Uh, and when I say short, I'm referring to the length of the relationship, not the length of his you know what." I smile at him and raise my eyebrows.

"What am I gonna do with you?"

"Just what you've been doing. Picking up the pieces of what's left of me."

"Dawson wants you back."

"Well, this is about what I want. And tonight I wanna get fucked up. In more ways than one. You in?"

"I'm always in."

"Good, tonight's gonna be fun."

Monday, October 17th

MAYBE IT WAS A LOT OF PUKE.

7AM

I WAKE UP feeling horrible. My head is pounding and I feel sick.

Last night. Oh, last night.

I don't think I want to remember it.

I lie in bed and look through my Facebook feed to see if there is anything on there I need to be embarrassed about.

Fortunately, I don't find anything.

Then I take a quick look at my emails. I scroll through all the sale ads and see one from Grandpa. It's one line.

—So, Hotshot, did you find yourself yet? Cause we haven't heard from you.

I feel bad that I haven't emailed Grandma and Grandpa for a while.

I reply.

—I'm working on it. Sorry I haven't emailed in a while. It's been busy.

Grandpa, I have a question for you. What's the difference between love and true love?

I want to add, *And why can't I seem to find it?*

But I don't.

My mind flits back to last night.

I'm pretty sure I was the life of the party.

And *not* in a good way.

I remember telling Bryce to go get the good stuff out of his room. Doing shots. Dancing with Jake and Bryce in front of Whitney and Dawson.

Kissing Bryce.

Kissing Jake.

No. Really, I was making out with Jake.

We were dancing. His hands were all over me. My hands were all over him. I didn't care who saw or what anyone thought. I had one mission.

To get laid and forget about Dawson.

To hurt him back.

Jake pulled me onto his lap. I was straddling him. Making out with him. Giving him a drunken lap dance. Dallas was putting dollar bills in my skirt.

Ugghh.

I throw my covers back, get out of bed, and turn on the shower.

I pull the hairband out of my ponytail and shake out my hair.

Oh gosh, my hair smells like puke.

Which makes me feel like I could throw up.

Again.

I SHOWER, GRAB a towel, and stand in front of the mirror and dry myself off.

I stare at myself in the mirror to judge how bad I look.

I'm going to have to dress nice today. Pretend that I feel fine. That I'm not embarrassed.

But as I dry myself off, I see that I have three little hickeys. One on the side of my neck and two more on my chest near my bra line.

I remember Jake was sucking down the side of my neck.

I remember giggling as he was kissing down the front of me.

I'm also pretty sure that's when Dawson got pissed and left.

I very clearly remember telling Jake I wanted to go back to his room. That we should have revenge sex. I even told him that I wanted to, um, do it. But I used the F-word.

And I never say anything like that. Not even with molten-lava-hot-asshole Dawson. I've said that I want him, but never used that word to describe it. Ever.

I remember Jake telling me we'd go soon.

I was feeling groovy, as Brooklyn's dad would say.

Well, I was until I wasn't.

All of a sudden, the alcohol I'd consumed hit me.

I remember telling Jake I didn't feel so good while we were on the chair kissing, but he didn't stop.

I'm pretty sure that's about when I puked all over Aiden's room.

Then it all gets blurry.

Riley holding me.

Riley taking me to his room. Riley holding my hair while I puked. Riley waking me up this morning at four and sneaking me behind the dorms and then through my window.

I put on a lot of eye cream and concealer to hide my puffy eyes, use the concealer to hide the hickeys, then go into my closet to try and find something to wear.

I dig through my closet and decide I just can't do it. I don't care what I look like today. I know Kym always says that looking good helps cure a hangover, but I just can't do it.

I grab the plaid skort, a long sleeved white T-shirt, and the black cardigan, since black fits my mood. I add some black knitted thigh highs to keep my legs warm and a pair of red suede fringe boots.

Okay, so those might make me feel a little better. I grab my red furry Longchamp bag and pet it. Decide it needs to come with me too.

I go back in the bathroom to throw on some powder and mascara and brush my wet hair.

I add some sea salt spray and scrunch it into waves.

I look in the mirror and decide that it's just going to have to do.

Katie had an early morning Spanish Club meeting, so she was gone before I even got up.

There's a knock at my door.

I open it and find Riley with *Revive* Smart Water, pumpkin bread, and Advil.

"You are a life saver," I say, grabbing the Advil from him and downing it.

As we walk to history, he says, "So, I'm thinking breakups and shots are not a good mix for you."

"No shit. Do I need to die of embarrassment now?"

"You have ceramics with Jake this morning. That ought to be interesting." He starts laughing. He seems to think this is just so freaking funny. "I think you may have gotten a little puke on Jake last night."

"Oh, god."

"Okay, well, maybe it was *a lot* of puke."

"Just kill me now, Riley. What would be a fun way to die?"

He tosses his arm around my shoulder. "Oh, no. I'm not killing you. You're too much fun."

"You held my hair while I puked."

"Yeah, baby, that's okay."

"Thank you. In case I didn't thank you last night. Like, during the puking."

"Oh, you thanked me. You bawled, thanking me."

"I bawled?"

"Oh, yeah. You had a drunken bawling meltdown. You kept thanking me for not being a stupid boy. You cried about the surfer and the orange, fake-boobed slut. You cried because you have a monkey nickname. I have no idea what that was all about. You cried about wishing on the moon and how since then your life has been shit. You cried about Dawson. About how you hate love. About how you are love cursed." He licks his lips and smiles. "You want to be embarrassed about something, that's what you should be embarrassed about. And that I changed your shirt. Did you even notice you were wearing my shirt this morning?"

"Uh, no."

"I swear. I didn't look." He laughs. "Well, not too much, anyway."

"I love you, seriously. You're still my hero."

"Yeah, I know. You told me that about a million times too."

"I owe you."

"Naw. That was me paying you back because my brother was an asshole. We're even, okay?"

"Okay. Riley?"

"Yeah?"

"Don't ever let me do that again."

HAVE FUN. NO STRINGS.

CERAMICS

I SHOULD SKIP ceramics, but I don't.

I drop my bag down on the table I share with Bryce and Jake. Neither of them is here yet. Maybe I'll get lucky and they'll both be sick.

But I'm not lucky today.

Bryce strolls into the room with Jake right behind him.

Shit.

What am I supposed to say? Do I apologize for puking on him? Or should I pretend I was so drunk that I don't remember. I mean, really, I don't actually remember that part. I could try to giggle and flirt with them. Go with the I-was-so-drunk routine that always seemed to excuse all the things Vanessa had done the night before.

Or maybe I'll go with how I feel. The poor-pathetic-feel-sorry-for-me-because-my-boyfriend-dumped-me-so-I-got-drunk route. And the best part of that route is I won't even have to act. It's just the truth.

Bryce pats me on the back. "How we feeling, there, slugger? Remember kissing me last night?"

I keep my head down and groan slightly. That way I don't have to look at them directly.

Jake bumps my side with his hip.

I look up at him then cover my face with my hand.

He says, "So . . . last night was, um, interesting."

"I'm told I may have puked on you. I'm very sorry and extremely embarrassed."

He pulls my hand off my face and smiles at me. "That's kinda my fault. You told me you didn't feel good. But I was pretty drunk and having too much fun."

"Hopefully that means you don't remember some of the things I may have said."

His blushes a little. "Oh, that I do remember. Revenge sex. Revenge sex. Let's have revenge sex. You're lucky I'm a nice guy."

"I didn't want you to be a nice guy last night. Why were you?"

"Umm, well, me and Dawes are friends. And it's cool we stayed friends even though I was dating Whitney. Kissing you was one thing, but sex would've been another."

"The whole *bros before hoes* thing, huh?"

"Well, you're my friend too. And you were drunk. You never get drunk. You always have fun and party, but you always seem like you know when to stop—before it gets ugly."

"I like to get tipsy, but I don't like that out of control drunk feeling, and I hate being hung over."

"You a little hung over today?" He laughs at me.

"What do you think?"

"So last night was just about getting back at Dawson?"

"No. I mean, maybe, kinda. Plus, I decided I just want to have fun. No strings. Strings do nothing but get you hurt." I sigh. A really big sigh.

Jake leans his arm on the table next to me and puts his fist under his chin. "You don't really seem like that type of girl."

"I never have been, but it makes sense."

"You're a good kisser."

"From what I remember, you are too. I heard when things didn't work out with Whitney and Dawson that she said she wanted you back."

"She did. And she was pissed I was kissing you. But what she did to both of us pretty much sucked. So, I don't really care."

"Do you want her back?"

"Not at all. Can I tell you a secret?"

"Yeah."

"This weekend, Maggie and I talked in the library for a really long time. You know, about you and Dawson. About Whitney. She is really nice. And really pretty. And making out with you was a whole lot of fun. I'm thinking I just want to be single."

Bryce asks, "So you gonna get back together with Dawson? He's miserable."

"I don't know. Right now it just hurts. He promised me that he didn't care about her anymore. So, no matter what he says now I'm not going to believe him."

"I'm glad you showed me the texts."

Bryce interrupts. "Plus, we got the video, so, ya know, some good came out of it."

"Everyone saw the video, didn't they? The video of me acting like a slut." I put my face back down in my hands and mutter, "I hate boys."

"Better not hate me," Jake says.

"Better never date me then."

I WAS HAPPY WITH YOU.

LUNCH

I SIT DOWN at a table all by myself. I don't want company today. I want to wallow in aloneness.

This is the kind of day when you wish you could stay home from school and pretend to be sick. I suppose I could've pretended to be sick. Maybe I still can.

Dawson sits down next to me. "We need to talk, Keatie. Seriously."

I take a bite of the calorie-laden fried chicken strips that I got for lunch today. They taste disgusting. "I'm really not in the mood to talk right now."

"When, then? After school? Please, Keatie?"

"Dawson, you don't even get it, do you? Do you know how embarrassing this is for me? I was going to take you home to meet my parents. You swore that you loved me and that you were over her. I have never felt so embarrassed of my decisions in my life."

"Jeez, I know, okay. How would you feel if your surfer dude did that to you? He was your first love. What would you have done if he had said he wanted you back?"

"He did. Remember? You were with me. I told him I was happy with my boyfriend. That I was happy with *you*."

"Oh, yeah. I forgot about that." He runs his hands back through his gorgeous dark hair. I try not to notice how his muscles flex or how sexy a gesture I've always thought it was. "Look, I'm so, so, incredibly sorry. I got caught up in it. It was like I wanted it for so long, and then when she finally wanted me, I just, I thought I needed to see. But what I realized is you are what makes me the me I am now. I'm so much happier with you than I ever was with her."

I get tears in my eyes. "Yeah, but not happy enough to tell her no. Not happy enough to go with me. What you did sucked. It hurt. And I'm not over it. Sorry. You chose the path. I'm just trying to deal with it. And I really would like to sit alone." I change my mind and stand up quickly. "Never mind. You stay. I'm leaving."

He grabs my arm. "You kissed Dallas and Bryce last night. You made out with Jake. You gave him a lap dance in front of me. Told him you wanted to have revenge sex."

"Yeah, I did. It was fun. Single girls can do that. And I know you kissed Whitney this weekend."

"No. She kissed me. Only once. She said we had to see if it felt the same, but it didn't. I'm not the same guy I used to be. I don't fit with her anymore. I fit with you. I love you, Keatie. Please, give me another chance."

"I can't do this right now, Dawson. Seriously, I can't. I feel like shit. And I don't want to start crying in the middle of the cafe. Please, I'm embarrassed enough by all of this as it is."

"You were drunk last night."

"No shit."

"Tonight. We're going to talk."

"I don't know what else there is to say."

"I'll think of something," he says, as I walk away.

SEAL OFF.
FRENCH

I LEAVE THE cafeteria and go into the bathroom and cry. Then I clean up my mascara and go to French class early.

Aiden walks in early too.

"Hey," he says, giving me a god-like smile and taking his usual seat behind me.

I don't reply. I just give him a *S'up* head nod and then lay my pounding head down on my desk.

Apparently, his godly smile has no effect on a hangover.

I feel a tap on my back. I roll my eyes and turn around. "What?" I say exasperatedly. I don't want to talk to him, or anyone else, for that matter.

He smiles at me and says, "Are you mad at me?"

"Are you happy that Dawson and I broke up?"

"Well, yeah, but I have my own reasons for that."

"That sucks, Aiden. Because I'm hurt and if you had even a remote desire to be my friend, you wouldn't want to see me hurt."

He winces. Like what I just said hurt him.

God, I'm being a bitch. I'm taking my frustration out on him instead of Dawson.

I'm getting ready to tell him that I'm sorry when he reaches out and hands me a little star.

I take it in my hand and look at it. It's one of the glow in the dark ones from his ceiling.

From his failed attempt to get the dream girl to go to Homecoming with him.

And that does make me mad.

I toss it back at him in disgust. "Why would I want this?"

He catches the star and lowers his head just a little. "I just thought, um, you said they remind you of your sisters and how you miss them. I just thought . . ."

"I don't need the leftovers from your failed attempt at asking your dream girl to Homecoming," I snarl.

"You're crabby today," he states.

"No shit."

"You probably shouldn't have drunk so much last night."

I hold my hand behind my head, flash him my middle finger, and say, "Seal off, Aiden," as Annie sits down.

She gives me an adorable look. The kind of look that makes me know she's on my side.

She leans over and says to me, "Girls' night tonight?"

"Abso-fricken-lutely."

MY LIFE HAS GONE TO SHIT.
3PM

AS I'M ABOUT to walk into the dance locker room, Whitney grabs me by the arm. "We need to talk."

"Talk about what? I'm not talking to you."

She looks around to make sure no one is near and admits, "I'm sorry, okay. He looked happy with you. I was jealous. Wished things could just go back to the way they used to be."

She gets tears in her eyes. "What you did at Homecoming. In front of my family. No one has ever stood up for me like that. Since I broke up with Dawson, my life has gone to shit."

"That happened to me too," I confide in her. "Last spring, I broke up with my perfect boyfriend. Except he wasn't perfect, and I wasn't happy. But I wish I could take it back, because since then, my life has gone to shit too."

"Your life has gone to shit? Everything you do here turns to freaking gold."

"I'm just trying to have fun. I don't want to be involved in all the drama."

"Do you think we could ever be friends? Dawson and I were never the way you are with him. We kissed. I made him. Told him that we needed to see." She dabs a tear from the inside corner of her eye. "But you changed him."

"No, you changed him, Whitney, when you broke up with him for reasons that had nothing to do with love. You broke his heart. Sometimes people just can't get over that."

She looks at the ground. "Yeah, I know," she says quietly and I know she's thinking about when Camden broke her heart all those years ago. "You should forgive him. It was all my fault."

"Actually, it's not all your fault. He could have told you no. And if he really loved me like he said, he would have."

"I feel bad. I don't usually feel bad about this kind of stuff."

"I'm pretty sure I feel worse, but thanks. It makes me feel so much better to know that your breaking us up was for nothing."

She puts her bitch face back on. "You made out with Jake last night."

I stand up straight. "And there's nothing wrong with that. Jake and I are both single. *Because* of you."

Peyton walks up to us. "Keatyn, are you okay?"

I shake my head at her and quickly walk into the dance locker room.

Because I am *not* okay.

A PEACE OFFERING.
6PM

I'M WALKING BACK to my dorm room, looking forward to having a girls' night when I get a group text from Annie.

> **Annie:** *Hey! We're all going to meet in my room tonight. My roommate has a swim meet, so we'll have the place to ourselves.*
>
> **Me:** *I just want to go back to my room. Can't we do it in my and Katie's room like we planned?*
>
> **Annie:** *No. You need a change of scenery. And I already ordered in food, have wine, and copious amounts of chocolate and junk food.*
>
> **Katie:** *Yeah, can't we just do it in our room?*
>
> **Me:** *PLEASE??*
>
> **Annie:** *Are you REALLY going to ask me to move ALL of what I've set up?*

I feel bad. Shit.

> **Katie:** *No, we won't. We'll all be there.*
>
> **Me:** *I'm going to stop, change clothes, and wash my face. I'll be there in a few :)*
>
> **Annie:** *Good :)*

I get to Annie's room and curl up on her bed. She sits on the bed, pulls me into a hug, and then hands me a piece of chocolate. "Here, eat this. It will make you feel better."

I look at what she handed me. A little purple foil wrapped square. The word *Bliss* written on it.

I hear Aiden's voice in my head. *Vos lèvres sont mon béatitude.*

I unwrap the candy, pop it in my mouth, and let the chocolate slowly melt. It really does taste like bliss.

"That's really good, Annie. Thanks for doing all this."

She brings three pizza boxes down to the center of her floor and hands out paper plates.

I decide to try and enjoy girls' night and not whine and bring everyone else down. Plus, I'm so incredibly grateful that I didn't have to show my face in the cafe tonight.

I get a text from Dawson reminding me that we're supposed to talk tonight. I tell him I'm having a girls' night.

"So, I need updates on everyone's weekend," I say to the girls.

Maggie giggles. "So what do you guys think of Jake? Do you think I could possibly have a chance with him? Is he getting back together with Whitney?"

"He is super hot," Annie says. "Keatyn, you know him the best. What do you think of him?"

I look at Maggie. "I kissed him last night. Made out with him. We were both drunk and trying to get back at Whitney and Dawson. It doesn't mean anything. God, I even puked on him."

"I heard about that," Annie says. "Aiden told me that you puked all over his room and he had to clean it up."

"Shit. I was mean to him in French, wasn't I? I should have thanked him or apologized. I think that's all I did today. Apologize for being an idiot."

Maggie lunges at me and wraps me in a hug. "You are not an idiot. You need to stop blaming yourself for what Dawson did. It's not your fault. Boys suck."

Katie waves her hand in the air. "I'll second that."

"Katie," Annie says. "We need to talk about your drinking."

"Yeah, we do. You would think that after what happened you wouldn't ever drink again. But you got drunk at the Cave *again* on Saturday night," Maggie says.

"Oh, so Keatyn can puke all over and it's okay with everyone, but I get drunk and I'm in trouble?"

"I think my situation is a little different, Katie," I say gently. "I hardly ever get drunk. You hardly ever *don't* get drunk."

She starts to tear up. "I don't know how it keeps happening. I plan on only having a couple drinks, but then when the guys offer me shots, I can't seem to say no. And when I do say no, they tease me about how I can't keep up with them."

"You can't keep up with the guys. You have to be able to say no. Have one drink then have a bottle of water. And try not to drink more than one drink per hour."

She nods.

Maggie gives her a hug. "We just want you to be safe, okay?" Then she turns to me. "Can we please talk about Jake? I don't care that you kissed at the party. What I care is that he didn't kiss me. Didn't even try to kiss me. He talked to me. Like we talked and talked for hours in the library. I think I fell a little in love with him."

"He said he had fun talking to you and thinks you are really sweet and pretty, but he also said he wants to be single for a while and just have fun. Basically, we both decided to become sluts."

Annie looks at me with wide eyes, "Really? You want to be a slut? Sleep with a bunch of guys?"

"Well, last night it sounded like a good idea but, the truth is, I can't do that. I have to like a guy. And I really only want to do it with a guy that I really like. Love, hopefully."

"Ace and I went a little further," Annie almost whispers.

"A little further?"

"Well, yeah, just a little. Like, I touched it."

We all scream and laugh.

"And?" I say.

"It seems very big. I didn't realize they get so big. I can NOT imagine that thing inside me."

Maggie hoots, "Oh, it will fit just fine. Are you thinking about doing it with him?"

"Well, I mean, I have thought about it. I'm not ready yet, but I've thought about it."

"Trust me on this," I say to her very seriously. "Wait. Wait until you think you can't wait any longer. And then wait some more."

"I'm surprised to hear you say that," Katie says. "I thought you would encourage her because it was so great with Dawson."

"It was great with Dawson. Sex stuff feels good. It can be great, but I think it makes you feel like you are sort of in love with the person. I think maybe Dawson thought he loved me because that part of our relationship was really exciting. But then when it came down to it, he didn't really love me. Same with my ex. He said he loved me, we did it, and then he didn't even respect me enough to not basically screw someone else in front of me. I think if I ever do it again, it's going to be with a boy that I know loves me."

Annie says, "But that's the problem, isn't it? The knowing."

"Yes, that's the problem."

"So, I should wait?"

"You should definitely wait."

"So, what are you going to do about Dawson?"

"He wants to talk tonight." I hold my hands up in the air. "What is there to talk about?"

"Didn't you read all his Facebook statuses while you were gone?" Annie asks. "If I were Whitney, I'd feel like complete shit. Everyone knew she wanted to get back together with him, and then he posted all those statuses."

"What statuses? I haven't looked at Facebook since I pressed the single button."

"I think you should read them," Annie says gently. "Actually, let's read them together."

She grabs her laptop and pulls up Dawson's profile page. "Do you want to read them, or shall I read them to you?"

"Read them out loud, so we can figure out what they mean."

"Okay, we'll start on Friday night. After you left, he said, *So confused.* Then later that night, *I really screwed up*, and then there is a little broken heart. Aww, that's so sad. Okay, so then I think this must have been after he saw the video. *Just threw my computer across the room, shattered it. Going to kill my brother.* Then at like two in the morning, he wrote on your wall, *Keatie, I'm sorry. I love you.* You didn't comment, but some people did. Jake said, *F you.* Dallas said, *Heard you liked the video.* I said, *Heart you, Keatyn.*"

"Aw, that was sweet, Annie."

"Let's see. Then on Saturday after I know they had lunch together, he posted, *I miss my Keatie.*

Maggie says, "If I was Whitney, that would have made me feel like crap."

Okay, so then he posted on your wall again. *I miss you* and another broken heart. Then we all know that he and Whitney were at the party together. Apparently, when he got home from that he posted, *The past is history.* Then on Sunday. *Counting down the hours until I can apologize in person.* Then Sunday night. *Love sucks.*"

"Wow. What do you all think that means?"

"It means he realized quickly that he screwed up. He was upset, but he still tried with Whitney, and it didn't work," Annie says.

"Plus, he knew she would read his status, and he didn't care," Katie says, defending Dawson. "They were all about you. I think you should take him back. He just made a mistake."

My phone vibrates. "It's him." I laugh. "His ears must be burning."

Dawson: *I thought of something.*

Me: *Huh?*

Dawson: *You told me we'd have nothing to talk about. I thought of something we could talk about.*

Me: *I just read all your Facebook posts from this weekend.*

Dawson: *We could talk about that. I'm out for a walk, wanna join me?*

Me: *I'm at Annie's dorm and I look like crap. Be prepared.*

I walk out, and Dawson says, "Casual, yes. Crap, no." He snakes his arm around my waist. "You always come out here with practically nothing on, then I have to give you my sweatshirt."

"Oh, sorry, I, um, I'll run back in and grab one."

"No, you're not. I love seeing you wear my clothes." He pulls his sweatshirt off over his head and pulls it down over mine. "This feels familiar," he says, then pulls the hoodie strings toward him.

"Did you really know right away you screwed up? Like before you even hung out with her?"

"I told you, the second you were gone, I knew I made a mistake. I didn't mean to hurt you. You're the last person I'd want to hurt."

"And after you hung out with her, when you said the past is history. What did you mean by that?"

"I meant that she's part of my past, not my future. You are my future. Well, I hope you are. Keatie, I love you."

"Please don't say that."

"Will you give me another chance?"

"I don't know."

"Can we start over?"

"I don't know, Dawson. Maybe. If we go anywhere, we'd have to go back to the beginning."

He gives me a sexy grin. "Our beginning was pretty amazing."

I lean in and give him a kiss on the cheek. "I have to get back in there."

I GO BACK inside and tell the girls about what he said. We dissect the entire conversation and consider the pros and cons of getting back together with him. And even though they come up with a lot of pros, I know I can't do it.

At least, not yet.

My phone buzzes.

Aiden: *I'm in the library. You're not here.*

Me: *You're gonna have to go it alone tonight. I'm not up for it.*

Aiden: *Just come talk to me.*

Me: *I have no makeup on. My hair is a mess. I'm not going anywhere.*

Aiden: *Then I'm coming to you.*

Me: *No.*

Aiden: *You missed the monthly birthday celebration at dinner tonight. I have cake for you. Double layer chocolate.*

Me: *Fine. But I'm warning you. I look scary. And I'm at Annie's dorm.*

Aiden: *I can handle it. And I know. Meet me outside.*

"Aiden is bringing me cake. I have to run outside."

"You can't see him with no makeup. Quick, put some on."

"Naw, I don't care."

Annie says, "You must be really upset about Dawson if you don't care."

"I am really upset about Dawson."

"Don't forget to apologize to him," she says, as she walks me to the door.

"SO, CAKE, HUH?"

"Come here." Aiden takes my hand like it's the most normal thing in the world and leads me over to a bench that is just off to the side of the entrance to Annie's dorm. He spreads a napkin across my lap, takes the plastic wrap off the cake, sets it on my lap, and hands me a fork. "Dig in."

I take a big bite.

I look like shit. I'm not gonna impress him with my manners either.

"Oh. Wow. Oh, yuuummm. This is goooood cake."

"Told ya."

I take another forkful and hold it up to his mouth.

He opens his mouth, so I give him a bite. "It is really good, but I already had a piece. This is for you."

"Why did you get me cake, Aiden?"

He touches my index finger with his. Runs it slowly up my hand. "I saw you weren't at dinner. Thought it'd be nice. Is it not nice?"

I take another bite, almost groan in ecstasy, and then say, "It's very nice. But a lot of girls missed dinner. Did you get them all cake?"

He frowns at me. "No, I didn't get them all cake. I'm sorry I made you mad today."

"It's okay. I'm sorry I was crabby. And I'm really sorry I puked all over your room. I've had a rough couple of days."

"That's why I brought cake, Boots. It's a peace offering. Get it? Piece of cake. Peace offering?"

I nod at him and smile. "I get it, and I like both kinds of peace."

He stops moving his finger across my hand and looks at me intently. "Good. Remember that in a few minutes."

"Why . . .?" I start to say, but I can't finish because his lips are on mine.

He gives me one of his long, slow, perfect, electrifying kisses.

Our lips touch.

They barely move.

They don't have to.

Just touching is somehow enough.

The kiss ends. He must have ended it.

There's no way I pulled away from a kiss like that.

I want to be kissed like that forever.

I'm frozen, holding my breath, and staring at his beautiful face. Those green eyes that make me feel emotionally naked every time he looks at me.

He touches my bottom lip with his finger.

Slowly glides it from one corner to the other.

"How are your lips?' he asks. And I know exactly what he's referring to. The night when he fixed my lips.

"Perfect," I reply, with a contented sigh.

"So you're not mad at me anymore?"

"How could I be mad?" I say.

But I want to tell him that I know it's all bullshit. The lines. The kisses.

I want to tell him that I'm not falling for him again.

That I was crushed when he didn't call me after our 29 dances.

That I saw our future.

That I just got hurt by a boy and I don't ever want to be hurt again. That I could never give him my heart.

For one reason.

He could destroy it.

If Dawson had the potential to break my heart, crack it in two, Aiden has the power to annihilate it.

And I would never be the same.

That's why we can only be friends.

That and the fact that he's hung up on someone else.

He gets up and says, "For once, I'm gonna end it on a good note. Goodnight, Boots."

"Night, Aiden," I say, trying to keep the wistful sound out of my voice.

I STOP BEFORE I go back into Annie's room and take a deep breath.

It's just cake.

He felt bad.

It's just cake.

He's a nice guy.

It's just cake. He's finally not failing French.

You are his tutor. It's just cake. A peace offering, so you will keep tutoring him.

I set the cake on the floor and let the girls dig in.

"Oh my gosh. We are *never* missing cake night again!" Maggie exclaims.

"It was sweet of Aiden to bring you cake," Annie gushes.

"I wish a boy would bring me cake," Katie says.

I touch my lip and say quietly, almost to myself. "He kissed me."

"Like made out or kissed?" Maggie asks, her mouth still full of chocolate.

"Just one of his super slow, lips-barely-touching, amazing kisses."

"But you're still done with boys?"

"Definitely," I say with conviction. "But, I mean, he brought us cake. He deserved a kiss, don't you think?"

"I'd do more than kiss for cake this good," Maggie laughs.

"You're bad."

She grins. "I wish."

IT'S A MESS.

10:30PM

KATIE AND I roll into our room just before curfew. I brush my teeth and walk out of the bathroom.

And see my side of our room.

There are books all over the floor by my desk. There are clothes piled high on my chair.

I slowly walk towards my closet and peek in.

It's a mess.

My shoes aren't in their boxes.

My expensive handbags are tossed in a pile on the floor instead of lovingly placed in a row on my shelf.

I back out of my closet and look at my bed. My bed, which I stopped making every morning.

Oh my god.

I've become Dawson.

I almost quit the play because of him. I almost gave up on my dream because of a boy.

Mom always says that Tommy encourages her to shine. That he'd never try to change her.

But Dawson didn't try to change me. I let myself change.

What did Kym say after I broke up with Sander? *I'm doing me.*

And I think that's exactly what I need to do.

Promise to myself #1: No more getting drunk and out of control. You are not that kind of girl. You've never been that kind of girl. You like being in control.

Promise to myself #2: You are single. But you don't need to act like Dawson did. Kissing everyone to make your ex jealous. No. You need to kiss whoever you want. Whenever you want. No apologizing for it.

There are too many hot guys here to apologize for it.

Oh, yeah, I'm going to like being single.

Welcome to my whoredom, boys.

I PICK UP my room while Katie showers. Then I call Mom.

"Hey," I say.

"Hey," she says. "Garrett is pretty upset with you."

"I was hoping he wouldn't tell you. Dawson and I broke up, Mom. His ex texted him and wanted to get back together. I was going to surprise you this weekend. I didn't tell anyone what I was doing. I chartered a plane and was going to just show up at your house. I thought we could stay in all weekend and no one would know I was ever there. I was bringing Dawson with me. I was going to tell him the truth on the plane. That's why I was so upset. Why I went to Miami. I needed to see Damian. I needed my friend."

"Oh, Keatyn," she says with a sigh. "I love you."

"I love you too, Mom. I'm done with boys. I just want you to know. I won't make any more mistakes. I won't see anyone or risk anything. I'll take better care of me. I promise. I'm sorry, Mom." I start crying. It's all catching up to me. I want my mom. I want her to come in my room and sit on my bed and talk to me and hug me when I feel like crying. I want to go to my sisters' room. I want all four of them to jump on me and hug me at once. I want Tommy to tease me. I can't do this here.

I just want to go home.

"Sweetie, you're seventeen. You wouldn't be normal if you didn't make a few mistakes. I think you have been beyond responsible. You left to protect the girls, right?"

"Yes. I love them so much. That letter in Avery's backpack freaked me out. I don't want Vincent to ever be anywhere near them. And, obviously, he is still looking for me. He's not just forgetting about me and giving up. But I was upset about Dawson. And I let it cloud my judgment. He told me he loved me, Mom, but he didn't really."

"You know, honey, you can't fully love anyone until you learn to love yourself."

I hear a blood-curdling screech from one of the girls, then Mom yells, "I've got to go! I love you!"

The call disconnects but I'm still holding the phone to my ear. Mom's words are resonating through my head.

You can't fully love anyone until you learn to love yourself.

I've been so worried about if a boy loves me or not. I give them my heart only to get it back stomped on and broken. I can blame Brooklyn and Dawson all I want for breaking my heart.

But the truth is, I let them.

I didn't listen to the nagging voice in my head. The voice that knew when we were on tour with Damian that things weren't right with B. The voice inside my head that knew all along that Whitney would want Dawson back and that he would want to go.

I didn't listen to them for one reason.

Love.

I kept telling myself that it wasn't true because they loved me.

I think it's time to figure out what I want out of my life.

It's time to learn to love me.

I LIE DOWN in my bed and close my eyes.

My bed feels so good.

I hear Katie brush her teeth, flip off the lights, and then get into bed.

"Night, Keatyn."

"Night, Katie."

I take a couple deep breaths and relax.

I'm so ready to go to sleep and have this day be officially over.

"Keatyn!" Katie exclaims a few minutes later. "They're so pretty! I love them!"

"Love what?" I say, keeping my eyes shut tight.

Please, just go to sleep.

"You mean you didn't do it?" she asks.

"Didn't do what?"

"Open your eyes, silly."

"I don't want to open my eyes. I want to go to sleep and forget today. Forget last night."

"Keatyn, you *need* to open your eyes."

"Fine," I say, as I slowly open them.

Oh. My. Gosh.

Oh my gosh.

Our entire ceiling is covered with hundreds of little glow-in-the-dark stars.

"They're beautiful," I tell Katie. "When did you find time to do that?"

"I didn't do it. That's why I asked if you did it."

"I didn't do it," I say again.

"Who do you think did?"

"I have no idea. Unless, it was Annie. Is that why she was so adamant that we come to her room tonight? Is she trying to cheer us up?"

"Could be. But she was with us the whole time."

My mind drifts to Aiden handing me a little star today in French. Me getting mad at him and tossing it back.

Then tonight. The cake. The peace offering.

Could Aiden have done this?

But that doesn't make sense.

They were for the dream girl.

But in class he said something about my sisters liking them. About how they reminded me of home. Was he just trying to get rid of them?

"I think it might know," I whisper to Katie.

I grab my phone from my bedside table and call Aiden.

"Hey, Boots, what's up?" he says, in his smooth delicious voice. "Get it? What's *up*?"

"Aiden, did you . . ."

He doesn't let me finish. "The answer to your question is yes. I did put stars all over your ceiling."

"They're beautiful. But I don't understand why you did it."

"I did it because I think it's time you finally knew that the stars were always for you. Always. Only. Ever. For you."

The End

About the Author

Jillian is a *USA TODAY* bestselling author. She writes fun romances with characters her readers fall in love with, from the boy next door in the *That Boy* trilogy to the daughter of a famous actress in *The Keatyn Chronicles* series.

She's married to her college sweetheart, has two adult children, two Labs named Cali and Camber, and lives in a small Florida beach town. When she's not working, she likes to decorate, paint, doodle, shop for shoes, watch football, and go to the beach.

www.jilliandodd.net

CPSIA information can be obtained
at www.ICGtesting.com
Printed in the USA
LVHW050230271218
601469LV00009B/325/P

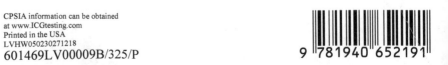

9 781940 652191